## About the Author

Peter Horstead spent his childhood in Lincolnshire, 'Bomber County', surrounded by RAF airfields. He spent eleven years in the armed services himself, and later took up flying. As a member of the RAFA Concert Band, he had the honour of entertaining and meeting, on many occasions, members of Bomber Command.

## Dedication

This story is dedicated to the 55,573 incredibly brave young men who sacrificed their lives whilst serving with RAF Bomber Command between 1939 and 1945.

Peter Horstead

# OPERATION PARLIAMENT

*To Dennis,*
*A pleasure meeting a veteran with so many wonderful stories*
*Regards*
*Peter Horstead*
*June '16*

**AUSTIN MACAULEY**
PUBLISHERS LTD.

Copyright © Peter Horstead (2015)

The right of Peter Horstead to be identified as author of this work has been asserted by him in accordance with section 77 and 78 of the Copyright, Designs and Patents Act 1988.

All rights reserved. No part of this publication may be reproduced, stored in a retrieval system, or transmitted in any form or by any means, electronic, mechanical, photocopying, recording, or otherwise, without the prior permission of the publishers.

Any person who commits any unauthorized act in relation to this publication may be liable to criminal prosecution and civil claims for damages.

A CIP catalogue record for this title is available from the British Library.

ISBN 978 1 78455 299 2 (Paperback)
ISBN 978 1 78455 300 5 (Hardback)

www.austinmacauley.com

First Published (2015)
Austin Macauley Publishers Ltd.
25 Canada Square
Canary Wharf
London
E14 5LB

Printed and bound in Great Britain

# Acknowledgments

I am indebted to my friend, Jon Glauert, for his editorial skills in correcting my appalling abuse of the English language and the rules of punctuation. I would also like to thank him for his enthusiastic encouragement and help when producing the presentable draft. David Evans of Mark generously allowed me to study his comprehensive library of material on Lancaster Bombers and Bomber Command. I thank Peter Higman for his considerable help on the production of the first draft of the manuscript. My grateful thanks go to the RAF Museum Hendon, Lincolnshire Aviation Heritage Centre and 'Lady Jane' at East Kirkby, Norman Groom and his Pitstone Museum and Flyingzone Publications, who all provided invaluable information and explanation. Finally, to the gentleman who farmed the old RAF Kelstern airfield in Lincolnshire in the 1950s. As a nine-year-old boy I heard him relating a story of a ghost Lancaster, hence, inspiring this book many years later.

# FOREWORD

## Tribute to aircrews of Bomber Command by Arthur (Bomber) Harris

'There are no words that can do justice to the air-crew who fought under my command. There is no parallel a period of danger, which at times was so great that scarcely one man in three could expect to survive his tour of thirty operations; this is what a casualty rate of over five per cent on each of these thirty operations would have meant, and during the whole of 1942, the casualty rate was 4.1 per cent. Of those who survived their first tour of operations, between six and seven thousand undertook a second, and many a third tour. It was, moreover, a clear and highly conscious courage, by which the risk was taken with calm forethought, for the air-crew were highly skilled men, much above the average in education, who had to understand every aspect and detail of their task. It was, furthermore, the courage of the small hours, of men virtually alone, for at his battle station the airman is virtually alone. It was courage of men with long-drawn apprehensions of daily 'going over the top'. They were without exception volunteers, for no man was trained for air-crew with the RAF who did not volunteer for this. Such devotion must never be forgotten. It is unforgettable by anyone whose contacts gave them knowledge and understanding of what these young men experienced and faced.'

**Air Chief Marshal, Sir A.T. Harris K.C.B., O.B.E., A.F.C., Air Officer Commanding-in-Chief, Bomber Command, Royal Air Force 1942-1945.**

# GLOSSARY of RAF TERMINOLOGY and SLANG

**A**
| | |
|---|---|
| Ack-ack | Anti-aircraft gunfire. |
| Angels | Height, i.e. Angels Ten = 10,000 feet. |
| AOC | Air Officer Commanding. (of a group.) |
| AFM | Air Force Medal. Awarded to NCOs for one outstanding action (immediate) or more usually for a sustained effort in battle. |
| ASR | Air Sea Rescue. |
| ATA | Air Transport Auxiliary. A civilian Organisation run by the Air Ministry to deliver new aircraft to the RAF from the factories. Many women were pilots for them. |

**B**
| | |
|---|---|
| Bought it | Killed. |
| Bowser | Petrol tanker. |
| Bus Driver | Bomber pilot. |

**C**
| | |
|---|---|
| Caterpillar Club | An informal association of people who have successfully used a parachute to bail out of a disabled aircraft. Once, you are awarded a silver caterpillar lapel badge twice, and you receive a gold badge from the parachute manufacturer. |
| Chaff | Slang name for 'Window', anti-radar device. |
| Camp | An RAF station. |
| Chop | Killed. |
| Cookie | Barrel shaped 4,000-pound bomb. |
| Chiefy | Ground Crew Flight Sergeant. |
| Crate | Aeroplane. |
| Crabbing | Flying slightly sideways. |
| Cans | Pints of beer. |
| Corkscrew | Evasive manoeuvres when attacked by a night fighter, sharp diving turn to port/starboard followed by a sharp climbing turn to starboard/port. |

| | |
|---|---|
| CO | Commanding Officer. |
| Coned | Being caught in the beam of many searchlights (a cone). |
| Computor | Wartime spelling for the first computers. |
| Ding Bat | High speed. 'Going like a ding bat.' |
| Duff Gen | Bad information. |
| Dispersal pan | A frying pan shaped concrete pad where bombers were parked. |
| DFC | Distinguished Flying Cross. Awarded to Officers for one outstanding action (immediate) or more usually for a sustained effort in battle. |
| DSO | Distinguished Service Order. Awarded to Officers primarily for leadership and dedication to duty as well as acts of bravery. |
| DFM | Distinguished Flying Medal. Awarded to NCOs as DFC above. |

**E**

| | |
|---|---|
| Elsan | Chemical toilet on board the aircraft. |
| ENSA | Entertainment National Service Association. A civilian theatre company that entertained the troops. |
| Erk | Ground crew member. |
| ETA | Estimated Time of Arrival. |

**F**

| | |
|---|---|
| FFI | Free From Infection, medical inspection for VD, etc. |

**G**

| | |
|---|---|
| Gen | Information. |
| Gone for a Burton | Missing/dead airman or crew. |
| Group | As in 1 Group. The administrative HQ for a number of squadrons in a geographical area, headed up by the AOC, an Air Vice Marshall. |
| Groupie | Group Captain. CO of an RAF camp. |
| Green House | Cockpit cover of a Lancaster. |

**H**

| | |
|---|---|
| Heat Wagon | Fire Engine. |
| Happy Valley | The Ruhr Valley industrial area in Germany. |

| | |
|---|---|
| Harbour Master | Station Commanding Officer. |
| H2S | An airborne radar bombing aid, displayed on a small screen in the navigator's position, giving a rough radar picture of the ground over which the aircraft was flying. |
| HCU | Heavy Conversion Unit. Here experienced twin-engine pilots and crews trained to fly four engined bombers |
| I/C, i/c | Intercom. Radio communication system on board aircraft to allow crew to talk to each other. |
| ID | Identity, i.e. Identity Card. |
| IFF | Identification, Friend or Foe, was a radar set designed to receive impulses from British ground radar sets, and to reply automatically with a coded pulse on the same frequency and thus protect British aircraft from British defences. Crews believed that if the 'J' switch were activated IFF would disrupt or turn off enemy searchlights. [It didn't!] |
| IP | Initial Point. The physical point that is the start of the final bombing run. |

**J**
**K**

| | |
|---|---|
| Kite | Aeroplane. |
| KIA | Killed In Action. |

**L**

| | |
|---|---|
| Ladybird | WAAF Officer. |
| Ludworth | Local market town. |
| LMF | Lack of Moral Fibre. A euphemism for cowardice, now known as Post Traumatic Stress. |

**M**

| | |
|---|---|
| Meat Wagon | Ambulance. |
| Mae West | Life jacket/preserver named after the film star because it 'stuck out in front.' |

| | |
|---|---|
| Main Spar | A structural element of an aircraft's wing, which runs across the aircraft, forming an obstacle to clear passage along the fuselage. |
| Milk Run | Easy operation. |
| MIA | Missing In Action. |
| Monica | Radar fitted in rear of bomber to provide some early warning of night fighters. |
| MT Section | Motor Transport Section. |

**N**

| | |
|---|---|
| NCO | Non Commissioned Officer, i.e. Corporal, Sergeant, Flight Sergeant, Warrant Officer. |

**O**

| | |
|---|---|
| Op/Ops | Operation/s. |
| Officer Ranks RAF | Pilot Officer, Flying Officer, Flight Lieutenant, Squadron Leader, Wing Commander, Group Captain, Air Commodore, Air Vice Marshal, Vice Marshal, Air Chief Marshal, Marshal of the Royal Air Force. |
| O.C. / | Officer Commanding. |
| OTU | Operational Training Unit. A follow on from HCU. |

**P**

| | |
|---|---|
| Pancake | Crash. |
| Plumduff | 4,000 impact fused HC bomb. |
| Piece of cake | Easy, |
| PFF | Path Finder Force. A small group of aircraft, which after finding the target, put down flares to guide the following bombers. |
| Plumber | Flight Engineer. |
| Port | Left side of aircraft. |

**Q**

| | |
|---|---|
| QFE | Airfield Atmospheric Pressure; i.e. altimeter setting at ground level, Elkington = 390 feet. |

**R**

| | |
|---|---|
| RDF | Radio Direction Finding (radar) |
| R/T | Radio Telephone. |
| RP | Rendezvous point. |

**S**
| | |
|---|---|
| Snowdrop | RAF Policeman. |
| Sortie | One aircraft making one trip to target and back. |
| Starboard | Right side of aircraft. |
| Scarecrows | Bombers exploding in flight, usually because of the bombs on board being hit by enemy fire. Crews were told, for moral purposes, that they were enemy ack-ack devices designed to look like aeroplanes blowing up. |

**T**
| | |
|---|---|
| Tail Spar | Structural element of the tail section. |
| Tour | 30 sorties made a tour. Airmen were then 'rested' for 6 months. |
| Toc H Lamp | Toc H (Talbot House) was a charitable Christian society for officers and men, who could go to a Toc H house for a break from the normal 'entertainments' they were attracted to! Its emblem was an old-fashioned candle lamp. 'Toc' was the army signal code for the letter T. Hence Toc H. |
| Tracer | Tracer ammunition contains a pyrotechnic attached to the base of the round. It is ignited by the burning powder enabling the path of the projectile to be 'traced'. Normally 1 in 5 bullets are tracer. |
| Two i/c, 2 i/c | Second in Command. |
| TIs | Target Indicators/Turn indicators. A bomb-like capsule that busts open at a given height releasing coloured burning candle flares. As they drop they ignite at different times, illuminating the target area for several minutes. |

**U**
| | |
|---|---|
| Undercarriage | Landing gear. |

**V**
| | |
|---|---|
| Vergeltungswaffen | Vengeance weapons. |
| Verey Gun/Pistol | Fires coloured flares. |

| | |
|---|---|
| VHF | Very High Frequency. |
| VC | Victoria Cross. Highest award for bravery. |
| VIC/Vic | Flight of three aircraft in an inverted V. |

**W**

| | |
|---|---|
| WAAF, Waaf | Women's Auxiliary Air Force. |
| Went in | Crashed. |
| Wimpy | A term used for Wellington Bombers. They were nicknamed 'Wimpy' after 'J. Wellington Wimpy' the Popeye Cartoon character that was popular in the cinemas at that time, and the name stuck. |
| Weaving | an uneven course for home. Drunk. |
| Wizard | First class, very good. |
| Window | Aluminium Strips of black-coated paper dropped by British aircraft to confuse German ground radar. |
| WingCo | Wing Commander. |
| Whizzed | Drunk. |

# OPERATION PARLIAMENT

## Prologue

Jack Richards's family had farmed the land around the village of Elkington for four generations, and he had kept the tradition alive and followed his father's footsteps on to the farm.

In the nineteen forties, the Air Ministry requisitioned four-hundred acres of the high land around their farm and two of the neighbouring farms, as it was one of the many suitable sites in the county ideal for conversion to an airfield for the modern Royal Air Force. The elevated plateau of flat land on top of the Lincolnshire Wolds had served before, in the Great War, as an emergency landing field for Zeppelin hunting bi-planes, the fighter-aircraft of the day of the Royal Flying Corps. However, 1942 saw it brought back into service. The Air Ministry created more than forty-five bomber stations in Lincolnshire alone in those days of uncertainty and apprehension, and Lincolnshire earned the sobriquet, 'Bomber County'.

For all Jack Richard's childhood he had been fascinated, and loved with a passion, any and everything about aircraft. He drew pictures of them, flew the balsa wood gliders he designed and constructed himself and read every book about aircraft he could lay his hands on. His passion for flying was the result of his father's exciting stories of the 'string bags' of the Great War which flew from the temporary airfield here at Elkington. He would thrill him with stories of heroic young fighter pilots attacking the giant blimps and bringing their wounded aeroplanes back to the field, and with stories of crash landings and explosions. He dreamed of becoming a pilot. However, when he was a small inquisitive boy, the iron-shod hoof of one of the enormous Shire horses, used on the farm, terminated those childhood dreams by crushing his leg, and the disability it left him with later disqualified him from service in the RAF. If things had been different, he knew he would have settled for nothing less than pilot's wings. However, it delighted him, when in 1942, his father told him the high land was going to revert to being an airfield once again. Even at twenty-one years of age, his passion for aircraft still burned.

It was in March of that year that Jack heard the unmistakable sound of four-engine Lancaster bombers as they arrived at the newly constructed airfield for the first time. They swept in from the grey skies with roaring engines, formidable giant, black, war machines that appeared indestructible, indomitable and invincible; an engraving of image and sound that would stay with him for the rest of his life. Whenever he could, over the next three years, he watched and admired the men and machines that flew above his head every day as he worked the farm.

The first time he became aware of the sound of the struggling Lancaster bomber, was just after dawn on a crisp, cold, misty mid-November morning in 1948. He was crossing the runway, pushing the pedals of an old upright bicycle that retained the scratched and chipped blue livery of its rightful owners, the RAF, when the noise of an approaching aircraft stopped him in surprise. Nothing had landed here since the RAF planes had left nearly three years earlier. He searched the residual night sky, staring through the early morning mist towards the sound, but the mist was all he could see in the greyness of the dawn. The sound he recognised, he had become very familiar with it over the war years, the roar of a Lancaster bomber's Merlin engines.

His family farmhouse, Beech Farm, was half a mile to the southeast of the perimeter track, and during the war he had learnt to recognise, instantly, the sound of any aircraft engine, be it fighter or bomber, friend or foe.

However, these engines were sounding very rough and were struggling badly. It was obvious the bomber was in trouble. The noise crescendoed as it approached from the southwest, heading towards the start of the old runway, banging and coughing in desperation. He dropped his bicycle and started to run; convinced the bomber was about to land or crash. Abruptly, the noise stopped. He whirled round, searching the sky, but there was no sign of an aircraft anywhere ... no noise ... nothing ... just a swirling, curling disturbance in the mist.

He remembered sitting at the supper table that night with his young wife and his father, after they had tucked up their young son snug in his bed, relating his early morning experience.

"I'm surprised you've not 'eard it afore?" said his father.

He had heard the clatter of a struggling Lancaster bomber approaching the runway every year since before the end of the war. It was always about this time of year and always first thing in the morning. He, and several other villagers, believed it to be the ghost of one of the Lancasters that crashed in '43 or '44, and it was trying to bring the lost souls of its crew back home.

"She'll bring 'em all back home safe and sound, one day. Mark my words, boy, mark my words."

# 1 ... Blooded

The Skipper, Johnnie Sanderson, said quietly to his crew, "Tomorrow night we will be on ops again. This time it is the real thing, our first bombing run over enemy territory. Germany!"

That night there were no drinking sessions in the messes, no 'booze ups' at any of the local public houses. Every member of the crew of 'G-George' lay in his bed deep in thought. Those going on their first operational bombing sortie ever, 'Dusty' Miller, the mid-upper gunner; 'Yorky' Ward, the tail gunner; 'Jan' Greasely, the air bomber; and the elegant 'Algy' Willoughby-D'Arcy, wireless operator, hoped their training would see them through and help them keep their nerve. They were not sure how they would react if attacked by anti-aircraft fire or a night-fighter. Being under fire for the first time, would they be able to master their fears? Would they be able to concentrate on their jobs? Would they let their friends and fellow crewmembers down? None of them slept well that night. They had volunteered for this job, but they were scared.

It was no different for those with operational experience. In many ways it was worse, they knew what to expect.

Johnnie felt a strange stirring inside. An excitement coursed through him. Instead of flying for hours on training sorties, he was going back to the task he had joined up for, back to flying against the enemy. Back to dropping bombs, back to the horror of flak and fighter, back to the stomach tightening fear of operational service. The waiting period between the final briefing and take-off was the time he hated most, when you had time to think, that was when the nerves were rubbed raw, and the memory of bad experiences came to the fore, the imagination creating 'what if ... '.

He knew that they would all be frightened and hope that 'Group' would abort the raid for some reason, but no one would have the courage to admit they were scared. It was always a relief when the time came to start-up the engines and taxi round to the threshold of the runway ready for take-off. Once in the air, all negative thoughts disappeared and the training and confidence would kick in. Even though he knew death accompanied most squadron sorties, flying into war still brought a nervous excitement to him. He had volunteered for this... he was scared.

Michael 'Paddy' Doolan, the navigator, had a love of adventure, and although he had completed eighteen sorties in Wimpy's, he still felt the same twinge of nervous excitement, that stomach-sucking moment when he thought about flying through the black night. Of being at the mercy of night fighters and vengeful anti-aircraft fire, of being responsible for navigating the exact delivery of the bomb load and the crew to the distant target and back home again. He had volunteered to do this... he was scared.

'Chalkie' White, the flight engineer, lay in his metal-framed bed listening to the night-time noises of the other occupants of his Nissen hut. The evening was warm, even with the doors of the bow-roofed tin hut propped open. His thoughts were of the baby son he never had the opportunity to get to know, never had the chance to play with, to teach, to love. His thoughts were also of his youthful bride, who had shown him so much unselfish adoration; and the strong, loving, cheerful father, who had guided and cared for him after his mother's death all those years ago? He could not wait to get back in the air; he could not wait to strike back, to wreak his revenge, to kill the bastard Germans. He was angry ... he was not scared.

The next morning found them on 'Battle Orders'. It stated, Pilot; 'JJ Sanderson, Aircraft; G-George', one of twenty Lancaster crews for that night's operation. Their first bombing run as a new crew in their new squadron, was to take place in a few hours. Johnnie met them all in the flight office.

"I thought that we might have a chat about tonight, just between ourselves. As you know, Chalkie, Michael and I, all have experience of operational bombing sorties. I would like to give you my idea of what it could be like tonight, and then I would ask that Chalkie and Michael give you their thoughts. First off, let me say this; we have been together as a crew for over nine months now, and I have every confidence in all of you. You have worked, to coin Yorky's favourite phrase, like 'buggers' these last few months and I am proud to serve with you and have the privilege of leading you," he said as he looked into the eyes of each crewmember in turn.

He had always felt the heavy weight of responsibility for his crewmembers. It was his decisions that could lead to their demise.

"Tonight you will see sights you never dreamt of. You have watched the training films and you have attended the lectures, but they cannot replace the real thing. The gardening op and the dinghy search we carried out, despite the fact it was in German territory, were a piece of cake, no flak and no fighters. We will inevitably meet flak tonight, and the first time is a terrifying experience, to say the least. You know the different types, and you know the damage they can cause. I think Jerry uses it, what Algy might say, 'to scare one shiteless'." They all laughed quietly. "Seriously, I know the sight of a wall of flak is daunting, but we will get through it. There is always a risk of night fighters falling on us, as you already know," he added with a smile, remembering their recent experience.

"But we know how to respond to these threats and we will combat them. If we corkscrew, I will do my best to tell you what action I am about to take so you can prepare for the violent movement. Do not chatter on the intercom; use it for business purposes only. We are a good team and I am confident we can face anything that Jerry can throw at us. We are well-armed, well-trained," he smiled. "And bloody-minded. All I ask is that you carry out your duties to the best of your abilities. Michael, would you like to add your thoughts?"

"Thank you, Johnnie. There is only really one thing I would point out. If you think flying in a giant tin tube is noisy, just wait until the flak and the guns are going off around you. It is sheer bedlam, so it is. It is so loud you cannot think, you cannot concentrate, you believe you are going to go to pieces, but by God, you have to think, you have to concentrate. Have confidence in your own abilities and those of your crewmates. Simply do the job you're trained to do, because I want to come home in one piece, and me arse still facing downwards."

They all burst out laughing and made one or two comments about the size of Paddy's backside.

"Thank you, Michael. Chalkie?" said a smiling Johnnie.

"Yes, Skip. Well lads, all I can tell you, is that the first time I went on ops, I shit myself. I was truly terrified. As Paddy says, the noise gets you as you approach the target. What with flak exploding around you, night fighters firing at you, the aircraft twisting and turning, your own guns filling the aeroplane with the stink of cordite, but ... you know you are delivering something even more terrifying to the Krauts, you know you are hurting them, blasting their cities, paying them back tenfold for what they have done to ours. You trained to do a job. Do it, no matter what happens. You will come back home okay, and feel that it was a job well done."

There was stillness and the crew was quiet.

Johnnie spoke again. "Thank you, Chalkie. A long time ago, it seems, I remember listening to Squadron Leader Leonard Cheshire talking about fear and courage. He said something like 'One man's thinking of the danger and he's frightened. The other man is thinking 'We've got to get there at all cost'. The second man will do the more spectacular thing, but I feel the first man has already done the braver thing'. He said, 'I cannot really see how you can have courage except where there is fear. It is the conquering of that fear, which what I think, is courage' ... I hope we haven't scared the life out of you," smiled Johnnie. "Any questions ... No? Okay. I suggest we meet in the crew room, kitted up at 1030 hours to take G-George up for a Night Flying Test."

Johnnie underestimated the effect his character had on people. He always had done. Those that knew him admired his polite modesty and lack of conceit. His friends and his comrades took confidence and security from his presence. He had proved his courage under fire many times and his calm, natural authority, helped and encouraged those around him in the terrifying trade for which they had all volunteered.

At the appointed time, they went out to their aircraft and checked their equipment thoroughly; radios, guns, bombsight, and radar, working OK? Emergency equipment, dinghy and flare gun correctly stowed and a hundred other pieces of gear and equipment checked and double-checked. They had carried out this routine hundreds of times ... .

The preparations for this sortie were the same as for any other sortie they had carried out in training and the two operational trips, the 'gardening' op and the dinghy search, both around the Friesian Islands. Nevertheless, this was different; they were to *bomb* the enemy. The job they had volunteered and trained for, this is what G-George existed for, and this was why the seventeen hundred people were there on the aerodrome ... to *bomb* the enemy.

The briefing was at 1800 hours. Two RAF policemen checked their ID as they entered the briefing hut. In the large room, placed either side of the central gangway, were rows of folding chairs and wooden benches behind trestle tables; a low stage-like platform was at the far end and on it, an easel, with a large blackboard resting on its wooden pegs smothered in multi-coloured chalk writing. A massive blackout curtain covered the wall at the rear of the platform.

The whole scene was familiar to the crew of G-George, but not the sense of occasion. This briefing had a distinct feeling about it. There were many crews attending that had never been in action over enemy territory before. They were edgy, apprehensive, worried. Although they laughed, it was with tight strained faces. Their eyes did not laugh. Everyone that smoked was smoking, whether needing a burst of nicotine or not. Smoke drifted up through the wooden rafters, slowly filling the roof void with its blue-grey swirls. All the new crews were anxious, nervous, excited. The more experienced crews tended to sit and talk quietly with each other, gaining comfort from the company of their trusted colleagues. They just wanted to get on and do the job. They were all scared.

Chairs squealed and clattered as one hundred and forty aviators rose to their feet and came to attention as the 'big wigs' filed in. The Senior Intelligence Officer (SIO) took his place on the platform and gripped the draw cords of the black curtain. A murmur of anticipation rose from the ranks of attentive aircrews.

"Sit down, gentlemen."

He waited, then, "Tonight, your target is ..."

The curtains fell away.

" ... Hamburg!"

An unsuppressed groan from those who had experienced Hamburg's well-organised defence systems earlier that year greeted his announcement

Johnnie looked to the floor. He had experienced Hamburg's vigorous greeting of night bombers before, and this would be a true baptism of fire for his new crew.

"This will be a maximum effort raid; nearly eight hundred bombers will be going tonight on the first part of what the Air Ministry has called 'Operation Gomorrah'. Hamburg is the second largest city in Germany and a vitally important one to the enemy, therefore a major target for the allies."

"It is their main Atlantic seaport and dockyard, with the shipyards of Blohm and Voss turning out U-boats as fast as they can. The other principal targets are the oil refineries, the big industrial areas, and the dynamite factory actually built by Mister Alfred Nobel! A target that should go with a bang, you might say."

Groans of derision rose from the aircrews at his attempt at humour.

They were unaware their 'Boss', Air Chief Marshal Sir Arthur (Bomber) Harris, or 'Butch' as they called him, had sent a message to the government's war committee two months earlier, on 27 May, 1943, stating that he believed destroying the city of Hamburg and its industries to be a vital part towards the Allies' victory. It was the second largest city in Germany, with a population of one and a half million. By devastating Hamburg, it would cut the industrial capacity to supply the enemy's armed forces and would have a dramatic effect on morale, playing an important role in shortening the war. He told them that he believed to eliminate the city they had to drop 10,000 tons of bombs in a concentrated, sustained attack.

Until there were enough hours of darkness to allow the medium bombers to take part, all available heavy bombers would carry out the first attack. Heavy daylight attacks by the American VIII Bomber Command, he hoped, would follow-up the night attacks. He had planned a series of daylight and nighttime raids over the next few days to achieve this 'process of elimination' and this was the start. His intention was to destroy Hamburg.

The SIO carried on.

"As some of you are aware, Hamburg is very well defended, both by guns and fighters. For your information, our Intel informs us, there are, in fact, fifty-four heavy anti-aircraft batteries, twenty-two searchlight batteries and three smoke-generating units. There are also some twenty ground controlled night-fighter boxes served by six major airfields covering the approaches to the port. As you can see, protection for Hamburg is very heavy." He paused. "However ... we have something that might help you. I have a special announcement to make, direct from Headquarters Bomber Command."

Here he referred to the sheaf of papers in his hand and read.

"'Tonight, you are going to use new and simple countermeasures, 'Window', to protect yourselves against the German defence systems. 'Window' consists of dropping packets of metal strips that produce about the same reactions on RDF (radar), as do your aircraft. The German defences will, therefore, become confused and you should stand a good chance of getting through unscathed while their attention is on the packets of 'Window'. When a good concentration is reached, 'Window' can so devastate an RDF system that we have withheld using it until we could affect improvements in our own defences and until we could be sure of hitting the enemy harder than he could hit us.'"

He put the piece of paper to the back of the bundle he was holding. After a momentary pause, the room filled with conversation. The SIO looked at the Wing Commander and let the chaps carry on talking as he received a nod.

"What the hell are they talking about?" asked Chalkie.

"Something that has been rumoured for months," said Algy. "It's strips of tin-foil that will confuse the ground radars that control the searchlights, flak guns and the night fighters. I heard about it months ago, Chalkie. I thought it was a jolly spiffing idea then. I wondered why they had not told us about it. I suppose they had to develop an antidote to it first before we let Jerry get his hands on it, 'cos he'll be using it as soon as he can, you can bet your bottom dollar on that."

"Gentlemen, gentlemen, thank you," the SIO waved them to quietness.

He held up a strip of silver paper.

"This is 'Window'. A strip of black paper coated on one side with aluminium. It is, in fact, exactly half the length of their radar wavelength, and confuses their radar system. It is exactly eleven inches by three-quarters, or, for those educated in European ways, twenty-seven centimetres by two centimetres. Yes, we now have something to help negate a brutally well defended target. You will receive your exact route later, but you will start dropping bundles of 'Window' every minute from eight degrees thirty minutes east, on the way to the target, until eight degrees east on the homeward leg. The protection you will get from 'Window' is not from the bundles *you* drop, but from the bundles dropped by the aircraft in front and above you. So it is vital to everyone that you adhere to your instructions for timing and course."

He then held up a bundle of 'Window'.

"The air bomber will drop the bundles, weighing one pound, down the flare chute. It will be a difficult and tiring task, as you will have to juggle a stopwatch, a torch, intercom connection and oxygen leads in the dark, along with bundles of metal strips. By the way, do not take the rubber bands off the bundles; they will spread automatically in the slipstream. The flight engineer will take over as you near the target area until after the bombing run. It is vital that you drop the bundles continuously, exactly every minute so they meet their full potential, even if they do cost fourpence a bundle." he added, with a smile. "When you go to your aircraft you will discover the boxes of 'Window' already stowed on board."

The Navigation Leader then took the stage, and with the aid of the giant map behind him and a billiard cue-like pointer, emphasized the course chosen, as shown by the red tapes stretching across the map. Assemble over the North Sea, fly on an easterly course, which would evade most of the German defences, and turn southeast to carry out the attack. They were to fly through the target and withdraw on a parallel course to that which had brought them in. All the pilots and navigators were furiously making copious notes despite the fact they would receive the exact details at the end of the briefing.

The Bombing Leader then explained that 'zero' hour would be 0100 hours. Three minutes before zero hour, twenty Pathfinder aircraft equipped with H2S radar will drop white illumination flares and yellow and red Target Indicators (TIs). From then on, every minute, all the way through the attack, fifty-one 'backer-up' Pathfinder aircraft would renew the target marking by dropping green TIs. The main force bombers should begin their attack at 0102 hours. All eight hundred bombers would be clear of the target by 0200 hours. They were all scribbling furiously on their pads now.

The bombing leader carried on, "Numbers one and five Group will provide the first wave of bombers after the PFF. (Path Finder Force). So we will be the first to go in at 0102 hours."

"Welcome to the party," said Paddy to Johnnie. "Talk about being thrown in at the deep end."

The Flying Control Officer (FCO) then outlined the starting up times and order of take-off and which runway to use. The met officer informed them that there would be winds of 17 mph from the northwest with zero cloud cover. The crews took this news with a pinch of salt.

"The buggers may get it right one day," remarked Yorky.

Wing Commander Harry Picton, the Squadron Commander, took the stage.

"To some of you, tonight will be a novel experience. Timing on night ops is vital. During the day you can see if the chap above you is about to dump on your head or you can see that you are about to do it to the chaps below you, but it is not that easy in the dark. It is imperative that you hold to your timings to make sure we all survive.

"Searchlights will also be a new experience for some. Look out for the single blue-white one that is on its own or staying upright. That is the master beam. As it lingers out there, it will be lining up some poor sod with its radar. It will suddenly lock on to an aircraft of its choice attracting ten, twenty, thirty of the regular beams along with it. Flak guns will then have a field day, 'a turkey shoot', as our American friends would say. Is that right, McClintock?" he said addressing the squadron's only American Eagle Squadron member.

"Sure is, Skipper." came the laughing reply.

"If the flak doesn't latch on to you, then beware, because obviously night fighters are about. The answer to that problem is ... keep looking ... keep looking ... and keep looking. Remember, gents, attention to detail, belief in your training and alertness at all times will help to keep you alive, and use 'banking searches' to stop night fighters sneaking up underneath you. Look out for other aircraft; remember there will be eight hundred other crews up there charging around the same piece of sky. Tonight is a first for all of us. 'Window', I am sure, will help bring us home. Thank you, gentlemen."

The Aldis lamp in the window of the red and white control caravan parked by the side of runway zero-six flashed green, illuminating the pale faces of the customary crowd of well-wishers, one of whom was Group Captain Thompkins, the Station Commander. He stood to attention and saluted as G-George, and every other aircraft passed him by. Johnnie released the brakes and G-George jumped forward to accelerate up to full power over one thousand five hundred and fifty yards until she reached one hundred and ten mph and lumbered into the late evening sky at 2306 hours. As she slowly climbed towards the east, the sky filled with bombers, their navigation and formation lights twinkling in the darkening night. They came from the north, the south and from the west. Lancasters, Halifaxes, Stirlings and Wellington bombers were assembling over the North Sea to form a mighty phalanx two hundred miles long and twenty miles wide. The leading Lancasters of this thundering herd moved at two hundred and twenty miles per hour on their mission of destruction.

# 2 ... Bombs Gone

They extinguished the navigation and formation lights as they passed four degrees east; they were approaching the domain of the German night fighter. G-George had climbed to 18,500 feet in the clear, cloudless night.

"Skipper," said Paddy. "Just double checking we have the same course and headings. I have the following; initial course is zero-seven-five until position fifty-four degrees forty minutes north, by seven degrees twenty minutes east." He then double-checked all the bearings and positions of the raid with Johnnie. "Copy, Skipper?"

"Yes, copy, Navigator. Thank you."

Johnnie always liked to double-check with the navigator just in case anything happened to either of them.

"We will have to adjust some of that, Skipper, as the Met boys have it wrong again. The wind forecast was seventeen miles per hour from the northwest, but over the last three checks, it was twelve miles an hour from the southeast! I'll adjust as necessary."

A click on the intercom,

"They couldn't forecast I'm gonna 'ave a pint tomorrow night, the useless buggers."

"Thank you, Yorky for your contribution. Just keep your eyes peeled for visitors," replied Johnnie, with a wry grin.

The mighty armada thundered onwards.

"Two minutes to first course change at 0020 hours, Skipper, turn on to one-one-seven."

"One-one-seven, OK, Michael," answered Johnnie. "Fully alert everybody, watch for other aircraft."

The great Lancaster banked to the right as it came on to its new heading, following the other squadron aircraft.

"Better start getting ready for the Window drop, Jan."

"OK, Skip, Willco."

Jan moved from his station in the front cupola, crawled under Chalkie's dials and switches, clambered over the main spar and made his way past the mid-upper turret. He opened up the flare chute, fitted the extension tube to it, and then opened the first box of Window bundles, made up of two thousand strips of aluminium-coated paper held together by a rubber band.

"Eight degrees thirty minutes, Skipper," announced Michael. "Its 0040 hours on the button, Skipper."

"Jan, start dropping."

"Willco, Skip."

"That should confuse them, Skipper."

"We shall have to wait and see, Michael."

Hundreds of bombers were now dumping tons of aluminium into the night sky. The German radar operators, who had tracked the bomber stream since the armada started to cross the North Sea, had known a major raid was imminent as their Luftwaffe listening service had picked up the ground test radio transmissions from the RAF bombers parked on their dispersal pads in the morning. A large-scale attack could be predicted quite accurately by heavy radio traffic in the mornings and very little in the afternoons. If there were no plans for an attack then the radio test transmissions were spread more evenly over the morning and afternoon.[1]

However, they were now flooded with false returns. Millions of aluminium strips were scattering across the sky. The enemy appeared everywhere. The whole of the German defence system was blind.

The radar-controlled searchlights wandered aimlessly looking for prey. Night fighters, alerted earlier, were up patrolling their combat boxes, but their ground controllers could not identify individual bombers. Their screens were a

---

[1] Because at this time the ground crews loaded the aircraft with bombs and fuel, and the aircrews received their briefing.

mass of unfathomable contacts, so they could not direct their charges to the bomber stream. Window was working.

As they crossed the German coast, the flak guns opened up on the bomber stream. Without radar guidance, they were shooting blind. Nonetheless, as experienced gunners, they put up a barrage where they expected the bombers to be, and they were not too far away. The first explosive bursts of smoke and fire that came near to G-George made Yorky, in his rear turret, jump with surprise, even though they were a hundred and fifty yards astern of the aircraft.

"Christ, the buggers are shooting at us!" he declared.

"What did you think they would do, Yorky? Invite you for afternoon tea?" laughed Algy.

"Jesus Christ!" exclaimed Dusty, in response to a large illuminating explosion close to the bomber stream. "What the hell was that? Someone's bought it, Skipper?"

"No, Dusty that was a 'scarecrow', an ack-ack shell designed to make you think just that, and scare us shitless"

"I've got news for Jerry. It works."

"Five minutes to target, Skipper. Turn on to one-eight-zero now," instructed Paddy.

At 0052 hours, Johnnie turned G-George on to the bombing-run heading. Jan returned to his prone position in the front and Chalkie took over his duties at the flare chute dropping bundles of Window every minute.

"Ready, Jan?"

"Yes, Skipper." A couple of minutes later, "Wow, the target is lit up like daylight ... Yellow TIs slightly to starboard, Skipper." He sounded excited.

Flak was bursting all around them now, but Johnnie thought it did not seem to have its customary deadly accuracy, being scattered and lacking its tight grouping that made it effective. The dreaded bright master searchlights that were usually seen shining bolt upright before swinging swiftly over to trap some unfortunate bomber in their blue-white glare, were wandering all over the sky groping to find an enemy.

Other lights were clinging to them to form their fatal cones, but tonight those cones were bare and empty. Without radar, they were lost.

"Red TIs going down, Skipper."

"OK, Jan, she's all yours."

"Open bomb doors."

"Bomb doors open," replied Johnnie as he pushed down the lever.

"Right a bit ... right ... steady ... steady ... steady ... steadyyyyy ... " Jan thumbed the tit and yelled, "Bombs gone!"

G-George leapt upwards as if in relief as over five and a half tons of explosives left the bomb bay at precisely 0104 hours. One 4000 lb 'Cookie' High Explosive bomb had followed three 1000 lb. HE's and 1,416 4 lb. incendiaries, packed into 'small bomb containers' (SBCs), which burst open as they departed the aircraft. The incendiaries tumbled through the air to add fire and destruction to the hundreds and thousands of other explosives that were already falling, exploding and burning among the docks, the factories, and the homes of Hamburg.

"Just caught a massive explosion to starboard of us, Skipper, bits, pieces, and smoke up to two or three thousand feet, I wonder if Mr. Nobel has lost his dynamite factory?" laughed Dusty.

Jan thought about the amount of bombs dropped that night. 'If we have just dropped over five and a half tons that means that eight hundred aircraft could be dropping anything between three and four thousand tons of deadly cargo'. It was not a thought he dwelt on for long. He had seen what the Nazi blitz had done to Plymouth.

For the next thirty seconds, Johnnie held G-George on a straight and level course, a heart pounding, and breath-holding time as flak banged and crumped around them. The photoflash flare, which Chalkie had loaded into the flare chute moments before the bombs had dropped, fell at the same time, its fuse set to go off before the bombs hit the ground. The camera, next to Jan, would then take its series of five shots, two before the aiming point, the aiming point itself, and two after, to show they had done their job and hit the target.

"Flash gone!" shouted Jan.

"Skipper, turn on to two-nine-seven for home," instructed Paddy.

Jan climbed out from the nose and replaced Chalkie at the flare chute; they would keep dropping Window for a while yet.

Chalkie returned to his 'dickie seat' next to Johnnie, turned and looked down at the sea of flames below him. Mile after mile of the city was burning. Thousands upon thousands of people were dying. The ugly sneering smile of revenge on his face was one he would not like his fellow crewmembers to witness. He could not help but think of his lost family. He felt no sympathy whatsoever for the Germans down below.

As Johnnie made the turn, heading northwest, Yorky yelled, "Corkscrew starboard now. Bandit starboard quarter!"

With that he opened up with his four .303 machine guns as a twin-engine Messerschmitt bf-110 night fighter swung in a curving attack from the starboard quarter five hundred yards away. Johnnie sent G-George into a steep diving turn. Dusty, in his upper turret, joined Yorky in his defence as the fighter sliced down the port side of the bomber without being able to bring his guns to bear, because of Johnnie's rapid evasive action. Dusty's fiery curving tracer stream chased after the fast-moving fighter until it vanished into the night.

"Okay, Skipper, he's gone. I don't think we hit him," said Yorky.

A few minutes later, he cried, "Oh my God, a Lanc has just blown up astern of us, and he's going down in flames, the poor bastards. I can't see any 'chutes'."

"Okay everybody; rubberneck the skies; and keep on your toes; we've got a long way to go yet."

Johnnie pulled G-George back on to the previous heading.

It was the first time that both Dusty and Yorky had seen what could happen when your luck runs out. They looked on in shock as the burning Lancaster spiralled down. Yorky bizarrely thought the falling, spinning bomber with its tail of fire streaming out behind, somehow looked like a tadpole wriggling through water. Searchlights picked up the burning beacon as if to illuminate its final exit as it plunged from the night sky to blow up on the ground below. Its fiery funeral pyre was lost in seconds among the scores of fires already burning.

Yorky looked down on his first sight of the horror of war brought by his comrades to this bustling metropolis. One and a half million people lived down there, loved, slept, and worked down there. Now they were dying down there, in their hundreds, in their thousands. The world was showing the Nazis of Germany the punishment for the devastation they had brought to Europe.

Chalkie smiled to himself whispering, "Serves you right, you bastards."

Although accompanied, intermittently, by flak all the way back to the coast, only once, as they passed near Bremerhaven, did it come close to them, exploding beneath the bomb doors and throwing the aircraft around the night sky. Jan was back dropping Window through the flare chute until they cleared the Friesian Islands and made their last turn for home. Window appeared to have helped protect them from the worst of the flak.[2]

After G-George had been flying for three-quarters of an hour, Yorky announced quietly over the intercom, "I can still see the red glow of the fires of Hamburg, even from all this way."

Dusty, swung his turret to face aft, and looked in awe at the glowing red sky behind them.

They did not see any other aircraft at all, friendly or otherwise, until nearing the Lincolnshire coast when navigation lights suddenly twinkled all around them, red, green and white, as the bombers gratefully swept towards their home fields. G-George came in over the creek at Saltfleet and cruised over the flat farmland towards the last turning landmark, the spire of Ludworth church.

She touched down at 0321 hours July 25, 1943, as it read in the navigator's log, and Johnnie announced,

---

[2] In fact only twelve aircraft were lost that night out of an attacking force of nearly eight hundred

"Home at last, chaps, home at last."

Their first bombing raid into Germany finished and they had survived. Flying as part of an operational squadron for the first time was unforgettable. They had experienced fear, horror, excitement, laughter and comradeship, all rolled into one highly emotional flight. They stood on the dispersal pan awaiting the crew bus to take them back to the interrogation and debriefing session. At first, nobody spoke. They lit up cigarettes and Johnnie stoked up his 'flying' pipe, Yorky filled his slim stemmed rosewood pipe and Algy fitted an exotic cigarette into his ivory holder, flicked his American Zippo petrol lighter and the perfume of roasted tobacco drifted among them.

He was the first to speak. "Well, Skip, that's the second sortie in the book. Good old 'Gloria' here behaved herself and brought us all back safe and sound, nobody injured and undamaged. Well done, old girl." He patted the starboard tail-plane affectionately.

As the crew bus took them back to the briefing room, realising they had survived their first bombing run, they were now bursting with conversation, the adrenaline pumping through their tired bodies. Each of the 'first timers' wanted to tell his comrades what he had seen, how he had felt, to talk about the tragic loss of comrades and the effect of their own bombs on the anonymous target. The excited buzz of their first bombing run was keeping them high, the nervous tension, the apprehension and the fear forgotten ... for now.

They reached the crew room where the CO and teams of intelligence officers de-briefed each crew. Checking on the weather over the target, the distribution of Window, the flares and markers, the timings of their drop, how close to the red or green TIs they dropped, the number of fires they saw, enemy action against them, the behaviour of the searchlights and ack-ack guns, evidence of night-fighters, descriptions of stricken aircraft. Interrogators wrote brief descriptive reports of their bombing run and the pilot, navigator and wireless operators had to fill out their log sheets detailing all the information the Intelligence Officers required. All this after six hours of highly energised action, the mug of rum-laced tea was very welcome.

They stowed their flying gear in their lockers, returned their 'chutes' and survival kits to the stores and enjoyed their first 'flyer's bacon and egg breakfast' as a combat experienced crew, and then fell into their beds. However, sleep did not come easily. The constant throb, vibration and noise of the engines were still with them. They were still in a state of excitement, still wound up after six hours of adrenaline-filled action. Maybe sleep would come tomorrow night.

Johnnie lay on his bed staring at the ceiling, the fires of Hamburg still flickering behind his eyes.

'Was it only nine days ago we arrived here at Elkington? It seems like we've been here forever.'

# 3 ... RAF Elkington

The four majestic Merlin engines are throbbing in perfect harmony as the Lancaster bomber levels off for her final approach. She slides out of the air, her natural habitat, and returns, be it temporary, to that world of earth-bound mortals. A double squeal of protest comes from the giant tyres as they make contact with the runway. The aircraft bounces back into the air and the tyres squeal again as they make their final contact. The engines' notes drop as the enormous aeroplane taxis towards the hard standing in front of the hangar. As the brakes come on, it rocks briefly and comes to a standstill. One by one, the engines hoarsely cough the spirit of life from the cylinders and rattle to a stop. Then there is silence, except for a tick ... tick ... ticking, as the engines cool in the fresh, morning air.

It is the early morning of Friday July 16, 1943.

Kit bags and suitcases surrounded seven young men who had just scrambled out of the back of a three-ton lorry and had watched the bomber's transition from sky to earth.

"Home at last, chaps, home at last," said a young Flight Lieutenant quietly to himself. The double winged brevet of a pilot sewn on to the chest of his battledress blouse, above two medal ribbons.

"Welcome to our new home, chaps, RAF Elkington." he said to his comrades.

"Thank you, *Flight Lieutenant* Sanderson." joked Algy.

The Skipper's promotion from Flying Officer occurred yesterday.

Flight Lieutenant Jonathan James Sanderson, Distinguished Service Order, Distinguished Flying Cross, known as Johnnie or Skipper to the other officers and sergeants that made up his crew, had dropped his kit bag and suitcase on the concrete beside the three-tonner. He was twenty-four years old, a vicar's son from a little village just outside Deal in Kent. His mother was the village schoolteacher and his fourteen-year-old brother thought he was a hero. He fell in love with flying at the age of seventeen and as soon as he could, he joined the RAF Volunteer Reserve at the nearby Manston airfield, so it was natural he would join the RAF. At six feet tall, with fair hair and bright hazel eyes, straight nose and an easy smile, he was the national newspapers' model image of the modern 'Hero of the RAF'. However, he certainly did not consider himself a hero, in any way, shape or form. He was a quiet and studious young man, an excellent pilot, calm and steady under pressure, as shown by the fact he had survived crash-landing a Wellington Bomber into the cold North Sea, and bringing home another, badly fire-damaged, and wore, on his chest, the ribbons of recognition for courageous behaviour.

He had completed his first 'tour' of thirty sorties in Wellington bombers and had volunteered to carry out another tour, but his second crash terminated this. He then spent time as an instructor at RAF Manby teaching colonial volunteers how to fly twin-engine bombers. But he soon realised he missed the buzz, the excitement and, contrarily, the danger of operational flying, so he volunteered again for active duty and had ended up at the Heavy Conversion Unit (HCU) at RAF Blyton, learning how to fly the magnificent four engine Avro Lancaster Mk.1 Heavy Bomber.

Over the last few months, the members of his crew had come to respect and trust him and they enjoyed his company. They liked him, but not when he drove his tiny, maroon, 1930s Austin 7 Ruby car. He drove like a maniac, even though its top speed was only forty-five miles per hour. His 'party trick' was to place a cushion on the driver's seat and try to drive the car with his head sticking out of the sunroof, terrifying passengers and passersby.

"I'm surprised you didn't squeeze 'Ruby' into the back of the truck, *Flight Lieutenant*," teased the navigator of the crew, Michael 'Paddy' Doolan.

"I would have done, Michael, but I don't think the WingCo would have been very chuffed to see an old Austin banger falling out the back of a personnel carrier. I wouldn't be a flight lieutenant for very long, would I?"

The rest of the crew laughed while surveying their new surroundings.

They had just come across the Lincolnshire Wolds from RAF Blyton, near Gainsborough, where they had first come together as a crew. Jan, Dusty, Algy, and Yorky had initially been a part of another crew on the twenty-four week Operational Training course. The exchange of three of their original members for more experienced aircrew after the first couple of weeks had surprised them. At first, they had been rather resentful that their other crewmates had suddenly vanished, but the professionalism and friendliness of the new 'bods' and acceptance of the mysterious ways of the services soon had them acting as if they had been together as a team for months. They had previously been training or flying in Wellington and Handley Page Hampden bombers, but they had all volunteered for the new four-engine Lancasters. The Conversion Course and the final twelve-week course, that was the Lancaster Finishing School, polished their skills as one of Bomber Command's front line weapons.

RAF Elkington was a large airfield situated high on the edge of the Lincolnshire Wolds, a few miles south-southwest of the busy little market town of Ludworth. It was now an important major airfield in 1 Group Bomber Command. It had the standard three runways in an 'A' shape, recently converted from grass to concrete. The prevailing wind, though, made the six thousand feet southwest-northeast runway the main one.

A long wooded valley close to the south and southwest of the runways made final approaches to the main and north-south runway a little hazardous for the unwary. The cold air trapped in the valley would cause the aircraft to sink unexpectedly, catching out many inexperienced pilots. Sat at the far end of the valley, an old windmill, its sails long gone, acted as a marker on the line of approach for the main runway.

Built around the perimeter track, there were thirty-six concrete dispersal pads, shaped like frying pans. Two hangars, one of them the larger B1 servicing hangar, were located to the west of the runway complex, a third was across the airfield towards the bomb stores.

The accommodation huts and messes were also on the west side of the airfield and the squadron administration huts, stores and offices were between them and the perimeter track, all spread out over many acres, as it appeared every RAF camp was.

The truck had dropped them outside the main guardroom, with its kerbs and brick pillar supports to the veranda-like entrance, painted a brilliant white. They all trooped in to report their arrival, and were then directed to the Camp Administration block opposite, where they completed several repetitive forms to prove they existed and were told which billet had been allocated to them.

"I suppose we should report to the squadron adjutant's office, if we can find it," said Johnnie. "Then you lot had better find the Sergeants' mess, I suppose, and check in to your new hotel rooms."

"Yeah, I'm sure, Skipper, it'll be some filthy, drafty Nissen hut in the middle of bloody nowhere," laughed Chalkie, the flight engineer. "I'll pop over to the MT section later and see if we can cadge a lift back to Blyton tomorrow to pick up your cars and my motorbike, if that's okay?"

"Good idea, Chalkie. I'll talk to you later."

Flight Lieutenant Jimmy Cook was the long-suffering squadron adjutant, responsible for all the paperwork and admin. He had seen a lot of action from the beginning of the war as a pilot; shot down twice within the first four months of 1940, captured by the advancing Germans in Northern France and then escaping to make his way back to England several weeks after Dunkirk. Now, it was better for his nerves and health if he served on the ground, away from the pressures of combat. He greeted them all with a cheery smile and a warm handshake, welcoming them to 599 Squadron, and after yet more form filling, pointed Algy and Paddy to the officers' mess and the SNCOs to theirs.

"Why can't the bloody RAF put the buildings next to each other, like the army does, instead of spreading them round the bloody county? We always have to walk miles just for a piss," complained Yorky, the rear gunner, as he and the other sergeants set off on the trek to find their Nissen hut quarters.

Jimmy gently warned Johnnie about 'The Boss' and then ushered him into the main office.

Wing Commander Harry Picton DSO DFC and bar, was not in a good mood. Early that morning, three more aircraft had arrived, but not the extra ground crews nor, more significantly, the spare parts, ammunition and extra fuel that should have come with them. As Johnnie entered his office, some poor supply officer was having his ears burnt at the other end of a telephone by the WingCo.

"Who the hell are you?" asked Picton, slamming down the phone.

"Flight Lieutenant Sanderson, sir. I came in from Blyton this morning," said a saluting Johnnie.

"Ah, yes, of course. Don't suppose you brought any petrol with you?"

"Er, only what was in the three-tonner's tank, sir."

"Yes, sorry, Sanderson shouldn't take it out on you. Welcome to Five-Nine-Nine," he smiled and offered his hand.

He searched through some personnel files on his desk and picked one up, glancing at it briefly to remind himself.

"By the way, I want you in 'A' flight to take Squadron Leader Chris Cooper, your flight commander, back up to flight strength. He could do with somebody like you. He does not have your ops experience, but he knows Lancasters. We are on ops for the next few nights, but I won't put you newcomers on battle orders until you have familiarised yourselves with your new kites. So for the next couple of days, let your crew find their feet and the local pub." Again, he smiled. "Jimmy will give you the details about your aircraft allocation and get your kite liveried up in squadron colours as soon as possible. You'll find Chris in the flight office next door." The 'phone rang. "I'll buy you a pint in the mess when I get back later."

He smiled and waved Johnnie to the door in dismissal as the 'phone continued to ring. He picked up the handset to stifle its demanding trill, shouting, "Yes!" into the mouthpiece, throwing the file back on its pile.

Back in the outer office, Jimmy, the adjutant, explained where Johnnie's billet would be and where the officers' mess was.

"You'll be part of 'A' flight, by the way, and your kite, which arrived this morning, will have the recognition code, 'G-George' with the squadron prefix of CD. The other new ones arriving today and tomorrow will be on 'C' flight, so they will carry CK as their prefix as we are now up to thirty-two aircraft, or will be when the rest of the new kites arrive next week. I will get the squadron 'artist' to paint her up for you tomorrow."

"The boys will be happy with another G-George. We were flying a good kite, 'G-George' at Blyton."

"Let's hope that's a lucky omen," said Jimmy. "If you report to the service hangar on Monday she will be ready for you, after the 'new boys' greeting from the old man at 08:30, that is."

"Where do I find the flight commander? The WingCo said next door."

"Yes, 'A' flight's office is out the door, second hut on the left. Make sure your tie is straight and your shoes are clean." He raised one eyebrow as a warning.

'A' flight commander, Squadron Leader Christopher Cooper, DFC AFM, welcomed Johnnie with a crushing handshake.

"Good to meet you, Sanderson, heard some good reports about you. Look forward to working with you."

His short, clipped way of address reflected his appearance. A young-looking face, sporting the obligatory moustache, trimmed to sharpened points. Dark, well-groomed, Brylcreamed short hair, swept straight back, his uniform neatly pressed, his tie tied in the regimental fashion required and his shoes gleaming like a guardsman's boots. The medal ribbons on his chest showed he was not lacking in courage. Altogether, an impressive figure of the smart, dashing RAF pilot he was trying to portray, and at twenty-three years of age, he was evidently destined for greater things as his relative rapid rise through the ranks displayed. This was his first command and he wanted to get it right. He had joined as aircrew back in '39 and qualified as a Sergeant Pilot in '41. He felt that success and efficiency would overcome his Grammar School background. His father's skill as a carpenter was not the background that heroes like Bader and Cheshire came from. He had to make his mark, he had to catch the eye of 'those that be' by having the best trained and the most efficient flight in the squadron, so he worked hard at it.

"You'll find us a cheerful lot. All the same, I like things to flow smoothly. We are lucky, we have some cracking crews, but they lack your experience, which is why I am glad to see you. When do you get your kite?"

"Monday morning, sir. Delivery was this morning, I believe."

"Ah, yes, it was, along with two others from the factory. Amazingly, women flew them all in. No navigator, no wireless operator, just a flight engineer, remarkable!"

"You have got to admire those ATA people, flying strange aircraft into strange airfields every day."

"Yes, especially as they're civilians and *women*?"

"We've been allocated one of the new ones, haven't we, sir? The Adjutant said it would be liveried up as G-George. We were flying a G-George out of Blyton and it would be nice if we could keep that going. You know how superstitious crews are."

"Oh, yes. I know that on most squadrons it is 'pot luck' as to which aircraft you fly, but the Groupie and the WingCo like their pilots and crews to have a particular aircraft allocated to them. They believe it helps with morale and boosts confidence if they can build up an intimate knowledge of their kite. But you will have to take 'pot luck' occasionally," he warned.

He chatted for a few minutes, in a friendly way, about the station and the squadron and the way he 'liked to get things done' efficiently and smartly. When Johnnie asked about the operations taking place over the next two nights, Cooper confirmed that he and the other new crews would not be included. He remarked that it would probably be the last free weekend for a while, shook hands, again with the firmness he thought conveyed strength of character, and returned to the paperwork in front of him.

The four Senior NCOs billet was one of the many accommodation Nissen huts. They would be sharing with five crewmembers of another Lanc from the squadron. The hut had ten beds in it and in the middle, a coke-fuelled 'Turtle' belly stove as its heating system. Paddy and Algy were given a room to share in the 'officers mess' huts, alongside Johnnie, who was sharing with a young Pilot Officer, Tony 'Ginger' Bere, another 'new boy'.

At ten o'clock that night, the crew of G-George, and several others looked on from the sidelines as eighteen Lancasters taxied round the perimeter track and one by one lumbered into the evening sky. The last ruby-tinged light of the day reflecting from the cockpit canopies as they set out on their latest sortie 'somewhere over Germany'. The following morning, the rising sun of a new day greeted the returning aircraft, one aircraft and its crew failed to return after crashing in flames as they fought their way home. Some of the other aircraft were shot-up and damaged, but the crews, although bone-weary tired, were safe.

# 4 ... The Crew

Two of Johnnie's crew had served with operational squadrons before, the flight engineer, Flight Sergeant Percival 'Chalkie' White AFM, and the navigator, Flying Officer Michael 'Paddy' Doolan DSO.

Chalkie White was twenty-four years old, a short, stocky, powerfully built man with a broad West Midlands accent. He answered to 'Chalkie', 'Brummie' or 'Percy', but definitely not Percival. That is what his mother used to call him if he was misbehaving and he hated the name.

He married his childhood sweetheart, Freda, soon after his eighteenth birthday in 1938. Together, with his father, they had run a small garage near the centre of Coventry. Freda coped very well with the paperwork and accounts, while Chalkie and his dad were excellent mechanics. In fact, his dad suggested he joined the RAF, as he knew the training for a mechanic would be better than in the army where he had learnt his trade.

Chalkie's call up was towards the end of 1939, and he did his forty-week RAF ground crew engineer training at RAF St. Athan on Barry Island in South Wales.

During the summer of 1940, his son, David, was born, but the Luftwaffe destroyed this cosy domestic world forever on the night of November 14, 1940, when they dropped thousands of high explosive and incendiary bombs on Coventry City, trying to destroy the engineering and aircraft manufacturing facilities situated around the city. The horrendous firestorm that destroyed and devastated the Midlands city also killed his wife, son and father, their remains now buried in a mass grave along with hundreds of others.

He had originally joined the RAF as ground crew, but that was not enough now. He wanted to avenge the death of his family, and he could only do that by re-mustering as aircrew on bombers. He wanted to strike deep into the heart of the enemy. Being part of the weapon that took death to the Nazis would help satisfy his need for revenge. He volunteered for an air gunner's course, but, typically, the RAF sent him on an air engineers' course instead. His promotion from Sergeant to Flight Sergeant came on completion of his aircrew course.

He then served as a flight engineer on Wellington bombers, completing a tour of thirty sorties in a remarkably short three months before they sent him to an OTU as an instructor. He hated this passive role and soon volunteered for a posting to Blyton HCU to convert to Lancasters and then on to complete the Lancaster Finishing School course with the rest of the crew. The Skipper had been using him, occasionally, as the second pilot, when needed, as he had completed many hours pilot training, like most of the crewmembers.

Chalkie had won his Air Force Medal, when he was a sergeant on ground crew. He saved many other lives and aircraft from destruction after the Luftwaffe had bombed and strafed his airfield. The aircraft next to one he was working on was hit by cannon fire, which set it on fire, killing the two ground crew about to tow it to the hangar for repair. Chalkie climbed onto a tractor and used it to pull the burning aeroplane onto the grass airfield out of the line of parked aircraft it was in, before jumping off and running clear. A few seconds after he had baled out of the tractor, the Wimpy exploded violently.

Not long after that, the RAF decided to disperse aircraft around the fringes of the airfield instead of parking them in lines, thus avoiding any more similar experiences.

He was an excellent mechanic and diagnostician, an ideal flight engineer. There was very little he did not know about Rolls Royce Merlin engines, and other engineers would consult him for advice and solutions to problems they could not figure out. Unlike most flyers, he was not superstitious, he did not believe in lucky charms or lucky routines before flying, he always just got onboard and started his pre-flight routines. The loss of his family had filled him with anger, hatred, and a wish for revenge; he had no other reason to exist now. He just wanted to get on with the job and 'kill the bloody Jerries.'

Flying Officer Michael 'Paddy' Doolan, DSO, the navigator, had served for a short time in a Wellington squadron, and had completed eighteen sorties before his aircraft had crash-landed. This happened early in 1942 on a return run from an operation over Mannheim in Germany. Flak badly damaged the bomber as they returned over the French coast, killing the waist-gunner and wounding the rear gunner. Elevators and rudder holed, losing height, they had diverted to an American airfield in Suffolk where the undercarriage had refused to lock down. It collapsed on touchdown and the Wimpy had crashed and burnt. He managed to pull his pilot and observer/nose-gunner out alive from the burning wreck, but the rear-gunner and wireless operator did not make it. He received the Distinguished Service Order for his bravery. Not long afterwards, he transferred to OTU to fly in Lancasters.

He was twenty-six years old and from Downpatrick, a small town close to the Mountains of Mourne in Northern Ireland. Although his 'Irish charm' made him very popular with women, he had remained single. His clear blue eyes highlighted his black hair and fresh-faced complexion. A very intelligent, knowledgeable, funny man, who was good at solving practical problems, a resourceful man, one you would want with you in a bad situation, thought Johnnie. His passion was for the sea, poetry and literature; he loved books.

Before the war, he had spent a great deal of time on the water. He was a keen sailor, even crossing the Atlantic with his brother and crew aboard their fifty-two foot ketch. His choice of the RAF had surprised his brother and friends; they believed that he would automatically join the Navy as his brother had done, but as he said, "I've *sailed* the Atlantic and now I want to *fly* the Atlantic."

Like most seafarers, he did believe in lucky mascots and always carried, what sailors call, a 'Monkey's Fist' with him. This was a piece of fancy cord-work, knotted into a tight, small ball, made for him by an old sea dog from the little fishing port of Ardglass in Northern Ireland. All the other members of the crew called him Paddy. The Skipper always called him Michael, because he did not like 'national' nicknames, like Taffy, Jock or Paddy, which he envisaged as bad luck for a reason he could not explain.

Later that morning found Johnnie, Chalkie and the wireless operator bouncing around in the back of a thirty-hundredweight truck on the road to Blyton to pick up their cars and motorbike.

The wireless operator was one Flying Officer Algernon Rupert Willoughby-D'Arcy, known as 'Algy', a twenty-five year-old single man used to 'the good life'. His father was a knight of the realm and a Member of Parliament for a rural constituency in Wiltshire, where the family home was a country house set in its own estate, and there was a flat in Mayfair, London, for 'entertainment'. Algy was a real 'Toff'. He played the role very well, smoking Turkish cigarettes through an elegant ivory holder and driving a 1934 open-topped J2 MG sports car. He was what you might call, a 'Ladies Man', tall, good-looking with debonair film star looks, and always wore the latest fashions, except for the white silk scarf he had worn on his first ever flight and now he wouldn't fly without it. In fact, he wore it all the time, in civvies or uniform, although not strictly a part of the uniform, unlike his typical RAF handlebar moustache.

Algy had joined the RAF Volunteer Reserve in 1940, when his father decided 'he had better do something useful for a change'. The impression he liked to give to people was that of a slightly dim, eccentric English gentleman, but, in fact, he was very intelligent, and when he came back from his aircrew training in Canada, he came top in his six-month radio-training course at RAF Yatebury, near Bristol. He was outstanding in grasping both the theoretical and mechanical aspects of radio and radar, also accomplishing a very good speed of eighteen words per minute in Morse code. When asked by one of his contemporaries why he was so proficient, he replied with a wink, 'Because I love spending time with Dit and Dah, old boy!'

He was a very accomplished pilot, but he always said, 'Only fly for fun, old boy.' He did not want the responsibility for 'all that metal and bodies'.

Despite all of his privileged background, public school, country house, Algy was happiest when up in the air and 'messing about with radio stuff'. Being part of a team was important to him. He loved being in the RAF, but he did not want to captain an operational aircraft, and had no ambitions for a higher rank; Flying Officer was high enough for him. It allowed him the freedom he needed for the style of life he enjoyed living.

On the way back to Elkington, bouncing down the narrow Lincolnshire lanes in his little Ruby car, Johnnie Sanderson wondered what would lie ahead for him and the members of his crew. They were now an active part of a squadron. The training had been long and hard over the last year, but they were a team, made up of competent professionals ready to take on the future, but what did that future hold for him and the crew? The other three members, like Algy, had never flown on an operational bombing sortie.

The baby of the crew at 21, was Sergeant Frank 'Jan' Greasely. His promotion to sergeant from AC2 (Aircraftman $2^{nd}$ Class), twelve months ago came on completion of his aircrew training, when he joined the rest of the crew at Blyton. He picked up his nickname, Jan, on his initial training course. All Cornishmen carry the nickname 'Jan' for some reason throughout the three services. He was the joker of the bunch; he could always see some comedy in most situations, even the more dramatic ones. His dark Cornish colouring gave him a piratical appearance, and women appeared to find this attractive, his broad West Country burr only adding to the attraction.

In civvy life, he had been an assistant gamekeeper to his father, who was Head Gamekeeper on the Mount Edgcumbe estate in Cornwall, just across the waters of Plymouth Sound from Devon. He was a first class shot with any type of weapon, but during his aircrew training, it was clear that it was probably best to leave flying an aircraft to those who had an aptitude for it, but he demonstrated an uncanny skill as an air bomber. Coupled with his love of guns, he was the obvious choice to fill the nose of a Lancaster bomber. He was very proud of his accomplishments as an air bomber and prided himself on hitting his bombing and gunnery targets.

Although he had an innate talent with guns of any kind, he was very clumsy in everyday life. This became obvious on the first day he became a member of the crew. They were standing around the NAAFI van in the hangar at Blyton on the crew selection day, when Chalkie asked him if he had the time on him, as he wanted to check his own watch. At that moment, Jan was holding, in his right hand, an enamel mug of so-called NAAFI cha, an indescribable lukewarm, brown liquid. Unfortunately, his watch was on the same wrist, so as he turned his arm over to check the time, the brown liquid, deposited itself down his uniform. He joined in with the hysterical laughter from his new colleagues. Nonetheless, they still took him on.

His father had given him, many years earlier, as a lucky charm, a foot from the first rabbit that he had ever shot, which he wore round his neck, threaded on a leather thong. He never went anywhere without it.

Sergeant James 'Dusty' Miller, the mid-upper gunner, was not much older than Jan was and they had become close friends during their training course. He was twenty-two years old, single, but had a girlfriend, Mavis, back in Crook, a little town in County Durham, where his parents ran a greengrocer shop and a small holding and where Dusty used to work growing the fruit and vegetables for the shop.

He had joined the RAF Volunteer Reserve two years earlier and trained at air gunnery schools at Morpeth in Northumberland, not far from his home, and RAF Binbrook in Lincolnshire, not far from Elkington.

His hobby, at home, when not growing vegetables, was playing the euphonium in Crook Town Silver Band. Johnnie's response to this was, 'What the hell is a euphonium?' Dusty had a habit of 'fingering' to a piece of music, playing an imaginary euph, as he called it, with the fingers of his right hand. On the shelf above his bed, in his Nissen hut, he had a brass, bell-shaped euphonium mouthpiece which he practised with constantly, making a musical squirting noise through it, which eventually, after a few weeks, drove the rest of his messmates mad, soliciting offers to ram the 'squirty thing' somewhere very private!

Since he had started the Lancaster Finishing School course, he had secretly been taking into the turret with him, a picture of his girlfriend, Mavis, which, for luck, he kissed each time he took off.

The last member of the crew was Sergeant Gordon 'Yorky' Ward, the rear gunner, or, 'arse end Charlie'. He was a tall, well-built twenty-three-year-old married butcher, from Seacroft, a village on the outskirts of Leeds. His broad Yorkshire accent was part of his character, that of a trusted, honest, hard worker with a wicked sense of humour.

He volunteered for aircrew because he wanted to pilot an aeroplane, but when he attended his initial pilot's assessment course at the Scarborough Flying School, he discovered he had no sense of height. He could not judge downward distances, and so he could not land the aircraft. When flying two-seater Tiger Moths with an instructor telling him what to do, he did not have a problem, but when he flew on his one and only solo flight, he almost crashed. As he came in to land he suddenly realised he did not know how high he was. After first hitting the ground, very hard, he bounced the aircraft up in the air and down again five or six times before veering towards a line of parked aircraft, stopping just short. His instructor hauled him from the aircraft and told him, in a flurry of very colourful language, never to get in the pilot's seat again. Consequently, he went to Walney Island Gunnery School, near Barrow-in-Furness, to train as an air gunner instead.

For some bizarre reason that Johnnie never understood, he always took a chicken wishbone with him for luck when he flew. His other crewmates believed it was to remind him that he was really still a butcher, not an aviator.

He smoked a pipe with a long thin stem and when he grew agitated, he used it to poke the people he was talking to and wave it around like a conductor's baton. His colourful conversations always seemed to contain the word 'bugger'. Bugger it! bugger them! What a bugger! In addition, his most favourite phrases were 'Well I'll be buggered' or 'Bugger me', to which the crew, as one, would answer, 'Not tonight Josephine. Not tonight!' After Algy had explained what the true definition was of his two favourite phrases, Yorky's answer to their cry would be an embarrassed flustering, 'No, no, I didn't mean it like that!' His broad Yorkshire accent, with hard 'Us, added an extra entertainment element to his favourite exclamations.

Although Johnnie had a lot of experience, as he had flown over thirty-nine operations in other bombers, some of the team were still green to combat flying and found night flying particularly stressful. Especially as they carried out their 'fighter affiliation' exercises, when Mosquito night fighters swept out of the darkness on mock attacks, shouting, 'Dagga-Dagga-Dagga, You're dead!' over the R/T.

Yorky's response was, of course, 'Bugger off!'

One aspect of training enjoyed by all the crewmembers was the low-level shooting and bombing runs they carried out on the firing ranges over the North Lincolnshire coast around Donna Nook. The beaches here were five to six miles wide from the sand dunes to the sea. On the sands were square, orange roofed, squat timber towers, used as targets. Here the gunners could blast away at something tangible, instead of shooting at clouds or using camera guns. As their great bombers banked over the beach, local kids would terrify the aircrews by standing on top of the sand dunes waving at the aircraft as they roared past, and they would be delighted when the rear gunner waggled his guns and turret in acknowledgement.

They would fly further down the coast, past Skegness, to the mud flats and wide beaches off Wainfleet (home of the brewery that produced 'Bateman's Good Honest Ales'), where there were more bombing ranges set up. They used practice smoke bombs, of course, dropping them from below a thousand feet and up to ten thousand feet, but most of the time they were lucky to drop them anywhere near the target, despite Jan's best effort.

'If we had decent bombsights like the Norden SABS that the Yanks have, we'd be laughin', my 'ansome,' was his constant excuse.

Their first sortie to the Wainfleet range had led to an official, but friendly, reprimand. The holiday camp at Skegness, set up by a certain Mr. Billy Butlin, had converted to the Royal Navy Officer training establishment, HMS Royal Arthur, soon after the start of the war. The crew received information in the mess the night before their exercise, that it was normal practise to annoy the Navy by 'buzzing' the parade ground at Skegness, especially if the officer cadets were on parade. So as G-George screamed north from the Wainfleet range, fifty feet above the ground at two hundred and fifty miles an hour, it seemed only natural to thunder over the parade ground causing hundreds of trainee officers to flatten themselves to the deck as the Lancaster swept dramatically over them at head height. The white ensign flying from the mast on the edge of the parade ground was in great danger of attaching itself to the bomber's wingtip. What Johnnie and his crew were not aware of was that there was one sailor who did not 'hit the deck'. That was the fist-shaking, inspecting Rear Admiral, who did not appreciate his 'young tars' being frightened out of their skin by some "damn young Johnnie-come-lately from the bloody Flying Corps!"

One day the crew received a real scare. They had been on a daylight exercise in Scotland ending in a high-level practise-bombing run over the Firth of Dornoch, some twenty-five miles north of Inverness. They had finished their exercise and were flying down the Yorkshire coast on their own late one afternoon around sunset. Algy had suddenly announced he had spotted an aircraft on his *Monica* radar repeater closing on them from their starboard quarter. Yorky, in his rear turret, spotted it quickly, recognised the aircraft by its yellow nose cone, and yelled.

"Fighter, starboard down, corkscrew right, now, ME-109, a thousand yards!"

His guns chattered for the first time in anger, but his tracers curved well to starboard of the banking fighter. Dusty, in his mid-upper turret, blazed away blindly in the same direction as Yorky's flailing bullets. He was not going to miss this opportunity to get his first chance of a 'kill'.

Johnnie started to put the aircraft into a right hand dive, heading for the coast.

"Skipper, it's turned away, it's turned away to port," reported Yorky.

He watched it dive away to the left, heading out over the North Sea as Johnnie pulled the heavy bomber back up to his original height and course.

"Aircraft approaching from starboard quarter!" shouted Algy, picking up a second image on his radar.

Yorky swung his turret round to face that direction and, again, quickly picked up this second aircraft. To his relief, he discovered it was a Spitfire.

"It's OK, Skip; it's one of ours, a Spit."

"Thank God for that," said Johnnie.

It came up along the port side of the Lancaster, the VHF R/T radio crackled into life.

"Spitfire to Lanc G George, Spitfire to Lanc G George. What is Auntie doing promenading out here on her own without a chaperone? Enjoying the evening air, are we? All sorts of wicked things could happen to a lady all by herself, you know. You are okay now; the nasty Hun has gone away. Prince Charming will escort you down to Spurn, if you like, over."

"Thank you, kind sir, you're so gallant. Spurn Point will be fine, out," replied Johnnie with a wry grin and a wave to the Spitfire pilot. The Spit moved in front of them and completed a slow victory roll. The RT crackled:

"How about having a go at that then, Auntie?"

"Very impressive." He switched to intercom. "Quickly, Chalkie, feather port outer."

Chalkie complied and one of the four props slowed to a standstill, its blades turning into the wind to stop the circular motion.

"Try copying that then, Prince Charming, out." retorted Johnnie over the RT.

The members of the crew who could see the events burst into laughter.

"That pissed on his chips, Skipper," laughed Jan, from his grand view in the nose.

Nevertheless, it was the first time the crew had experienced the adrenaline-producing effect of an enemy fighter being close to them.

"Well done, gunners. Brilliantly picked up, Yorky, and great backup, Dusty, well done both of you. You got that radar working at last, Algy, well done."

The way the crew had handled that little emergency pleased Johnnie. Okay, it had not come to the fighter opening up on them, but that could have been because of the quick reactions of Yorky and Dusty that frightened him away. They had all worked well as a team.

As he followed the Spitfire down the coast, he realised that his hand had shaken when the guns began their noisome violence. Six machines guns blasting away in a flying metal box is an awesome level of sound. He remembered his last operational sortie in a Wellington over Germany some eleven months ago, the one after his crash-landing in the sea.

A night-fighter had strafed them, killed his wireless operator, and injured the navigator. The sudden invasion and the explosive impact into his secure world, the incredible noise, the stink of cordite and hot metal, the sudden metallic smell of warm, fresh blood, the gut-sinking feeling of *déjà vu,* the terror of crashing. The shock of the attack had disturbed him, so the posting to the unit at Manby, as an instructor, had secretly pleased him, a break from fifteen months of constant active duty, but he had felt guilty about the sense of relief. He would be okay now though, he thought, of course he would. Wouldn't he?

As they crossed the neck of Spurn Point the Spitfire pilot waggled his wings, called 'Cheerio!' and, with a flourish, banked and roared away up the Humber.

As they set down at Blyton, Johnnie announced,

"Home at last, chaps, home at last."

There was a certain amount of banter in the sergeants' mess that night, as the Senior NCOs of G-George related the Skipper's response to the Spitfire's challenge and their first encounter with the enemy. Yorky did confess that he had discovered the true colour of 'adrenaline'.

# 5 ... The Final Test

Everybody was apprehensive about the final test of the Lancaster Finishing School; it was an active sortie into enemy territory. For those members of the crew, Algy, Jan, Dusty and Yorky, who had no experience of operational service, all the months of training, all the hours of concentration, and all the hours of practice, had led them to the final test. Those sortie-experienced members, who had known the apprehension, excitement, and the gut-wrenching fear that operational service can bring, braced themselves and attempted to cover up any signs of nervousness. They knew it was up to them to put up a 'good show' for their less experienced comrades. Their brief meet with the ME 109 earlier had brought home, with hindsight that the enemy was not that far away and could appear at any moment. It certainly had made their reactions sharper, and their concentration, when carrying out training exercises, more intense. It could well save their lives one day.

"Do you reckon we're ready to take on the Hun again with our new crew, Johnnie?" asked Paddy, with a smile, whilst standing at the bar of the officers' mess, a dimpled glass mug of beer gripped in his fist. "Tomorrow will be the last Monday here at Blyton. Next Monday we will be in Elkington, living in wooden huts and dropping bombs for a living."

He raised his glass and silently toasted their future.

Johnnie laughed, "Yeah, I guess we will. I think the lads have done well. They have worked hard and I shall be more than happy to fly into action with them. Can you be happy to go back to war?" he grinned at Michael. "We have a good, strong team, Michael. There is only one person I am worried about- me! I can't say I'm looking forward to being under fire again, but I suppose we'll get used to it ... again."

They knew that they would be flying their first offensive op, as a crew, tomorrow night, if the weather was suitable, and tomorrow was their last lecture, on air-to-ship sea mines.

\*\*\*

"This, gentlemen, is the Mark one-stroke-four, sea mine. It is one thousand five hundred pounds in weight, including seven hundred and fifty pounds of Amatol high explosive. It is seventeen inches in diameter and nine feet long including the fairing on the front." The armaments officer informed them, as they stood outside the armoury maintenance unit staring down at a dark green metal tube on a multi-wheeled trolley.

"I was expecting a round thing with horns sticking out of it," said Yorky jokingly.

"They are the ones dropped by the navy from on board a ship, sergeant," lisped the rather effeminate armaments officer. A shining example of how a flight lieutenant should look. 'All bull and neat creases,' thought Yorky, but is he ...?

"Please feel free to sit on the mine. Have a good look at it. You will be flying with a few of these strapped to your bottoms tomorrow night," he patted the mine affectionately and laughed, in a way that you could only describe as a guffaw. No one else laughed.

"When you drop the mine, a small parachute releases from this end," he indicated the back of the mine. "This facilitates vertical entry into the water. The wooden fairing on the other end prevents deflection during its flight, and then disintegrates when it hits the water. After a short while in the sea, a soluble plug activates, and enables the parachute to release. This then floats away and the mine sinks to the seabed and becomes active. We will now go into the staff lecture room for detailed info'. Follow me; we should squeeze all seventy of you in there with a crush." Again, he guffawed.

"For detailed info'?" whispered Jan. "What the 'ell was that lot, then?"

The flight lieutenant was not wrong, the ten aircrews did get into the lecture room, just, and it was a crush.

"These are non-contact mines." He indicated an exploded diagram of the mine they had seen outside, pinned to the back wall. "The ones we normally drop are either acoustic or magnetic. They do not have 'horns' sticking out of them, as our friend expected," he said, glancing at Yorky, who was sitting on the front row with the rest of his crew.

"Is he ... ?" he whispered to Johnnie.

"Shush ...,"said Johnnie, with a smile.

"Acoustic mines!" declared the flight lieutenant. "All ships have a sound signature, a mixture of engine and propeller noise. A microphone inside the housing of the mine can home in on those sounds and differentiate between a large or small vessel, then detonate on that pre-selected signal."

"Magnetic mines!" he announced. "All metal ships have a magnetic field, but even though the builders try to disguise it by the use of electrical cables running round the perimeter of the ship, that does not eliminate it. Here again, the mine is fine-tuned to identify the strength of the magnetic field passing overhead and it will detonate to its pre-selected signal."

He swung a leg over and sat on the mine lying on the floor in front of him resting on wooden chocks.

"But that is not all; oh golly, no. We have a few more tricks up our sleeves. Recently, the 'Boffins' ... " he said 'Boffins' as if referring to a superordinate heavenly being, " ... have come up with some super little gems. Like the 'Acoustic-Magnetic mine' and the 'Magnetic-Acoustic Mine'."

By now, his energetic style of presentation and slight lisp were causing many in his audience to giggle and smirk.

"What's the bloody difference between a *Magnetic*-Acoustic Mine and an *Acoustic*-Magnetic Mine, for God's sake?" whispered Yorky to Dusty.

"BUT, that is not all." carried on the excited flight lieutenant. "It is possible to set a 'Period Delay Mechanism' to hold open the firing circuit allowing the mine to work off all the pre-selected delaying operations. The 'PDM' can be set to allow two or three ships to pass over, before blowing up the next one. The thinking behind this is that the first few ships could be *speerbreckers*, minesweepers to you and me, or patrol boats and the next one could be a large warship or even an aircraft carrier. This action can confuse the minesweepers when they are escorting vessels through a minefield, and we hope the jolly old *speerbreckers* get *blown* to bits as well, brilliant, what?"

"I don't know about confusin' the *speerbreckers,* he's bloody well confusin' me," sniggered Jan.

The flight lieutenant then spent the next hour explaining, in his own unique and effervescent style, the ins and outs of his obvious favourite subject. How the explosion did not sink a ship, but the powerful, dramatic pulse-wave from the gas bubble it created ripped a ship's hull apart. How the type of seabed dictated the strength and direction of the blast, and the damage the plume of water could do to anything in the air up to three hundred feet above. However, he assured the crews the mines were quite safe to transport, in fact, even if they crashed with mines on board their aircraft, they would not explode, and they would still be safe. The ironic jeering that greeted this appeared to confuse him a little, so he struck the nose cone end of the mine a mighty blow with a heavy engineering hammer. That produced several squeals and cries of 'Hit the deck!' from his stunned audience. When they had recovered their somewhat chagrined composure, he explained that they had a very clever device to prevent accidental arming. A safety fork prevented the closing of the arming switch, along with a safety switch with a soluble plug; this operated hydrostatically and kept the mine in a safe condition until a predetermined period had elapsed once the mine had submerged below thirty feet of water.

As they rode back to the flight hut in a crew bus, Jan mimicked the armaments flight lieutenant, "We'll blow the jolly old *Speerbreckers* to bits, brilliant, what?" With his broad Cornish accent, it was even more comical.

"Well you couldn't call the flight lieutenant boring, now could you?" laughed Paddy. Nonetheless, they all now knew how aerial mines worked. All they had to do was drop them.

Johnnie informed them they would take 'G-George' on a Night Flight Test (NFT),[3] used to check that all systems were working okay in the air, and that there were no 'gremlins' hiding in the system.

"It's funny where they come from," said Chalkie to Johnnie. "You can never predict their appearance and they always come when you least need them."

They exercised NFTs before all active operations, whenever practical. It was no good finding out the bomb doors wouldn't open if you were sitting above a German city at eighteen thousand feet, surrounded by flak and night fighters, and the only thing you could drop on them was the contents of the Elsan toilet! Therefore, they went for a 'quick trip round the block', tested their systems and thirty minutes later landed.

"I can never understand why they call it a Night Flying Test when we do the bugger in daylight!" exclaimed Yorky.

At 1730 hours that afternoon, RAF Blyton's tannoy system reminded them that the briefing on their target was at 1800 hours tonight in the briefing room. Ten crews were about to embark on their first-ever active raid into enemy territory, and after that they would be dispatched to their squadrons to become part of the front line against Hitler and Nazi Germany's onslaught against the free world.

They filed into the room, through the double doors guarded by two RAF policemen. It was a large room within the main administration block, with a raised platform at one end, and the Intelligence Officer's office at the other. They entered amid the murmur of nervous chatter. People laughing too loudly at stupid comments, their laughter sounding forced and contrived. The crews tended to crowd round their Skippers for comfort as they settled into their seats, arranged in rows of seven behind folding trestle tables either side of the central aisle.

The SIO called them to attention, and clattering chairs accompanied the senior 'bods' entrance and their procession down the room to sit in the front row of seats.

---

[3] See appendix for a copy of the NFT form

The Station Commander took to the low platform. His four rings of rank on each arm reflecting the chest full of medal ribbons that gave him the authority and respect he was due.

A tall man, with a thin stiff moustache and strangely neat eyebrows, he tapped his right thigh with his leather-covered swagger stick and addressed the gathered ensemble.

"Good afternoon, gentlemen." There was a mumbled nervous reply from some of the aircrews. "You are about to start your last challenge and pass out of the Lancaster Finishing School. That phrase always sounds to me like we are referring to a posh girls' school." Raucous cheers and laughter greeted this, and immediately the atmosphere changed.

"Knowing airmen, as I do, I suspect that most of you would prefer being there than here!"

Again, laughter and ribald comments filled the room. He held up his hands to regain control.

"This will be your last sortie in our command. After this you will join your squadrons and become operational members of the world's greatest air force." The room had fallen quiet. "The skills you have learnt over the last few months will enable you to take this damned war to the heart of our enemy. For some of you this is the first time you have flown 'in anger', so to speak. Tonight you have the first opportunity of fighting back. High explosives, incendiaries and mines are all part of our arsenal. Tonight you also will become part of that arsenal. Your training is over. You are now weapons of war. Good luck, and thank you, gentlemen."

He stepped off the platform and the Intelligence Officer (IO) then took the stand.

"Your target for tonight is ... "

He pulled back the black curtain that covered the wall behind the podium to show a giant map of Europe, crossing from Lincolnshire to Holland and up to the coast of Denmark; red tapes indicated the route there and back.

" ... the shipping lanes of the Friesian Islands. Tonight, gentlemen, you are going 'Gardening', that is the code word for mine laying, as you know. The area code-names are Nectarine A, B and C," he used a wooden pointer to show the areas. "All the sea-lanes around Holland, Denmark, Northern Germany and Poland have plant code names, and this is where you *sow* your mines, hence the term 'Gardening'."

"You will be sowing your mines along the shipping lanes from Terschelling to Wangerooge." The pointer followed his words on the map. "These are vital routes for Axis shipping, both military and civilian. They are the southern approaches to Wilhelmshaven, Bremerhaven, Bremen and Hamburg." Again, he indicated each port. "These are vital ports to the enemy. If we can disrupt their supply chain by sinking their ships or by driving their ships into the waiting arms of the Royal Navy, then we could be shortening the war. You are not flying over enemy occupied land, so no flak. Some of the gunners on the islands may try to have a go at you, but you will be way out of range of their guns. But keep a sharp lookout for Jerry night fighters, especially in Heligoland Bay." He indicated the area off the mouth of the River Elbe with his pointer.

The Navigation Officer then briefed them on their course.

"Gentlemen, let me take you through the routes and headings for tonight, and this, of course, is mainly for the Captains of aircraft and Air Bombers. The Navigators, as you all know, have already gone through this in detail earlier."

They were to approach the islands from the southwest so they could plant their mines in the shipping lanes to the northwest of the group of islands. Their course was zero-eight-seven to a turning point southwest of Terschelling where the Path Finder aircraft would drop a green Turn Indicator flare. They would then turn on to zero-seven-five degrees to take them to their individual dropping positions. He stressed how important the accuracy was of their navigation to these points. When they had dropped their mines, they were to turn for home on a heading of two-six-two degrees. [4] Collection of their TI arrival times, individual target co-ordinations and timings would be at the conclusion of the briefing.

"To avoid being picked up early by the German radar, you will fly low, two hundred feet from take-off until you cross the

---

[4] See appendix for courses and routes navigated.

coast at Saltfleet. Remember the seventy-foot high windmill there; the locals like it with its top on! You will cross the North Sea at one hundred feet until you see the first TI, you will then climb to fifteen hundred. After you have dropped your mines, you will start to climb to eight thousand feet for the journey home."

The Bombing Leader was next, a tough looking Wing Commander, with a chest full of ribbons.

"I am your Bombing Leader and one of the Path Finders for tonight. The first aircraft will take off at 2200 hours and that will be me. Pilots come and get your take-off times from the board after the briefing," he indicated the blackboard on its easel at the edge of the platform. "Tonight you will be planting six Mark One, fifteen hundred pound aerial acoustic mines."

"Is that one of the round ones with spikes?" Paddy asked Johnnie with a smile.

The Bombing Leader emphasised the accuracy of position, timing and height. They were to drop their mines from fifteen hundred feet exactly, and fly at one hundred and eighty mph exactly. This was a precision mission, not a training jolly over the North Sea. Johnnie and Michael were making furious notes on their pads as he spoke.

"It is very important that we know where the mines are. If you drop them in the wrong place, you could be responsible for blowing up a friendly ship. If, for some reason, navigators, you have to jettison your mines, it is vital you plot where they fall."

The Meteorological Officer, a nondescript, wingless Flying Officer, then informed them that the wind would be ten to fifteen knots from the northeast, intermittent cloud with a base of five to six thousand feet would be with them over the target, but could start to lift by the time they were on the homeward leg.

The Group Captain returned to the platform.

"You have spent the last few months putting the final touches to your skills as bomber crews; tonight you put that all together when you make your first strike as an effective weapon of war." Here he paused and looked all round the room at the attentive audience. "Some of you have experience in combat;

most of you are going to war for the first time. Remember, this is what you have trained for, good luck."

The Intelligence Officer took the stand again and called them all to attention as the senior officers filed out of the room.

"All right, gentlemen, please be seated. Wireless operators will report later to the Communications Officer, there at the back," he indicated a flight lieutenant seated at a desk, "to get the signals and codes for tonight. Pilots and air bombers collect your information from the board and collect your maps and charts from the map store. When you have done that, go and get your egg and chips." He smiled as an ironic cheer went up. "Issue of parachutes and rations, etcetera will be at 2000 hours. Good luck chaps."

The pilots, air bombers and wireless operators collected their information and returned to their accommodation huts, each with their private thoughts. After the now traditional meal of egg, chips and baked beans in the aircrew mess, they went to the crew room and took their flying gear from their lockers, heavy flying suits, flying boots, Mae West life jackets, parachute harnesses and leather helmets. Paddy came in piled up with boxes of survival kits and ration packs. The crew shared around flasks of coffee, sandwiches, chocolate and boiled sweets. The more experienced crew members among them had made up their own survival kits, dispersed over different parts of their flying gear. The top part of Johnnie's flying boots had zipped sides, but when cut off, this left the wearer with what looked like an ordinary pair of shoes. One of his metal trouser buttons had a red dot on it and when balanced on a twig, nail or pencil, the red dot would always point to north.

Silent nervous tension had reduced the normal banter and jokey behaviour. Each member of the crew checked and double-checked his equipment and clothing as he waited for the crew bus to take him out to dispersal. Most men smoked cigarettes or puffed on pipes. Algy was always at the end of friendly banter because of the ivory cigarette holder he used, but not tonight. At last, buses and lorries arrived and the WAAF drivers asked them the recognition code for their aircraft and the dispersal pan number. Johnnie and his crew climbed on a bus and joined the crew of F-Fox. They travelled round the perimeter track in silence.

"G-George!" the WAAF shouted, as the bus jerked to a halt.

The crew jumped down and collected their gear and boxes. The WAAF drove off with a wave: F-Fox was standing on the next pan seventy yards away.

Darkness would come early tonight. Thick grey cloud stretched from horizon to horizon. It looked more like a November afternoon than a July evening.

They gathered round the starboard tail-plane in the failing light while Johnnie did his pre-flight inspection with the ground crew flight sergeant, and Jan, the air bomber, inspected the open bomb bay and his babies, six massive green cylinders suspended from their brackets. Johnnie checked that the wheel chocks were in place and the covers removed from the airspeed indicator Pitot head, the static vents, cockpit and wheels. He checked that the tyres were okay and that the white paint marks on the wheel rims and walls of the tyres matched, showing there had been no tyre creep. If there were, this could mean a tyre could fail on take-off or landing with catastrophic effect. He checked the leading edge of the wings and tail and signed the flight sergeant's airworthiness document, Form 700, and the fuel state form, and took possession, be it only temporary, of G-George from him.

Aircraft were the ground crew's property, aircrews only borrowed them occasionally, usually leaving them in a pitiable state, or so the ground crew believed. Woe betides any pilot that brought back a damaged one; sucking of teeth and a tut-tut-tut would greet him.

Johnnie joined the rest of the crew while they waited for the green flare to appear over the control tower, which meant 'Get on board, prepare for take-off'.

He pulled out his pipe, his 'flying pipe' as he called it. It had a short stem and an apple-shaped bowl; in fact, it looked like a squashed apple with the top cut off. He tamped down some tobacco and struck a match, joining the other smoking members of the crew. It was strictly against the rules to smoke around an aircraft, as it had on board one thousand-five-hundred gallons of highly flammable aviation fuel! However, the ground crew flight sergeant would turn a blind eye as long as they were to the back of the aircraft. The little conversation there was was very stilted; they were finding it difficult to keep eye contact; their nerves jangled with anticipation.

Suddenly eerie wavering green light bathed the scene, as the flare burst above the airfield.

"Git on board, liddle doggies, git on board," sang out a nervous Yorky, in a mock cowboy accent, as he knocked out the remains of 'baccy' from his slim-stemmed pipe on the side of the tail fin.

"You've been watching too many 'shit kickers', Yorky," laughed Dusty. "I'll just 'water the wheel'," he said as he relieved himself over the tail wheel for luck.

# 6 ... Gardening

Over the last few months, they had fallen into a logical unspoken ritual when it came to boarding the aircraft. Jan Greasly, air bomber, climbed in through the starboard side door first, and felt for the rabbit's foot around his neck; then Johnnie Sanderson, pilot; Chalkie White, flight engineer, went straight to his flying station without ritual; followed by Michael (Paddy) Doolan, navigator; Algy Willoughby-D'Arcy, wireless operator; Dusty Miller, mid upper gunner and finally, Yorky Ward, rear gunner.

Jan swung himself under the switches, gauges and buttons of Chalkie's station and entered the Plexiglas world of the nose cone. He stowed his parachute on the bulkhead at the back and, lying prone on the green leather-covered cushion over the escape hatch in the floor, carried out his checks on the bombsight-head in front of him, the bombsight computor on his left and the bomb-release selectors on the panel to his right. With these switches, he could select which bomb to drop and the timing of the stick of bombs. Below this was a smaller panel that controlled the release of the photo-flares from the flare chute near the main door in the fuselage. On the port side, looking downwards, was the F.24 camera installation, although they would not be taking any photographs of the target tonight, but would be when they were dropping bombs. Then standing up and sitting on the adjustable metal seat, he checked the twin machine guns in the turret directly above him, making sure that the guns and the turret moved freely on their hydraulic mountings.

Johnnie put his parachute behind his seat and secured it, settled himself and tightened his seat straps. He felt under his Mae West life jacket and touched his breast pocket that contained his still warm 'flying pipe', smiled, and then began his complicated pre-flight checks ensuring he had turned the radio to intercom. Then he carried out the engines' start-checks. Brake pressure, the idle cut off to down, battery ground/flight switch to ground, signal ground crew to plug-in external accumulator/battery trolley, boost cut-out lever up, switch on undercarriage warning lights and flap indicators. Open the throttles to three-quarters, set the supercharger, lock the undercarriage, close bomb doors, check flaps are neutral, set propeller levers to max rpm and air intakes to cold, switch on fuel gauges and check levels. Switch off master cocks, switch pumps in No. 2 tanks on and select the master cock required, switch on the ignition and booster coil and then prime the engines.

Chalkie checked that all the fuel cocks were correctly set, that oil, fuel pressures and temperatures were okay. He slid back his side window and shouted down to the corporal of the ground crew,

"Ready for starting."

"Undercarriage locked down?" he asked,

"Undercarriage locked down."

"Brakes on?"

"Brakes on."

"Switch to ground?"

Chalkie responded to each call. "Switch to ground."

The corporal then called,

"All clear. Contact starboard inner."

"Contact starboard inner," replied Chalkie.

Johnnie pressed the starter buttons and, one by one, the engines roared into life, starboard inner, port inner, port outer, starboard outer. Five thousand eight hundred and forty horsepower produced from four Rolls Royce Merlin 24 engines were ready to pull over thirty tons of war machine, metal, fuel, high explosive and people into the night sky on the crew's first operational sortie.

Paddy settled behind his light-shading curtain, switched on his little angle-poised lamp and sorted his charts, protractor, compasses and the other bits and pieces he needed to do his job.

He checked his repeater instruments were on, altimeter, compass, airspeed indicators, and his radars.

He fingered the 'monkey fist' in his pocket, just to make sure it was there.

It was Algy's duty to check all the safety equipment, the Verey signal pistol and flares, dinghy stowage, fire axes and extinguishers. He then sat in his seat next to the portside window facing forward and arranged his signal books and pad for ease of use, checked again the signal codes for the night, made sure that the radios were working and his '*Monica*' radar was operative. He checked the direction-finding equipment and the IFF. [5] He tucked his white silk scarf more comfortably round his neck, enjoying the sensual feel of the material.

Dusty clambered into his mid-upper turret, pulling himself up into the cupola on the top of the aircraft. His feet stuck into the stirrups safely inside the new armour plated, semi-circular 'skirt' of the lower end of his turret. He tried to make himself comfortable on his canvas sling of a seat, knowing he had many hours ahead stuck in this place.

Swinging his turret sideways and guns up and down felt good; they moved smoothly and responded promptly to his touch on the control handles. He checked that the guns were on 'Safe' and locked the turret fore and aft for take-off. He placed the photograph of his girlfriend, Mavis, at the side of his starboard gun, kissing his fingers and placing them on her face for luck.

Yorky slid over the aft tail spar, closed the draft-proof bulkhead doors and secured his parachute just aft of the starboard side door. He eased himself through the sliding doors at the rear of his turret and settled into his seat, reaching behind him to slide the doors shut and remembering to lock them. It was a very tight fit for a man of his size; he always described it as 'cosy'.

---

[5] This is a radar that identifies whether an approaching aircraft is Friendly or Foe; hence IFF.

He checked that the four Browning machine guns were not loaded, set them to safe and tested their lateral movement and the horizontal movement of the turret. Then he cocked the guns and returned the safety catches to 'safe'. Before he fastened his harness, he felt inside his heated flight suit to check that the chicken wishbone was still there in his tunic breast pocket.

They were all trying to get used to the roar and rumble of being inside a metal tube again with four great thundering engines trying to shake them out.

"Right, chaps, all ready for the joy ride?" said Johnnie through the intercom. "Strictly by the book tonight chaps. We want everything as right as possible. Communications check people! Flight engineer."

"Engines OK. Oxygen connected."

"Bomb aimer."

"Photo Leads OK. Camera isolation switch 'on'. Bomb selector's numbers OK. Feed clear. Oxygen connected. Intercom OK when turret rotated."

"Navigator."

"Instruments and lights OK. GEE set off. Oxygen connected."

"Wireless OP."

"Wireless OK. Batteries charged. Spare batteries OK. Oxygen connected."

"Mid upper gunner."

"Turret elevation and rotation OK. Feed clear. Oxygen connected. Intercom OK when turret rotated."

"Rear gunner."

"Turret elevation and rotation OK. Feed clear. Oxygen connected. Heated clothing OK. Intercom OK when turret rotated."

"All eyes watch for possible trouble. Jan shine the Aldis lamp ahead of the aircraft. Yorky watch the tail."

"Ground/flight switch to flight."

"Ground switch to flight," answered Chalkie, switching over from the mobile accumulator used to start the engines to the aircraft's own 24-volt batteries.

He signalled the ground crew to unplug and remove the accumulator and the wheel chocks, and then checked the oil pressures and temperatures.

As Johnnie warmed the engines, he checked that the navigation lights were on and the altimeter read correctly. He pushed the throttles forward, released the brake and eased G-George on to the perimeter track to join the line of throbbing aircraft slowly making their way to the runway 'in use for tonight'.

Chalkie had his window pulled back on the starboard side and watched that Johnnie did not get too close to the edge of the 'peri' track as they travelled round to the runway.

They halted on the threshold line of the runway as the aircraft in front roared down the concrete strip and clambered into the night air. A green signal light flashed from the control caravan ahead on the port side of the runway, the signal to prepare for take-off.

Johnnie checked that the wing and tail navigation lights were on and announced, "Take positions for take-off. Flaps twenty."

"Flaps twenty," reported Chalkie.

Jan's normal take-off station, the one he preferred, was lying prone in his front dome watching the ground race beneath him. He explained to Johnnie that it made him feel alive and excited and, of course, he could watch for any obstructions on the runway ahead. Johnnie's answer to that was that if there were any obstructions, his warning would be too bloody late anyway. But tonight it was 'by the book', so Jan stepped up into the cockpit, scrambled over the main spa and along with Paddy went to sit on the floor with his back to the aft side of the main spar that ran across the fuselage behind the radio and navigator's positions. Algy left his seat and stood up with his head in the astrodome bubble just above his station to act as a further pair of eyes when they taxied and then joined his other two crewmembers sitting on the floor.

Johnnie waited for the second green, which meant 'clear to take-off'.

It flashed a few seconds later.

"Running up," he called over the intercom and opened the throttles against the brakes.

"Running up," answered Chalkie after a small pause.

Applying the brakes restricted the aircraft's fight to leap forward as the engines picked up their power. The airframe vibrated and thrashed desperate for release like a giant tethered beast.

"OK for take-off."

Chalkie checked the engine gauges, temperatures, oil pressures; he switched off the booster coil, checked that the coolant temperatures were correct and placed the radiator override switches down.

When satisfied that everything was ready, he declared to Johnnie that he was okay for take-off.

"OK for take-off"

"Taking off!"

Johnnie released the brakes and slowly opened the throttles as far as they would go.

"Full power."

"Full power."

Chalkie checked the engine gauges again and slid his hand below Johnnie's on the throttles to make sure they did not slip back when Johnnie put both his hands on the control yoke to pull her into the air.

The bomber thundered down the airfield, the enormous wings flexing alarmingly as the giant pneumatic tyres absorbed the unintended undulations of the concrete runway. Every part of the aircraft vibrated, jostled, bounced, juddered and shook as it accelerated through the darkness. The vibration would have rattled the back teeth of the crew if adrenaline had not locked their jaws. The crescendoing roar of the engines, the rattle and vibration of the aircraft numbed their brains. Their bodies tensed, waiting for the inevitable. Distantly, in their headphones they heard Paddy starting to call the airspeed every three seconds when his airspeed indicator repeater showed seventy miles per hour. As soon as the throttles were at maximum, Johnnie pushed the yoke forward gently to raise the tail wheel, his feet still dancing on the rudder pedals to keep G-George straight, to stop her veering off the runway.

"70 ... 80 ... 90 ... 95 ... 100 ... 105 ... 110!"

Johnnie eased back on the yoke and G-George rose majestically off the ground, crabbing slightly to port in the northeast wind, well before the end of the two thousand yard runway. The sudden smoothness and relative quiet, brought on by the wonder of flight as they became airborne, came as a glorious relief to the crew. Their adrenaline levels, along with their heart rates, started to return to something near normal as they returned to their flying stations.

Paddy made a note in his navigation logbook, 'Take-off 2217 hours.'

"Wheels up."

"Wheels up," came the reply as Chalkie raised the undercarriage and Johnnie nipped the wheel-brake lever to stop the wheels from turning and causing damage and excessive wear as the main gear retracted with a clunk under the engine nacelles.

"Climbing power."

"Climbing power," Chalkie decreased the engine revs to 2,400 rpm when they had reached 500 feet.

"Flaps up."

"Flaps up."

Chalkie slowly raised the flaps.

"Cruising power."

"Cruising power."

Chalkie lowered the revs to 1,900 rpm as she settled into a steady climbing turn to starboard to join the circuit of the other Lancasters above.

Their first op had attracted the normal attention for a mass take-off.

A group of people had gathered by the control caravan, among them several WAAFs, waving to the crews or to their boyfriends in particular as they took to the air, wondering if they would see them again. Chalkie always thought it was comforting that at least someone cared enough to see them leave.

When all ten of the training crews and the two Pathfinder aircraft were in the air, they turned towards the coast and levelled out at two hundred feet. They had practised low-flying tactics many times, but hurtling through the dark night at one hundred and eighty miles an hour two hundred feet above the ground was exciting and exhilarating.

"Now this is what you call flying, Skipper," said an elated Chalkie, looking at the other aircraft in close harmony at the side and in front of them as they skimmed over the Lincolnshire Wolds and then dropped to cross the flat plain towards the coast.

Johnnie laughed. "Yes, as long as nobody puts a bloody great pylon in the way."

"Now don't you worry, Skipper," charmed the navigator in his broad Irish brogue. "Would I let a thing like that happen to you? I'd have to walk home myself if I did."

They flashed safely above the windmill at Saltfleet, and reduced height down to one hundred feet as they pounded out across the North Sea.

They were on their first sortie against the enemy, their first experience as a full crew, thundering across the sea on the way to drop their first explosive load for real.

After flying two hundred uneventful miles, the intercom clicked.

"Three minutes to turning point, Skipper." called Paddy.

"Thank you, Michael. Keep an eye out for the TI chaps."

Within seconds a cascade of green flares, several miles to their front, burst into life and appeared to hover in the air several thousand feet up.

"That's the indicated colour for tonight, Skipper," said Jan from his forward station.

"Turn on to zero-seven-three and climb to fifteen hundred feet, Skipper," said Paddy as they passed under the TIs.

"Okay, Michael. Eyes skinned everybody. I'm sure that Jerry knows we're here now."

He turned to port, eased back on the control yoke, and levelled out at fifteen hundred feet.

"Was the TI in the correct position?"

"According to my calculations, indeed it was, Skipper."

Dropping the mines in the correct place, at the correct time, meant that accurate navigation was critical. A burst of red and green hanging flares from the pathfinder miles in front, indicated where the first of the timed runs was to begin.

Johnnie had always thought that these flares looked like some bizarre aerial Christmas tree.

He could see the three Lancs in front of him and presumed the others were in their correct line astern of G-George. The coastlines of the Friesian Islands were to starboard about four miles away. Some light flak was creeping into the sky like strings of brightly coloured beads over the coast of Norderney Island, but it was obviously way out of range.

"Seven minutes to target drop zone."

"Okay, Michael. Jan, everything okay? Are you ready for your big show?"

Jan, lying prone behind his bombsight, had double-checked his bombsight computor's calculations and then checked them again. The mines were to drop at five-second intervals.

"All okay, Skipper," answered the remarkably calm, warm burr of a Cornish accent.

Johnnie had to fly straight and level, not just to drop the mines, but also afterwards for at least another five minutes to confuse the Germans as to where they had dropped their mines.

"Three minutes to drop zone," intoned Paddy.

"Jan, she's all yours," said Johnnie.

"Ok, Skipper. Steady as you go."

Johnnie smiled to himself. Jan's accent made it sound like a command on a pirate ship out on the Spanish Main.

"Open bomb doors."

"Bomb doors open," he replied.

"Two minutes to drop zone," said Paddy.

Jan turned, and looked through the inspection hatch to the bomb bay behind him and checked that the bomb doors had fully opened.

"One minute to drop zone."

"Drop zone ... NOW!" called Paddy.

"First mine gone!" shouted Jan. "Second ... third ... fourth ... fifth ... sixth mine gone!"

He checked through the viewing hatch of the bomb bay again to make sure all the stores had gone.

G-George, as if in relief at losing the weight of six 1500 pound mines, had tried to leap up in the air as each mine had left, but Johnnie was ready and held her 'straight and level' for a few more minutes.

"Close bomb doors."

"Bomb doors closed," intoned Johnnie, as he reached down to the left of his seat and pulled the lever to its normal position.

"Time to turn, Skipper."

"OK, navigator, course for home?"

"Two-six-four."

"Let's go home, chaps, but keep a sharp look out, everybody."

He pulled the aircraft round to port in a steep climbing turn heading for a height of eight thousand feet; he steadied her on 264 degrees.

They had dropped their first weapons of war. The only person to witness their efforts was Yorky from his rear turret. He had watched the mines float down and splash in the sea. What would trigger their fuses, he wondered -- a cruiser, a destroyer, a battleship even? He hoped it would not be a poor Dutch fisherman, but then satisfied his conscience that they only had small wooden boats so they would be safe. A fleeting shape in the darkness brought him out of his reverie and he was just about to shout a warning when another Lancaster slowly passed to port a thousand feet below.

"Lanc to port quarter down, Skipper," he reported.

"Thanks, Yorky."

The night was clearing and by the time they were approaching the English coast, bright moonlight bathed the scene and they soon realised they were not alone. Wingtip and tail navigation lights were appearing around them like fireflies on a summer night, as the rest of the night's adventurers came home. Crossing the coast just north of Saltfleet, they flew their final circuit and Paddy noted in his log 'Landed 0221 hours Tuesday 13.7.43. RAF Blyton'.

"Home at last chaps, home at last," murmured Johnnie.

Their first operational sortie complete, only another twenty-nine to go to complete their tour. However, when they arrived back in the briefing room for debriefing, the de-briefing officer informed them that training ops did not count towards their tour.

"So, that was a free one for the bloody RAF, then?" complained Jan.

"I suppose so, Jan," laughed Johnnie. "Well done everyone and thank you."

"No problem, Skipper. Now where are those bloody bacon and eggs?" said Dusty.

Later, in the aircrew dining room, just off the crew room, Algy asked Paddy how he felt before the op.

"I don't know really, Algy. I admit I was shit-scared the night before. But then again I'm always shit-scared when Johnnie's driving anything mechanical, including Ruby," he laughed.

"You were scared?" asked a surprised Dusty. "But you've done all sorts of mad bloody things, like sailing across the Atlantic and back. Not to mention the ops you did on Wimpys. Christ, you got a DSO. I admit to being a little nervous," he joked. "But I wouldn't have thought that you, Chalkie or the Skipper would have been."

"It takes a brave man to be scared, Dusty. Courage is conquering that fear and saying 'get on with the job', just like you did today. You're a hero, Dusty and you didn't know it."

"What about you, Algy? You're a calm and peaceful man, so you are." asked Paddy.

Algy swept up the handlebars of his moustache with the back of his fingers and, in his best public school cut-glass accent said,

"Ai has got to aidmit I was shite-scaired on the way out and I was shite-scaired on the way back and between those two points, I was also shite-scaired."

They all laughed.

As Johnnie laughed, he put his arm round Dusty's shoulder.

"By God, Dusty, I wish I wasn't scared, but believe me, we all were. It comes with the job. You know the old saying, 'If you can't take a joke," but before he could say any more the others all chorused, "You shouldn't have joined!" and burst into happy laughter. They were safe, fed and watered and relieved they had made it home in one piece.

\*\*\*

Johnnie's mind snapped back to the present as he drove Ruby through the main gate of the camp. He thought the last twelve weeks of the Lancaster Finishing School course had pulled them all together well, they had become a well-moulded crew, and operational experience would bind them together even more. Thoughts of the training the crew had been through faded; it was behind them and a new adventure was about to begin here at RAF Elkington. They were going to war as part of an operational squadron, as Michael might say, "Once more unto the breach, dear friends, once more."

# 7 ... G-George

At 0830 hours on Monday 19 July, 1943, Johnnie and the rest of his crew joined the other 'New Boys' in the briefing room where the 'whys and wherefores' and the 'dos and don'ts' of 599 Squadron would be explained.

Wing Commander Harry Picton, DSO DFC and bar, was the Squadron Commander, a hard-nosed professional aviator. He joined the RAF in 1935 and totally believed in Bomber Command as the instrument that will win the war. He was one of the first to fly the Avro Lancaster when it came from the factory of Mr Alliott Verdon Roe (Avro) at Chadderton, near Oldham in Lancashire, and believed it was the best bomber ever built. He drove his crews long and hard to perfect their operational skills. He knew that badly trained crews are the first to die on sorties. He was also a golden member of the 'Caterpillar' club.

"Gentlemen, welcome to Five-Nine-Nine. We, as you know, are part of One Group Bomber Command, to give it its Sunday name. The seventeen main airfields in the Lindsey district of North Lincolnshire are home to all the squadrons of One Group. The Air Officer Commanding (AOC) is Air Vice Marshal Rice, and he resides at the Group HQ, Bawtry Hall in Bawtry, near Gainsborough. He is of the old school; he earned his wings on the battlefields of France in the Great War and above the deserts of Mesopotamia in the twenties. He is an efficient, enthusiastic and competent boss. He expects and demands high standards from his Squadron COs and his crews. So do I, gentlemen, so do I."

He paused before carrying on.

"As you have been aware, the squadron, or part of it, has been on ops this weekend and we have been lucky: only one crew failed to return out of the eighteen that took off on Friday night. We believe that most of the crew baled out over the Italian coast; they are probably gobbling up ice cream in some cosy Italian POW camp by now. Let us hope so," he smiled and looked round the crews present, remembering he had welcomed that crew just eight days ago. "We have no ops planned for the next few days, so you people can carry out some familiarisation flights in your new kites."

He spent twenty minutes explaining his thoughts and beliefs on the workings of a successful squadron. By the time he had come to his finale, his honesty, enthusiasm and belief in 599 Squadron had impressed the new crews.

"Sanderson, as you know, you will be in 'A' flight, and so will you now, Bere. Unfortunately, 'A' flight needs a replacement for the weekend's loss. The rest of you will form the new 'C' flight under Squadron Leader Joe Kendrick. I suggest you all report to your flight commanders and those whose kites are ready have my permission to go and play with them. Do not bring them back dented or with lumps missing. Welcome to Five-Nine-Nine. Dismissed, gentlemen."

"Hello, Jimmy. Is our kite ready yet do you know?" asked Johnnie of the squadron adjutant.

"Yes, it is," he smiled. "I wish you buggers were this keen to go on the battle orders. Log your flight plan, Johnnie, go and get kitted up, and then speak to the Chiefy."

After kitting up in the crew locker room, drawing their parachutes and survival packs, Johnnie and his crew made their way to the technical area hangar to find the flight's 'Chiefy', the Flight Sergeant in charge of the flight's aircraft and ground crew.

"Morning, Chiefy. Is G-George ready?"

"Yes, Mr. Sanderson, she's ready. We have also updated the new *Monica* radar in her, all fitted and checked out. I'd be grateful if you would test the system while you're up and give me a report when you get back."

"Yes, no problem, Chiefy."

"'Rembrandt' Roberts, over there, has done a good paint job on 'er, sir."

A chap in dirty blue overalls with oil up to his elbows waved towards them with an oily rag in one hand and a giant wrench in the other. He gave no impression of being a budding Rembrandt.

"We'll wheel 'er out for you, sir."

He signalled the driver of an RAF tractor connected to the rear wheel of the aircraft. It pushed the aircraft slowly out of the hangar on to the vast hard standing outside.

"She's been thoroughly checked, sir. All systems are OK. All guns loaded but not cocked," he warned.

Johnnie carried out his pre-flight ground checks and signed the 'Form 700' and fuel state report, which meant he took responsibility for the aircraft from the ground crew and accepted she was full of fuel, armed up and ready to fly. Jan checked that the open bomb bay was clear of any ordnance.

"Thanks, Chiefy," Johnnie said as he handed back the flight sergeant's clipboard.

The crew gathered round the nose of the aircraft and inspected the new livery. On each side of the fuselage, in red, were the large letters CD, and then on the other side of the yellow rimmed red white and blue roundel the letter G; G for George. In smaller red letters towards the tail-plane was MH393, her personal identity number. Just below the cockpit, on the starboard side, was a shield announcing that 599 Squadron's emblem was a winged bomb and their motto was, 'Acta Non Verba', 'Deeds not Words', translated Algy. An apt motto for a bomber squadron thought Johnnie. On her port side, just below and to the rear of the front turret, was the round, yellow gas detector patch. Just behind the air bomber's side windows was a smaller letter G.

"She'm look beautiful, Skipper, I thinks we should give 'er a name," burred Jan.

"We'll have to see if she is a friendly old girl first," said Paddy.

"You're right, Michael, let's wait until we have completed a few sorties in her," suggested Johnnie.

They climbed aboard in their customary order of entry, Jan, Johnnie, Chalkie, Paddy, Algy, Dusty and finally Yorky.

They checked over the next hour all the systems and equipment on board.

When everybody was happy with their situations Johnnie asked the control tower for permission to taxi to the runway and take-off.

He lifted her into the bright morning sky, an endless blue, cloudless sky, a perfect English summer's day, a perfect day to fly. His flight plan was to stooge around the airfield for a while in case the air test brought to light a problem that meant a speedy return to the ground, and then, if everything was okay, a cross-country exercise. Everything was fine initially, so they set off on their first jolly in their brand new bomber. Johnnie had asked Michael to plot a course that would take them across the Pennines and over the Irish Sea up to Carlisle and then follow Hadrian's Wall to Newcastle, hug the coast all the way back down to Norfolk and finally back up to Elkington. On a beautiful day like today, you did not really need a navigator. Just a map would suffice.

They flew over the rolling green hills of the Wolds and watched the green countryside gradually turn grim and dark as the South Yorkshire coalfields and steel mills passed below them, replaced by the granite and heather of the rugged Peak District as they passed over the Pennines. Soon the long bright waters of the Howden, Derwent and Ladybower reservoirs glistened below them.

"If you look to port, chaps, you can see the dam that Guy Gibson and Six-One-Seven practised their raid on," informed Johnnie. "Let's take a closer look."

He turned hard to port and pushed the control yoke forward putting G-George into a diving turn.

"Do you think you can show Six-One-Seven a thing or two, Jan?"

"You bet, Skipper. Take her down to sixty feet and I'll drop one right on the button," said Jan from his prone position in the nose blister.

"You mad buggers," was the comment from the rear turret.

Johnnie laughed. "Just testing our low flying skills, Yorky, that's why it's called a familiarisation flight."

G-George roared down from the high moorland above Derwent Water to flash across the reservoir at two hundred and twenty miles an hour sixty feet above the blue waters. Jan lined up his sights on the twin castellated towers of the dam ...

"Right a bit ... right a bit ... steady ... steady ... left, left a bit ... steady ... steady ... bomb gone!" he shouted down the intercom.

G-George thundered over the dam wall missing it by some thirty feet. Chalkie burst out laughing at the faces of two workers erecting scaffolding on the starboard tower.

"Did you see their faces, Skipper? They wondered what the hell was happening, they almost fell off their scaffolding," cried Chalkie.

"Brilliant flying, Skipper! I hate to piss on your chips, Jan, but you missed the bugger," cackled Yorky.

"You Englishmen, you're all bloody mad, ye really are," laughed Paddy.

Twisting and turning, Johnnie put the aircraft through the Derwent Valley with the high hills on either side, and then pulled up in a slow climbing turn to starboard to return to his original course. Not wanting exclusion from the fun, Algy commented that he could not remember hearing the order to 'open the bomb-bay doors', so that if it had been for real they would by now be scattered over the Derbyshire moors.

In a mock cut-glass accent, Dusty said. "Oh don't be such a bore, old boy. Six-One-Seven Lancs did not have bomb bay doors on the Dams' run. Anyway, do you want to live forever?"

They flew south of the Manchester conurbation towards Liverpool. Jan called from his prone position in the nose blister.

"Barrage balloons ahead, Skipper,"

"Got them, Jan."

Johnnie skirted Liverpool's docks in case the local artillery boys decided to carry out some practise on them, and crossed into the Irish Sea.

In front of them, a mass of merchant and Royal Navy ships was slowly moving northwards in columns that formed a gigantic block of forty or fifty vessels. In the middle, they could clearly see the flat flight deck of an aircraft carrier surrounded by several fast-moving frigates, their white wakes standing out against the brown sea. On the outside of the armada, little corvettes, the sheep dogs of the fleet, were chivvying the tardy and out of line merchantmen. Johnnie did not envy their perilous journey across the treacherous North Atlantic.

Paddy was standing between Johnnie and Chalkie watching the convoy two thousand feet below.

"I don't fancy their journey, Michael."

"No," said Paddy. "The North Atlantic is a big cruel place, to be sure. And I know from bitter experience," he said grimly.

"I was going to exercise the bomb doors, but the gallant sailor boys down there might get a bit jumpy if we fly over with them open, so, we're going to bomb the Isle of Man, gentlemen," Johnnie informed the crew. "Your target, Jan, is 'The Tower of Refuge' in Douglas Bay. That is the castle-like building on the island in the middle of the bay. OK people; treat this as a serious exercise. We have done it a hundred times, but the opportunity may not arise to practise again before the real thing. Give me a course to target, navigator."

"Willco, Skipper," said Michael. One minute later, "Turn on to three-one-five, Skipper, twenty-two minutes to target."

"Three-one-five, thank you, Michael."

Johnnie turned and climbed to ten thousand feet. The chitchat that had passed between the crewmembers over the intercom had died out; it was back to business again, even if this was only an exercise.

Their run in to Douglas Bay was perfect. Jan was confident his calculations on his bomb computor were spot on and they would have delivered their load very close to the target.

"Well done, everybody, course for Carlisle, Michael, please. Gunners, when we turn to our new heading I want you to test your turrets and guns, including you, Jan, but only short bursts. You can test them thoroughly later over the North Sea."

Fifteen minutes later, they turned into the Solway Firth, a wide funnel that led them past the bombing range of Drumburgh to their right, then on north of Carlisle. They picked up the distinct line of Hadrian's Wall as it snaked across fell and vale towards the east. Jan was thinking, if only keeping the bloody Jerry out was as easy as that. On reaching Tynemouth on the northeast coast, they turned south following the sandy beaches, staying two or three miles offshore.

"OK, boys, you can test your guns again now."

A cacophony of sound immediately greeted Johnnie's words. Eight Browning machine guns were spewing lead in every direction. Johnnie flinched at the suddenness of the barrage, his memory flicking back to his last operational sortie, when men and aircraft had died. Yorky had ten thousand rounds at his disposal while the other two gunners had two thousand each. However, they knew not to waste the ammunition. They might be on a test flight, but there was still a war on and marauding Jerry fighters were not against 'popping over' for a bash at a susceptible target or two. Their experience with the ME-109 not long ago had taught them that.

They carried out several more exercises as they flew south, including ditching into the sea, escaping by parachute and the drill for fire on board. However, the mid-upper and rear gunners were ever vigilant searching the skies for the black-crossed vermin that could deliver a very nasty bite.

G-George crossed back over the Yorkshire coast at Withernsea, with its strange lighthouse a mile from the sea halfway down the main street of the town.

"You're now flying over God's County," said Yorky. "Isn't it beautiful?"

The flat, featureless coastal plain of the East Riding of Yorkshire is not what you might call the most attractive of vistas, a point made by Cornishman, Jan.

"'Tis borin' this. Now, if you go to Kernow, youm'll see boo-iful countryside, me 'ansome."

"Kernow, where the 'ell is that?" asked Yorky.

"That be paradise next to Deben," Jan replied, in his broadest West Country accent.

"Thank God you're not the navigator," laughed Dusty.

The next lighthouse they saw was that at the end of Spurn Point, that curling hook of land that protects the river Humber, opposite the tall red brick Fish Tower of Grimsby docks. They swung round Ludworth church spire and came in to Elkington on final approach. The controls of G-George were still a little stiff and Johnnie put her down quite hard, bouncing back into the air and coming down hard again prompting Yorky to comment, "Bugger me, Skipper. Remember what the WingCo said 'Don't bend it'. We 'aven't paid for it yet, the bloody paint's still wet!"

"Home at last, chaps, home at last," laughed Johnnie.

'We are as ready as we ever will be,' he thought later. 'We've trained hard, we work well as a team, we've had our first gardening sortie and now we are operational. Now the true test; bombing Germany. Let's hope this bloody war is over soon.'

They spent the next few days at RAF Elkington carrying out familiarisation flights, getting used to their new aircraft and checking their knowledge of systems and routines in the air. When they returned from each test flight, each member of the crew reported any glitches or malfunctions of their equipment or systems and recorded it in the F707A 'Flight Snag Book', and handed it to the Chiefy for the ground crew to sort out and rectify. There had been, occasionally, some small problems, but no major ones; MH393 was a new aircraft after all.

On the Thursday morning at 0800, the tannoy system called them and Pilot Officer Tony 'Ginger' Bere and the crew of F-Freddie to 'A' flight's office where Squadron Leader Chris Cooper briefed them for a sortie.

"Your two crews are on stand-by today. The Air Sea Rescue launch from Grimsby has gone to sea to search for the crew of a Lanc that came down in the North Sea. They think they could have ditched somewhere near the Friesian Islands, off the Dutch/German coast, on their return from a raid on Germany last night, and they hope that the survivors have clambered into their dinghy."

He turned and indicated the islands on a large map pinned to the wall.

"You were both out there last week at OTU, weren't you, gardening?"

Johnnie answered, "Yes, sir, last Wednesday."

"The week before, for us, sir," answered Ginger.

"Right. ASR will signal us if they think they need us, after the rescue launch has gone as close to the islands as it can without attracting too much attention. You will go, carry out a square pattern search, and if you spot them drop a large survival dinghy and contact the ASR on RT. I want you to go and get your aircraft ready, and then be ready to scramble anytime this afternoon. There will be an update and weather briefing before take-off."

The tannoy announcement had them rushing to the crew room in the late afternoon. The ASR Launch had not located the lost aircrew, so this air search would be the last chance for the ditched airmen.

The Met officer's brief informed them that over the next few hours, the weather would be deteriorating fast, and they could expect low cloud, high winds and heavy rain; flying conditions would not be good.

"I'm afraid there is no further update on the ditched crew," said Chris Cooper. "Take-off as soon as possible, Johnnie. As the most experienced, you will lead the flight. Good luck."

Within the hour, they had left a sunny airfield behind them and were thundering over the Lincolnshire coast at close to two hundred and fifty miles per hour. As they crossed the North Sea, the Met Officer's forecast, for once, started to come true. Cloud cover was dropping, the skies were darkening and it started to rain. The wind was coming from the northeast and was growing in strength.

Three-quarters of an hour after leaving the Lincolnshire coast behind, the two aircraft positioned themselves one mile apart, reduced their speed to one hundred and fifty miles per hour and started their sweep from just south of the island of Terschelling. They had been on this exact patch before, gardening. They swept east by northeast to the seaward side of the islands, but there was no trace of the dinghy. The weather was deteriorating fast, cloud level was down to five hundred feet, the rain was now very heavy and the northeast wind was endeavouring to put yet more airmen in the storm-lashed waters below. Just flying the aircraft and turning at that low height demanded total concentration on flying, never mind trying to search the huge waves of a grey, heaving sea for a tiny yellow dinghy.

For the next few hours, the two Lancs patrolled up and down. In the fast fading visibility, despite the danger of attack, they showed their navigation and formation lights, the landing lights and even the coloured approach lights in case the ditched airmen could see them and could send up a flare. All members of the two crews were straining to scan the angry sea through the foul weather. After some four hours of fruitless search, fuel was getting low and dusk was approaching. Johnnie gave the order to abort the search and return home.

The crews were reluctant to leave the search area, but they had no other options. They were thinking that it could very easily be them tossing around in a tiny rubber dinghy, in great danger of perishing in the cold storm-cursed North Sea. They had not seen any signs of a bright yellow dinghy or even a bright burning flare.

"Poor sods," said Yorky as they turned for home. "Poor bloody sods. Can't we do another sweep, Skipper? You never know."

"We've done the best we can, Yorky. Course for home, navigator."

Johnnie sadly turned off all the lights, "God bless, lads."

They returned through the atrocious weather to a rain-lashed Elkington lost in their own thoughts.

As they taxied to a halt, an exhausted Johnnie said, quietly, "Home at last, chaps, home at last."

The rest of the crew was thinking exactly what was going through his mind that the crew they may have left out there, most probably would never be coming home. The crew of a lost Lancaster.

The next day the WingCo informed Johnnie and Ginger, that because the weather during the search was so bad, and they had been within striking distance of enemy territory, exposing them to obvious danger, and they had stuck to their task diligently, the op would stand as their first sortie of their tour of thirty. ASR had reported nothing had come from further searches carried out that day.

"And you can tell your crews that there will be an op tomorrow night and they will be on it. I can't tell you what the target is, but it will be a bombing op flying over German territory," said Harry Picton.

When told the news about the dinghy search op, Chalkie said, "One down, twenty-nine to go. Shame it wasn't against the Krauts. Any news on the ditched crew?"

"No, unfortunately ... Now more news, chaps. You are going to get your wish, Chalkie," Johnnie Sanderson, the Skipper, said quietly. "Tomorrow night we will be on ops again, this time it is the real thing, our first bombing run over enemy territory. Germany!"

## 8 ... Feuersturm

Late in the morning, after the Hamburg raid, their first bombing sortie under fire, Johnnie went to see the flight sergeant in charge of G-George's ground crew.

"Morning, Chiefy. Much damage to her from last night?"

"Mornin', Mr. Sanderson. No sir, just had to patch up the bomb doors a bit; you collected a few shrapnel holes, but nothing serious. How was it out there, sir?" he asked with a concerned note in his voice, knowing it was the crew's first bombing op.

"It was okay, Chiefy, it was okay. Not much flak and we only saw one night fighter. It seems that Window worked. Let's hope it continues to work for a long time yet."

"Amen to that, Mr. Sanderson, amen to that."

Johnnie climbed the ladder and entered the Lancaster; made his way forward, ducked under the bottom of the mid-upper turret, scrambled over the main wing spar and climbed up to sit in the pilot's seat to carry out some post-flight tests. When he had completed them, he sat and looked around at the cramped interior. He had flown several Lancasters now and every aeroplane was different. The same workers and engineers may have assembled them in the same factory, they may have the same engines and equipment, but every aeroplane was an individual with its own quirks and foibles, its own character, and MH393 was an individual; she had her own little quirks.

Johnnie knew that on take-off he had to check her tendency to swing to port by advancing the port throttles slightly more than normal. Most Lancasters' rudders become heavy and sluggish when flying at high-speed, but G-George responded quickly to the rudder pedals. They were so sensitive that with three wheels on the ground when building up speed for take-off, she wagged her tail like a dog and his feet had to dance on the pedals to keep her straight on the runway, so he tried to get the control yoke forward to get her tail wheel up as quickly as possible. Her elevators were light and responsive, and only became heavy in fast sharp turns, and when applying the brakes on landing, she always pulled a little to starboard; yes, she had her own little ways.

Her controls were still stiff with newness, but Johnnie knew they would ease up with time, but it was still hard physical work flying a thirty-ton bomber. There was no hydraulic help to the flying controls; it was hard muscular effort that made G-George change attitude or direction. At the end of a long flight, especially in bad weather, the pilot of a Lancaster would be very relieved when the flare path of home came into sight and the tyres kissed the runway. The constant noise and vibration of flight drained the energy and taxed the concentration powers to the limit. After flying over enemy territory, forming up on the bombing run, the bombing run itself, the suicidal thirty seconds flying straight and level waiting for the photo-flash flare to go off, avoiding flak, searchlights and night fighters, the pilot would be exhausted after many long hours 'at the office'. That is why every six weeks or so they went on six days' leave, and after thirty ops, they had six months away from active duty.

That night, the 'Royal Oak', in the village, resounded to the many aircrew members roaring out ribald songs of 'daring do' and the escapades of ladies of uncertain moral character, all accompanied by copious pints of 'Hewitt's Ales' and the well-bashed pub piano. It had been out of tune since the last war when many of the same songs had raised the rafters sung by the same young flyers that flew their wood and canvas bi-planes from the grass field that was RAF Elkington then. They all celebrated the relief of surviving a day's wartime flying. The crew of the newly named 'Gloria' was among the most prominent.

"Why, 'Gloria', Algy, and not just plain old 'George'?" slurred Jan after his third pint.

"Because, old son," said Algy, sagely. "You can't use a male name for an aeroplane. It doesn't sit right. Now something sensuous and alluring like 'Gloria' does. Gloria reminds me of my favourite film star; she is sleek, shapely and seductive and responds to the kindest of touches. Now who would you rather caress, eh, Jan, a 'George' or a 'Gloria'? I am sure she will be a bitch at times, but treated with tender loving care she will always look after us. I, for one, would love Gloria Swanson to look after me, old boy. Nudge nudge, know what I mean?" He roared with laughter at his own jest.

A little later, a christening ceremony gave MH393 G-George a new name ... Gloria! All members of the crew duly shared a pint bottle of Hewitt's Brown Ale when the flight's resident artist, 'Rembrandt' Roberts, finally unveiled the painting, on the port side nose of the aircraft, of an evocatively posed young woman, wearing nothing more than her stockings and underwear. He had also painted the images of two bombs just below the cockpit canopy on the Skipper's side of the fuselage to show they had completed their first two sorties, their first trophies of war.

Two nights after their first bombing run, they found themselves on 'Battle Orders' again.

"The target for tonight is ... Hamburg again," announced the SIO at the briefing that afternoon. "Our American cousins have been busy over there for the last two days and a flight of Mosquitos went on a bombing run last night just to keep the German fire-fighters on their toes. The bombing of Hamburg has caused great damage to the German industrial machine, but we are not finished with them yet. Tonight is the next stage of 'Operation Gomorrah', the next step in Air Chief Marshal Harris's 'process of elimination' of Hamburg's participation in the German industrial war machine. Tonight is another 'maximum effort'. You will be part of an armada of some eight hundred bombers again."

The weather was very warm, as it had been for a few days. It was a dry heat, almost desert-like. The crews were sitting in their shirtsleeves listening to the instructions for the night. The SIO carried on,

"We believe that the Jerries have moved a great many more ack-ack guns and searchlights into the Hamburg area to try to combat our use of Window. You will be using it again tonight, by the way. When you go out to your kites, you will notice a new chute fitted to the starboard side of the air-bomber's compartment. You will use this instead of the flare chute back in the fuselage; it will make the job of dropping the bundles much easier. You will begin dropping them at nine degrees east on the way out and stop dropping them at nine degrees east on the way home. Again, I must emphasise that dropping them every minute is the only way to get the greatest effect, it is your lives that are at risk ... Your route tonight, as the navigators already know, is to rendezvous over the North Sea at 2300 hours, then fly just north of Heide, which is west of Heligoland ..."

He used the wooden pointer.

"A geography lesson as well," muttered Paddy.

"Well, you are only a navigator, old boy." smiled Algy.

" ... then on towards Kiel, southeast of Lübeck and finally, southwest to the target. Yellow TIs will mark all the turns. Make sure your timings are as instructed."

When they went out to the dispersal pan and inspected 'Gloria', Jan found a new square-shaped chute protruding from his compartment, exiting just in front of the bomb bay doors.

"At least I won't have to scramble up and down the bloody fuselage. Mind you, I will probably be crammed in with 'chaff' boxes."

He checked the bomb load secured in the bay and found it was the same combination as on their last raid, one 4000 lb 'Cookie', three 1000 pounder HEs and six SBCs. As he scrambled through the main door, he checked the flare chute and the photoflash flares secured to the flank of the aircraft. These were about three feet long, six inches in diameter and were the deadliest thing in the aircraft. They developed over one million-candle power of burning light and could blow the bomber to bits if they went off inside the fuselage. He made his way to the front cupola. The rest of the crew climbed aboard in their normal order, took up their stations and went through their pre-flight checks. They had all carried out their own personal pre-flight routines.

Johnnie could feel the residual warmth of his 'flying pipe' in his breast pocket; Jan had felt the smooth comfort of his rabbit's foot; and Paddy gently rubbed the 'monkey fist'. Algy tucked his white silk scarf more comfortably around his neck; Dusty gave Mavis a kiss; Yorky patted his pocket feeling the reassuring shape of his 'wishbone'; and Chalkie got on with his job.

Three quarters of an hour later, 'Gloria' heaved herself and her crew into the summer night to join the hundreds of other crews making their way back to Hamburg, whose defences would be waiting for them tonight.

They were again in the first wave of Lancasters and were due to drop their bomb load at 0112 hours. As they made their final turn near Lübeck, marked by the yellow TIs, there were no flak or searchlights scarring the night sky from the town's defences that would have highlighted its location, and Johnnie only knew he was over Lübeck by Michael's instructions and the yellow turn indicators. The town was cowering in complete darkness, as if it were in hiding, as if terrified of what was going to happen again to Hamburg, its neighbour, would happen to them.

It had every right to feel terrified.

Jan spoke on the intercom, but still carried on dropping Window through his new chute.

"Skipper, is that Hamburg, forty miles or so, up front?"

He could see a column of smoke rising thousands of feet in the air; and the red glow of fires was already visible and the attack had only just started.

What he did not know was that the fires started with the bombings of the last three days and nights, had overwhelmed the fire-fighting department of the Hamburg Civil Defence Force. They were struggling to attend to fires spread throughout the city. Most of the serious fires were on the west side of the city and that was where most of the fire-fighters were. Now the 'Terrorflieger' were back to drop more high explosives, which blasted open the buildings and allowed the incendiary bombs to set fire to the flammable interiors. The next few hours would be terrifying for the people of Hamburg, and they had every right to be terrified.

Never before in the history of warfare had anybody seen what Germany's second city was about to receive.

The first bombs fell at 0057 hours and the last of 2,326 tons of high explosive and incendiaries fell at 0147 hours, fifty minutes later.

Weather in Hamburg over the last few days had been very warm with hot bright sunshine and low humidity. The city had already suffered from the fires created over the last few days and the rubble and wreckage were now tinder dry. On this night, within fifteen minutes of the attack, the citizens of Hamburg heard a strange and chilling sound. A shrill howling, almost animal-like, was spreading through the city; a howling that had never been recorded before in a fire. They called it 'Feuersturm' or Firestorm. The high temperatures and low humidity and the fact that most of the fire-fighters were on the west side of Hamburg allowed the newly started fires in the east to grow and join together, sucking at the night sky to draw in more oxygen. Hundreds of acres of the city were now burning out of control. Thousands of apartment blocks were burning, their residents trapped in the cellars, suffocated by carbon monoxide. The ferocious firestorm generated so much heat it melted and buckled the metal blast doors that guarded the entrances of the cellars and air raid shelters. It hungrily sucked out the fuel of life from the very bodies of the thousands of trapped occupants, feeding on the oxygen, feeding its own insatiable destructive appetite. Tens of thousands of people had fled from the city that day, and now the asphalt of the roads had become a boiling, clinging trap for anybody trying to run away. Bodies incinerated where they had fallen, mothers holding children burst into flames as they tried to escape the terror, the elderly and infirm trapped in their homes, burnt or choked to death.

The fire raged miles into the air above the city and winds of fire were travelling at over one hundred and fifty miles per hour, and reached temperatures of 1,400 degrees. It engulfed anyone and everything in its path. The firestorm raged and roared until there was very little combustible material left for the fuel-hungry monster to consume. The fire-winds finally subsided sometime after 0400 hours, but it was many hours before the fire-fighter teams and rescue squads could enter the area because of the immense heat.

The bombers turned their backs on the devastation and left the incinerated, choked and charred bodies of over 45,000 people.

"Jesus, Skipper, it's nothing but a sea of flames down there. Everything is on fire. No bugger could live through that!" cried a stunned Yorky.

A column of smoke towered to 20,000 feet above the city, taking with it the stench of death.

Because Yorky's turret was partly open to the elements, where he had a pane of Perspex removed from directly in front of him to allow better visibility, he was the first to catch the nauseating smell pervading the air, even at that height.

"My God, what's that bloody awful smell?"

Very quietly, Paddy said, "That's burning flesh, Yorky."

"Bugger me," was the only answer Yorky could give.

Chalkie turned round and looked back along the cockpit canopy down over the starboard wing to the city in flames. He wondered if the German bomber aircrews had watched Coventry city die in that 'Feuersturm', as he was watching their city of Hamburg die. A grim smile of revenge flickered across his face.

Johnnie noticed that other bombers were clearly visible in the reflected glow from the fires, even though they were fifty miles from Hamburg. The night was very clear with bright moonlight, ideal night fighter conditions.

He was just about to contact his gunners when:

"Skipper, I'm picking up a bandit thirteen hundred yards astern and slightly to port," reported Algy who thankfully, thought Johnnie, was concentrating on his 'Monica' radar screen.

"Thanks, Algy, sharp lookout, gunners."

Algy spoke again.

"Still there, Skipper, eleven hundred yards and closing slowly." A few seconds later, "Nine hundred yards."

"Any sign of him yet, gunners?" asked Johnnie.

"Can't see a sign of the bugger," came back Yorky.

"Nothing yet, Skip." said Dusty.

"Six hundred yards and still closing," called Algy, starting to sound a little anxious.

"Any sign yet, Dusty?"

"No, Skip, nothing."

"Yorky?"

"Nope."

Johnnie swung G-George to port and tipped the wing down to vary his flight pattern.

"Got him, port down!" cried Yorky, "Corkscrew port, go!"

"Got him!" called Dusty.

"The bugger was trying to get underneath us, Skipper."

The fighter opened fire, but Johnnie's rapid reaction to Yorky's order, by diving and turning hard to port, had frustrated the Luftwaffe pilot's aim and the lethal tracer shells screamed just inches under the starboard wing and fuselage. The fighter banked away and dived to port to turn and renew his attack.

"Keep searching for him. Climbing to starboard," Johnnie informed the crew, pulling Gloria hard up.

After a while, "Coming back on previous heading."

Everyone's nerves were now at full stretch, their senses fully alert, the fires and devastation of Hamburg forgotten. Johnnie knew it was no good telling everyone to keep their eyes peeled. They already were.

"Coming in from starboard, high, twelve hundred yards," called a remarkably calm- sounding Algy, eyes glued to his small radar screen. "One thousand yards and closing fast."

"Corkscrew starboard, GO!" cried Dusty, opening up with his twin machine guns.

The giant Lancaster tipped and fell to the right, losing height rapidly. The JU-88 twin-engine 'Nachtjagd' (Night hunter) could not correct his curving, diving attack and swept down the port side without firing. Yorky swung the turret in line with him and empty shell cases rattled down the dispersal chutes underneath his guns, as four lines of tracer from his guns followed the fighter, but were always just that bit behind him as he dived away crossing underneath the bomber to disappear from the crew's sight.

When seven hundred feet had unwound from the altimeter, Johnnie heaved the control yoke back to his stomach and turned to port in a gravity-defying climb. Informing the crew of his move, he regained the height and levelled off.

"Any sign, gunners?"

"Nope"

"None Skip. He may have had enough," commented a hopeful Dusty.

"Corkscrew starboard, go!" ordered Yorky, then immediately. "No! Hold it hold it, Skipper."

The chatter of his four guns began. "He was almost underneath."

Yorky's weapons then hammered non-stop.

"Got the bugger, got the bugger! He's going to port, falling away. He's in flames!" he cried excitedly. "He's goin' down in bloody flames. It's a Junkers eighty-eight!"

"Where is he?" asked Johnnie.

Algy stood up with his head in the astrodome above him to join in the search.

"Down to port, I can see him spinning. There's a 'chute. No, two, yeah, two 'chutes!" shouted Yorky.

"He's definitely going down, Skipper, well alight," commented a very calm and relaxed Algy.

"I got the bugger!" shouted Yorky excitedly.

Johnnie tipped the bomber's port wing and looked back through the blister in his canopy just in time to see an explosion several thousand feet below them as the stricken JU-88 smashed to the ground. He could see the two grey parachutes floating through the clear night air.

"Good show, chaps, good show! Brilliant shooting Yorky. Well done, everyone. First blood to us. Log the time and position, Michael."

"Will do, Skipper."

The intercom literally buzzed as the crew excitedly ran through the action again with elation and relief that 'it was them and not us'.

"Ok, chaps, let's settle down. Well done, but let's get home before any more of them find us."

He put Gloria's nose down, increased the revs and thundered towards home through the moonlit night.

When they were nearly two hundred miles from Hamburg Yorky came over the intercom and said solemnly, his excitement drained:

"Bugger me. I can still see the glow of Hamburg."

An hour and ten minutes later, the tyres squealed in protest as they bit into the concrete of Elkington's main runway.

"Home at last, chaps, home at last."

They wearily entered the briefing hut, where, distributed around the rearranged tables and chairs, were packets of Woodbine cigarettes and ashtrays. The Station Commander was always there to greet them as they filed in, as he was always standing by the runway control caravan to see them off, no matter what the weather. Some pretty, young WAAFs handed out mugs of hot tea laced with the customary rum. Tired and distressed crews collapsed into the chairs to relate the night's affairs. They told of the exploding bombers, the attacks of night fighters, and the death of comrades. Briefly, their spirits rose as they told of their victories over the fighters. Nevertheless, the dreadful stench of burning flesh and the sight of the devastated, burning city had affected them all. Its glow and stench had followed them back over the North Sea.

One Lanc from 'C' flight was missing. As no one had seen it go down the hope was it had diverted to another airfield somewhere.

"Who was it?" asked Paddy.

"D-Dog, the Canadian, Charlie Bowden's kite," answered Johnnie.

"I was only talking to their navigator last night, just before the briefing. He was from Kilpatrick, just a few miles from home. God bless the poor boy," said Paddy.

This time their 'flyers' bacon and eggs' did not seem so special.

As the day wore on, news came through that the missing Lanc from 'C' flight had not diverted to another field. In fact, Yorky and Dusty had witnessed, unknowingly, its destruction. It was the one they saw explode in midair.

The aircrews, including the crew from Gloria, drank the Royal Oak dry that night as many of them tried to dispel the ghosts of the raid and wash the stench of death from their nostrils.

# 9 ... Ginny

"Are you going to the thrash tonight, Johnnie?" asked Algy as they walked back to their accommodation hut from the flight office the next Saturday morning. "It could be a whiz, old man. They have the 'Squadronaires' playing, you know, the RAF dance band. They are jolly wizard so I hear, and there will be lots of totty. It's an all ranks bash so there will be stacks of juicy waafs."

"Where is it?"

"They've cleared the front part of number two hangar, setting up a bar, decorations and everything."

"Yes, it could be a laugh, I suppose, why not? We could end up weaving an uneven course for home, if we can get enough beers."

"Let's hope they don't run out like the Oak did on Thursday night."

The evening was warm as they made their way to the dance. Johnnie looked to the heavens as the bright moon slid out from behind a cloud, bathing the airfield in an ethereal light.

"A bomber's moon tonight, Algy. I wonder why we're not on ops."

"I don't care why we're not on ops, I am just jolly glad we are not, old boy. Come on, here we are."

They entered the hangar through a canvas tunnel rigged to block the lights, which were flooding the inside, from breaking the blackout regulations. A blast of swing music greeted them and a large crowd of airmen and WAAFS were dancing in front of the stage, where a trumpeter from the 'Squadronaires' was playing a solo break from the well-known Glen Miller tune 'Little Brown Jug'. It looked like the entire station had attended and were enjoying themselves. They spotted the rest of the crew at a table close to the bar.

"Here you are, Skipper," called Dusty. "We got you some chairs. What are you drinking? Pints of wallop?"

"Yes please, Dusty."

He plonked two pints of bitter on the table before them. Algy took a mouthful.

"That's what I've been looking forward to, a warm, flat pint of wallop. Thank you, Dusty."

"I'm sorry, Algy, they didn't have any chilled champagne."

"Oh well, c'est la vie." He took another deep draft.

Johnnie watched them as they all laughed and gulped down their well-earned beers. It had been one hell of a week, three ops, flak, night fighters, exploding Lancs. Yes, they deserved their few days off ops and a chance to relax and have some fun and celebrate their first 'kill'.

A couple of pints later, he stood up to get a round of drinks for them all.

"Right, chaps what is it, pints all round?"

"Yeah, Skipper, but I don't think Algy will want one yet – look!"

Yorky pointed to the crowd dancing in front of the band. There, in the middle was Algy, wrapping himself around a young WAAF corporal and they were both oblivious to the world around them.

"That's not dancing," said Jan, "That's probably illegal and certainly against King's Regulations."

They all laughed.

As Johnnie turned to go to the bar, he collided with someone.

"Oh, I'm terribly sorry I ..."

He stopped speaking, stunned by the beautiful face of the WAAF Section Officer standing before him, who was now holding a glass with just the remains of a drink, the rest of it had splashed down her arm and skirt.

"I'm so sorry. Here please, let me dry you off."

He produced his handkerchief and attempted to dry off her arm, but she stopped him and smiled.

"No, it's all right. I can do that myself, thank you."

She took the handkerchief from him and wiped her skirt and arm, returning the damp cloth back to him.

"I'm so sorry; please let me get you another drink. What was it?"

"No, that's fine, don't bother."

"No, please, I insist. It's the least I can do. What was it?"

"Well okay, it was a gin and orange."

Johnnie was soon back clutching a small glass for her and a pint of beer for himself. She was wiping, with her own handkerchief, at the damp patch on her uniform skirt.

"I am so sorry. I hope it won't spoil your evening."

"Please stop apologising; it was an accident," she smiled.

"Skipper, are you getting the pints, or what?" shouted Yorky.

"Oh, I forgot. I was about to get the chaps a beer."

She laughed. "You carry on, Flight Lieutenant."

"No, no, please call me Johnnie."

She looked at the wings on his left breast above his medal ribbons.

"Is that your crew over there?"

"Yes and a thirsty set of beggars they are. I'd better get them a beer."

"Yes, and I had better find my girlfriend. Thanks for the drink, 'bye."

She turned and was soon lost in the noisy, throbbing crowd.

Johnnie stood there for a while before turning again to the bar. When he returned to the crew with a tray full of foamless pints, Yorky demanded, "Who was that ladybird, Skipper? She was a luscious piece of Waffery, she was. What's her name? What section does she work in?"

"Oh, blast," said Johnnie, looking up quickly searching the crowd, "I forgot to ask. Yes, she was quite a looker, I must agree."

In fact, he was thinking how beautiful she was. He had been a fool not find out her name or where she worked or even if she was from this camp.

'I must discover who she is,' he said to himself.

Chalkie leaned across to Yorky.

"Didn't get her name, didn't find out where she works. He's a great pilot and Skipper, but as far as women go, he's as dim as a TocH lamp."

"Come on, Johnnie, join the party!" called Paddy.

Johnnie gave up his fruitless search and sat down.

The Squadronaires carried on playing, the beer carried on arriving, and disappearing, and Johnnie and many others that night ended up weaving an uneven course for home.

The next evening, Johnnie was working late in the flight office with Chris Cooper, the Flight Commander, after a day spent trying to shake off an unaccustomed hangover.

"OK, Johnnie, let's call it a day, shall we? You're not getting any better, are you?" laughed Chris. "Go to the mess and get something to eat before they shut up shop and then I would recommend an early night."

"Yeah, I think you're right. I'll come back to these training schedules tomorrow morning."

He made his way to the officers' mess to find it deserted except for two WAAF stewardesses chatting beside the kitchen door.

"I know it's late, but I don't suppose there is any chance of something to eat, is there ladies?"

"Certainly, sir. We're expecting a few more of you soon anyway; they've been to some meeting in the ops room. What can we tempt you with, sir? Bangers? Spam fritters? Or a meat curry?"

"I don't think my stomach could survive an attack by the curry. What meat is it, anyway?"

"I think I'll 'ave to decline an answer on that one, sir." she said with a smile.

He was attempting to carve an insipid banger when a female voice addressed him from across the table.

"Hello again."

He looked up to see the beautiful girl he had admired at the dance standing there. As he stood up to greet her, his foot connected with the leg of the table, jolting it violently, knocking a jug of water over on its side. Water cascaded over the seat opposite and the jug rolled over the edge of the table to crash noisily on the floor. Ironic cheers rose up from the dozen or so officers who had just entered the mess hall.

"Oh no, not again!" she laughed. "You do have this uncanny knack of throwing liquid at me."

"Oh dear, I'm terribly sorry ... I do apologise ... I'm so sorry," he flustered, his face burning red with embarrassment.

"Please, do stop apologising. It's all right; you missed me this time."

They both burst out laughing as he replaced the wet chair and indicated to it as an invitation to join him. She removed her hat, hung her gas mask case over the back of the chair, sat down, and shook out her hair.

"I do hope you are a little more careful with your aeroplane," she said smiling.

"I can assure you I am most careful with His Majesty's aircraft, Ma'am."

"Been 'avin' a bit of an accident 'ave we, sir?" said the stewardess. "Never mind, I'll clear it up. What would you like, Ma'am, bangers, Spam or curry?"

"I think I'll try the Spam, looking at those sausages, and I'm not brave enough to try the curry," she smiled.

"Look, I'm terribly sorry, but I don't know your name. By the time I had come to my senses last night you had disappeared like Cinderella at the ball."

She smiled at him and offered him her hand. "Hello, Johnnie, I'm Ginny ... Ginny Murphy,"

He suddenly found himself lost in her aura and was very pleasantly surprised she had remembered his name.

"Can I have my hand back, please?"

"Oh, yes ... I'm sorry." He reluctantly released her hand, thinking how soft and delicate it was.

Her raven hair fell over her ears in a series of dark, soft, velvet waves. She pushed a strand of hair gently away from her emerald-green eyes, which reflected the origins of her surname. Her lips were glistening with freshly applied red lipstick that was most probably against King's Regulations. Her cheeks were flushed by the laughter they had both enjoyed as she looked directly, almost daringly, into his eyes.

"Hello, Ginny, Jonathan Sanderson ... er ... Johnnie," he stumbled.

"Yes, I know," she said mysteriously.

"How ... how did you ...?"

"Don't ask, as I may have to confess to some spying. I can do that, spying that is, as I am in Intelligence," she laughed.

They shared their meal and talked non-stop. He discovered she was just twenty-one and came from Lincoln where her father was the manager of an up-market furniture store. However, his constant complaint was, she said, that all they sold now was 'utility furniture' made from 'tea chests and knotty pine'. She had an elder sister called Charlotte, but known by the family pet name of 'Charlie', serving as an officer in the Women's Royal Naval Service in Chatham dockyard.

They were so engrossed in each other that they did not realise they were the only ones left in the dining room and carried on chatting until the lights suddenly started to go out.

"Oh. Everyone has gone!" she exclaimed.

They both looked at each other guiltily and giggled.

"Look, it's still early," he said looking at his wrist watch. "Why don't we go down to the pub in the village? I've only been there once, but it seems like a good show."

"Yes, all right, but I must go to my quarters first."

"OK, I'll grab my car and meet you back here."

When he pushed open the door to the lounge bar of the Royal Oak, he was dismayed to find it heaving with aircrews, his own among them. He was hoping for an intimate cosy fireside drink, and to continue their earlier pleasant conversation, but there was no chance of that, especially when Algy spotted them by the door.

"Johnnie!" he shouted across the cheerful bedlam, "Come and join us, come and join us, and bring that gorgeous young lady with you, you sly old dog. We were wondering where you had got to. Now we know!"

Johnnie and Ginny exchanged a brief disappointed glance, seeing that the hope of an intimate quiet drink had gone. She held on tightly to his arm as the crew surged towards them.

After introductions all round to the crew of G-George and several other young women attached, they entered reluctantly into the spirit of the evening with a smile.

# 10 ... Death

"We're on Battle Orders for tonight, Johnnie," said Paddy as he came into the flight office after breakfast the next morning.

"Yes, I just found out myself, Michael. Meet in the crew room at 1030 hours for the NFT. Spread the good news would you?"

By the time they had come out of the briefing hut, the weather had closed in. Rain was lashing the open land that was the airfield, dark grey clouds were hurtling across the sodden sky.

"Bloody Hamburg again," said Algy as they all ran across the grass to the crew room after the briefing.

"Do you think we'll go with this filthy weather, Skip?" asked Jan.

"They said it won't be this bad over there, but we'll just have to wait and see. I can't see them standing us down just for the sake of a bit of rain, Jan."

"I suppose not, Skip, wishful thinking, eh?"

Sitting at the end of the runway with rain streaming down the cockpit canopy, and the wind rocking Gloria, Johnnie peered through the grey evening light also wishing the order would come through to stand down. His stomach churned at the thought of fighting Gloria, as he also called her now, into the stormy, howling night and out across the frightening North Sea.

Suddenly the green 'go' light from the caravan cut through the greyness. Brakes off, throttles to full, she thundered past the caravan, its normal accompanying crowd reduced to two windswept WAAFs waving from the sheltered side of the caravan and the Group Captain standing on his own out in the foul weather, saluting. Johnnie had a feeling that one of the WAAFs was Ginny, but no, it couldn't have been. Why would she do that? They had only just met! She must have been waving off someone else.

The pilots were to rendezvous at a given position six thousand feet over the North Sea, but as Johnnie fought Gloria slowly up into the storm-ridden sky, he realised he would not be able to see any other aircraft and would have to try to rendezvous solely on timing.

Paddy had just recorded in his log 'Take-off 2103 hours 2 August, 1943'. The intercom crackled:

"Michael, we will have to rendezvous by timing, there is no chance we will be seeing any other aircraft tonight. Keep me up to date on our progress."

"Ok, Skipper. Twelve minutes to RP."

"Ok."

As they fought their way across the storm-tossed sea and closed on the German coastline and their target, the weather grew worse with each mile. Sheets of lightning briefly illuminated the rods of wind-driven rain, accompanying thunder sounding like distant guns as forked lightning searched for anchor points to secure its tearing prongs. Johnnie fought to keep Gloria on her intended course as she bounced and jolted around the sky, up and down, side to side. The crew were clinging to whatever they could to save themselves crashing against the many obstacles that occupied their space. Gloria broke through the rainstorm and they found themselves underneath towering, turbulent cumulus nimbus thunderclouds, where the air tossed them around like leaves in an autumn gale. Suddenly the cockpit and the nose cupola filled with a weird, but beautiful dancing blue light.

"What the hell is that?" said Chalkie, pointing to the electrical flowers dancing on the windows and the large luminous rings that were encircling the starboard propellers.

"Look at the wing tips. It's St. Elmo's fire, Chalkie."

Every pointed surface on the aircraft had flickering blue flames leaping from or around them; ethereal light bathed the gun muzzles, radio aerials and tail-planes. Sparks were shooting across Algy's radio sets and Paddy's navigation aids, filling the fuselage with its tremulous light, transfixing the crew with its slightly disturbing alien beauty. After a few minutes it disappeared as suddenly as it appeared, leaving the crew with a feeling that some unearthly presence had visited them.

"I've never seen that before, Skipper," said a bemused Chalkie. "I've heard about it, of course, strangely beautiful, really, if not a bit creepy."

The storm grew worse. Johnnie was now worried that Gloria could be damaged by the constant violent movement. The darkness closed back on them as the thunderous rain returned even heavier.

"Skipper, the temperature of the starboard outer engine has shot up and oil pressure is down. I can't see anything outside, it's too dark?" reported Chalkie peering through the storm-lashed canopy.

"OK, keep monitoring."

The engine took away the need for any decision; it started to misfire and splutter, and as lightning lit up the sky, Chalkie saw flames coming from under the cowling.

"Fire in the starboard outer, feather it, Skipper?"

"Yes. Feather and extinguish," ordered Johnnie.

Chalkie turned the fuel cock off and pressed the feathering button in front of him and the propeller slowed and stopped. Johnnie shut down the throttle and switched off the ignition to that engine.

"Master fuel cock off, prop feathered, fire extinguisher on," said Chalkie calmly. After a while, "Fire's out, Skipper."

"Ok, Chalkie, well done."

At that moment, lightning struck the port tail fin causing the aircraft to yaw and buck violently. Johnnie fought to bring her back on course.

"Bugger me, Skipper, it's getting a bit larey back here. Isn't it time to go home yet? It really is getting a bit lumpy and bumpy. I've cracked me 'ead about five times already." complained Yorky.

"Well that could help knock some sense into 'ee." laughed Jan. "Its fine up 'ere, lovely sunny day, it be."

"Bugger off!" came the reply.

"Ok, chaps, I think it would be wise to abort this op, we'll never find the target in this weather and we've now lost the starboard outer. Algy, signal group our plan. Michael, give me a course for home. Do not relax chaps; there is still a war on out there. I'll drop down to see if I can get under this weather a bit, but keep on oxygen everyone."

Johnnie fed the yoke gently forward, his hands and arms aching with the tremendous effort to keep Gloria flying. He gradually dropped from eighteen thousand feet through the furious black storm clouds with lightning illuminating their opaque angry interiors. At just over eight thousand feet, they slipped from the cloud base and as they did so, lightning again lit up the sky.

"I just saw a Lanc two hundred yards to our front and one hundred yards below us, Skipper," reported Jan, "crossing from port to starboard. What the ...!"

Johnnie and Chalkie watched horrified, as four curving arcs of red tracer swept up towards them from the dark. Bullets splattered on the doors of the bomb bay and in the blink of an eye, the Plexiglas turret cupola and Jan's nose cone shattered as the machine gun bullets, trailing fire, tore through them. Two of the tracers smashed into Jan's chest, a third fire-tailed lead slug ripped through his throat and a fourth one crashed through his oxygen mask exiting through the back of his leather helmet. The force of the impact threw his body back and up to smash against the underside of his turret, spraying a mist of red and grey gore around the compartment and on to Chalkie's trousers and boots. Jan's blood soaked, broken body crumpled back down.

Johnnie's immediate reaction was to throw G-George violently down to port shouting,

"Corkscrewing port!"

The freezing night air blasted through the nose cone and the entry port underneath Chalkie's instrument panel. Paddy's and Algy's charts and papers scattered down the body of the aircraft in the sudden gale.

The Lancaster below them had disappeared back into the rain and gloom like an evil spirit of the night.

"That was a fucking Lanc!" shouted Chalkie.

"I know! He must have thought we were a night fighter. Stupid bastard!" said Johnnie, as he pulled Gloria from her downward rush. "Check what the damage is, Chalkie. Jan, can you hear me? Jan ... Jan, can you hear me?" he called over the intercom, but all that there was to hear was the hiss and crackle of radio silence.

Chalkie noticed for the first time the blood spattered over his trousers. He folded back his 'Dicky' seat, bent and stepped down into the nose cupola. The bloody scene that greeted him made him recoil in shock. Looking at the bloody mess in front of him, he knew Jan was dead. No one could have survived such wounds. He placed his hand on Jan's foot, briefly.

"Poor bastard, what a way to go, killed by your own mates."

He shook his head sadly and patted the boot affectionately, then scrambled back through the entry port and pulled down his seat from the fuselage side

"It's no good, Skipper, he's dead. The nose cone and turret cupola are badly damaged and Jan has taken two or three hits, he's dead, Skipper. The bombing selector board, computor and sight are totally u/s, the turret cupola is a bloody mess as well."

"Jesus Christ! Poor Jan. Are you hit?" said Johnnie in alarm as he saw the blood on Chalkie's lower body.

"No, it's Jan's, Skipper."

'What a stupid way to die,' Johnnie thought, 'another crewmember lost, how many bloody more must I lose?'

The night air was roaring through the damaged nose into the cockpit. "Skipper to crew, we have been hit by gunfire from one of our own Lancs and I believe Jan has bought it. The nose and front turret have been badly damaged; we will go down low and try to make it back home. Report in, everyone."

One by one, the rest of the crew confirmed they were all right.

"Are you sure Jan's bought it, Skipper," asked Dusty.

"I'm afraid so, Dusty. Chalkie has checked him out."

"We've been together since we went to Blyton. He was a good mate," Dusty added softly.

He and Jan had hit it off as friends' right from the first day they had met. Jan reckoned it was because they were both men of the soil, so to speak, him being a gamekeeper and Dusty a nurseryman. They had drunk many a pint together over the last year or so. Dusty remembered one night when ...

Gloria fought through the storm and flew over the tempestuous North Sea to take Jan's broken body home.

Their orders had been that if the operation had to abort they were to jettison, over the heaving sea below them, the high explosive bombs and keep any incendiaries they were carrying.

"Chalkie, jettison the HE's, we've not got incendiaries on board, have we?"

"No, Skipper, open bomb bay doors."

"Bomb bay doors open."

Chalkie pushed the jettison control button, but nothing happened, he tried again, still nothing happened.

"The circuits are probably damaged. They should have dropped, but they haven't, Skipper. I'll try the 'T' bar."

He pulled the 'T' handle on the instrument panel in front of him to jettison the load manually, but again nothing happened.

He pulled the 'T' handle again, nothing. "No joy, Skip. I'll go back and check through the viewing window."

He scrambled down the fuselage and peered through the small viewing window aft of the main spar, seeing a bomb bay full of deadly explosive. He made his way back to the cockpit.

"No, they're all still there, Skipper."

"We'll just have to go home with the eggs still in the basket then, won't we?"

He closed the bomb bay doors and flew on through the foul weather, Gloria bouncing and shuddering violently. Thoughts of his ditching in the sea washed over him, briefly. Lifting his right hand up towards his face for a few seconds he realised that there was no trembling, no shaking to show that, yes, he was scared, but was in control of his fears.

"Skipper to crew, we have a further problem. We can't jettison our bomb load so we are going home with them. Now, because of the damage and we only have three engines, the landing could be a bit dicey, especially with a few tons of H.E.

sitting under our arses. My options are as follows. One, we ditch the aircraft after baling out over the North Sea. Two, we ditch the aircraft after baling out over Blighty, but that means dumping Hitler's little packages on some poor English village. Three, we stay with Gloria until we are over Blighty and you all jump and I will land her. I suggest that option. I'll give you a couple of minutes to think about it, and then come back to me with your choice off the menu."

Paddy spoke first:

"Skipper, we have to take Jan back home. We can't just drop him in the cold sea on his own. I would like him with us when we land."

"Skipper, I agree with Paddy, we take him home. And I'll be buggered if you think I'm swimmin' in this bloody weather, be buggered if I will, I'm stayin'."

"Staying," said Dusty.

"No options, old man, got a date with a pretty little Popsie tonight."

"Okay, you mad 'buggers'," said Johnnie, imitating Yorky's accent. "We go in on three and a basket full of rotten eggs," in a more sombre voice. "We will take Jan home."

As they made their final approach, Algy used the Verey pistol in the roof, just behind his radio station, and fired off the flares that notified flying control that they had damage and needed the emergency teams to meet them.

"'Woldimp' control, one nine, finals. Have live load on board, nose canopy damaged and a casualty, suggest 'meat and heat' wagons follow us," radioed Johnnie.

"Okay, one nine. Understand, you're clear to land on runway zero six," answered the tower.

They came in over the long wooded valley and Johnnie put Gloria down on the runway as if he were landing on thin ice. The tyres gently kissed the ground and the 'eggs' in the bomb bay stayed exactly where they were, to the immense relief of the crew.

"Home at last, chaps, home at last," said an exhausted and saddened Johnnie.

A fire engine and an ambulance raced up behind them on the runway.

The dejected and saddened crew stood by the tail-plane in the rain and watched the 'meat' wagon take Jan's dead body away.

The war had now become something much more personal; Jan's death brought home to them that in war, friends die.

A crew bus picked them and their gear up and took them back for the debriefing, a sad and difficult exercise for them all.

"Oh, Johnnie, I'm so sorry. He was a lovely boy," said Ginny when they met the next night. "To think I watched him take off last night."

"So it was you standing by the caravan, I thought it was, although all I got was a very brief glimpse as we flashed by."

"Yes, I just wanted to wish you luck," she said shyly. "The other girl was one of the waafs that have fallen under the magic spell of Algy's charms. I think he's building a harem."

"Look, I don't think I will be much fun tonight, I've got to write to Jan's parents. Can we meet tomorrow night?"

"Of course, how insensitive of me. I'm sorry, Johnnie. Yes, I'll look forward to that." She stood on tiptoes and kissed him on the lips.

When she had gone, he touched his lips softly with his fingers. That was the first kiss.

Meanwhile, Jan's parents, down in Cornwall, were reading the soulless official telegram from Wing Commander Harry Picton, which informed them their son, Sergeant Frank Greasely, had died as the result of air operations on the night of 2 August, 1943.

# 11 ... Goodbye

"When did you and your crew last have any leave, Johnnie?" asked Chris Cooper, 'A' flight's OC.

"It was about two months ago, I think. I'm not quite sure."

"Not to worry; I'm sending you all off on seven days' leave for a break. You have had an eventful start with the squadron. By the way, Sergeant Greasely's parents have asked if they can bury him on the estate where he lived in Cornwall. The Groupie has agreed and his funeral will be next week."

"I would like to attend, please sir, and so would Sergeant Miller, they were close friends."

"I'm sure that will be fine. I'll drop a line and tell them to expect you."

Dusty was sitting on his bed in the Nissen hut he shared with his friends, Chalkie, Jan, and Yorky. He was watching the Adjustment Officer, a young pilot officer, and an RAF police corporal, folding and packing away all of Jan's possessions, his uniforms, shirts and socks, shoes and boots. The officer placed Jan's private and personal items into a cardboard box after checking to see that they were suitable to send to his next-of-kin.

"I will arrange to settle any mess bills, and I have filled in his log book," said the Adjustment Officer, holding out Jan's flight logbook. It was clearly marked, KIA.

"Was he a friend of yours or just a colleague?"

"You obviously don't fly, sir, do you?" answered Dusty sourly.

When they had gone, Dusty folded back Jan's mattress and pushed it to the top of the metal bed, and as he did so, something caught his eye on the floor next to the wooden folding chair beside the bed. It looked like a dead mouse, but when he bent down he realised it was Jan's 'lucky rabbit's foot', its leather thong snapped. He picked it up and absently rubbed the soft fur with his thumb.

"This didn't do you much good, bonny lad," he said sadly.

Johnnie and Ginny went down to the Royal Oak the next night. As was the way of the service, Jan's death was toasted and the conversation moved on. There would be time for grief and remembrance at his funeral.

"I'm going on leave tomorrow, Ginny; I'm going to see my family; I've not seen them for almost a year. I hope you don't mind?"

"Mind! I only wish I was coming with you." She stretched out her hands and held both of his. "I know you flyers have a rough, tough and 'devil may care' attitude and death is part of the job, but I get the feeling that Jan's death means something more to you. What is it?"

Although it was August, the thick walls of the ancient pub made the warmth and joviality of a log fire welcome. It hissed and crackled in the massive inglenook in front of them. Johnnie stared at the flickering flames, mesmerised by their constant movement.

"Jan is the seventh person to die flying with me. I just don't want any more deaths on my hands," he said quietly. "I always seem to get out alive, but others die. Why is that, Ginny?"

"Oh, Johnnie, it's not your fault, you don't cause it. It is the luck of the draw; it's being in the wrong place at the wrong time. It is ... it's many things. It's this damned war; it's Hitler's madness. One thing that is certain, Johnnie, it is not your fault. Bomber crews are lost every day, yes, sadly some die, but some become POWs, some survive, and some carry on, inspiring and leading other men. You're one of the latter, Johnnie, I know."

"Maybe you're right," he smiled sadly. "How can I think such dark and desperate thoughts with a beautiful girl sitting here holding my hands? You are enough to inspire a whole squadron, a whole bomber command." Then reflectively, "I wish you were coming to Kent with me, my mother would love you."

"I wish I could meet her too. Maybe next time, eh?"

Before he went off to Kent, Johnnie arranged to meet Dusty at Paddington station in London to catch the early morning train to Plymouth the following Tuesday.

They met at seven o'clock on the forecourt of the station underneath the large clock. The ticket collector, who clipped their travel warrants, warned them that getting out of London would be slow because of a Luftwaffe raid the previous night. After several stops and starts, the train finally started to pick up speed leaving the grey grimness of a bomb-scarred city behind. It emerged into the countryside, which appeared to Johnnie totally devoid of the signs of war, bright with sunshine and blue skies. Fields of wheat and barley were starting to turn golden in the summer sun. Cattle and sheep grazed in green fields, and waving Land Army girls harvested the hay as the train steamed on its way to the West Country. After stopping at Exeter, they thundered along the Exe estuary and the dramatic coastline of Dawlish and Teignmouth, arriving at Plymouth station before lunchtime.

"We had better get a taxi to Stonehouse for the ferry across to Cornwall," said Johnnie to Dusty.

"You know this neck of the woods then, Skip?" he asked.

"Yes, we used to come down here for holidays when I was a nipper. We used to stay at a wonderful place called Burgh Island, back along the coast. My father was at university with the chap that owned the hotel on the island."

The ancient taxi took them through Plymouth's devastated streets. It had once been a charming, if not cramped, medieval city, with a richness of Tudor timbered buildings and narrow cobbled streets leading down to the Barbican harbour and up to the famous Plymouth Hoe! The scars of the Luftwaffe's raids were still raw and visible. Piles of rubble heaped on street corners; while whole areas of the city had disappeared, in fact, nearly four hundred acres of the city was in ruins. The bombed-out St Charles church stood like a black skeleton overlooking the ravaged city and the ancient harbour. They travelled down the infamous Union Street with its many pubs and theatres, a few of them were islands in a sea of destruction now. Piles of rubble bordered the cobbled roads leading up towards Millbay

Docks. The shops, pubs, houses and warehouses of a vibrant and historic district had disappeared.

Both Johnnie and Dusty wondered if this is what Hamburg would look like now. Turning left up Durnford Street at the end of Union Street, by the Earl Grey pub, they passed the brewery that backed on to Stonehouse Creek. Then they drove past the granite might of Stonehouse Barracks, the home of Plymouth's Royal Marines and just after the arched gatehouse to the barracks, they turned down Admirals Hard where the taxi dropped them at the top of the cobbled slipway. From here, the small, steam-powered ferry, The Northern Belle, crossed to Cremyll on the Cornish side of the Tamar Estuary.

"There's a café over there, Skip, or there's the 'Vine' opposite, if you fancy a pint! I don't know about you, but I'm bloody starvin'."

"Yes, good idea, Dusty. The café, I think; it's been a long time since breakfast."

A small café stood at the end of the row of terraced cottages that led down to the slip, where according to the weathered sign hanging on the quayside wall, the ferry departed 'Every half hour, quarter to and quarter past the hour'.

Maybe it was because they were the only customers, and the old woman who served them confessed to having a son in the RAF serving overseas, had something to do with the surprise offer of ham sandwiches. They downed them, and mugs of hot strong tea, with gratitude.

They climbed aboard the little boat and the ferryman collected his sixpence fare from both, tooted his whistle and put the ferry astern from the stone jetty, swung her round and steamed away. They went past the imposing granite buildings of the Royal Navy's clock-towered Royal William Victualling Yard and half a dozen various sized naval warships tied up alongside the wall, and steamed across the narrow channel to Cornwall.

"You'm for the funer'l, gents?" asked an old man sat on the seat of an ancient pony trap, an old seaman's cap well back on his head, the pony's head stuck in a nose-bag of oats.

"Er, yes we are," answered Johnnie.

"Climb aboard, Skipper, I've bin' sen' to collect 'ee."
"Oh, thank you."

They clambered up into the high-wheeled pony trap, the old sailor took the nosebag off the pony, climbed back to his seat, and they set off towards the stone-ball topped pillared gates that guarded the long straight drive up to Mount Edgcumbe House.

The trap driver informed them, in an indignant tone, that the house had received a couple of direct hits from Jerry bombers back in '41. They were trying to hit the nearby naval dockyard, but had hit the house, and the subsequent fire had gutted the interior of the beautiful medieval building. They drove around the blackened ruins of the house, in a clearing in the woods behind stood the estate's small chapel. A ruddy-faced older version of Jan met them, wearing what was obviously a rarely worn tweed suit that gave off a slight smell of mothballs and damp. He wore a black armband on the sleeve of his jacket.

"Thank 'ee for comin', sirs," he said touching his cap, "we're very grateful you both could make it. It's a very long way from Lincolnshire and Frank would have appreciated you comin'."

He led them into the small chapel and showed them to the front pew to the right of Jan's coffin, which rested on two rustic trestles in front of the low altar. The chapel filled up with local people and a white-haired, ancient vicar conducted the short service in a gentle and soft Cornish accent. Johnnie and Dusty felt like interlopers in this very parochial and close community until the vicar asked if Johnnie would like to say a few words as Frank's commanding officer.

He stood and faced the gathered mourners their weathered country faces expectant. He began, hesitantly.

"Err, Jan ... erm ... Frank, was a vitally important member of our crew. Without him, there was no point in taking off and flying over Germany. He took great pride in his status as an air bomber and gunner ... and he was very good at his job, a perfectionist with great dedication and skill. He always said he owed those skills to his father and his experience in the countryside of his beloved Cornwall, or Kernow as he proudly called it. He was also a very popular member of the crew and we came to look at him as a bit of a mascot as he was the youngest at twenty-one. I felt privileged to serve with him and to call him a friend. We miss him very much."

A few days earlier, he had copied out part of a poem he had found in a newspaper as he thought it was very apt and moving. He was going to ask Jan's mother if she would like to keep it, but he decided to read it now, he pulled it from his pocket, unfolded the piece of paper and cleared his throat, nervously, and read to the little gathering in a tiny Cornish chapel hundreds of miles away from the scene of Jan's violent death.

"I would like to read this poem, written by an air gunner, about an air gunner, and I thought it might serve as a tribute to Jan ... erm ... Frank," explained Johnnie hesitantly. "'Requiem for an Air-Gunner' by Sergeant R.W. Gilbert," he began.

*My brief, sweet life is over,*
*My eyes no longer see,*
*No summer walks,*
*No Christmas trees,*
*No pretty girls for me.*
*I've got the chop.*
*I've had it.*
*My nightly ops are done.*
*Yet in another hundred years,*
*I'll still be twenty-one.*

He folded the poem and handed it to Jan's grieving mother. She accepted it shyly and started to read it, but her eyes started to fill with tears. She spoke to him in her warm round accent:

"Thank 'ee, Flight Lieutenant. Frank would have loved that."

"Thank you, sir, I'm sure Frank would 'ave appreciated it," said Jan's father as he put a comforting arm around his wife.

After the funeral service in the chapel, the congregation moved to the graveyard to lower Jan's body to his final resting place. A red and blue-capped Royal Marine Bugler, sent from the nearby Royal Navy training barracks, HMS Raleigh, played the Last Post and Reveille over the grave. Johnnie and Dusty stood to attention, saluted their fallen comrade and friend, and said their final goodbyes.

They all filed into the small hall next to the graveyard, which served as the estate school and had, in fact, been Jan's first ever school. It surprised the two airmen to find the amount of food laid out on the trestle tables for the 'funer'l tea'. Ham sandwiches, pork pies, scones and cakes and other local delicacies graced the tables. There were even pots of clotted cream and jam. Johnnie knew the war had come to this tiny corner of England, but the locals had spared nothing for the funeral of one of their own, 'Jan' Greasely.

# 12 ... Jock

Back in Elkington, the next day, Chris Cooper, the OC of 'A' flight, called Johnnie to the flight hut.

"Ah, Sanderson, everything go okay in Cornwall, I presume?"

He carried on without waiting for an answer, "A couple of bits of news for you. Your rear gunner, er...Sarn't Ward, he is to get an immediate DFM for that JU-eighty-eight he got the other week, well done. Awards like that are very good for the flight ... and the squadron of course. Yes ... well done."

"It's nothing to do with me, sir. He got the Jerry on his own, a first class effort and I'm delighted he's got the gong. Is there any news on the Lanc that shot us up?"

"No, not a word. If it had been from this squadron, we would have heard by now. However, I have news of Greasely's replacement; he is a member of the squadron, as it happens. He was one of the survivors of your kite's predecessor, G-George. His name is Flight Sergeant McGuffin, you can find him out there," he indicated the crew room beyond his office door. "He's got a lot of experience; should fit in well, I think."

"Is that the chap with the fearful red hair and stunning handlebar 'tache?"

"Yes, he does have a somewhat striking appearance," he smiled, "but don't judge a book by its cover ... and all that. Here is his service record for you to read, experienced chap. By the way, Chiefy says your kite is all fixed and ready for a test flight."

"Thank you, sir."

A while later, after reading the flight sergeant's service record, Johnnie went through to the crew room.

"Hello, Flight, I'm Johnnie Sanderson. Welcome home, as it might be."

"Hello, sir. Ay, thank 'ee," he said with a smile.

"Have you met the others yet?"

"I've met Mr. Doolan there, sir," he indicated Paddy, who was reading a newspaper while slumped in one of the overstuffed armchairs that somehow graced their flight's crew room. He put up his hand in recognition on hearing his name.

"Hello, Skipper. Good leave, besides Cornwall, I mean?" he added quickly.

"Yes fine, thank you, Michael," he turned back to the flight sergeant. "Walk with me over to the service hangar and tell me all about yourself. Rouse the rest of the chaps will you, please, Michael? Have them all here in say ... an hour. Gloria's ready for an NFT, okay?"

"Certainly, Skipper."

The two airmen walked down the gravel pathways towards the hangar. 'Jock' McGuffin was a little shorter than Johnnie was, but not by much, his flaming red hair escaping from underneath his Glengarry-style side cap.

"Now, what have you been up to?"

"Not a lot to tell you, sir; I'm just a typical bomb aiming gunner that's been around a bit," he answered in his thick Glaswegian accent.

"It's the 'round a bit' I want to hear about. What do we call you, anyway?"

"Well ma' name is Finlay Lachlan James McGuffin in full, if ye like, but everyone calls me Jock, sir."

"I'm not keen on calling people by their national names, except our rear gunner, Yorky. I don't think he has ever been called anything else," he laughed. "I'll call you Finlay, if that's all right by you? And by the way, forget the 'sir' out of earshot of senior officers, the other chaps call me Skip or Skipper, okay?"

"Ay, that's okay, sir ... I mean Skip."

"So, what have you been up to for the last few years?" asked Johnnie.

He had read the service record, but as that was an impersonal set of facts, he would sooner hear the man's story from his own lips.

"I joined up in '39 before the start of the fun and games and ended up as a gunner on Blenheims. I was too thick to qualify as a navigator," he smiled. "We were sent to France with the Advanced Air Striking Force in support of the BEF, but a Jerry fighter shot us down just before Dunkirk. We baled out, my pilot and I made our way to the coast, we ended up on the beach at Dunkirk, and managed to cadge a lift with the Navy on the very last day, June the 4th. The rest o' the crew were captured."

He paused as if in remembrance. "We turned up at Manston in Kent and were 'returned to unit' with a DFM, well, the Skipper got a DFC actually. Went back on Blenheims for a while until I found out they were creating the new trade of Bomb Aimer-Gunner, so I re-mustered, but I did'nee wanna be an 'Arse End Charlie'. After air bomber training, I got posted to the HCU at Hemswell and ended up on Lancs with the newly formed Five-Nine-Nine here at Elkington."

He stopped talking and just walked quietly beside Johnnie. After a while, he carried on with his story.

"Four weeks ago, my Skipper, who had been on ops for eighteen months nonstop, was bringing us back from Essen on his forty-third sortie, when the aircraft became 'unserviceable' as they like to call it. We had taken so much damage that the bloody thing couldna fly anymore. We jumped, but something stopped the Skipper from getting out. We all came down around the field here, but the Skipper and G-George went in, a few miles away up by the Grimsby road. They sent us on extended leave and now I'm back wi' a golden 'Caterpillar' badge."

He hooked his thumb under the flap of his tunic pocket to show the little gold badge, which indicated that twice a parachute had saved his life. "So with all due repec', I hope you can keep a kite in the air, Skipper," he laughed. "I no fancy any more jumping."

Johnnie burst out laughing and clapped 'Finlay' on the back. "I'll do my best, Finlay, I'll do my best."

"Seriously, though, sir, after losing two kites, I hope I'm not going to put a jinx on your kite?"

Johnnie stopped walking and put his hand on Jock's shoulder.

"Finlay, I don't believe in all that gobbledegook and neither should you. You have just been in the wrong place at the wrong time." He briefly remembered Ginny's words. "That red hair and remarkable handlebar of yours are bound to bring us good luck," he said with a smile. "She all ready, Chiefy?"

"Ay, Mr. Sanderson, all okay. Hello Jock."

"Chiefy."

"Your mid-upper is on board, sir. We'll tow her down to your dispersal pad soon."

"Fine, Chiefy, we'll take her up for an NFT later this morning."

Johnnie and Finlay clambered on board and worked their way forward. As they reached the cockpit, Dusty was emerging from the nose cone.

"Hello, Dusty," said a surprised Johnnie. "Do you want to convert as well?"

"Pardon, Skip?" said Dusty, confused. "Oh, no, I've just hung up Jan's rabbit's foot in there. I hope you don't mind, Skip. He forgot to take it with him on his last op …"

"No, of course I don't mind; it's up to Finlay here really. He is our new air bomber. This is Dusty Miller, mid-upper, Finlay."

"Hello, no, I dinna mind at all; we need all the luck we can get," he said, producing a rather tatty piece of white heather from one of the top pockets of his battle dress blouse. He added, in a rather embarrassed way, "My mother sends me a piece every month, where the hell she gets it from in the middle of Glasgie, I dinna ken."

The two smiled and shook hands.

"I've seen you around in the mess a few times. I'll buy you a pint later," invited Dusty.

"I'll leave you two boozers together," chuckled Johnnie. "Be in the flight crew room at 1100 hours ready for an NFT, okay?"

"Sure thing, Skip," they said together, looked at each other and laughed.

'He'll fit in fine,' thought Johnnie as he made his way aft to talk to the Chiefy again.

"I see you've won Jock McGuffin," said the Chiefy.

"Yes. Hard to miss, isn't he?"

"He's a good lad, Mr Sanderson, very dedicated to his job. He was always down here checking on his guns and aiming gear, making sure everything was tickety-boo in the nose, one of the best. By the way, I can assure you he is a true redhead. His party piece, in the mess, is walking on his hands down the bar. Unfortunately, he does it when he's wearing his mess kit kilt, and he's a true Scotsman, if you know what I mean, not a pretty sight," he laughed and Johnnie shuddered and grimaced.

"Oh, by the way sir, would you mind telling Mr D'Arcy he owes me two bob. He forgot to wind in the trailing whip aerial when you brought her home last, so we had to spend bleedin' hours rewinding a new one!"

Johnnie kept a straight face, because he knew that ground crews had better things to do than to correct Algy's 'cock ups'. Hence, the 'fine' of two shillings for the ground crews beer fund. "Yes, certainly, Chiefy, I'll tell him."

A few nights later, the four sergeants were sitting round a table in the sergeants' mess, celebrating Yorky's DFM, pints of beer and a crowded ashtray in front of them. When the Skipper had informed him that morning of his award, Yorky's reaction had been predictable:

"Well, I'll be buggered!"

Which did the normal chorus greet: "Not tonight, Josephine, not tonight!"

Now he was puffing away on his slim-stemmed pipe using it to emphasise most of the points of his conversation.

"Stop poking the nice new flight sergeant with your pipe," laughed Chalkie.

"I was just about to ask what's the old man like; he seems like a decent sort?" asked Finlay, brushing Yorky's spittle from his battledress blouse.

"Yeah, he is," said Chalkie. "Bloody good pilot too. Got quite a few sorties beneath his belt, even ditched a Wimpy in the drink, the North Sea."

"That's what he got the DFC for, isn't it?" asked Yorky.

"Yeah, it was back in May forty-two, on the way back from Berlin," carried on Chalkie. "A night fighter attacked them. They already had flak damage and some of the crew wounded, so he put it down in the sea. He pulled two of his crew out and got them in the raft even though he had broken ribs. The Air Sea Rescue boys were out on patrol tied up to a channel buoy in the mouth of the Humber when they got the signal that a kite had ditched. They pulled them out after they had been in the water for about six hours. The other three crew members went down with the Wimpy."

"And he only got the DFC?" said a surprised Finlay. "What did he get the DSO for then, for God's sake?"

"A couple of months later he brought home a badly damaged Wimpy. Most of the linen fabric skin round the arse end had burnt off, the rear gunner had burned to death and the wireless op killed by gunfire from a night fighter, and two other lads wounded, but he got them home. He got his DSO for that, but that's not all, on his first sortie after that, a night fighter killed his navigator."

"Jesus! Jerry's determined to get him, isn't he, and I thought I had some bad luck," said Finlay.

"We all joined up to fight, didn't we?" asked Dusty. "We didn't join up just because we get better pay than the Pongos, and the RAF is the only service to issue bed sheets as well as blankets, and shoes as well as boots. Then again, wearing a 'wing' certainly helps when chatting up the girls, but we still joined up to do our bit, didn't we? If Jerry's determined to get the old man, then we, as the important members of the crew," he said puffing his chest out, jokingly, "had better make sure they don't."

"Well said, Dusty. I'll drink to that," said Yorky, raising his pint. "'Oo would 'ave thought you were a speech-maker, me old mucker."

"That was one hell of a trip last night," said Dusty, putting four new pints of beer on the table.

"Yeah, I never thought I would get the chance to go to Milan, not in my life," said Yorky.

"We did'nee actually go bloody sight-seeing, did we?" laughed Jock.

"Oh, I don't know. How many people get the chance to go to Geneva and then view the majestic beauty of Mount *Blank*, and then climb the snow-covered Alps, with the Matter'orn Mountain shining in the moonlight, all in one night."

"Very poetic, Yorky, quite h'eloquent, if I say so myself," said Dusty. "But I was freezin' me 'what-nots' off for nine bloody hours."

"You were alright, but my heating suit was on the blink. One minute I had Betty Swallocks and the next Breezy Falls. It was a bloody nightmare, I can tell yer," moaned Yorky.

"Talkin' about freezin', the Skipper did well," added Chalkie. "Although the ground crew had put de-icing paste, you know, that thick white gunk, on the props and the leading edges, as we were going over the Alps the wings started to ice up badly, and she became heavier and a pig to handle. He was fightin' to keep her in the air for a long time; it took some flyin' that did. We were both grateful to start sliding down the other side."

Yorky asked, "What was that mountain where the Stirlings and Halifaxs peeled off?"

"It was called Mount Paradiso or something like that."

"I presume it was an 'Eyetie' mountain?"

"Yes. How many peeled away then, I couldna' see from up front," said Jock.

"There were about two hundred or so, wasn't there?"

"Yeah, they were goin' to Turin, I think."

"What were they bombing in Turin, then," asked Dusty.

"Factories, they said," answered Yorky. "Aircraft factories, same as us in *Milano*, some Lancs went with them as well; I don't think they were ours though."

"No, they were all from Three and Eight group. I tell you what, dropping bloody Window didnee stop that flak. It was a bit heavy and accurate, unusual for the Eyeties," said Jock. "I saw at least one Lanc go down. Did you see any more, Yorky?"

"No, but I was glad when we turned for home. Bugger doin' trips like that again, the views might be nice, but try sitting in that turret for nine and a half hours. It was bloody murder."

"Well, it's another sortie towards the tour," said Chalkie.

# 13 ... Peenemünde

The tannoy outside their Nissen huts rudely awakened them the next morning, summoning them to attend the briefing hut at 0900 hours. By the number of grey faces and hangdog looks, most of the squadron appeared to regret their indulgence the night before. They shuffled to their chairs and lit up the customary cigarettes before the flight of senior officers entered.

"Welcome, gentlemen, be seated," greeted the Station Commander.

Group Captain Charles Peregrine Thompkins MM DSO DFC and Bar, was a Great War veteran. Very much of the old school, his cut glass accent had graced the mansions and palaces of the good and great. He was the perfect English Gentleman, but not a man to cross by sloth or deception. He demanded the highest standards from everyone, including himself, and his dedication to his 'young warriors', as he called his aircrews, was never in doubt.

"I have called you here this morning, because the squadron has had the honour of being selected by Air Chief Marshal Sir Arthur Harris, to participate in a vital operation. We are combining with squadrons from Five Group for this special mission, while the rest of One Group will be attacking a different section of the same target. Wing Commander Picton will explain what will take place over the next few days. Wing Commander?"

"Thank you, sir. As the CO says, we are joining Five Group for this one, but before we do, we have to consider a different way of delivering our bombs instead of simply dropping them on a TI. On this op, the accuracy of our bombing is the top priority; therefore, we will be using a time and distance system to deliver our ordnance. Very simply, the PFF will drop a marker over a point of visible land from which the timed run will begin. At a known given time from that marker, you will drop your bombs on the time dictated. This will guarantee greater accuracy if enemy smoke screens or bad weather obscures the target or the target indicators cannot be seen. Sounds simple, gentlemen, yet nevertheless, we have to get it *exactly* right, to the second, not *approximately*, but *exactly*," he emphasised. "So, for the next few days that is *exactly* what you will be practising."

Gloria and her crew joined the rest of 'A' flight on their practise runs over the bombing ranges at Donna Nook, near Saltfleet. They knew this bombing range well. During their training, they had offloaded hundreds of practise smoke bombs on the enormous wide expanse of sand flats that stretched for miles down the coast and from the sand hills to the sea at low tide.

Their 'point of visible' land, where the first TI would be dropped and where they would start their timed run, was the lighthouse at the end of Spurn Point, that extraordinary hook of land that penetrated the North Sea east of Kingston-upon-Hull and protected the River Humber. The orange-topped structures that were the bomb targets were the second point of aim for the bomb-aimers; green TIs would mark these. Paddy was responsible for the timing from the first 'visible point of land' and told Jock the exact time to drop the practice bombs.

They made their first bombing runs at eight thousand feet and Yorky's comment from his grandstand seat in the rear with regard to their accuracy was:

"Missed the bugger by a mile, Jock."

However, as the day went on the timing became more accurate as they adjusted speeds accordingly; bombs crept nearer and nearer to their target, but were still around two to three hundred yards away.

The next day Gloria's crew carried out another twelve attacks on the now tide-washed sands of Donna Nook. By their last run, the speed was right, the timing was right, the height was right and they dropped their bomb load of thirty-pound practise smoke bombs within one hundred yards of the marked target. They went back to base happy.

"How did the practise go today, Johnnie?" asked Ginny as they sat in the officers' mess bar that night.

"'Careless talk costs lives', young lady," he laughed, pompously quoting one of the Ministry of War posters. "No, it went fine, really. I think we have the idea now. We will find out tomorrow, won't we? We are going to a different range and I hope we'll get it right first time, but I very much doubt that. Anyway, enough about that, look, there's a new movie on at the briefing hut, 'Phantom of The Opera' with Nelson Eddy, Susanna Foster and Claude Rains. Do you fancy going? It starts in about fifteen minutes."

"Oh, I love Nelson Eddy. Yes, let's go."

They walked over to the briefing hut that also acted as the camp's cinema, church, and recreation hall, and it provided the venue for the concerts given by that eager, enthusiastic and willing group of entertainers from ENSA. Algy said that ENSA stood for Every Night Something Awful! Nevertheless, they did their best.

The station's Padre greeted them and relieved Johnnie of sixpence for two tickets, and waved them to the rows of benches and seats. The seats were more towards the back of the makeshift theatre, so Johnnie steered Ginny towards the back row, which was actually half way down the hall. The temporary screen on the platform concealed the massive map of Europe that normally displayed the routes for their bombing missions.

They laughed and forgot the trials and tribulations of war as they enjoyed 'Tom's' discomfort at the hands of the cartoon mouse, 'Jerry'. The lights extinguished and the main feature began. The film's story developed, but provided a mere distraction as Johnnie was trying to pluck up the courage to move his right hand. He had flown many sorties over Germany. He had faced the might of the enemy's flak. Their determined fighters had shot him out of the sky, he had entered the devil's lair, but the thought of trying to hold Ginny's hand scared him to death. He felt like a nervous schoolboy. Eventually Ginny came to the rescue when she placed her hand on his, and he grasped it eagerly in relief. She giggled softly at his reaction.

That night, as he walked her back to the WAAF officers' quarters, they kissed. Gently, slowly, holding each other's hand and just quietly said, "Goodnight."

The next morning, Monday, found the crew of Gloria far out to sea making a sweep to drop their practise bombs on the mud and sand flats off Wainfleet, south of Skegness. This time their 'Point of visible land' was none other than the white towered Skegness Pier. Their first run was abysmal, with Squadron Leader Chris Cooper, who was watching their efforts, coming over the radio telephone (RT) informing them that their efforts were less than desirable and needed to improve a little, but he used a more direct language.

"You couldn't hit a pig in t' arse wi' a banjo, Jock. Shockin' that was," Yorky chuckled.

By the time they had finished the third run, the smoke bombs were falling across the target well within one hundred yards.

"Well done, everybody, well done," commented Johnnie. "Remember we will only get one chance on the op. So let's make the next few runs perfect."

Getting bombs to within one hundred yards of the target from eight thousand feet was considered 'on target'.

When the bomb bay was empty, they turned for home well pleased with their efforts for the day.

"Well done, G-George, good effort," came the call from Chris Cooper.

"Fancy a trip to Butlins, Skipper?" asked Dusty, with a smile, remembering their 'fly past' the last time they were here.

"Are you trying to get me busted, Dusty? I don't think that Admiral was very chuffed last time."

The whole crew laughed and smiled, except Jock:

"What was that all about, Skip?" he asked.

"I'm sure the chaps will tell you the story in the bar tonight, Finlay."

"Yeah, we scared the Navy shitless, Jock," said Chalkie.

\*\*\*

"Battle orders, Johnnie," said Ginger Bere, Johnnie's roommate, as he came out of the flight office the next morning. "Briefing at 1500 hours. Looks like this is the op we have been working towards."

The crew took Gloria up for an NFT for twenty-five minutes, then checked in with their section leaders and double-checked their personal equipment. Gloria was now showing more trophies painted on the side of her nose. Alongside the three bombs was an ice-cream cone showing they had visited Italy and a swastika to acclaim Yorky's JU-88.

What surprised them as they approached the briefing hut were the twelve to fifteen Snowdrops circling the building instead of the customary two standing guard outside. At the door, an imposing flight sergeant and a corporal checked their 12-50s (ID cards) and the Skipper had to vouch for each member of his crew.

"Something big is on, Johnnie," said Paddy with a smile as they passed through the doors. "God, there's more of them inside."

Around the perimeter of the room, more service police stood surveying the aircrews as they took their seats.

"The last time I saw this many Snowdrops, they were carpeting a woodland floor, so they were, and very pretty too," he commented.

As the senior officers entered, it surprised Johnnie to see Ginny bringing up the tail end of the party, a sheaf of papers in her hands.

"Sit down, gentlemen," instructed the Senior Intelligence Officer, (SIO). "Thank you, Section Officer Murphy." She passed him some of the papers she was holding. A wolf whistle sounded from the gathered flyers and a chorus of comments made Ginny's pretty face blush. "Okay, you animals," laughed the SIO. "Have you never seen a woman before?"

"Not such a cracker as that one."

More catcalls and laughter followed.

That Ginny was subject to such behaviour made Johnnie feel very protective and slightly jealous.

"That's your little Popsie, isn't it, Johnnie?" asked Algy, but Johnnie waved him to silence.

"Right, settle down you lot," smiled the SIO. "Tonight, your target is …" the black cloth covering the giant map fell away "… the Baltic coast."

"In fact it is the German island of Usedom, or part of it, the area called Peenemünde," he indicated it with his cue-like pointer and turned back to his captive audience,

"Six hundred miles away, gentlemen, the Germans are developing highly specialised radar equipment that will greatly improve their defence systems to find, identify, and destroy British bombers in the dark. The scientists at Peenemünde are carrying out the development and testing of this equipment. If we allow them to continue with this, we can expect bomber command casualties to increase … dramatically."

He now had the absolute and complete attention of everyone in the room.

"If you do not destroy this facility tonight, you will go back tomorrow night. The night fighters and flak positions will not expect you tonight, but they will tomorrow night or the night after and all the other nights that you will have to go back, if you do not get it right tonight. This operation is of extreme importance. You will go back regardless of casualties, until you meet the aim of the operation. Wing Commander Milson is Air Officer on Air Vice Marshal, Sir Ralph Cochrane's staff, the AOC of Five Group, with whom you will be flying. Wing Commander Milson will give you the details of the operation, which has the codename 'Hydra'."

He stood down and sat next to Ginny in the front row, giving back his papers.

Milson stepped forward.

"Good afternoon, gentlemen. Welcome to Five Group." Ironic jeers greeted his opening words, which he accepted with an indulgent smile. "As the Senior Intelligence Officer said, tonight's sortie is part of Operation Hydra. We are to cut off the heads of this particular monster, which is hiding in

Peenemünde. There are three sections of the target, and three waves of aircraft will attack them. Your rehearsals of time and distance bombing, and your accuracy were very impressive, as reported to Sir Arthur, so you will be going in with squadrons from Five Group as the last wave. Thank you, Flight Lieutenant."

He turned to his aide, standing next to the large blackboard and easel on the side of the stage, who unrolled a huge map of the island of Usedom and the surrounding area, showing three coloured sections.

"You will drop your HE bombs on the red section here, which is the experimental section of the site." He used the pointer to indicate the northern part of the target area on the very northeastern tip of Usedom Island. "The other waves will have gone in before you to hit these other important areas, factory workshops and the power plant," he pointed to them. "Do not be confused by their flares and smoke, stick to your bombing instructions on timing."

He removed his glasses and frowned at the assembled aircrews.

"We are not expecting too much interference from German night fighters, but they have three smoke screen batteries protecting the site and many flak guns. There will be a diversionary raid by a separate force of Mosquitos and Beaufighters on Berlin, who will fly ahead of the PFF and peel away to divert and confuse the German defences by also dropping Window. Tonight, the weather forecast is ideal, because we, or I should say, you, need a clear moonlit night to help identify your first visible point of land and to find your target. You will be using, for the first time, another new system. That is a 'Master Bomber', whose job is to direct the Pathfinders and 'Backers up' to ensure accurate marking with the TIs. He will also be advising the bomber stream on to their target areas. Obey his directions implicitly. He will relay his instructions by RT, on button ...." He looked down to the SIO.

"Button B, sir."

"Does that mean we'll get our money back if we miss, sir?" shouted Yorky.

"Okay, thank you," Wing Commander Wilson carried on amid some laughter. "An inordinate amount of intelligence work and effort has gone into the planning of this operation, and I cannot underestimate its importance. As I said before, welcome to Five Group, Gentlemen." There were no jeers this time. "Good luck."

The Navigation Officer took the stage.

"You will rendezvous with the stream over the Wash and descend to two hundred and fifty feet for your flight across the North Sea. Ten minutes before the Danish coast, you will climb to your bombing height of eight thousand feet and start dropping Window. Your 'point of visible land' will be Rugen Island, marked by yellow flares," he used the pointer. "That is the start of your timed run towards your target. You are to bomb on your timed distance." He emphasised. "Green TIs will follow red markers as your confirmation of target. Do not overrun your timing; an allied civilian worker accommodation camp is very close by."

The Met Officer and the Flying Control Officer gave their reports and instructions then the CO of the squadron, Wing Commander Harry Picton, took the podium.

"As you can imagine, this operation is highly confidential. If Jerry gets a whiff of this through a leak from this briefing, vigorous pursuit to find the source of that leak will follow and the strictest punishment summarily executed."

"We have been selected for this op because we are good, damn good! Your results over the past few days have been remarkable, well done everyone. However, first prize goes to Johnnie Sanderson and his crew. They actually put two practise bombs within fifty yards of the target. Remarkable!"

Whistles and jeers greeted this; Jock stood up with hands clasped together over his head and bowed to all around him in victory.

"I might add, I think, that it was probably two flukes, if I know Jock McGuffin," finished off Harry Picton and smiled at Jock's shocked look of disbelief.

\*\*\*

At two hundred and twenty miles per hour, two hundred and fifty feet above the sea, five hundred and ninety-six heavy bombers were thundering across the North Sea like a herd of stampeding buffalo. Leading them were twenty-eight Mosquitos and ten Beaufighter light bombers of the diversionary force. Bringing up the rear were the Lancasters of Five Group and 599 Squadron including Gloria. Thirty-three miles from the Danish coastline, the armada popped up to eight thousand feet and completely surprised the German radar watchers as their screens filled with echoes. Six hundred and thirty-four aircraft had started to drop their 'chaff', Window. They crossed the Danish coast, clear in the bright moonlight chased by light flak.

"First course change in two minutes, Skipper," announced Paddy. "Heading is one-one-nine."

"One-one-nine, thank you, Michael."

Forty minutes later:

"We shall be going over Rugen Island a little early, Skipper. We need to lose about two minutes. Suggest a sixty degree dogleg to port."

"All right, Michael, will do."

Johnnie turned to the left and flew on that course for two minutes then turned through a hundred and twenty degrees for another two minutes coming back on to his original heading. Flying a four-minute equilateral triangle lost them the two minutes required.

"That okay now, Michael?" said Johnnie as he came back on to his course. "I wouldn't like to do that again with all these other kites around us."

"Yes, that's fine now. Five minutes to first markers."

As they turned on the yellow markers over Rugen Island, Paddy announced:

"Time to target exactly six minutes forty seconds, keep it at two hundred and twenty miles per hour, Skipper and we will be perfect."

"You heard the man, Chalkie."

Chalkie already had his hands on the throttles and his eyes glued to Johnnie's airspeed indicator.

Meanwhile, the light bombers, the Mosquitos and Beaufighters of the diversionary force, had turned way ahead of the bomber stream and were now dropping flare markers on their approach to Berlin. Their diversion and use of Window had pushed the night fighter squadrons up over the capital city and away from the main stream at Peenemünde, one hundred and ten miles away. The small RAF team of light bombers dropped more TIs and HE bombs on the city, but it soon became obvious to the German defences that the allied bombers had fooled them and they sent urgent signals to the fighter controllers to send their charges back up to the Baltic coast. Their orders were to patrol the air combat boxes off the east coast of Denmark and the northern shores of Germany. By the time they arrived, the first two waves of the attack had dropped their ordnance and had long gone. 5 Group became their targets in the clear, bright moonlight.

"Green TIs on red flare markers dead ahead, Skipper. Open bomb bay doors," called Jock from his prone position behind his bombsight.

Johnnie pushed the lever down:

"Bomb bay doors open. She is all yours, Finlay. Release on Michael's shout."

"Thirty seconds," called Paddy.

"TIs are wrong then, Skipper they're too far away," shouted Jock. "They must have drifted!"

Johnnie's headphones crackled as the Master Bomber, Group Captain Searby, shouted:

"All Hydra Three aircraft, all Hydra Three aircraft, ignore the green TIs. Ignore the green TIs. Bomb on timed distance, bomb on timed distance. We will remark with yellow. We will remark with yellow TIs."

Johnnie commanded Finlay, "Bomb aimer, ignore green TIs, ignore green TIs. Release on Navigator's shout, on the Navigator's shout!"

Unfortunately, a few bombers had believed they had their timing wrong and had dropped their bombs on the green TIs.

What they were not aware of was the concentration camp full of Polish forced workers, directly underneath the markers. Over five hundred of them perished that night.

"Counting down from now, ten ... nine ..." called Paddy.

On one, Jock shouted:

"Bombs gone, photo flash gone!"

They had bombed exactly on target, on time and within their allotted time bracket. It was 0051 hours.

There had been very little flak for the first two waves of aircraft, but the artillery batteries had come alive and were pumping shells up at the aircraft at the end of the stream. Johnnie flew straight and level for another twenty seconds until the camera operated at the same time as the photo flare. As soon as he could, he put Gloria in a diving turn to starboard and ordered Chalkie to push the throttles hard up to the very gate of the emergency power. A cluster of yellow TIs drifted slowly down exactly where they had dropped their bombs.

"Well done, everybody, yellow TIs going down on our bombs. Well done."

The diversionary raids and the use of Window had kept the deadly night fighters away, as suggested at the briefing, from the first two waves of bombers attacking the other target areas. The third wave now became the target of the frustrated German defences, as they realised the diversifying tactic had fooled them into thinking the target was Berlin. Their night fighters raced back to the skies over the North German and Danish coast to take their revenge.

"Night fighters, Skipper. I can see three of them... A Lanc has been hit!" Yorky shouted. "It's in flames. God, there's another one hit!"

"Jesus! There's a Lanc right above us!" yelled Dusty. "Christ that was close. It couldn't have been more than fifty foot away."

His Northeastern Geordie-like accent was very broad at moments like this.

"Another Lanc crossing from port, Skip, about five hundred feet above us. Jesus, an 'ME One-Ten' is attacking him

... He's right underneath him firing upwards ... Christ, the Lanc's exploded! It's in flames! You bastard!"

Dusty opened up with his twin Browning machine guns and the German night fighter dived quickly away to port and was lost to an angry and upset Dusty. The fireball that had been the Lancaster above them was spinning in a fiery spiral below to their starboard side.

"Bastards!"

"Any luck, Dusty?" called Johnnie.

"I don't think so, Skip, the bastard dived away too quickly. He was directly under the Lanc when he began firing. They must have a cannon or something on top of the fuselage."

Johnnie made a mental note to keep checking the airspace around and to use 'banking searches' more to check underneath the aircraft.

Ribbons of coloured beads stitched the sky around them, tracer bullets from fighter and bomber were patterning the night and white flares dropped by the fighters augmented the bright moonlight. They saw three more Lancasters fall to earth smothered in life-stealing fire. Johnnie put Gloria down to six hundred feet and pushed her as fast as she would go. Within the hour, they were turning over Denmark on to their directed heading for Elkington keeping well clear of the flak defences of the Kiel Canal and the heavy anti-aircraft guns of Sylt Island. They skipped over the sea at wave top height, the moon reflecting brightly from the rolling waters, and touched down at 0410 hours on the morning of Wednesday, August 18 1943.

"Home at last, chaps, home at last."

Ginny was on duty in the control tower when G-George touched down. As she said a silent prayer, a smile of relief brightened her face.

Jock asked Yorky later on the crew bus. "Does the 'old man' always say that when we come back?"

"Yeah, he always has done. Superstition, I suppose."

That lunchtime, Johnnie walked into a quiet, subdued 'A' flight hut, a group of fellow pilots were slumped in the scattered armchairs. Ginger Bere came over to him.

"Have you heard about Chris and George Palmer?"

"No. You mean the boss, Chris?"

"Yes. Both failed to come back this morning. We thought they may have had to put down somewhere else, but nothing has been heard."

The telephone in Chris's office rang, the flight clerk, a Cockney corporal called out quietly:

"Mr. Sanderson, can you report to the CO, soonest, please, sir?"

Johnnie made his way to Harry Picton's hut and spoke to the adjutant, Jimmy Cook.

"Do you know what the Old Man wants me for, Jimmy?"

"I think so; you'd better go straight in."

"Is there any news on Chris and George Palmer?"

"None yet, that's what this is about."

The admin sergeant and his staff looked up briefly as Johnnie knocked and pushed open the WingCo's door.

"Ah, Johnnie, close the door. Sit down. Cigarette?" he offered.

"No thanks, sir."

"No, you smoke a pipe, don't you? Flash it up if you want. I like the smell of a good tobacco."

Johnnie pulled the pipe from his battledress pocket and proceeded to fill it from his kid-leather pouch.

"As I'm sure you've heard Chris and George didn't make it back last night. In fact, forty aircraft were lost last night, twenty-three Lancs, fifteen Halifaxes and two Stirlings. Most of the Lancs were from Five Group, two from us, unfortunately."

He threw the piece of paper he had read from on his desk.

"Until we hear to the contrary, we must presume our two are 'missing in action'. Therefore, I need a new Flight Commander, Johnnie, and you are my choice."

Johnnie stopped lighting his pipe and held the lit match in mid-air until it burnt his fingers. He recovered enough to say:

"Me sir? But I've only been on the squadron a few weeks!"

"You have the experience and the knowledge to do a good job. It will be an acting position until we have news about Chris and if that news is negative then the position will be substantive. Are you in agreement?"

It was more of an order than a request.

"Yes sir, as long as it doesn't affect my crew."

"No it won't. It just means more work for you," he smiled and offered his hand. "Oh, by the way, if it is made substantive then it will be Squadron Leader Sanderson."

"Oh! Thank you, sir."

"There's a message from on high you can pass on to your chaps ... came in just now." He picked up two signal forms from his desk. "I quote, 'Peenemünde, Congratulations boys, on a job well done', ACM Sir Arthur Harris, and one from AOC of Five Group, 'Excellent performance Five-Nine-Nine, well up to Five Group standards', AVM Cochrane. Cheeky bastard! The squadron did do well last night though Johnnie. The early reports are saying we did some major damage to our target. We'll know more tomorrow when we get the photo results."

Johnnie left Harry's office with mixed feelings, a sense of elation at the chance of promotion and the opportunity to lead his own flight, but offset by concern for his two missing colleagues. He decided to keep the news to himself for now.

The next day, Harry Picton shared copies of the photographs taken by the squadron aircraft with Johnnie. The results were good. The whole squadron had dropped their bombs within the perimeter of their target area.

"Did you see these?" said Harry, indicating three large circular features on one of the photographs, just to the south of their target.

"Yes, I saw one; the others must have been under the smoke screen they put up. What do you suppose they are?"

"I don't know," he said slowly. "I didn't see them, the smoke was too thick. They are too big for radar dishes, don't you think? I might have a word with intelligence to see what they think."

He collected the photos together, tapping them on the desk to square them off.

"I'm afraid there's no news of Chris or George, nothing at all. We have officially posted them as missing. Therefore, I shall be announcing your elevation to Flight Commander and acting Squadron Leader today. You take over now, Johnnie, good luck. Have a chat with Jimmy; he will show you the ropes as will Joe and Bill. It's not an easy job, Johnnie, but I know you'll do your best."

The news delighted the crew when he informed them of his new position and rank; they bowed and saluted, calling him 'Squadron Leader, Sir'.

The next two days, Johnnie talked through his situation with the other two flight commanders, Bill Askin and Joe Kendrick, taking their advice and warnings. He was the one responsible now for selecting the crews for battle orders, for sending crews out on ops, selecting the crews who may not come back. He was the one who would wipe their names from the flight board hanging in the flight crew room. Harry was right; the job would not be easy.

He spent time getting to know his fellow pilots and their crews. On the Friday afternoon, he had the extra half ring sown on to the jacket sleeves of his uniform and the epaulettes of his battle dress. He felt quite proud of himself looking at his reflection in the mirror. It also meant a pay rise of one shilling and one penny per day, 7/7d a week extra! The crew insisted he spent that pay rise on beers that night down at the Royal Oak, where they noisily celebrated his promotion. They were very chuffed that their Skipper was the 'boss'.

"Did you see the papers today, Johnnie?" asked Algy, over the top of his pint.

"No, why?"

"You know you were asking about those round features you could see at Peenemünde? Well, the chap from the Daily Telegraph informs us that we dropped one thousand eight hundred tons of bombs on their secret radar sites where the Krauts are researching and developing aircraft radiolocation and armaments. So that might answer your question?"

"I don't think so, Algy; they looked too big for radar scanners. But if the man from the 'Daily Telegraph' says it's true, it must be, eh!"

# 14 ... Mablethorpe

On the Saturday night, Johnnie invited Ginny out to dinner to celebrate his promotion. He had booked a table in the restaurant at The Mason Arms, the grandest hotel in nearby Ludworth. When he went to pick her up in 'Ruby', he wore his 'walking out' uniform, with its extra rings showing his promotion. When he saw Ginny, he was speechless. She was wearing a dark green dress, just low enough to give a hint of décolletage and the pencil straight skirt emphasised the natural flare of her hips. Her dark hair piled up, held with a silver multi-toothed diamanté comb, and accompanied by matching drop earrings, around her neck a diamanté-clasped black velveteen choker. Her eyes were sparkling like polished emeralds, her high cheekbones softly highlighted with the slightest trace of rouge and her red lips glistened in the evening sunlight.

"My God, you look stunning. You look beautiful. You've done all this for me?" he asked, amazed.

"No, I've dressed up like this for the waiter, you chump."

She laughed delightedly, hitting him with her clutch bag and blushing coyly at his heart-felt compliments.

All the way through the meal, he hardly took his eyes off her. The old waiter watched them and smiled to himself. With this war and destruction happening all around, it was so nice to see two young people so obviously in love. He thought about his own sweetheart who had waited for him when he came home from the last lot. Sadly, no longer with him, but it did his heart good to watch these two.

When the meal had finished, they moved from the restaurant to sit in the lounge area and he ordered two expensive brandies. As they were waiting for them to appear, he watched a young flying officer and a young woman approach the nearby reception desk and obviously ask for a room. The receptionist was a rather plain woman in her late forties, her fingers empty of jewellery. Greying hair pulled back in a tight bun at the back of her head and her grey tweed two-piece suit probably reflected her character. Her dry, sharp voice caught almost everybody's attention in the lounge area.

"I'm sorry, sir, but we do not let our rooms to couples who cannot offer proof of their having taken the sacred vows of marriage. Which I presume you and this ... er ... lady, have not. Good night ... sir!"

The red-faced couple scampered away, giggling.

It had crossed Johnnie's mind of maybe trying to do something similar and asking Ginny to spend the night with him one day soon, but his face must have given his intentions away as he looked at her.

"I know what you're thinking, but I'm not that type of girl," she said in a mock American accent, and laughed. Then softly, putting her hand on his, "Not yet, Johnnie, we will know when it's the right time, I'm sure we will."

Although Johnnie blushed horribly, he was secretly pleased she had clearly understood what was going through his mind. He had realised, tonight, that he was hopelessly in love with this beautiful, wonderful girl, and, at this moment, he did not want to break the magic that they shared. However, when would it be the 'right time'? How long did he have left to enjoy these wonderful moments they were sharing? Should he tell her how he felt? Would it be fair to her? After all, a bomber pilot's chance of survival was very small; look at Chris Cooper and George Palmer. How long before his logbook carried the mark MIA or even KIA? How long would it be before someone wiped his name from the flight blackboard? How would she know when it would be the 'right time'? The questions tumbled through his mind, but he knew she was right.

"You're absolutely right, you very clever girl, you. You are right. Let's just enjoy the time we have together."

Their brandy arrived and they both sat quietly for a while, not really knowing what to say next.

"Look," he said, "I've scrounged some petrol for the car; why don't we take her for a spin tomorrow? The coast maybe; what do you think? You're not on duty, are you?"

"Yes, but not until six o'clock and yes, that would be a lovely idea," she smiled, relieved that the conversation had moved on. "I haven't been to Mablethorpe since I was a girl. Can we go there?"

"Mable Thorpe? That sounds like the name of some second-rate Lancastrian music hall act," he laughed.

"No, silly, it's a nice little seaside resort about fifteen or sixteen miles away."

"Yes, I know, sweetheart," he said kindly.

She blushed slightly with pleasure realising that was the first time he had used an endearment instead of her name.

The next morning found them bouncing down the lanes to Ludworth, past the majestic church and its towering spire and on through the sunlit summer lanes of the Lincolnshire countryside towards the coast.

"I love the wide flat views here," said Ginny. "The skies are so big, and the horizons go on forever. Oh do stop. Look! They're using horses to gather the harvest."

They pulled into the side of the road, got out, walked to a field gate, and stood leaning on it, watching a farmer using a pair of bay-coloured heavy horses to pull a sail-reaper-binder, harvesting the tall, golden wheat. The farmer was sitting at the rear of the reaper controlling the magnificent horses, while the horizontal wooden sails pushed the wheat on to the scissor-like cutting blades. The broad canvas belt carried the corn through the harvester and tied it in to sheaves with binder twine, then released them through the back of the machine. He waved to them as the horses pulled the harvester past the gate. A woman and two young girls were following the reaper picking up the fallen sheaves and 'stowkin' them in threes to allow them to dry out in the warm summer breeze ready for threshing.

As they leaned on the gate, the sun was warm on their backs and the scene in front of them was ancient and peaceful. The only sounds were the clatter of the sails as they spun round, the chatter of the cutting blades and the regular clump of the horses' feet on the summer-dried land. When the farmer stopped to clear a blockage, there was silence, broken only by the jingle of brass-adorned horse tack, the lazy buzz of a bumblebee and the beautiful sound of a rising lark, singing high above them as it soared in the blue cloudless sky. The gay tinkle of the children's laughter floated cross the field. Ginny leaned her head on Johnnie's shoulder and took hold of his hand.

"If only it could always be like this, it would be perfect, wouldn't it – no bombers, no war, no Hitler."

"I suppose it will be one day. Unfortunately, the Nazis are making us fight for it. God knows why they want to 'conquer the world'. I don't think jack boots and a funny moustache would suit me, do you?" He put his finger across his top lip and 'goose stepped' in front of the gate, laughing. "Come on, let's go and see the sea."

They waved to the farmer and the girls, turned and walked back to the car hand in hand, just as a vic of three Spitfires roared above them at low-level, as if to emphasise the reality of the present time.

They continued weaving down the lanes, passing an RAF camp that no doubt had been the take-off point for the Spitfires. A long straight road through the drained marshlands led them into the outskirts of Mablethorpe, a large coastal village that was once just a small fishing village. 'Sea bathing' had become popular before the war and had made these little seaside villages into a haven for factory workers and their families from the East Midland industrial cities. They could hop on a train in Nottingham or Leicester and get off half a mile from the sea and the sandy beaches of Mablethorpe ... paradise.

As they drove down the High Street, the 'sea bank' flood defence was directly in front of them, rising up to block the view of the sea. He parked the car and they walked hand in hand up the concrete slope to the top of the sea wall. On either side, sand dunes stretched away forming the natural sea defences. In front of them were the war defences. Barbaric barbed wire covered the beach. Sprouting from the tide-washed sand were curly pigtail-like rusting iron stakes that held a maze of wire, and further down the beach, scattered like children's tossing jacks, were giant, rusting, anti-tank devices, and signs warning of mines and death. Exposed by the outgoing tide was a bombed out wreck of a cargo ship stranded half a mile from the shore, a familiar sight to Johnnie as he had flown over this stretch of beach many times. The whole scene was a reminder of war and the dangers of Nazi rule.

They turned north and walked along the track that topped the sea bank, the warm day slightly chilled by the onshore sea breeze. They were quiet with their own thoughts.

Hesitantly, she broke the comfortable silence, "Johnnie? I hope you didn't mind what I said yesterday ... you know ... in the hotel after dinner."

"Of course not, I understand how you feel and I will respect that. I know that lots of couples aren't bothering to wait and are rushing into a ... physical relationship because of the war, but ..."

"No, it's not that, Johnnie," she interrupted him. "It's not that. It's just that ... it's just ... Johnnie, I've never done ... you know ... I've never been with a ... a man," she stopped walking and bowed her head releasing his hand.

Johnnie stopped, turned and took her face in his hands, his whole being bursting with love.

Softly he said, "Oh my darling," he kissed her lips gently. "Oh my darling, what a fool I've been. I now understand why you said we would know when the time was right. Yes, we will know, and I don't care how long it takes. I am more than happy just being with you. I sometimes pinch myself to make sure I'm not dreaming when we're together, just to make sure that we are together. You do want us to be together?"

"Oh yes, Johnnie, of course I want us together, but I thought that if we didn't ... you know, you would lose interest in me, and I didn't want that to happen," she added shyly.

Johnnie picked her up and spun her round, laughing happily.

"Do you know? You say the most wonderful things, Miss Virginia Murphy."

A soldier on 'wandering patrol duty' passed them by, his rifle slung on his shoulder. He smiled to himself at the scene before him. He did not bother to throw up a salute, the officer would not have noticed anyway.

They walked back to the car totally lost in each other.

"Let's go up the coast a bit. I would like to see this windmill at Saltfleet that I keep trying to knock over and we can find somewhere for lunch."

They followed the narrow road that went north through little hamlets; passed red brick farmhouses with windows and doors weather-worn from the almost constant northeast winds off the North Sea, and finally the tall tower and sails of the mill came in sight a couple of miles away.

"There it is," cried Ginny, pointing.

As they arrived, a lorry was just pulling away with a load of white-dusted sacks piled in the open back. They climbed out of Ruby, and looked up at the slowly turning sails; a man in a dusty apron came out the door, his clothes and body covered in a fine white powder. He took off his soft peaked cap and beat it against his leg; the breeze took clouds of flour away. He sneezed noisily, wiping his nose with a big coloured handkerchief.

"Bloody flour gets everywhere," he sneezed again. "Not a lot of good if you got 'ay fever, is it?" he laughed. "Can I 'elp you?"

"No, thank you. We just stopped to admire the mill. I normally see it from up there," he pointed to the sky.

"What do you fly then, or shouldn't I ask?" he smiled; he had already recognised the uniform and the set of wings on Johnnie's chest.

"Lancaster, out of Elkington, we use your mill as a navigation point."

"So you're the buggers that thunder o'er 'ead and shake the old place wicked, are ye?" he said with a glint in his eye. "It takes bloody 'ours to let the flour dust settle."

"I'm sorry about that, but yes, sir, I'm afraid it is us."

"Well, no matter. You boys are doin' a grand job. Is this the missus?"

Johnnie blushed and stammered, "No, sir, we're just ... er ... friends."

"I bet you are," the miller said with a grin and a wink.

"We'll be on er ... our way," flustered Johnnie. "I'll try not to shake you up too much next time I pass over."

"Aye, give us a waggle o' your wings next time. I wish the pair of you all the best then. G'bye"

They climbed back into Ruby and drove off, giggling at the miller's presumption.

"I'm starving," said Ginny. "Can we find somewhere to get lunch?"

They tried The New Inn, the pub next to the mill, but it had the window shutters pulled over and the front door locked and bolted. He turned Ruby round and retraced their steps until a lane on their right appeared, going in the right direction towards Ludworth. The road was arrow-straight, bordered by reed-edged dykes that drained this former marshland. After a couple of miles, opposite the strange sight of a squat-towered church that appeared abandoned in the middle of a field, standing on its own sat an old redbrick pub. A faded sign swinging from an old-fashioned gibbet post proudly announced it was the 'Prussian Queen' and informed passers-by that 'Bateman's brewed Good Honest Ales'. They crossed a little bridge over the dyke and drove on to the stoned area in front of the pub.

"Do you think it will sell food?" asked Ginny.

"I don't know, but let's hope so."

They pushed open one of the narrow, glazed double-doors and found themselves in a small bar furnished with wooden stools, scrubbed tables and old pine settles. The only person visible was a weather-faced old man sitting next to an unlit fire. He nodded and said, "'Ow doo," baring his toothless gums in a smile. Johnnie shook the little brass bell on the small bar and it tinkled brightly. After a couple of minutes, a round, red-faced, smiling woman came rolling from behind a floral curtain that separated the private quarters from the bar. She was wiping her hands on a cloth and there was evidence of flour on her arms and face.

"Oh, I'm sorry, duck, I didn't realise we 'ad customers," she beamed at them. "What can I get you, duck?"

"What would you like, Ginny?"

"A gin and orange, if I can?"

"And a pint of bitter, please."

"Certainly, I think we've got some orange cordial somewhere, duck. Ah, here it is."

She poured the drinks and set them on the bar.

Johnnie asked, "Is there any chance of something to eat? We're both starving."

"Well ... I've just made some meat pies. I could cook some taties I suppose," she said to herself. "Well, if you don't mind waiting a bit I could do you pie and taties... potatoes," she corrected herself quickly, "if that's all right?"

"That would be wonderful, thank you," said Ginny.

"I think you'd be more comfy in the snug, duck. It's just through there. Bit more private, like," she smiled at them and indicated a door in the corner of the bar.

They went through and settled in two comfortable, ancient, wooden high-backed chairs, their arms polished by decades of use. They put their drinks on a rickety, green-tile topped table in front of an arched, small-brick fireplace. On the red-clay tiled mantelpiece were two ashtrays made from the bases of brass four-inch artillery shell cases, from that other war, the one supposed to stop all wars.

When they settled, Johnnie drew out his 'flying pipe' and filled it with tobacco, struck a match and inhaled the fragrant smoke.

Ginny said shyly, "Johnnie, I know that most aircrew have lucky mascots, like your pipe, or special pieces of clothing they take with them when they fly, like Algy's silk scarf, and I wondered if you would like this ... as a good luck token."

She reached into her handbag, pulled out a little envelope, and passed it to him.

"It's just that I thought that if you have it with you when you fly, it would mean that a bit of me was flying with you, you know, for luck."

He took the envelope from her and opened it. A curl of raven black hair tied up with a tiny scarlet ribbon fell into his hand.

"Yes, I would love to have a piece of you with me," he said admiring the shining lock of Ginny's hair. "I shall keep it next to my heart."

He laughed and unbuttoned the left breast pocket of his tunic and slipped the beribboned lock into it and gently patted it, saying, "For luck. Thank you darling."

He took her hand and kissed her.

They chatted and sipped their drinks and sooner than expected, the landlady came bustling through the door with a large wooden tray.

"Here you are, then."

She placed the tray on the table; put the two steaming plates of food in front of them, each contained a large piece of pie, boiled potatoes, and what looked like spinach, all swimming in a rich looking gravy. Putting down the knives and forks, salt and pepper pots, she said:

"Well I hope you enjoy the pie. I pinched my old man's potatoes he was going to 'ave for 'is tea." she giggled.

"It looks wonderful, thank you," said Johnnie. "What kind of pie is it, by the way?"

"Oh, didn't I say? It's rabbit. The old man shot a couple yesterday," she turned and left the room, saying, "Enjoy your pie."

"Oh, my God, I've never eaten rabbit before, Ginny. Have you?"

"Yes," she laughed at him. "Many times, it's good country fare. You used to live in the country, didn't you?"

"Yes, but we didn't eat the local population."

When the landlady came through to check that everything had been all right with the meal, her face lit up with delight to find two plates scraped clean.

"You enjoyed that, by the looks of it," she beamed.

"Yes, that was wonderful. It is the first time I have ever had rabbit, and it was delicious, but what was the green vegetable? I didn't recognise it ... it was very nice though. Thank you."

"My pleasure, duck, that were Samphire from off the beach."

"Oh ... Samphire?"

As they left the pub:

"I really did love that rabbit pie, but what the hell is Samphire? And I can't get used to being called 'duck'."

"They're both Lincolnshire things," said Ginny with a smile. "Duck is a term of endearment. Some people call you 'love', but round here; it is always 'duck'. I think it is quite sweet really. Samphire is a plant that grows on the beach; it spends half its life under the sea, full of iron, good for you." She flexed her muscles like a prizefighter: Johnnie grimaced.

"Good honest country food, rabbit and 'tates' from the fields, and Samphire from the beach, duck," said Ginny, in a broad Lincolnshire accent, both laughing at her mimicry.

They drove back to Ludworth and on to Elkington in a pleasant sated contentment, enjoying the warm summer afternoon breeze flowing through the car windows and the open sunroof, happy just in each other's company.

The growl and roar of aero engines greeted them at the gates of the camp, the time and place destroying their reverie.

They were back to the real world, but they knew their future was together.

# 15 ... The Big City

"The target for tonight is ... Berlin ..." revealed the SIO, the next afternoon. "... the Big City."

The announcement generated despondent groans from the experienced crews at the briefing, but Chalkie smiled and muttered to himself:

"At last."

Gloria's crew had not yet attacked 'the Big City', as the aircrews had nicknamed Berlin, although both Johnnie and Paddy had experienced the Nazis' almost fanatical defence of their capital, and knew they could expect a very warm reception from flak and fighter.

"We've not hit Berlin hard for several months, but our illustrious leaders have decided it's time we did. This is a maximum effort raid; it will involve over seven hundred aircraft. We are going to hit Jerry hard, very hard. I have a message to read out from ACM Harris."

He unfolded a sheet of paper and read.

"'Tonight you go to the 'Big City'; you have the opportunity to light a fire in the belly of the enemy and burn his black heart out. Good luck.' Air Chief Marshal Harris."

He looked round the room to judge the reaction.

"Burn, you bastards, burn," muttered Chalkie.

"Those of you who have been to the Big City before know what to expect. Heavy flak and very active fighter cover. We are going to try to fool them by approaching under the cover of Window and from an unexpected direction, as you can see from the tapes. You will cross the Dutch coast near Groningen, turn southeast just north of Osnabruck, then turn north-northwest as your final approach. Hopefully, by attacking from this unusual direction, south-southeast, it will keep the fighters away from the bomber stream as it approaches."

He indicated with his pointer the course that brought the bombers into Berlin from the south-southeast instead of either the northeast or the southwest, which were the normal approach routes.

"Again, a Master Bomber will accompany you, he will make sure the TIs are correctly placed and direct the operation. PFF Mosquitos will also guide you to the target by marking the route to keep you on the correct track. Do not think you can make your own way there: the effect of seven hundred bombers is only maximised if they stay together in a stream. The weather forecast is not good; the Met Officer will give you the details of the headwinds."

The Met Officer warned them of a storm coming in from the east with very strong winds and heavy rain. 'Unusual for this time of year', he informed them.

"Unusual if they get the bugger right," whispered Yorky to Dusty with a smile.

Berlin is a long way from Elkington: at least three to four hours flying by the route they were going, nearly seven hundred miles. 'Z' hour, the start of the bombing, was 0100 hours in the morning, so take-off would be around 2100 hours, it meant a very long night for the crews.

As they boarded the aircraft, they carried out the normal pre-flight checks, and each member that believed in 'lady luck' checked his lucky charm. This time Johnnie had a piece of Ginny with him. He took the lock of ribbon-tied hair from his breast pocket and touched it to his lips saying softly, "For luck."

Gloria lifted off into the balmy late summer evening at 2046 hours on Monday 23 August, just over five weeks since they had joined 599 at Elkington. A lot had happened in those few short weeks and the crew had shared together the fear, the dangers and the sorrow of being in the front line of the war in the air. They trusted and depended on each other, not just for friendship, but a much closer, indefinable emotion, comradeship. They were responsible for each other's survival. If one fell down on the job, it would mean the lives of the whole team could be in jeopardy. Every one of them was vital to the efficient and successful operation of the giant war bird.

As they crossed the Dutch coast at 19,500 feet, the signal came through to close up into a tighter formation and to begin dropping Window. Their instructions were to keep close order with the other aircraft as they crossed the Dutch coast, to make sure the stream of bombers spent the least time possible flying through the band of radar-controlled searchlights and flak guns that stretched from Hamburg down the coast to the south of Belgium. 'The Kammhuber Line', a formidable array of anti-aircraft guns and searchlights fed with night fighter stations, a deadly area for hundreds of heavy, relatively slow bombers. By narrowing and shortening the stream, they could pass through one section of the Kammhuber line more quickly than the radar operators could plot the individual aircraft, and Window helped to confuse the defence forces even more.

"Keep a sharp lookout, chaps," said Johnnie, as the sky around started to fill with aircraft. "Jerry might start thinking this is his lucky day with all this lot bumping across his territory."

Keeping Gloria steady had started to become a wrestling match for Johnnie. The wind had increased steadily over the last three-quarters of an hour and had changed direction and the 'dirty' turbulent air from hundreds of other bombers did not help.

Searchlights were scything through the darkness seeking to pick up the bombers. Blue-white 'master lights' would suddenly pounce on a radar-targeted aircraft and ten, twenty, thirty yellow lights would be compelled to attack the moth-like bomber trapped in the beam. Then exploding bursts of dirty, orange-red centred flak would creep nearer and nearer to the doomed aircraft, until man-destroying fire engulfed it, and it fell to earth like a burning angel. Nevertheless, with the help of Window, the stream came through relatively unscathed and thundered its way on to Berlin.

"Skipper, because of this head wind we've lost fourteen minutes, making us very late for Z hour," reported Paddy.

"Yes, Michael, I thought we were. Increase air speed as best we can, Chalkie, OK?"

"OK, Skipper, but I think we will be lucky to catch up with this wind."

Chalkie adjusted the throttles and propeller pitch to increase the airspeed.

"I calculate that we should turn on to our bombing approach in two minutes, Skipper, but with this wind it's about the best I can do."

"All right, Michael, what's the heading, three-four-zero?"

"You had better make it three-five-zero, Skipper, compensation."

Johnnie turned Gloria to port in a long banking turn towards her target twenty miles away in the darkness. Clouds covered the bright moon now and Johnnie could not see any other aircraft in the sky. For hours, he had been conscious that he was part of a great armoured armada, but now he could well be flying on his own. For a moment, a flash of panic crossed his mind, was the mission aborted and had they missed the recall signal? Were they truly on their own?

"CORKSCREW PORT NOW!"

The scream from Dusty snapped him violently back to reality.

"Corkscrewing left!" he cried.

Gloria filled with the sound of machine guns, the reek of cordite sharpening everyone's senses as Dusty and Yorky pumped streams of lead after the diving night fighter that Dusty had spotted off the port side. The stutter of shells hitting their fuselage caused Johnnie to react like lightning.

"Climbing left," he called, dragging the heaving Lanc up into the sky before throwing it hard down to the right. "Diving right," he called.

"Okay, Skipper, he's pissed off," said Dusty.

"Everyone all right?" asked Johnnie. "Report in."

The attack by the night fighter had everyone alive and buzzing with the effects of adrenaline. All their senses tuned to the highest frequency, their nerves jangling with fear and excitement.

Algy was the last to confirm he was okay.

"We've got a few holes aft of the mid-upper, Skip, but nothing too bad. Can't see any serious damage, but I'll go and check."

"Okay, Algy. How long to target, Michael?" he asked as he brought Gloria back on to her true heading.

"Three minutes."

Johnnie looked out at the burning city in front of him. Hundreds of incendiaries were burning in long narrow rectangles of bright white light that swiftly blossomed into a rose of fire. It was strange to see the flames reflected on the aircraft. It appeared almost as if Gloria was on fire herself, with the red glow dancing up and down the wings.

"Skipper, we've got a few new ventilating holes in the port side roof, just behind Dusty's turret, and similar in the starboard flank. One shell bounced off the armoured skirt below Dusty's turret, and the first aid kit is all over the floor, but nothing serious. I've looked through the astrodome, but I can't see any damage to the tail-planes," reported Algy.

"Okay, Algy. Let's get the job done everyone, and bugger off home."

"Two minutes to target," called Paddy.

"All yours, bomb aimer."

"OK, Skipper. Steady ... steady ... right ... right ... left left ... steady ... steadyyyyy ... Bombs gone! Close bomb bay doors," said Jock.

Johnnie flew 'straight and level' for the thirty seconds or so that it took the photo flare to illuminate their efforts. This was the heart-stopping period of the bombing run, the most terrifying. Flak creeping closer, closer, and he had to stay on that fateful course for a few seconds more. He was unaware he had held his breath expecting the inevitable until Jock cried 'Flash gone!' He then expelled it in an explosive burst of relief and necessity, diving and turning Gloria away from the bombing run.

He found himself reciting a verse from a poem that had stirred his blood as a boy at school, and now it seemed very fitting for the crew of a bomber over Berlin. Alfred Lord

Tennyson's epic tale of courage and daring; 'The Charge of the Light Brigade:'

*Cannon to right of them,*
*Cannon to left of them,*
*Cannon in front of them*
*Volley'd and Thunder'd;*
*Storm'd at with shot and shell,*
*Boldly rode and well,*
*Into the jaws of Death,*
*Into the mouth of Hell*
*Rode the six hundred.*

A eulogy written for them?

It crossed his mind that Tennyson had lived not twenty miles from RAF Elkington; he had published his first poems in nearby Ludworth.

The target below was glowing with thousands of fires. The wind was creating tornadoes of fire that were roaring through the 'Big City'. Chalkie's smile was not pretty.

"Skipper!" cried Dusty urgently, "There's a Lanc crossing directly above us from the port quarter, about three hundred feet. JESUS! He's opening his bomb doors. Dive port! Dive to port! Oh God!"

"I've got him, Dusty," said Johnnie, putting Gloria into an immediate dive to port.

"He's dropping his load!" shouted Dusty from his turret cupola on the very top of Gloria.

The first one thousand pound high explosive bomb, dropping from the Lancaster above them, passed within three feet of Jock's terrified face staring from the nose cone. The second hit the starboard wing outboard of the outer engine. Both Chalkie and Dusty watched with horror as the green-painted bomb ripped through the wing as if it were paper. Gloria lurched violently to starboard. The other four one thousand pound bombs fell harmlessly to starboard of them.

Johnnie, Chalkie, Dusty and Jock realised at the same moment that the next bomb to leave the Lancaster above them would be the nine-foot long, three-foot diameter, dustbin-shaped, four thousand pound 'cookie' high explosive bomb. If that hit the aircraft it would smash her out of the sky, most probably in a flaming spiral dive to earth, which meant that no one would get out alive.

Johnnie fought Gloria back to port as hard as he could. His left foot felt as if he were trying to push the rudder pedal through the floor; he forced the yoke forward and turned it as far to the left as it would go.

"Please God! Please God!" pleaded Dusty, as he stared at the lowering bomb bay of the Lanc, now only a hundred and fifty feet above his head. Gloria was starting to move from directly under the bomb bay when the giant green two-ton dustbin started to tumble towards them. Dusty sat in frozen silence as death came straight for him, seemingly in slow motion. He watched as it slowly turned and fell from the belly above him. Rolling and tumbling so slowly through the sky. There was no sound in his world, nothing else to see in his world, no other thoughts were in his head until he screamed as death flashed by the side of him and fell away to carry its destructive explosives to the enemy below.

"Oh my God ... Oh my God!" he sobbed. "That was bloody close. That was bloody close."

"Are you okay, Dusty?"

"Yes, Skip, but that was bloody close. You couldn't have got a fag paper between us."

Gloria lurched to starboard again as Johnnie tried to bring her back on an even keel.

"What the hell is he doing coming from that direction? The attack approach was from the south-south-east not the bloody south-west!" exclaimed Chalkie

"They were probably late getting here, like us, but I guess they took a shortcut," said Johnnie. "Oh my God, there are more of them, look!" he pointed forward above them. "I'm climbing to get above them. More power, Chalkie."

He adjusted the pitch of the propellers and pushed the throttles forward.

"What's the damage, Chalkie?"

"We were hit outboard of the engine, Skipper, through number three tank, but it was empty, thank God. It's forward on the wing, it shouldn't have affected the ailerons or flaps. How do they feel?"

"Okay, but she's flying like a pig. I don't think she can climb over that lot; we are starting to lose height as it is. Skipper to crew, Skipper to crew, we have had a bomb strike from a friendly Lanc that was above us. It went through number three tank on the starboard wing, but we are okay. Gloria is objecting to the damage, but I am sure she will get us home. We cannot climb above the stream that is crossing us; we will go low and head for the coast. Keep a sharp look out for fighters; they'll be very active for the rest of the night. And for God's sake keep a look out for other bombers!"

"Two-seven-seven is the direct heading for Elkington, Johnnie. Avoiding most of the hot spots for flak and night fighters," informed Paddy.

"Thanks, Michael, two-seven-seven it is then."

He turned Gloria on to the new heading away from the threat of more bombs falling on them. He had to fight her starboard drag by constantly pushing the port rudder pedal and very soon the ache of effort turned to cramping pain in his left foot and calf muscles and he knew he had nearly six hundred miles to go before they reached home. That meant at least three more hours, if not more, flying with a hole in the wing and a crabbing aircraft. To ease his foot he carried on with the banking searches, banking to starboard and port to check that the night fighters were not creeping underneath them. He also varied his height, but the damage to the wing was not helping him manoeuvre easily.

Algy suddenly came on the intercom and asked where they were.

"Just getting away from Berlin, Algy. Why?" asked Johnnie.

"Because I'm going out tonight, going out for dinner at the Savoy. Can you drop me off at the next station, please, driver."

"What the hell are you talking about, Algy?"

"Do you know Pinky Bevis? Jolly good shooter you know, jolly goo …"

"Michael, quickly, check Algy, will you? That fighter may have hit him. He's talking gibberish."

Paddy came out of his seat and spoke to Algy, who stared at him.

"Algy, Algy, are you alright? Are you hit, are you hit?"

Algy carried on staring.

"Jesus, it's his oxygen, Skipper. There is a bloody great split in his supply pipe. I'll try and fix it."

He crawled over the main spar and found the remnants of the first aid kit scattered across the aircraft's floor. He found what he was looking for, took the reel of sticking plaster back to Algy's seat and bound up the ruptured oxygen pipe leading to his facemask.

"There 'old boy', you'll be fine now. Speak to me, Algy, speak to me."

He clicked Algy's intercom switch to talk.

"What, what, what happened?"

"You were away with the fairies, you were, but I've brought you back to this world. Are you okay, now?"

"Yes, yes, I'm fine old boy. What happened?"

"Your oxygen pipe got cut by that fighter and you were rambling about going to the Savoy for dinner."

"Are you okay now, Algy?" asked Johnnie.

"Yes, thank you, Skip, must remember to take you and Paddy here to the Savoy when we get back, as a treat for saving the old bacon."

"Is it you that'll be paying then?" asked Paddy with a grin.

"Me! Paying! Oh …Oh … I'm wandering again … Oh I'm going …"

They all laughed. Even in the middle of a battle young men can laugh.

Ack-Ack fire constantly harried them as they left the suburbs of Berlin. Jock would have normally taken station in the forward turret as an extra defence against fighter attack, but dropping Window was part of the bigger defence plan against both flak and night fighters. He was the most exposed to the beaded streams of coloured tracer zipping across the skies around them, as he explained to Algy later that day in the Royal Oak over another flowing pint of bitter.

"The old 'flaming onions' comes at you as if in slow motion, all nice and bonny like, red, white and yellow balls swaying thro' the night in long waving lines. It's almost hypnotic, you know, you canna tak your eyes off it. Then it suddenly flies by you at a hell of a speed. That means its bloody close. That's when you start shittin' ye sen."

Johnnie brought Gloria down to a thousand feet. She had been losing height all the time, but by slowing her down and bringing her into thicker, warmer air he hoped she would handle better.

As they passed south of Bremen, heading for the island of Texel, the radar-controlled searchlights of the Kammhuber defence line tried desperately to pick them up. Their low-level passage and Jock's distribution of Window appeared to make them elusive.

"The starboard outer oil pressure is dropping and the temperature is starting to climb, Skipper. I think there might be some damage from the bomb strike after all."

"Let me know when it starts getting critical, Chalkie. I would like to keep as much speed as we can."

"This vibration from the wing can't be doing a lot of good if that engine has a problem. We may have to shut it down and throttle back the other starboard engine as well. Are you okay, Skipper?" asked Chalkie noticing Johnnie flinching as Gloria juddered.

"It's just my left leg hurting like hell, trying to keep pressure on the port rudder."

"Do you want me to relieve you for a spell?"

"No, it's all right, Chalkie, I'll manage."

"Oh, you're such a hero, Skipper."

They both laughed.

"Maybe when we get over the sea then, Chalkie."

"Do you want some more trim on the rudder tab?"

"I don't think that there's any left."

The light flak that had chased them through the dark had faded away, but for a reason.

"Bandit above to starboard front!" called Dusty, "One thousand yards on starboard quarter up."

"I'll get the bastard. Come to me ye Kraut bastard," encouraged Jock.

He quickly stood up and readied his guns, and then proceeded to describe what he wanted to do to him in his own Gaelic tongue, which fortunately the rest of the crew could not understand.

"Okay now," said Johnnie. "Keep the intercom clear."

"I don't think he's seen us, Skipper."

"No firing unless he turns towards us, gunners. Understand?"

"Ok, Skip," was the reply from the three watching air-gunners as they tracked the fighter through the bright night.

"He's seen us!" shouted Dusty. "He's turning and diving! Corkscrew to Starboard now!"

His two guns clattered into life. Jock joined in with his, cursing like the heathen warrior he was at that time. Yorky raised and rotated his guns as far as he could to the starboard side. The single engine fighter came into his view as it curved round to bring its guns to bear. Bright balls of tracer curved towards them and the deadly twenty millimetre shells zipped over the top of Dusty's turret. Yorky's four machine guns joined Dusty's to put up a wall of fiery lead in front of the yellow-nosed, black-crossed attacker.

"Got the bastard!" yelled Dusty, as the fighter suddenly flipped over to port and black smoke appeared in a trail as it dived away underneath Gloria.

"Yes, I see him," said Jock. "But I canna get to him. He's heading off home wi' his arse on fire!"

Johnnie brought Gloria back up to a thousand feet and resumed his course.

"Everyone okay?" he asked, his heart pounding and sweat running into his facemask from the exertion and the adrenaline-pumping fear of the attack.

The crew reported they were all right. Algy complained that the excited gunners were disturbing the peace and quiet with their noisy commentary and smelly guns.

"You be bloody grateful we're here or you would be pickin' twenty mil lead from your ear'ole," laughed Yorky.

"Just his ear'ole, Yorky?" asked Dusty.

"I'm getting another signal, Skipper, about fifteen hundred yards back, fine on the port quarter, and another high on the starboard, but they're not gaining on us very quickly," reported Algy.

"Are they ours, do you think?" asked Johnnie.

"I don't know, they're coming up very slowly."

"Keep an eye on them, Algy. Gunners, can you see anything?"

"Nothin', Skipper."

"No, nothing," reported Dusty.

"Starboard signal is still closing, thirteen hundred yards and closing slowly."

"Still can't see anything," said Yorky.

"A thousand yards now, he's closing fast. It's definitely a bandit."

"Got him, Skipper. Stand by to corkscrew starboard ... Go! Go!"

"Up the revs, Chalkie."

Gloria's engines drummed with more emergency power as Johnnie threw her in a downward curve making it difficult for the fighter to bring his guns to bear.

"He's broken away, Skipper," called Yorky.

"Port one's coming in, nine hundred ... eight ... seven."

"Christ! He is trying to catch us at the bottom of the curve. Hang on everybody!"

As Johnnie pulled Gloria out of the starboard dive into a climbing turn to port, he pushed the control column forward violently, which made Gloria drop her nose briefly, and then she lumbered back into the port climb. This caused massive air turbulence that rocked and buffeted the fast closing fighter. This, combined with Yorky and Dusty's streams of tracer rushing towards him, was enough to frighten him off; he broke away without opening fire to search for easier prey.

"He's buggered off, Skipper."

"Yes, he's turned to port and is well behind us now," reported Algy.

"Thanks, Algy, well done, everybody, but keep a sharp lookout. How is number four engine, Chalkie?"

"That engine is going to seize, Skip, those acrobatics didn't help it. Oil pressure's right down now and the temperature has rocketed. I'd sooner close it down than let it blow up."

"If you must, Chalkie. Dusty, we have to feather the starboard outer so you won't have any hydraulics, okay?"

"I'll put the turret facing aft, Skipper."

"Okay. What about the inner engine, Chalkie?"

"Oil and temperature are OK. Closing fuel cock, feathering starboard outer."

Chalkie held the feathering button until it stayed in by itself. Johnnie closed the throttle and switched off the ignition when the propeller swung to a stop. He adjusted the air speed to one hundred and forty miles per hour and tried to trim the rudder tab to take the pressure from his painful left leg, but there was nothing left to trim.

"Finlay, Yorky, we've had to shut down number four engine; Dusty's turret is on manual now so he will be covering the tail only. Let's hope the night fighters stay away."

"Where's the bloody foul weather when you want it? I told you the buggers wouldn't get the forecast right," grumbled Yorky.

"Is anything happening with that wing, Chalkie? All that snaking about won't have done it a lot of good."

Chalkie looked along the wing, clearly seen in the bright moonlight.

"There's bits flapping about, but it looks okay. Let's hope it lasts."

"Dutch coast coming up, Skipper," Paddy informed him.

"ETA, Elkington, Michael?"

"About one hour twenty-five minutes at this speed."

Chalkie was watching Johnnie struggle to keep the aircraft flying straight and level and as they passed just north of Texel Island off the Dutch coast, he suggested to Johnnie that he took over the flying for a while.

"Okay, I could do with a break. I'll try putting her on 'George' for the change-over."

However, as soon as he turned on the automatic pilot, Gloria yawed violently to starboard and dipped her starboard wing alarmingly.

"Forget it, Chalkie, she obviously wants me to fly her." They both smiled and Johnnie took charge of the yoke again, his foot and leg crying out for relief.

"Light flak to port," reported Jock from the front turret as red tracer whipped up towards them. "It must be a ship. Yes, I can see it now. Kraut navy, Skipper. Can I give it a burst?"

"No, Finlay, they're only firing at our engine sound. We don't want to show them where we are."

They left the waving strings of tracer behind them as they headed for the Lincolnshire coast.

As they made their first approach to the airfield, Algy sent a message telling the control tower they had damage and may need the 'meat and heat wagons' to greet them. Johnnie eased his foot on the rudder and let her sideslip to take some of the speed off her, then kicked her straight at the last minute and touched down safely.

"We've got company," said Yorky, watching the fire engines and ambulance following them down the runway. "Sorry lads, but no business for you tonight, so you can bugger off." He puffed out his cheeks with relief that they were down in one piece.

Johnnie cut the port outer engine and taxied to their hardstanding on the two inner engines, where he applied the brakes, cut the engines and eased his foot from the rudder pedal.

"Home at last, chaps, home at bloody last."

"Well done, Skipper. You brought her down a treat," complimented Chalkie.

"Just get me out of this bloody seat, will you? I can't feel my leg."

Chalkie helped him through the aircraft to the doorway and down the ladder.

"Christ! Are you wounded, Skipper?" asked an alarmed Algy.

"No," laughed Johnnie. "It's just my leg has seized up after three hours of pushing that bloody rudder pedal."

They all stood round the tail in a close group, lighting up cigarettes and pipes, and there was a strong feeling of comradeship, of togetherness, their conversation excited and noisy in relief. They had come through a battle together and won, albeit with Gloria wounded. They were relieved they were back home and not scattered over the fields of Germany.

In the control tower, the tension in Ginny's face disappeared. She smiled. He was back. Late. But he was back.

Two other crews from the squadron were not.

# 16 ... Cherry Stone

The next morning, Johnnie was in his office, 'A' flight's office, studying a list of repair reports from the Chiefy, including one for Gloria. She would be out of action for five days while the team of engineers from AVRO, stationed on the camp, repaired the wing and the bullet damage to the fuselage. There were no spare aircraft at the moment as a few of 'A' flight had suffered damage from flak and fighter on the last raid and no crews were due leave for a couple of weeks. Therefore, no flying for his crew over the next few days, it would give them a welcome respite from the tension of ops.

Two crews had failed to return from Berlin, but luckily, he thought guiltily, not from 'A' flight. One each from 'B' and 'C' flight had gone missing over the target. John Welcome and his crew in O-Orange from 'B' flight, had exploded in midair after taking a direct hit from heavy ack-ack and Flight Lieutenant 'Jack' Jones, an Australian, and his crew in C-Charlie from 'C' flight, crashed, after a night fighter shot them down in flames. Members of the squadron had seen and confirmed both losses and no parachutes.

He received a telephone call from the squadron adjutant, Jimmy Cook, telling him that the squadron CO, Harry Picton, required his presence as soon as possible.

"Good morning, sir," said Johnnie, throwing up a salute as he entered Picton's office.

"Morning, Squadron Leader," said a smiling Wing Commander.

"I beg your pardon, sir?" asked a surprised Johnnie.

"Just been confirmed this morning by the 'Old Man', you're no longer *acting*, you are now *substantial*. Congratulations!"

He held out his hand, which Johnnie shook.

"Sit down, Johnnie that is not the only news I called you in for. The other two flight commanders will be joining us in a couple of minutes. When will your kite be airworthy again? Has the Chiefy told you?"

"Should be ready by Monday, hopefully, I wanted to ask you about that, sir."

Harry Picton interrupted him,

"I think it's time you started calling me Harry, don't you?" he said smiling.

"Certainly, sir ... Harry. There are no spare aircraft at the moment, so what would you prefer me to do, stand down one of my crews or just one of my pilots and take his place if there are any ops this week?"

"No, I want you here. In fact, I want all of you here. You'll find out why when the others arrive."

With that, there was a knock on the door and the two flight commanders, Squadron Leaders Bill Askin and Joe Kendrick entered.

"Grab a chair, gents."

He indicated the two wooden fold-up chairs propped against the wall under a very large chalkboard, which showed a list of aircraft recognition codes, the names of each pilot and the number of sorties they had completed.

"First of all, I'm sure you would like to congratulate Johnnie here; his promotion to Squadron Leader has just been confirmed."

They congratulated him and shook his hand.

"Right, gents," said Picton. "The reason I've got you here this morning is to prime you before we go and see the 'Old Man'. The AOC has selected us for some special ops that will mean we will be mostly working on our own. For the next few weeks, we will be attacking very selective targets and not taking part in the normal Bomber Command raids. Alongside us will be our very own Mosquito squadron, or I should say, part of a squadron, who will be our personal pathfinders. The Groupie will give you more details in an hour." He looked at his watch. "In fact at eleven o'clock in his office in the admin block. I believe the squadron was selected for this job was because, would you believe it, the boss of Five Group, Air Vice Marshal Cochrane, was very impressed by our performance at Peenemünde and sent a letter of commendation to 'Butch' Harris. However, when we get in front of the 'Old Man', you don't know that, okay?" he said, tapping the side of his nose and smiling. "It's a feather in our caps, gents. You never know, we could be up there with Six-One-Seven."

He smiled sardonically.

"Why? Are we going dam-busting then, Harry?" laughed Bill.

"I don't know about that, but we will be doing a great deal of precision bombing practise over the next few days. Right, I will see you at five to eleven outside the Groupie's office. Thanks, gents."

The three flight commanders piled out of his office and stood outside in the warm balmy summer sun, smoking. Johnnie lit up his pipe as Joe asked:

"What do you think this is all about, Bill?"

"God knows. I thought that Six-One-Seven, over at Scampton, were the special ops boys?"

"They are, aren't they, but that's Five Group," said Joe. "I hear they've got a new CO by the way. George Holden has taken over from Gibson. Tip-top chap, I hear, and for some reason they have moved to Coningsby.

"No! George Holden 'bought it' last week over the Dortmund-Ems canal. I hear Leonard Cheshire is now the CO," said Bill. "Maybe every group is going to have its own special ops squadron, that's how the Pathfinders started," he said, dragging hard on his cigarette. "What do you think, Johnnie?"

"You may be right, Bill. Maybe we are going to find out the truth behind all these odd sorties we have carried out. It'll be interesting to see what the Groupie has to say."

"Sit down, gentlemen, sit down. Smoke if you like."

Group Captain Thompkins leaned back in his comfortable leather chair and slowly lit his large Meerschaum pipe; its bowl turned a dark honey-brown colour with time and handling. He puffed clouds of fragrant blue smoke to the ceiling of his sparsely furnished office. Wing Commander Ray Britton, his second in command, was sitting to his right.

"First of all, I would like to congratulate Johnnie on his promotion. Saddened that I am at losing two fine crews, but congratulations, well deserved. I know that a few of you and your crews are mystified and curious about some of your recent sortie targets. This may clarify things for you. I recently had a meeting with Sir Arthur, AVM Rice and some chaps from the Economic War Committee or some such damn thing – Boffins, in other words. They have been working with something called ..." he pulled a piece of paper towards himself, "The Central Interpretation Unit, or CIU as they call it, and some of their chaps, er ... photo interpreters ... PIs, Damn acronyms! They have uncovered some very interesting material, confirming what they had suspected for a long time. I am talking about rockets. Not bonfire night rockets, but big buggers that go bang, very loudly!" he looked over the top of his spectacles at the assembled officers and tossed a set of photographs towards them.

"Have a look at them and tell me what you think."

Johnnie picked up one he thought he recognised and showed it to Harry.

"Look, sir, that's Peenemünde; there's those circular features we talked about," he said, pointing to them. Britton picked up another set of photographs of some of the buildings at Peenemünde and showed them to the officers.

"This is a photograph taken by you on the raid and this by reconnaissance Spitfire the next day," he said, showing them two clear pictures with no smoke cloaking the scene. "And these, taken a few days later, see any difference?"

He handed them two more photos.

After a while, Bill Askin said, "But the second set seems to show more damage than the first. How can that be?"

"Yes, very interesting, isn't it?" said Ray Britton. "You're quite correct; it does show more damage than you photographed on the night or the Spit the day after. We have since found out *they* actually blew up some slightly damaged buildings, painted blackened beams on roofs, spread rubble around non-damaged buildings and created some more craters in the sandy soil! Now why on earth would they do that? We think it simply means that this site is much more important than we first thought. They are going to the trouble of camouflaging the site after we have bombed it, trying to convince us there is more damage than we thought. What's their reason?" He paused for effect, and then declared, "Rockets! Intelligence knows the site carries out rocket research, which is why we raided it, even if the official version was we were destroying highly specialised radar equipment. This latest set of photos confirms that they are still testing them on this site. We believe those circular features are actually test pads for some type of intercontinental missile."

He looked towards Thompkins.

"But, gentlemen," said Thompkins, "we have been advised that they are still months, if not years away, before they will be able to produce workable weapons of that ilk. However, on the same site, and elsewhere, I might add, they have researched, tested and built a smaller jet-engined weapon. The Ministry believes that at this time this is a bigger and a more urgent threat than anything else the Hun is developing."

He tamped down the tobacco in his pipe with a blackened finger then carried on.

"The Germans have code-named them 'Kirschkern' or 'Cherry Stone' and they are part of what they are calling 'Wunderwaffen', Wonder Weapons. We believe this refers to the rocket and jet-propelled weapons they are developing. The 'Cherry Stone' is a flying bomb, a pilotless aircraft that has the range to bring havoc to Britain and her allies. It can fly at around four hundred miles an hour, carries a two thousand pound warhead and could easily hit London from its proposed launch sites."

He leant forward and stared at the four young officers in front of him, suddenly reminded of a briefing he had received some thirty years ago from his RFC commanding officer, whose 'squadron office' was a shell damaged farmhouse somewhere in the mud of France.

"Bomber Command has selected our squadron to spearhead the bombing attacks on their research and manufacturing sites, their storage and transport facilities and, probably the most important, their proposed and existing launch sites. Thankfully, this weapon is still in its development stage, although a very advanced development stage. We have to try to stop or at least slow down that development to the final stage."

Ray Britton now took over.

"If you look closely at the photographs we gave you, at the top left you can see a series of straight lines. The PIs of CIU have looked at these in 3D and have come up with what they are calling, 'Ski Sites', because the buildings resemble snow skis lying on their side. Now they have found similar constructions in Holland and along the coast of France. They seem around 240 to 270 feet long and could be some kind of storage facility. In these photos, they have also identified what seems to be a launch system or ramp about 300 feet long. The ones in France and Holland have barn-like structures and other small buildings associated with them, possibly storage facilities and barracks. These will be some of your first targets."

He handed round some more photographs that clearly showed a concrete-walled ramp system with these strange 'ski-like' buildings near them.

"The French Resistance has done a cracking job to confirm these sites for us and I believe they have even sent some sketches of a site over to our intelligence people who confirm these photographs are showing potential flying bomb launch sites. The photos you are looking at now are from a site in northern France, near Abbeville. The launch ramps are directly aligned towards London."

"And this, gentlemen, is what we are talking about."

The Groupie passed over a single photograph to Harry Picton.

"My God, it's a flying torpedo!" he exclaimed.

The rest of his officers craned to look at the photo of a long, sharp-nosed torpedo shaped bomb, with short, straight, stubby wings, the tail-plane and rudder of a small aircraft, but with a long, open-mouthed, cylindrical tube attached on top of the back half of the bomb's fuselage.

"The 'Cherry Stone'! It is just over twenty feet long, has a wingspan of seventeen and a half feet and stands nearly five feet high. We believe the engine is a kind of pulsejet. But I leave that to those who have a greater understanding of these things than I do," declared the Group Captain. "The Dutch Resistance very kindly gave us one, after the Germans carelessly lost it during a failed test flight. Damn good job they did too, because that is not all they have done for us. Between them and the *Maquis,* they have also discovered which Luftwaffe unit is responsible for operating these sites and the names of the scientists and military personnel that make up the 'Kommission Für Fernschieben', roughly translated as 'The Commission for Long-range Firing or Bombardment'."

The Groupie enjoyed demonstrating his fluent German.

"These people are the ones responsible for the research, development and operation of not only these hideous things," he waved a derisory fluttering hand at the photograph, "but the whole kit and caboodle of the *Wunderwaffen*s. These people are our targets. Cut off the head and the body dies!"

He slammed his hand on the desktop to emphasise his point causing his brass inkwell and collection of fountain pens to jump into the air.

"As you know, Six-One-Seven squadron has built up a reputation in the last few months since the raid on the dams as an efficient and effective low-level attack unit. Over the next few months, they will concentrate on certain targets to combat these German threats. We, meanwhile, have our own specific targets set out by Sir Arthur Harris, the Air Ministry and Winston himself. 'Bodyline' is the codename chosen to cover all the forthcoming operations against the rocket sites of which ours is one part. Ray?"

The Groupie mopped up the spilt ink with his large blotter as Ray Britton spoke.

"As you can imagine, this is top-secret, of course, and your crews cannot be told the full story. The cover story is still the same as Peenemünde; you have been and will be attacking secret radar installations and their research and testing facilities. However, your first target is very different.

Johnnie interrupted, "When is the op, sir? My kite is at the menders until Monday, and I certainly wouldn't like being left out."

"Don't worry, Johnnie, we wouldn't do that," smiled Thompkins. "We need all the experience we can grab. The flight ground crew chiefs instructions this morning were to make sure all available aircraft are airworthy by 0800 Monday, because that is when you will start a few days of special training."

Britton continued. "As I said, your first target is very different from the squadron's normal ops. It will be a fortified château near Paris. Normally, for a job like this, we would send in the 'wooden wonders' in a high-speed, low-level strike. However, the restricted bomb loads of the Mosquitos would not be enough to damage or destroy the target and achieve our objective. Therefore, the task is ours. It will be a squadron maximum effort, every available aircraft and crew."

He paused and looked at his boss, who nodded.

"Intelligence informs us that there is a conference or a meeting arranged at the château for the *very* senior members of the 'Wonder Weapon Commission' and the chief scientists involved with project 'Cherry Stone'. Our job, gentlemen, very simply, is to destroy that meeting and as many delegates attending as possible, thereby cutting off its head, hence 'Operation Decapitation'."

He collected the photographs from the seated officers as if to stress his next words.

"And, as I said before, you will treat this information as top-secret. The briefing for your crews will be as for a normal operation, but it will take place only a couple of hours before take-off. Operation 'Decapitation' is planned for twelve days' time on the evening of Monday 6 September."

## 17 ... Decapitation

For the next two days, Johnnie was busy in his office working on the new training schedules they would be using from Monday morning for the sortie the following week. His crew, and those of the rest of the flight, was enjoying the break from the fear-sodden sorties over war-torn Europe. The Royal Oak and the other pubs around the villages and Ludworth were doing a roaring trade. On Friday afternoon, he threw the last forms and reports into the filing tray on his cluttered desk and walked round to the squadron office.

"Hello, Jimmy, what's the latest? Anything brewing?"

"Not at the moment, Johnnie. But I'm sure Mr Schicklgruber and his chums will be up to mischief again soon and we shall have to pay them a visit and drop a ton or two on their bonces!"

The phone on his desk burst into life.

"Yes, sir, I'll put you through to him now," he pushed the intercom button and said, "Skipper? Got the CO on the blower. I'm putting him through now."

He slowly put the phone down. "Mmm ... that was strange. Groupie has never phoned late on a Friday before, and there was something in his voice."

"What do you think?"

"Don't know, an op maybe?"

His 'phone rang again. "... Ok, Skipper ... Johnnie is actually standing in front of me... OK." He put the phone down. "You're to go in. I've got to get the other flight commanders."

Johnnie knocked on the door and entered on Harry's call.

"You wanted me, Harry?"

"Yes, old man. Been a change of plans. That was the Groupie on the blower. 'Decapitation' has been brought forward."

"To when?"

"To *this* Monday night."

"*This* Monday night!" exclaimed Johnnie. "So, that's the training up the Swanee then."

"Well, that's the problem. We have to use the next two days to get the chaps whizzed up for this op. You've been working on a schedule, haven't you?"

"Yes, I have, but I intended to try it out on my flight first."

"Could it be extended to the squadron?"

"Yes, but with different timings, obviously, I had planned to carry it out over five to six days."

"You've got two days now!"

There was a knock on the door.

"Come in you two, grab a chair."

The other flight commanders sat down.

"Operation 'Decapitation' has been brought forward to Monday night ... *this* Monday night."

The two newcomers looked at each other in surprise. Bill attempted to say something, but Harry held up his hand.

"According to Intelligence, the meeting of the 'Kommission' is starting this Sunday and all the principals will be there on Monday night. Therefore, we have two days to put this together. Johnnie has been working on a training plan as I asked him to. He has worked out the details for his flight, but we will now use it for the squadron. The basics of the raid are simple enough. The château is more castle-like than country house, which is why it is our job. Built in the days when they built castles to last. Lots of towers and turrets, made from solid granite. Because it is relatively small, we will be bombing from 1,000 feet and going in line astern in pairs. The load will be all high explosive, no incendiaries. Now go away and put Johnnie's training plan into action, starting tomorrow morning. He has all the info you will need. If you need any help to get things moving, just refer people to me. Come back to me later this afternoon, Johnnie, to keep me up to date. Okay, gents, sorry to mess up your weekend, but, as they say, 'press on regardless'."

Johnnie called in his captains of aircraft to the flight office late that afternoon after going through his training schedule with the other flight commanders, with a few changes; they agreed with his suggestions and called in their captains.

The eleven other pilots that made up 'A' flight's Skippers crammed into the flight office.

"Gentlemen, unfortunately your weekend plans have gone out the window. A sortie we did not expect to carry out until ten days time will now take place on Monday night. I know your lads will be completely cheesed off, but 'duty calls'. We have the luxury of two days' preparation and training, which we will start from 0800 tomorrow morning. It is nothing out of the ordinary as far as the crews are concerned, just another sortie across the Channel. We will be dropping HEs on a VIP target, and that will mean going in at tree top-level, popping up to one thousand feet and delivering our ordnance.

"We will use the next two days to get used to that exercise and to practise our approach to the target. It is vital that we are accurate in our bombing. The target is relatively small; very little room for error; precision is paramount. We will be flying in close formation in line astern and flying side-by-side one hundred feet apart. I mean close! Heavy flak protects the target and there is a fighter airfield less than three miles away. We have to get in, out and away, as fast as possible. Therefore, tomorrow morning, we will be flying up the Bristol Channel trying not to bump into each other and then having approach practise against a similar target in South Wales. There will be a briefing for all the crews at 1900 hours tonight. You had better go and find your crews and prime them. Would Peter Mee and Jim stay behind please when the others have gone? Thank you, gents."

The Skippers filed out, their conversations buzzing with questions.

'Geordie' Pilot Officer Peter 'Pity' Mee and Flying Officer Jim Baker stayed behind.

"You know that G-George is in the mender's shop at the moment and there are no spare kites available, so I am going to requisition your kites over the next couple of days. Peter, I will take K-King tomorrow and Jim, I will take I-India on Sunday. It just means you and your lads will have a day off over the weekend, lucky you. My kite will be ready on Monday. You will both be on the sortie. You're both experienced pilots with good crews. That's why I picked you. I'm sure you will cope on the op with only one day's training."

At the briefing that night, Harry Picton outlined the operation to all the crews; he explained the reason for the training over the next two days and called on Johnnie to impart the details.

"Tomorrow we will be practising flying in pairs a hundred feet apart and a quarter of a mile between each pair at two hundred miles an hour at one thousand feet. That is five seconds apart! Lundy Island, in the Bristol Channel, is our formation point; from there we form pairs in line astern to hit our target sixty miles up the channel, Flat Holm Island. From there we swing round over South Wales, back out to sea to come in over St. Govan's Head at two hundred feet from the south-southwest, on 10 degrees true. Pop up to one thousand as you pass east of Pembroke and follow the Cleddau Estuary to your target of Picton Castle."

He turned and smiled at the squadron commander as catcalls, whistles and comments came from the crews.

"We're going to bomb the family home, boss?"

"Make sure the servants know we're coming, sir. We'll be there in time for tea!"

"Will one be at home, m'lud?"

"All right you heathens. If it was mine, you lot would be the last people in the world I'd invite for tea."

More whistles and cheers of derision greeted Harry Picton's words.

When the laughter had died down, Johnnie carried on.

"The castle is a fair copy of the target we will be going against on Monday. The approach is very similar, following a shallow valley with hills behind the château. We only have two days to get it right. Let's get it right tomorrow and perfect it the day after."

Wing Commander Harry Picton led them on their first pass up the Severn Estuary with Tony Rance in C-Charlie as his partner alongside. 'A' flight fell into line astern, the aircraft flying in alphabetical order two hundred feet above the grey-brown sea as they passed over Lundy Island. The other flights followed suit as the flight commanders badgered the pilots to 'close up, close up' and keep together, keeping 440 yards between each pair. The front aircraft were approaching a small convoy of merchant vessels with two Royal Navy corvette protection ships, when a burst of light ack-ack suddenly whipped towards them from one of the trailing merchantmen. Their 'Pom-Pom' guns aimed so low that some of the shells were bouncing off the water. The two front bombers, Harry and Tony, hurriedly ordered their bomb aimers to signal with their Aldis lamps the day's recognition code, but the tracers still kept pumping into the sky around the aircraft. Suddenly C-Charlie's port outer engine started to pour black oily smoke and Tony Rance, the Canadian pilot, pulled across the channel towards Wales, away from the guns. Other aircraft were now frantically flashing their Aldis lights and the nearest corvette to the firing ship veered towards her with its giant signalling lamp clattering out a cease-fire message. The sprays of deadly lead stopped as the rest of the Lancasters swept above the little flotilla. Many of the sailors were on deck waving at the aircrews; the response from the aircrews was shaking fists and vigorous applications of 'the finger'!

"C-Charlie, this is leader, can you make it back to home?"

"Leader, this is C-Charlie. Yes, we are feathering the engine now. No fire."

"OK, C-Charlie, return to base. Will see you later. Leader out."

"Leader to all aircraft, carry on as planned. I will be talking to our Navy friends later." He clicked off the RT, muttering to himself, "Fucking idiots!"

They spent the next two hours concentrating on getting the aircraft to fly in the tight formation that might save their lives over France. The pilots were fighting hard to keep the giant bombers stable as the 'dirty air' from the prop wash and slipstream of the aircraft in front of them buffeted and tossed them around.

"Leader to all aircraft, leader to all aircraft, after this next run through, we will decant towards the assembly area to attack the main target. Remember to approach on a heading of 10 degrees and up to 'angels one' at Pembroke. We will carry out the two approaches as planned, and then home for tea."

"Have you got enough parking spaces in the grounds for all the squadron, Boss?" was the cheeky question from Australian, Flight Lieutenant Mike Hunt, in H-Harry.

"No, sorry, Mike, the gardeners haven't finished cutting the lawns yet."

There was laughter throughout the squadron.

Two hours or so later, all the aircraft touched down safely at Elkington. Johnnie went to see Harry in his office.

"Ah, Johnnie, just the man! How do you think it went today?"

"Beside Tony Rance's experience, you mean? I hope you have given the Navy what for. He was bloody lucky to come out of that at that height. Is he okay?"

"Yes, he's fine. Chiefy says his kite will be okay for tomorrow morning."

"I thought it went well today. It was a bit chaotic at first, but once they had grasped what a hundred feet between them and a quarter of a mile gap between each pair was, they did well. The only thing I'm not sure of is the height of the hills behind the target."

"No higher than a thousand feet. Shouldn't bother us at all. I think the real worry is the flak. Because it is the HQ of the main flak regiment, we are expecting a very lively reception; hence, we are going in under the radar until the last-minute. If we go through at a quarter of a mile between us at two hundred miles an hour, we'll be done and dusted in just over a minute. The flak boys won't even have woken up by then, hopefully."

Johnnie and his crew switched to I-India the next day amid the customary bickering about aircraft being inferior to Gloria.

"Don't worry, chaps, we'll be back in Gloria tomorrow," said Johnnie. "Let's just get on with the job like good little boys, shall we?"

By the time the squadron had completed their last mock attack on Picton Castle in the middle of the afternoon, and the WingCo was happy, the thoroughly fed-up residents of Pembroke and the surrounding areas were glad to see the departure of the roaring low-flying Lancasters.

The battle orders the following day showed the briefing would be at 1700 hours, and NFTs ordered for both the morning and the afternoon to make sure all aircraft were 'A1' for the op.

The Senior Intelligence Officer pulled the blackout cloth from the giant map as he said:

"Tonight the target is … Château-Thierry, France. The town of Château-Thierry lies on the north bank of the River Marne, between Paris and Epernay. Your target is the Château that is within the grounds of the medieval castle in the centre of the town."

Section Officer Ginny Murphy handed him some papers, then blushed as the whistles and cheers erupted. The SIO waved them to silence, ignoring their catcalls.

The red route tapes showed a track overland to Reading, crossing the coast at Beachy Head then across the French coast east of Abbeville and then directly to Château-Thierry. An outward journey of three hundred and eighty miles; the home route was almost a reverse of the outward route.

"The target has been selected by the ACM and his committee, because it is the regional headquarters of one of the main Flak regiments of the Wehrmacht. They are the people developing the latest weapons and detection systems that could have a disastrous effect on future Bomber Command operations. Therefore, we must take them out! We have selected a route staying clear of the obvious flak concentrations, but at such a low height you will be a target for any trigger-happy Kraut," the SIO carried on. "Around the target, there is a heavy concentration of medium and heavy flak batteries. In the last few days, some ten extra batteries have moved in. We estimate there are now some thirty to forty batteries protecting your target. That is not counting the heavy and light machine gun batteries of which there could be ten to twenty. It is vital that you stay as low as you can only going up to your bombing height of one thousand feet, no more than five miles from the target. This will give your air bomber time to get his fix. If you come up earlier than that, their radar will pick you up and the searchlights and guns will pick you up."

The Navigation Leader then detailed the route and confirmed the position for the target as 49 degrees 02 minutes north and 3 degrees 24 minutes east.

"As normal, we have routed you the Reading-Beachy Head track because of our busy American friends filling the skies of East Anglia with their fighters and bombers. Talking of Americans, your approach is directly over the American Great War Memorial. You cannot miss it, a couple of miles west of Château-Thierry town."

The Bombing Leader explained that two Path Finder Force Mosquitos would mark the target with red ground markers; two more Mosquitos would confirm this with yellow explosive incendiary Target Indicators.

"One of the Mosquitos will act as a Bombing Master and confirm the markers as the bomber stream comes in by RT and redirect you if necessary. Your ordnance will consist of two types of loads. The first twelve aircraft will carry one High Capacity 4000-pound 'Cookie' and four two thousand pound H.E. Penetration bombs. The second twelve aircraft will carry a mixture of six one thousand and three two thousand pound H.E penetration bombs. The back-up aircraft will carry six two thousand pound HC – HEs, all on short-time delay fuses, a heavy and very effective load."

The Met Officer confirmed clear skies with a good moon.

The Flying Control Officer clarified the times and order of take-off. They would lift off in close order of twos and form the stream in loose formation until they gained their bombing height when they would then move into line astern in pairs. He confirmed that 'Z' hour was midnight exact.

"The signal to move into line astern will come from the squadron leader, Wing Commander Picton. He will broadcast one word, 'Trafalgar'. The wireless operators have already been given the wavelengths and codes for the night."

Group Captain Thompkins then took the stand.

"Gentlemen, Five-Nine-Nine's selection for tonight's prestigious mission was deliberate. This is the first of many critical sorties against vital targets to combat the terror weapon systems that Germany is preparing for the future. I shall not stand up here spouting how good we are, or how dedicated we are to bringing the Hun to his knees, I shall just wish you good luck, God speed and a safe return. Thank you, gentlemen."

He was pleasantly surprised to get a round of applause accompanied by wolf-whistles.

"He's got the cheer because he was brief," commented a cynical Yorky.

The sun had shone all day and now reflected its promise for tomorrow as the western sky blazed in red glory. As night closed in on the thirty-two Avro Lancasters parading majestically round the peri track, their boss, Wing Commander Harry Picton in A-Apple, led them. His port wingman was Pilot Officer Tony Rance in the repaired C-Charlie. Johnnie and his crew, alongside Mike Hunt in H-Harry, were the fourth pair to throb round the peri track. The boss waited for his second green light from the control caravan on the side of the main runway, which would release him from the threshold to thunder down the two thousand yard concrete strip, followed closely by his wingman, and launch into the darkening sky.

Half an hour later, the small armada had streamed in formation and was pounding high over the English countryside at nine thousand feet and at just over two hundred miles an hour towards Beachy Head, where they would drop to just one hundred feet above the English Channel.

Yorky, in his little enclosed world back in the tail, watched, fascinated, the twinkling navigation lights of the aircraft following on behind and beside him. Normally, by this time, they would be thundering over the North Sea with no lights around them. It always appeared they were flying on their own, lost in the darkness of the night. Sometimes, he never saw another bomber until they got home; it was a comforting situation having close neighbours. However, as they raced over the English Channel, they extinguished the twinkling lights, and every gunner in the flock of war-birds concentrated on the velvet darkness for that tiny glow of hot exhausts that could mean a stalking night fighter. They crossed the French coast without incident. No flak opened up on them and no searching beams illuminated them.

"Two minutes to go before we go up to 'angels one', Skipper," reported Paddy.

"Okay, Michael. Stand by everyone. We are about to start the bombing run. Are you ready, Finlay?"

"Aye, Skipper, no problem."

Then over the radio came, "Trafalgar ... Trafalgar ... Trafalgar."

All the bombers tightened up their formation on Harry's leading Lanc. Now they had to climb to one thousand feet and put a quarter of a mile, 440 yards, between each pair in turbulent, disturbed air, as well as flying with a hundred feet between partners. It was not easy. Gloria was bouncing and yawing, fighting Johnnie's efforts to keep her at her station as she flew through the prop wash and slip stream from the bombers in front. He thought it must have been hell for those aircraft further back in the line.

"This is like being on a bleedin' big dipper!" was the cry from the tail.

"Flak ahead, Skipper. They woke up bloody quick," said Jock.

Streams of coloured tracer were weaving the sky in front of them and every second more guns were joining in. Within a few short seconds, heavier flak was bursting above the leading bombers.

"Jesus Christ! The buggers were waiting for us!" cried an alarmed Chalkie. "How the hell did they get on to us that quick?"

440 yards in front of Gloria, 'Chin' Pettersen's D-Dog's starboard wing erupted in flames as the petrol tanks exploded after a direct hit by flak. It dived towards the ground, but disintegrated as the high explosive ordnance on board took

another direct hit. G-George jerked violently upwards as they flew through the smoke, flames and debris. Johnnie fought hard to keep Gloria under control, while Yorky watched in horror as the remains of D-Dog fell to earth in a fiery fountain. The stutter of machine gun bullets sounded on the side of the fuselage and Algy instinctively ducked as rounds passed over his head to punch an exit through the roof. Dusty joined Yorky by opening up on the gun positions below, filling the aircraft with even more clamouring noise. Burning bombers, flying flak and yammering guns were creating scenes from Hell, but Johnnie and his crews pressed home their attack.

"Red TIs ahead, Skipper," called Jock. "Yellow ground markers have gone up, confirmed target."

"Master Bomber to all aircraft, master bomber to all aircraft, bomb on red and yellows, repeat, bomb on red and yellows, out."

"You got that, Finlay?"

"Yes, Skip, got it. Memorial is directly ahead. Open bomb bay doors."

Johnnie pushed the lever down.

"Bomb bay doors open. She's yours, bomb aimer."

"Come right a bit ... right ... left left ... right ... right ... steadyyyyy ... Bombs gone!"

Gloria leapt upwards as the five and a half tons of high explosive left her belly. Johnnie used this springboard effect to power climb away from the barrage of anti-aircraft shells that was now bursting in a curtain of steel around the château.

"Another Lanc gone down behind us, it was one of the third pair behind us, I don't know who that was, Skipper."

"Okay, Yorky. Everybody who can, start rubber-necking the sky, because if those guns were waiting for us, you can guarantee there will be fighters around. Keep sharp, everyone."

He turned Gloria away from the burning target and climbed away to the east, back towards the coast, leaving the sky behind a cauldron of tracer and exploding flak. Searchlights had now joined the party and were sweeping the darkness in search of the impudent intruders. The delay-fused bombs now commenced their demolition work. In a series of rapid explosions, the 4000 lb 'cookies', identifiable by their deeper boom, and the other high explosives, blasted Château-Thierry into ruins. A castle that had stood over seven hundred years and had withstood the ravages of countless sieges and attacks, succumbed in less than one minute to weapons of modern warfare with the Château reduced to rubble and burning timber. Flame, smoke and debris punched hundreds of feet into the night sky.

As they thundered towards the coast, the calm voice of Algy came over the intercom.

"Skipper, I've got two signals astern on 'Monica', one to starboard and one to port. By the way they're moving, I think they're bandits."

"Can you see anything, gunners?"

"Nope," said Yorky.

"Nothing yet, Skip," said Dusty.

"The one high on the port side is coming in, definitely a bandit. Range about a thousand yards," called Algy.

Dusty spotted him first.

"Got him, about eight hundred yards high on the port quarter, Yorky. Can you see him?"

"No ... Yes! Corkscrew port, now!"

"Corkscrewing port, up the revs, Chalkie."

"Twenty-seven-fifty, Skip." said Chalkie.

The engines throbbed with more power as Gloria went down in a turning dive making it much more difficult for the fighter to turn inside the curve and bring his cannons to bear.

"He's broken off, climbing to port," said Yorky.

"The starboard one's coming in, Skipper. Eight hundred ... six hundred ..." reported Algy.

"Got him!" called Dusty.

His guns chattered and tracer stitched the night. Yorky joined in and six streams of deadly tracer coned in on the twin-engine night fighter. He obviously did not like the odds and swept underneath the bomber to safety.

"Turning and climbing to starboard," announced Johnnie.

Gloria pulled sharply up to the right and then levelled off.

"Bandit high to rear port, Skipper."

Algy's radar screen was working well.

"Corkscrew port, now!" screamed Dusty. "The sneaky bastard crept up on us."

"Corkscrewing to port."

Again, Johnnie plunged Gloria downwards to the left and she filled with the stench of rotten eggs as six machine guns hammered away at the black-crossed attacker. This time, the night fighter kept coming, his 20-mm cannons pumping fiery shells at them. Gloria's battle team won the day. The starboard engine of the JU-88 twin-engine fighter burst into flames as it dived away streaming smoke.

"We got the bastard!" shouted Dusty from his lofty perch.

"He's going down. He's spinning. He's gone in!" Yorky's voice had gone up an octave with excitement.

"Well done, chaps, well done, all of you, well done. Still keep rubbernecking; they may come back for revenge. Twenty-six-fifty revs, Chalkie."

"Twenty-six-fifty revs and all is okay, Skipper."

"Bandit closing fast, high and rear starboard side," called Algy.

"Corkscrew starboard, Go-Go-Go!" shouted Yorky.

Again, accompanied by a chattering Browning serenade and the reek of cordite fumes, Johnnie pushed Gloria into another violent diving turn calling Chalkie for more power. The fighter blazed away at them, but his shells passed harmlessly to port. He overshot them and Jock opened up on him from his nose turret, following him as he climbed and banked to attack again, Dusty opened up as he crossed his sights as well. This time, the fighter swept in a long curve out of range of Gloria's chattering guns, coming at them from below, but not low enough, for Yorky depressed his four guns as far as they would go and met him head on. Both aircraft were spitting fire and venom at each other in a deadly duel. Johnnie pulled her back up into the night sky twisting to port to try to evade the deadly cannon fire, and succeeded. The pilot canopy of the fighter disintegrated and it dived and rolled to port. The roll got faster and faster as the twin engines screamed on their downward journey to destruction. No pale parachutes broke in the moonlight.

"YEE-HA!" shouted Yorky. "Got him, got the bugger! I got the bugger! Well I'll be buggered!"

"You most probably will be, by all of us, for that nifty piece of shooting!" called Dusty.

"Well done, Yorky, well done. There'll be a gong for both of you from tonight's efforts, I'm sure there will," said Johnnie. "You'll soon have more than me, Yorky."

The whole crew joined in to sing Yorky's praise, but the Yorkshireman had already returned to work.

"Christ, another Lanc's hit, Skipper. About a thousand yards on our port rear quarter. He's going down now."

"See if you can spot any 'chutes, gunners." said Johnnie, "Everybody okay? Report in."

The six members of his crew all came back confirming no injuries or damage.

"Need to go on to three-one-five for the coast, Skip," came from Paddy.

"Three-one-five it is, Michael. Keep a sharp look out everybody, just because we've had some success doesn't mean we can go to sleep, keep your eyes skinned," warned the Skipper. "We're going down to two hundred feet to get under the guns and lights as we approach the French coast, keep rubbernecking for more fighters. Let's have some more knots from her, Chalkie. Let's get her home as fast as we can."

Four Merlin power plants increased their throb at Chalkie's demand as they blasted their way over the French countryside. As they swept towards Abbeville, probing columns of searing light searched for them, but they dropped even lower and escaped over the sea towards Beachy Head without discovery. The sky was very clear with a big bright moon reflecting in the burnished steel of the flat calm sea, their headlong rush towards home mirrored in the shining water. Johnnie warned the crew that they would be climbing rapidly when they flew up the giant white cliffs of Beachy Head. Algy stood up to watch their dramatic approach through the astrodome above his head. Johnnie left it to the last moment before pulling hard back on the control column and sending Gloria rocketing up the famous giant cliffs.

Jock shouted in excitement, "That put the shits up the bloody bluebirds she keeps singing about!"

"Do you mind, Jock, that's my beautiful Vera Lynn you're talking about. She is England's salvation from Marlene Dietrich. It was the White Cliffs of Dover she was singing about anyway, not Beachy Head," protested Algy.

Gloria came to rest just after 0231 hours on the morning of 31 August, 1943, according to Paddy's log.

"Home at last, chaps, home at last."

As the others departed the aircraft, adrenaline still pumping high from their success against the Hun night-fighters, Johnnie sat on his seat, high in the greenhouse-like cockpit, surprised to see his kid-leather gloves soaked with sweat; he had not even realised his hands had sweated. His thoughts lingered on what had happened tonight. The shock of the aircraft directly in front of him blowing up, the lives of seven comrades, people he knew well, people he had drunk with, laughed with, snuffed out in the blink of an eye. 'Chin' Pettersen and D-Dog's crew decimated and spread over the fields of France. He had not found out yet who else had gone down. The two JU-88s destroyed was a remarkable feat. The gunners had done a great job of defending the bomber, but it was more lives thrown away, even though they were German ones.

"Come on, Johnnie! The transport's here." called a voice.

With one more thoughtful look at his hands, he scrambled out of the odorous bomber, glad of the fresh night air to wash away his melancholy.

Later that morning, as the crew was inspecting the damage from their expedition to France, Algy realised just how close to his head the night fighter's shells had passed. As he sat in the chair at his station, four inches above his head, next to the astrodome, were three ragged holes allowing the morning sun to light up the worktable in front of him.

"I say! Do you think that nasty little Jerry had something against me last night? Maybe I shagged his mistress last time I was in Berlin?" he said, as he poked his fingers through the holes.

"Aye, you shagged his mistress all right. The last time you went to Berlin, you dropped five tons of high explosive on her head," laughed Chalkie.

The debriefing, after they had touched down in the early hours, confirmed the two JU-88s as kills. One credited jointly to Dusty and Yorky, and the second to Yorky on his own. The station commander, Group Captain Thompkins, always in attendance 'when his boys came home', heartily congratulated them and agreed with Johnnie that 'a gong or two wouldn't go amiss'.

"Well done, you two," congratulated Harry Picton, "Brilliant work."

"It was all of them, Harry, the team was magnificent. It's a privilege to fly with them," said a very proud Johnnie. "Tonight the beers are definitely on me!"

"I'll hold you to that, Sanderson. I presume you mean for the whole squadron?" laughed Harry.

Then in a cheerless voice he said, "We lost three aircraft. Four 'chutes were seen, we think from P-Popsie, none from the others."

"Who else did we lose, Harry?" asked a sombre Johnnie. "We saw Chin Pettersen go down."

"Yes, so did we. Jim Baker in I-India blew up."

I-India, the bomber Johnnie himself was flying twenty-four hours earlier, had spun into the ground, a burning wreck.

"God, we were flying I-India yesterday. Makes you think, doesn't it?"

"Twenty-one young men, it sure does, old man, it sure does."

Harry wandered away from the briefing room by himself, back to the squadron office to send the telegrams and begin to write the dreaded letters to wives, mothers and sweethearts.

"It is with the deepest regret that I…"

Later that night, the walls of the Royal Oak resounded to the raucous singing of celebration, young men celebrating, knowing they have survived for yet another day. They remembered, but did not mention the names of those whose kit and personal possessions already sat in cardboard boxes, ready for 'return to stores' or for sending to their next of kin. Their faces would soon blur with those of the new young replacements.

Ginny had joined Johnnie and his crew to help Yorky and Dusty celebrate their gladiatorial victories. After several pints of 'Hewitt's 4X bitter', Yorky declared his undying love for her in his beer-slurred voice.

"I think you're wunnerful, you're so beauful, I'm totally in luv wiv you, you know? Why are you seein' tha' ugly ole bugger, when you could 'ave sum 'on like me?"

"But what about your wife, Yorky?" laughed Ginny.

"Oh, she wun mind; shis very unnerstandin, shis luvly like that. In fak shis wunnerful, I luv 'er dearly, I do, yer know, I really do. Les drink t' wife, ev'ry wun, lets drink t'my wifey," he shouted across the pub, hanging on to a none too sober Johnnie, "To my wifey, to…was' her name, Johnnie?"

"Fanny."

"Thas right, Fanny. Les' drink t'my Fanny!" he shouted.

To which the pub echoed, "To Yorky's Fanny!" Then fell about in hysterical laughter.

"Look after him, chaps," said Johnnie, passing him over to the capable, but slightly drunk Paddy.

"Let's go and sit down, shall we?"

"Yes, I think we should before you fall down," said a smiling Ginny.

## 18 ... Operation Bodyline

The crew room in 'A' flight's hut the next morning looked and sounded more like the sick quarters, with bodies slumped in overstuffed armchairs. Dusty was actually lying on the 'ping pong' table and various pathetic moans and groans were coming from many other members of the flight.

Algy burst through the door bouncing with energy, a large smile on his face, showing no signs of a well-deserved hangover.

"Morning chaps; beautiful day; didn't see many of you at breakfast. Not hungry? Morning, Skipper," he said as Johnnie came out of his office.

"Morning, Algy, nice to see someone still alive. Come on you lot, all kites to go on NFTs this morning. There is no transport to dispersal, so you will all have to walk to your kites ... do you the world of good. On your feet and off you toddle; come on, move yourselves!" he shouted, smiling broadly.

"And I thought you were a caring, understanding and generous-hearted human being. You're naught but a slave-driver," bemoaned a grey-faced Paddy.

By the time the crews had collected their parachutes and flying gear and walked across the airfield, Johnnie, via the crew bus he and Harry Picton shared, had arrived at the dispersal pad in time to greet the now almost mutinous crews.

"There you are, chaps, the walk did you the world of good, didn't it?"

More mutinous mutterings greeted his cry.

He chuckled, "If you can't take a joke, you shouldn't have joined." He had to scramble up the ladder into Gloria quickly to avoid the various pieces of kit aimed at his head.

When everyone had completed their equipment checks and reported on the intercom, he informed them that they were on 'battle orders' for that night, the NFT was not a joke.

\*\*\*

"The target for tonight is ... Watten. North-eastern France, just north of Saint-Omer," the SIO had informed the crews at the briefing in the late afternoon. "Our noble allies, the US Army Air Force, attacked this site in a daylight raid two days ago. Although they did a splendid job, Bomber Command has asked that we go in and do the job properly."

As he expected, loud cheering and whistling greeted this.

"Seriously, they have done a magnificent job. Their target was a very large concrete emplacement still under construction. We believe it is probably some sort of forward command bunker or ammunition dump. Reconnaissance photos show the northern section of the site badly damaged, but the road, rail and canal connections to the site showed little damage. Therefore, we are going in to rectify that situation. There was very little flak when the Yanks went in, but we suspect Jerry has moved some ack-ack troops into the area over the last twenty-four hours. The other high activity flak area is, of course, between Calais and Boulogne-sur-Mer. So, as you can see ..." he pointed to the giant map "... we have routed you north over Veurne."

The bombing leader, an experienced flight lieutenant, now took over the pointer and the platform; he unveiled a huge air reconnaissance photograph of the area and used the pointer to highlight his words.

"The approach to the target will be from the northeast to avoid dropping our ordnance on the French population of the village of Watten. This will bring you on to the main target, which is where the canal, rail spur to the bunker site and a road meet. Beside this is what we believe to be a supply dump where they store the materials and possibly armaments after being off-loaded. Before the American raid, the Jerries have been floodlighting this site and the bunker itself to allow work to carry on twenty-four hours a day, this is obviously an important site. It would be very convenient for us if they went to bed and left the lights on, but do not bank on it. Further to the southwest is where the rail spur joins the main railway line, and another spur's off to the bunker. That is your second target. Air bombers have already received instructions to set up their bomb control boards to hit both targets on the same run-in. 'Z' hour is 2400. Let's show the Yanks how it's done."

The navigation leader went over the course and the headings for the outward and homeward flights. The Met Officer informed them it would be a dry, moonless night with light cloud from eight thousand feet and the Flying Control Officer confirmed their order and times for take-off and designated the 'runway in use'. Harry Picton and Group Captain Thompkins now took the stage.

"This tonight is another example of Air Chief Marshal Harris's faith in this squadron," said the Groupie. "A high priority, low-level sortie that ..."

A massive window-shaking explosion abruptly interrupted Thompkins. Two hundred or so airmen leapt to their feet in alarm. Someone shouted, "It's an air raid!" The cry, taken up by several others, caused dozens of them to rush towards the doors at the back of the hut to try to get out quickly and seek access to the air raid shelters outside.

The doors crashed open and Flight Sergeant Pidkin of the station's RAF police, who had been on duty outside with some of his staff, entered. Perched on his razor-scraped scalp was a crisp white-topped cap, shaped to a point in the front above the guardsman-like slashed black peak that partially obscured his all-seeing eyes. A red-veined nose, which could sniff out breaches of the King's Regulations across the other side of the airfield, fronted his thin-lipped florid face; a sharply pointed waxed moustache underlined it. His tailored tunic fitted his barrel-chested figure like a second skin. The cross strap, belt, pistol holster and gaiters that adorned his immaculately pressed uniform were blancoed a startling snow-white. His boots sparkled and shone like polished black mirrors.

He cleaved his way through the fleeing aircrews as if he were a knife-prowed ship in Arctic iced seas.

"Gentlemen!" he roared, immediately gaining their attention. Ignoring the fact, that most present out-ranked him, he then addressed the gathered squadron in the way of a patronising schoolmaster in front of a classroom filled with naughty boys.

"Now, gentlemen, there's no need to panic. It ain't an h'air-raid; it seems it h'is an h'incident on one of the dispersal pans. So you can all calm down and carry on wiv' your business. Go on, gentlemen, sit down and pay h'attention to the Station Commander. Sorry to disturb you, sah!" he addressed the Group Captain with an immaculate salute.

The Group Captain, slightly embarrassed at his youthful 'air-warriors' reaction to the explosion, replied.

"No ... no ... not at all, Flight Sergeant Pidkin ... erm not at all."

Harry Picton promptly took charge of the situation.

"Could you please investigate the h'incident, erm ... incident, Flight Sergeant, and report directly to me, soonest?"

With an arm-quivering salute, the blancoed bloodhound answered,

"YES SAH!"

He executed an impossibly robotic, foot slamming about-turn and the hut shook. He set off, leaving a ghostly cloud of white Blanco powder in his wake. Under his left arm, his silver-topped cane was held straight fingered and perfectly parallel to the floor as he marched back through the airmen scattering them like farmyard chickens in front of a tractor. As he passed through the doorway, he commanded,

"SECURE THOSE DOORS!"

As if by spontaneous obedience, the double doors slammed shut!

The immaculate figure, straight right arm swinging shoulder-high, marched across the airfield towards his American-style Jeep and drove off, bouncing over the grass towards the flame-flecked column of smoke that was rising from the dispersal pads on the east side of the main runway. Thompkins watched him through the window, again, slightly embarrassed. He commented to his Wing Commander,

"To misquote the Duke of Wellington, Harry, he scares the shite out of me, God knows what he would do to the enemy if he ever came into contact with them."

"All right, gents, let's just calm down and sit down. We will discover what it was all about soon. Sir?" he turned to the Group Captain.

"Ah, yes. Where was I?"

"High esteem, high priority, low-level sortie, sir."

"Yes, ahem, as I was saying, the op tonight reflects the high esteem AVM Harris has for Five-Nine-Nine. This high priority, low-level raid against a vital target ordered at such short notice is a true compliment to your abilities as a leading squadron of Bomber Command. Good luck and God speed."

He touched his cap with his leather-bound cane and left the platform. Harry called the men to attention as the Groupie left the briefing hut.

"All flight commanders please stay and see me after this briefing."

He then addressed the re-seated aircrews.

"Right, gents, we shall be keeping as low as possible as we approach the French coast to try to fool their radar, but as we cross the coast we will go up to our bombing height of three thousand and start to drop Window. The outward journey will be in vic formation, and I want you in those bombing formations as we make the turn over the North Sea. We will stick in vic formation as we bomb, because the target area is not very wide. Once you have dropped your load, it is down to the deck and get back here. Okay, gents go and collect your gear. Dismissed."

The three flight commanders approached the platform.

"For your ears only," said Harry, "this op is part of 'Bodyline', okay? The official cover story about this site is that we do not know what the hell is going on there, but it could be something to do with 'Cherry Stone', that's why Butch Harris has selected us. Further news from our sortie to Chateau-Thierry, the photos taken the next day show that nearly ninety percent of our bombs fell inside the curtain walls of the castle and the Chateau itself was badly damaged. But! We missed our real targets. Intelligence sources now tell us that the people we were after weren't there."

"What!" exclaimed Bill Askin, "You're telling us it was a waste of time?"

"No, it wasn't a waste of time, Bill. We did get an artillery general, some of his senior officers and some of the scientists involved with this 'Cherry Stone' thing, but we did miss the big boys. I did not know this myself, but the main people attending that meeting were Herman Goering, head of the Luftwaffe, of course, Albert Speer, the Minister of Armament and War Production, Professor Werner Von Braun and Doctor Martin Schilling, the two main scientists developing Germany's 'Vunder Veapons'. They were at the Chateau, but Hitler called them to Berlin the day of our op. We missed them by hours. You can now see why it was such a vital and prestigious operation."

A vehicle's brakes squealed outside the hut followed by the flight sergeant policeman entering and marching up the room. He slammed to attention in front of the small group of officers and saluted Harry Picton.

"Sah, I'm afraid I am the bearer of bad news. The h'explosion we 'eard was the result of a thousand pound bomb dropping from the bay of H-How and setting off the rest of the bomb load, which 'as destroyed that h'aircraft and badly damaged the one on the next pan, F-Fox, both from 'C' flight. Unfortunately, sah, four armourers are missing and three 'ave been injured. They 'ave been taken to sick quarters. The fire teams have the blaze under control, but it's an 'ell of a mess, Sah."

"What do you mean, missing, Flight?"

"Missing, sah, their bodies cannot be found, but the Chiefy saw them and knows they were there as 'ee was working on F-Fox with the three injured ones."

"Is he Okay?"

Yes, sah, 'ee's Ok."

"Right, thank you, Flight, return to your duties, I am sure they will need your help."

"Sah!"

He saluted, executed his about turn and marched away.

"I suppose the lads would just be vaporised. What a way to go, though," said Joe Kendrick, 'C' flights OC. "I'll get over there and see what I can do."

"I'll come with you, Joe. You two can give your flights the gen. The op still goes on. I'll just phone the Groupie."

As the now depleted 599 Squadron took to the air later that night, there was a reflective quietness about the crews. Death and destruction were their daily business, but the loss of the ground crew and the two aircraft that afternoon had appeared too close to home, more personal somehow. They expected people to die flying bombers over enemy territory, but they did not expect it to take place at 'home'. That night, they all made a conscious effort to double-check their lucky charms, and Johnnie kissed the red-ribboned lock of Ginny's hair and carefully replaced it in the pocket next to his heart.

"The first turning point coming up in five minutes, Skipper; your heading is one-eight-zero," announced Paddy, bringing everyone back to the business in hand.

"Okay, Michael."

Dusty, from his lofty tower, watched as the giant bombers manoeuvred themselves into their vic formations around him, navigation lights twinkling in the moonless summer night. They extinguished them as they crossed 53° north, the turning point sixty miles off the Norfolk coast, and the aircraft became shadowy ghosts in the night as they skimmed over the English Channel.

"Two minutes to French coast, Skipper. Then turn on to a heading of two-three-zero and climb to angels three, which should take us directly to the target in eight minutes."

"Okay, Michael. Pilot to crew; stand by everyone, turning on to target heading, ETA eight minutes. All ready down there, Finlay?"

"Aye, Skipper, ready and willing, as the actress said to the Bishop! Coast a mile ahead, yellow TIs going down as planned. A-Apple and Co are starting to climb."

"Thank you, Finlay, start off-loading Window,"

Johnnie eased back on the control column and Gloria started to slide up to three thousand feet on her new course, the yellow turn indicator flares gently drifting down several thousand feet above them. As they swept inland, heading southwest, light flak, like strings of coloured beads, came weaving up to meet the flight of bombers, but the stream of throbbing aircraft soon passed the hopeful gunners. Within five minutes lights appeared in the distance ahead of them.

"Looks like they have left the bedroom lights on, Skipper," said Chalkie. "They deserve being bombed lit up like that." As he spoke, the floodlights turned off, the night sky returned to darkness, and the flash of guns, and the crump of anti-aircraft fire reminded the crews that this was not just a night-time jolly.

"Two minutes to target."

"Red marker flares ahead, Skipper. Bomb doors open."

"Okay, Bomb Aimer, bomb doors open. You've got her,"

Johnnie reached down to his left-hand side and pushed the bomb door lever down. The bomb aimer turned and opened the viewing panel behind him to check that the doors were fully open, and then turned back to his prone position behind his Mark XIV bombsight.

"Steady as you are ... steady ... steady ... right ... right ... steady ... steadyyyyy ... First bomb's gone! Hold her steady, Skipper."

The exploding flak buffeted Gloria. "Steady ... steady ... Second bomb's gone."

The three bombers in their vic formation, led by Gloria, dropped their high explosives in unison.

"Right on the button, Skipper. Both targets hit. Good shootin', Jock!" cried Yorky from the back. "Someone's been hit. He has an engine flaming. The port kite of the vic behind us; he's pulling up and away to starboard."

"That's 'Pity' Mee in K-King, Skipper," reported Paddy.

As they crossed the ridge of higher ground and flew over the giant concrete bunker, the flak became very intense. Heavy guns had joined the light flak as the lightened bombers, on full power with throttles slammed wide open, roared away under the safe, comforting blanket of darkness.

"Right chaps; well done, Finlay; well done everyone. Now those that can, keep rubbernecking the sky, we have probably woken up a hornet's nest."

He pushed G-George down low as he turned for home, down to fifty feet across the short hop to the sea. He scared the life out of the watch-keepers on a Royal Navy corvette, patrolling a couple of miles off the French coast, as he roared over them, ten feet above their radio mast. There was no time for challenges and replies.

Yorky whooped in surprise as the ship flashed in front of him.

"That's the second time you've upset the sailor boys, Skipper. Do it three times and I think the punishment is keel hauling," he cackled.

They completed their final circuit of the airfield and touched down at 0135 hours in the morning of September 2, 1943.

"Home at last, chaps, home at last."

As they waited by the tail of G-George for the transport to take them back for de-briefing, Lancasters were returning and taxiing to their dispersal pans. The wreckage of the two 'C' flight aircraft was still just visible in the moonless night further round the perimeter track.

A red flare lit up the approach to the runway as a Lanc came in on three engines. They all turned to watch his attempt to land.

"It's K-King," said Yorky.

"That's Pity Mee's kite, isn't it, Skipper?" asked Algy. "Christ, he's only got one leg down; look, his port wheel's still up."

The inner port engine was still, its propeller feathered and stopped. The undercarriage below it had not come down as the starboard one had. With hearts in their mouths, they watched as the giant bomber's one wheel touched down. Peter Mee kept the port wing high until gravity forced it down. It bit into the concrete of the runway and K-King slewed round, travelling at close to a hundred miles an hour. The wing crumpled and broke. The petrol tanks ruptured and the contents, several hundreds of gallons of high octave aviation fuel, ignited on contact with the red-hot engines. The explosive shockwave hit the horrified watchers as a physical assault. A ball of black-cloaked, yellow and orange flame engulfed the aircraft and its crew. The sound of the explosion was terrifying and it continued to echo round the airfield for several seconds. Clanging bells of the racing fire engines and ambulances, flickering flames that lit the night, the towering column of black smoke, created a horrific scenario of fire and death. Twice, within twelve hours, tragedy had struck RAF Elkington. Another seven brave young men had perished in the service of their country when they thought they were safely home.

Johnnie took breakfast early that morning. What was the point of sleep? It only brought images of the previous night to mind. He had lost another crew; more men had died under his command. He knew that casualties were inevitable, but it was still very difficult to except the unrelenting responsibility of command.

Ginny slid on to the seat next to him before he even realised. When he did, he beamed in relief at her presence.

"Hello, darling." She threaded her arm through his, conscious of mess ethics that said 'no touchy'. "How are you?"

"All the better for seeing you, believe me," he smiled at her and squeezed her hand.

"I had a feeling you might be here early. I am so sorry about Peter Mee and his crew. Do you know why it happened?"

Bluntly, he said, "Yes. His luck ran out."

He was silent as she ordered her food from the stewardess, and then he said, almost desperately, "Look, can we try to get away this weekend? I just want to spend some time alone with you. Just the two of us away from this bloody war."

"Oh, darling, I can't, I'm on duty all weekend; in fact, I'm on duty from today until Tuesday morning. I am so sorry.

There's nothing more I would rather do than spend the weekend with you ... alone."

Her meaning was not lost on him and he squeezed her hand gently, raised it to his lips, and kissed her fingers softly.

"Would you like more coffee, sir?" asked the stewardess.

"Er ... no, er, thank you," he stumbled, as she walked away with a grin on her face.

Ginny giggled delightfully at his embarrassment at being 'caught'.

"What time do you finish tonight?"

"It depends if there are ops tonight. Do you know if there are any?"

"No, I've not seen any battle orders yet. You'd see them before me anyway."

"I'll try to get a message to you later to let you know, all right?"

"Yes, if there is no op let's meet anyway, even if we only end up down the 'Oak', I would just like to spend some time with you."

Harry waved away his offer to write the letters to Peter Mee's family and those of his crew.

"Thank you, Johnnie, but it comes with the job. Unfortunately, it is a much more regular occurrence these days. I think we should drink their health tonight, old son, how about it?"

"Yes, I think you're right, Harry."

The 'three tonner' dropped off the dozen or so officers outside the Royal Oak later that night after they had dined in the mess and then gathered in the bar afterwards. However, the atmosphere was too depressing and they needed a lift. The Royal Oak, with its mixture of locals and aircrews, both officers and NCOs and some pretty WAAFs, was the ideal place.

Ginny found him there, later, stationed at the side of the piano with Harry, mugs of beer swaying in their hands, singing their heads off with the rest of Gloria's crew and many others from the squadron, telling the morbid story of a dying airman, to the old army tune, 'The Dying Lancer'.

*'The young Aviator lay dying,
And as in the hangar he lay, he lay,
To the mechanics who round him were standing,
These last parting words he did say.*

*Take the cylinder out of my kidneys,
The connecting rod out of my brain, my brain,
The cam box from under my backbone,
And assemble the engine again.*

*When the court of enquiry assembles,
Please tell them the reason I died, I died,
Was because I forgot 'twice Iota,'
Was the minimum angle of glide.'*

She smiled fondly at him and retired to the snug with a couple of other abandoned girlfriends.

Johnnie and the survivors carried on, as is the way of RAF aircrews, celebrating life and the sudden death of their friends, because this time next week, their friends could be doing the same for them.

The next few weeks saw many new faces joining 599. Replacement crews and aircraft appeared nearly every day until the squadron was back to its complement of thirty-two heavy bombers. Experience and skill were the criteria for selecting the new crews. Their aircraft were updated with the latest technology in bombsights and radar as 599 was fast becoming one of the top squadrons in Bomber Command.

Dusty asked what the new dome was underneath the rear of Gloria, towards the tail. Johnnie explained it was the new H2S radar navigational aid.

"Remember, Michael, Algy and I went on that course at Woodhall Spa a few weeks ago."

"I think I was off sick then. How will it help us?"

"It's a downward looking radar system that can distinguish easily between water, land and even built-up areas. It helps to identify the target more precisely and is a great aid for Michael and his navigation. The Pathfinder Force has used it since earlier this year, but the crack squadrons like Six-One-Seven and us, now warrant it. It also provides a better watchful eye, 'Fishpond', for identifying attacking fighters from behind than the current 'Monica' radio pulse system. Algy has a small screen in front of him and this reflects the signals from the unit. It transmits a radar beam from the rotating transmitter in the bulge that points down and backwards sending out signals in a giant fan shape. If an aircraft comes into that fan, Algy will see it. We'll show you how it works while we're doing the NFT, okay?"

"Sure, Skipper. The trophies are adding up nicely," he said, pointing to Gloria's nose art.

Nine black bombs and a red one for the sortie to Berlin, an ice cream cone for Italy and three swastikas for the night fighters shot down, were now painted alongside the scantily dressed 'Gloria'.

"Roll on when there's thirty on there, Skipper."

"Amen to that."

The next two weeks were relatively quiet for 599 Squadron. Ginny and Johnnie started to spend as much time as possible together; their friends and colleagues started making comments about them, saying if you wanted to speak to one, look for the other.

Harry Picton had the crews carrying out training flights over varied terrain, flying in close formation and at low-level, both in daylight and at night. He and his crew joined them in constant bombing practice and 'fighter affiliation' exercises, making sure the new pilots were as competent as the rest of the squadron at low-level precision bombing that was now one of their specialities.

\*\*\*

"Hey, Yorky, you're goin' to realise your dream again," said Dusty as they left the briefing hut. "We're going to Italy again. Do yer think we've got time to pop into Venice and have a bash at a gondola?"

"Very funny, it just means I'm gonna freeze me bollocks off as we go over the Alps again."

"Yeah, but you'll warm them up again when we land in North Africa. Have you been there, Yorky?"

"No, but a fellow from 'C' flight reckons it's full of sand, flies and scorpions, and is bloody 'ot, I don't fancy that bugger. I don't understand if we're goin' to bomb Friedrichshafen in Germany why the 'ell do we have to go all the way to Africa if they want us to bomb La Spezia in Italy as well?"

"Well it's sort of on the way back home, isn't it? It cuts down the hours we're flying, which can't be a bad thing."

"Did the SIO say we were bombing the Zeppelin factory in Friedrichshafen? I didn't realise they still had them old things."

"No, you clot," laughed Dusty. "They make aeroplanes there now and probably something to do with this rocket thing. He did say something about radio dishes as well. I don't know, we'll just carry on regardless, me old cocker."

"What about Italy then? Are we after the docks?"

"Were you at that bloody briefing or not?"

"Yeah, but I wasn't really paying attention. I was trying to figure out what was wrong with my upper port gun; it's been misfiring a few times lately."

"We're after the naval base there and an oil depot. I wonder what the flak will be like there. I don't think the 'Eyeties' are any good, are they? It'll be a hot reception in Friedrick-what's-um-call-it though. An air gunner from Scampton was telling me he was there a couple of months ago and he said the flak was hell."

The 'air gunner from Scampton' was right. The flak was heavy. They had planned to bomb from 8-10,000 feet, but the flak had driven them up to 15,000 feet, but the eighty Lancasters escaped unscathed and turned south towards Algeria.

They didn't have long to enjoy the warmth of Africa – just a few hours of snatched sleep, a meal and by eight o'clock the next night they were airborne back over the Mediterranean heading for Northern Italy, refuelled for the long journey home, and rearmed with high explosive for their diversion to La

Spezia naval base. As Dusty predicted the 'Eyeties' were not very good and the desultory flak that came up at them was not a serious threat. Nine hours after taking off from Blida in Algeria, they touched down at Elkington, exhausted, but unmolested. Paddy logged 'Landed Elkington 0515 hrs Sunday 19.9.43'.

Algy greeted Johnnie's 'Home at last, chaps, home at last,' with, "Thank God for that, Skipper, I thought we'd never get here."

Over the next two weeks, even as people and aircraft were joining the squadron, the special raids continued, with ops against more massive bunkers and one against a probable 'Cherry Stone' launch site in northern France called Mimoyecques, and then another in Holland. The aircrews still did not know, officially, that their targets were rocket related. They believed they were development or manufacturing sites for Germany's special radar and defence systems, but that was soon to change.

The news that they were going back to Peenemünde caused a few raised eyebrows at the ops briefing.

"To the northwest of the target we so brilliantly hit the last time we were there are some strange-shaped buildings," explained the SIO. "They are shaped a little like snow skis laid on their sides. There are other structures there as well. We are not sure what they are, but we suspect they could be some type of experimental launch ramp for attacking bombers. They were not touched last time, so we want to destroy them this time. Hence, this little sojourn has the code-name 'Ski Jump'. Again, we think there are links to the secret defence systems that the Jerries are trying to develop; to find, identify and destroy British bombers in the dark," he lied smoothly. "So, it is in your interest you get this one spot on."

The Navigation Leader had briefed the navigators in detail before the main briefing, but now went through it again for captains of aircraft and air bombers. They were to cross the western Danish coast at Ribe, then go between the islands of Zeeland and Funen flying out over the Baltic as if the target was Danzig in Poland. But as they passed the southern tip of

Bornholm Island, they would start dropping Window and abruptly turn due south until they crossed the Polish coastline, before turning northwest to come up to the target from a completely different direction from the last attack in August. Some of the accompanying Pathfinder Mosquitos would also start dropping Window, but they would carry on and drop illumination flares and incendiary bombs on Danzig, further up the Baltic coast, as a diversion to attract and confuse night fighters.

The squadron would then turn and fly up the peninsular that was Peenemünde, directly to their target on the northwestern tip. The remaining PFF Mosquitos would drop green TIs to mark the Target. Navigation was much simpler now they were using H2S; they had used it for the last few ops. It could clearly define the difference between land and sea, making navigation much more positive and accurate.

Johnnie had not been able to see Ginny all day, until he caught up with her briefly, just before she went on duty the night of the sortie. They promised each other time together in the coming weekend. She watched him board the transport to take him to Gloria out on the dispersal pan and, half jokingly, said to herself, "He spends more time with her than he does with me. Look after him for me, Gloria."

As Gloria approached the coast of Denmark, Paddy asked,

"Do you believe this bull-shit about 'secret radar' sites, Johnnie?"

Johnnie remembered the briefing when the Groupie had described the 'Wunderwaffen' for the first time.

"I don't know, Michael, I suppose it could be a cover story."

He hated having to lie to his friend and crewmember, but he was under strict orders.

"It just doesn't sit right with me. I believe there is more to it, so I do. Steer zero-nine-three degrees in two minutes, Skipper."

Just under two hours later, at a height of eight thousand feet, they turned on to their bombing heading marked by the Pathfinder Mosquitos with red Wanganui sky flares. Through the partial covering of cloud, Johnnie caught occasional glimpses of the barren, cold Peenemünde peninsula below them.

"Five minutes to target."

"Thank you, Michael. Stand by, Finlay."

"There's some thicker cloud up ahead, Skipper, but I don't think it will block the TIs ... Jesus Christ! What the hell is that, Skipper?" shouted Jock in alarm.

# 19 ... Vergeltungswaffen II

Lifting out of the patch of thick cloud, five hundred yards ahead, was a giant rocket! A black and white chequered rocket, looking every inch like the typical drawing a child might make of a space ship. As it left the cloud on its thrust to the heavens, a tail of flame, two, three times the length of the missile blasted from its base, transforming the night sky into glaring daylight, and vaporising the cold night air in to a turbulent, twisting column. On the side of the rocket could clearly be seen the markings V-49.

The noise it produced was the loudest thing Johnnie had ever heard in his life. The whole of their aircraft was shaking and vibrating as if being shaken by an invisible mighty hand. Algy leapt to his feet and stuck his head into the astrodome and stood there looking up, transfixed. Yorky had shouted, 'What's goin' on, what's goin' on?' until he too could see the frightening sight of the future roaring heavenwards above his head. Frozen in shock in his Plexiglas bubble, Jock stared in disbelief. Dusty, was facing aft, but swung his turret round, terrified by the glaring light, the thunderous noise and vibration that stunned him into silent shock to see the rocket speeding upwards directly in front of them,

"I told you it was bullshit!" cried Paddy. "I told you!"

In the few brief seconds they watched, the rocket accelerated upwards away from them at a terrifying speed until it had blasted out of sight. The only proof that it ever existed was the white vapour trail, its churning column stretching through the night sky, curving away over the Baltic Sea.

Chalkie stood next to Johnnie with his mouth wide open pointing at the empty sky as Gloria broke through the thick vapour trail, leaving swirling eddies behind her.

Astounded by what had just taken place, Johnnie realised that for the last few seconds Gloria had been flying herself. He jerked back to reality and started to fly his bomber again, and took charge as the intercom filled with shocked and frightened voices.

"Okay, everybody, that was bloody terrifying, I know, but we still have a job to do, let's get on with it," he ordered, "Michael, how long to target?"

"Two minutes to target, Skipper."

"Bomb Aimer; get ready for the bombing run. Gunners, rubber-neck the skies for fighters."

"Green TIs dead ahead, Skipper; more going down. Open bomb doors."

"Bomb doors open."

The control lever went down and the two thirty-three foot doors swung smoothly open.

"Left left a bit ... left left ... left left ... steady ... steady ... steadyyyyy ... BOMBS GONE!"

After the nerve jangling seconds Johnnie had to fly 'straight and level' for the execution of the photo flash flare, he dived Gloria to starboard out over the Baltic Sea as the dreaded black, fire filled ack-ack balls started to explode all around the squadron, and ribbons of tracer decorated the sky. Other Lancs copied his actions and they galloped away across the sea leaving the arching vapour trail of the rocket scarring the sky.

"Now we know why we came back here," said Paddy. "And it wasn't for fucking radar scanners!"

"Why didn't the bastards tell us the truth? Can't we be bloody trusted?" shouted Yorky.

"In all my time in the RAF, I've ne'er bin' so shite scared as that," said Jock. "Is that what we're fightin'? 'Cos if it is, we have fucking lost! That bastard must have been fifty-sixty foot long, for Chri'sake!"

"All right, all right, calm down everyone!" said Johnnie firmly. "That was a shock to us all, I know, but we are still over enemy territory and we have a job to do ... well done on the bombing everyone, well done."

"Did you know about that, Skipper," asked Algy, very calmly.

"I did not know that a bloody great rocket like that was down there, and I do not believe Group knew either. The flight commanders were aware there was suspicious activity going on down there, but Group thought it was something to do with small flying bombs. Not bloody great things like that, and we could not tell you anything about that because it was top-secret; we had to feed you some duff gen; I am sorry; there was nothing I could do."

"Aye, Skip, I can see that. Sorry fo' loosin' ma' rag."

"That's Okay, Finlay."

"Yes, I'm sorry, Johnnie, I should have kept my mouth shut."

"That's all right, Michael, we were all in shock, I think. Those that can, write down everything you saw; every detail, no matter how small; it could be useful for the SIO. Michael, can you work out where, exactly, it came from and what its course and speed were."

"Will do, Skipper."

"Gunners keep sharp. They know we have seen that; night fighters could be chasing us all the way back home. Finlay, man the front turret. Algy, send a coded signal to Group saying, 'Operation complete; have interesting Intel; confirm Wunderwaffen'; nothing more than that for now. Now let's concentrate on getting home. Max throttles, Chalkie, you okay?"

"Yea, just a bit shook up, I suppose. Was fucking scary tho' Skipper."

"Succinctly put, Chalkie," he laughed.

Three hours later, they had made Elkington without any more unpleasant surprises. The only surprise was the lack of night fighters over the Western Denmark coast.

"Home at last, Skipper, home at last," said Chalkie, beating Johnnie to the point.

Ginny was watching from the control tower as the squadron came home, checking each Lanc as it touched down. Thirty had gone out and she counted them all back in. With immense relief in her heart, she heard that G-George had touched down. Over the last couple of weeks, she had realised how much Johnnie meant to her, and now when he left on an op she was on edge and fretted until his beloved Gloria gently kissed the runway and brought him back home to her.

"Thank you, Gloria."

The briefing room was alive with sound as all the crews were trying to tell their own version of what they had witnessed. The buzz had gone round the camp that something special had taken place and the SIO had pulled in every member of his staff and every senior officer available to record the crews' experiences. None was more valuable than G-George crewmembers' stories. Ginny tried to make sure it would be she that talked to Johnnie and his crew, but the SIO insisted on getting their story himself. They had been the front aircraft nearest to the rising rocket.

Harry Picton spoke to Johnnie after sitting in on his debrief.

"Trust me to miss the most exciting thing to happen in years. Well, we knew something special was happening there, but not this. Now we know what those large circular features on the photos were for."

The Station Commander joined them.

"Harry, we have a potential security nightmare situation here. Word of this must not, I repeat, must not go out of this room. I am just going to contact Group. How do you propose to stop the gossip?" said Group Captain Thompkins.

"Me?"

"Yes, you. You are the Squadron Commander, are you not?"

"Yes, sir. I'll talk to the Senior Security Officer and we'll come up with something."

"Okay. Nevertheless, it must not leave this building. There would be absolute panic if the public got a hold of this."

He walked away from them and, on his way out, talked to the terrifying RAF Police Flight Sergeant, emphasising his point with his leather-bound cane and pointing to the door.

"Johnnie, can you find the SSO while I find Ray Britton. We'll meet in the SIO's office."

Five minutes later, they were all sitting in the small office in the corner of the briefing room. The other two flight commanders had joined them.

"I've given Flight Sarn't Pidkin instructions that no one leaves here until we have decided how to handle this," said Harry.

"The crews are knackered, hungry and tired, sir," said Joe Kendrick. "We need to let them go as soon as possible."

"I agree." said the station second-in-command, Wing Commander Ray Britton. "A quick answer to the problem, Wing Commander, would be to talk to everyone now and clarify the situation and the consequences of a breach of security. Short, sharp and to the point, agreed?"

They all agreed and went back into the briefing room. Harry climbed up on the raised platform and commanded attention.

"No, it's all right, Wing Commander, I'll speak to the crews."

Ray Britton climbed up next to Harry, who called for order.

"Gentlemen, what you saw tonight, besides being a shock, is of immense national importance. We have suspected for a long time that Jerry had something like this up his sleeve, and if we, Bomber Command, are to combat it, then absolute security is essential, word of this *must not*, *must not* go outside of this room without express permission. Besides scaring the locals to death, it could jeopardise the plans we already have to tackle this threat to the progress of this war. Any mention of what you saw at Peenemünde to anyone else outside this room will result in a Court Martial and subsequent execution of the most severe of punishments." He raised his voice and said firmly. "Do you understand me, gentlemen?"

"Yes, sir," came the reply from all.

"Good! Well done tonight, an excellent report from your flight commanders on how you all reacted and how you carried on with your job and carried out, what seems to have been a successful op. Go and get your bacon and eggs."

A cheer went up as crews filed into the aircrew mess for their, now traditional, breakfast.

The next morning, the tannoy system blared out the message for all aircrews to attend the briefing room at 1100 hours.

"For security reasons, it has been difficult to keep you informed of the true purpose of some of your ops. I am afraid that situation will carry on. I will tell you what I can about your ops, but the nature of the beast means that security will remain tight."

Group Captain Thompkins went on to explain that the squadron was now part of a special team of squadrons put together to combat the rocket threat from Germany. Their last few ops had been exactly that, and for the next few months, they would continue being part of that spearhead group. He praised them for their results and their bravery and announced that three DFMs, one bar to a DFM, one DFC and two 'Mention in Dispatches' would be awarded to members of the squadron in the next few weeks.

"I'm sure that you understand why we have had to keep a lid on the real reasons for selecting your recent targets, but I am confident that you will not let this affect your performance as one of the top squadrons of Bomber Command, nay, the Royal Air Force. Thank you, gentlemen."

A chorus of whistles, cheers and applause echoed round the room as he walked down the central aisle smiling and touching his cane to his hat several times in salute.

"You've got to hand it to him," said Paddy to Algy. "He knows how to butter them up, so he does. And they love him."

"I am delighted to announce that the bar to the DFM is going to you, Yorky, for bagging one and a half JU-eighty-eights on the Berlin raid. Well done," announced Johnnie. "So the beers are on you tonight, Yorky."

Gloria's crew all gathered round a grinning Yorky, clapping him on the back and shaking his hand.

"Oh, by the way, Dusty, you'll be paying a third of the beer bill tonight," said Johnnie, with a smile.

"Why me?"

"Because you're one of the 'Mentioned in Dispatches', well done."

Yorky was the first to grab his hand and pump it up and down.

The Royal Oak's rafters rang again that night to the sound of brave young men being young men. Ginny and a few of the other WAAFs joined in the celebrations and the songs. Dusty had brought his brass 'euph' mouthpiece with him and was squirting out popular and ribald service songs with it, accompanied by Pilot Officer 'Doc' Whaites on the pub's battered old piano, while Johnnie pretended surprise that Ginny and the WAAFs knew the words to many of the risqué songs.

"Ginny, shocking! What would your mother say?"

"My mother taught me the words," she cheerfully laughed back. "And Betty the barmaid knows them all too, look at her."

Betty was singing her head off as she pulled pints of beer. She had been the barmaid in the 'Oak' since the camp on the hill had opened. The statuesque, buxom farmer's daughter from the next village, just up the road, could handle any airman's song no matter how crude it got; in fact, she could handle any airman no matter how crude *he* got ... full stop!

The party went on all night until 'Bob' Down, the landlord, rang the bell at ten o'clock and thankfully threw the towels over the pumps as he shouted, 'Time, Gentlemen, Please! Time, Ladies and Gentlemen please!'

Half an hour later, he could still hear the strains of 'Barnacle Bill' as the last truck carried the happy airmen and women over the hill to the camp a mile and a half away.

"Had a good night, Bob?" said another Bob, Bob Vickery, the local policeman who rode up on his rickety old bicycle.

"Not bad at all, Bob. They were celebratin'. Some of the lads 'av been awarded medals, DFMs, I think?"

"Ay, the buggers deserve 'em an' all. Bit different to our war, eh, Bob, all this flyin' and bombin'."

"Yar got time fer a pint, Bob?"

"Well ... seein' as yer askin'," he smiled. "Anybody in?"

"Just Jack Richards and his dad."

PC Vickery took off his bike clips and helmet, and joined the landlord and the two farmers at the bar of the darkened pub for a welcome out-of-hours pint of bitter.

# 20 ... Most Secret

The message was short and simple, addressed to Squadron Leaders W. Askin, A.I. Kendrick and J.J. Sanderson, 599 Squadron RAF Elkington. The three flight commanders of the squadron.

'You are to report to Group Head Quarters at 0900 hours tomorrow, Saturday 9 September, 1943.'

An RAF policeman showed them into the operations room at Bawtry Manor, the country house used by 1 Group, Bomber Command, as their HQ.

A large table dominated the central space, surrounded by twenty or so chairs. At the end of the room was a low platform with steps leading up from the side. A giant map of Europe covered the wall at the rear of the platform and blinds covered the four sets of windows. Green shaded electric light bulbs glared brightly from the ceiling, flooding the room with a hard, stark light.

They all spun round as the doors crashed open and their boss, Wing Commander Harry Picton, led in a group of five senior RAF officers and two civilians. The three flight commanders came to attention at the sight of so much 'top brass', who made their way to the top of the table and settled themselves in the chairs, except Picton, who remained on his feet.

"Sit down, gentlemen," said Picton, after a pause, indicating the chairs in front of them.

"Let me introduce the Air Officer Commanding One Group, Bomber Command, Air Vice Marshal Rice, Air Vice Marshal Nelson from the Air Ministry, and of course, you know the CO of Elkington, Group Captain Thompkins. Group Captain Woodfield is from Air Intelligence and these two gentlemen," turning to the two civilians, "are Professor Richard Kemble and Doctor Charles Ankers." He paused, and looked straight at his flight commanders. "Treat the information you will hear today in absolute confidence; it's top-secret, gentlemen. Air Vice Marshal Rice?"

"Thank you, Wing Commander. Gentlemen, you may smoke if you must," intimated the AVM, but nobody took up his offer. "I apologise for the short notice of this meeting, but we only got clearance from the Air Ministry yesterday. You and your squadron recently experienced a unique event. You unwittingly witnessed an extraordinary development of modern warfare, the launch and flight of a ballistic missile, a dramatic and terrifying weapon in the hands of our enemy. This is one of what Mr Albert Speer, the German Minister for Armament and War Production, has called, 'Vergeltungswaffen', vengeance or retaliatory weapons. They consider these 'Wunderwaffen' as retribution against the mass bombing of German cities. You are aware of the smaller rocket-powered weapon, 'Cherry Stone', and you are successfully carrying out operations against installations related to that."

He leant forward and placed his folded arms on the table.

"Because of what you saw at Peenemünde this week, the War Cabinet has decided to bring forward an operational plan, which has been developing over the last few weeks, to combat these threats. Because of your excellent record recently, you have earned the right to carry out a vitally important mission, even more important than the raid on Chateau-Thierry. The tactical and technical details you will receive later. I am here to emphasise the vital importance of this event. Your squadron will carry out a bombing raid that will alter the course of this war if you succeed. That is not an exaggeration; that is a fact. If you fail … well, that is not an option, as you will learn. There are great difficulties and dangers to overcome on this sortie, but with training, dedication and courage, you will earn the gratitude of, not just this nation, but also the western civilised world."

He paused to allow the magnitude of his words to permeate their slightly shocked brains.

"Let me introduce to you one of this country's finest scientists, Professor Richard Kemble, who will explain further. Professor?"

"Thank you, er, Vice Marshal er, sorry, *Air* Vice Marshal," he corrected himself, with a smile.

Kemble was something that a cartoonist would have drawn if he were drawing a 'boffin'. He was tall and thin, wearing a shapeless, tweed suit. His greying hair had obviously declared its independence years ago and was probably a stranger to a comb. His long, horse-like face had the colourless pallor of a long-term prisoner and his sharpened nose had a permanent dampness about the end, which he kept dabbing at with a violently coloured handkerchief. However, his eyes were the windows to his true character. They were a sharp piercing blue; light appeared to emanate from them as if he was trying to send out his own brightness and intelligence. They commanded attention.

"Gentlemen, we are in grave danger."

The three observers looked at each other in alarm. He ignored their reaction and carried on.

"Not only of being left behind in the technological war, but also of losing the war itself. German scientists have advanced their aviation technology much quicker than we anticipated. Raids on Peenemünde and other rocket weapon development-sites over the last few months have been a great success. We now know that those raids set back their 'Vergeltungwaffen' rocket production and experimental programme by many months. The Fieseler One-O-Three Flying Bomb, 'Cherry Stone', was the first Vengeance weapon, the V-One if you like, and the A Four rocket, the one you saw, is the second, V-Two, but, we believe there are many more in its family."

Here Group Captain Woodfield coughed, nervously, purposely. The professor glanced at him then carried on.

"Some people believed that the German rocket programme was dead in the water. I did not, and after your exciting experience, I am sure you do not either. I know it is even more advanced than it was in August. But, the first raid on Peenemünde, I do believe, delayed their use of devastating rocket weapons that could be capable of attacking Russia and the United States of America for a few short months only." He paused and glanced at AVM Nelson. "What *you* witnessed over Peenemünde, gentlemen, is, but the tip of the iceberg.

"You are pilots. You are aware of the developments in aircraft design, engine advancements and deadlier, more powerful weapons. However, what you are probably not aware of is the giant leap in technology that German aviation scientists have made. At this stage, to prevent Group Captain Woodfield perhaps succumbing to a cardiac seizure," he said smiling towards him, "I will only give you the basic facts to underline the consequences of your mission."

He paused and rubbed his chin.

"Britain has, for the last four or five years, been working on Wing Commander Frank Whittle's idea of jet propulsion. A simple small jet engine is easy to make, but it remains a simple small engine with limited power and use. We have seen the effects in the V-One Flying Bomb trials in Germany. However, a jet engine that could turn a three hundred and fifty mile an hour Junkers Eighty-eight into a six hundred and fifty mile an hour fighter plane and a lumbering Dornier bomber into a five hundred mile an hour deadly weapon, three or four times its current size, is a frightening and terrifying image. Ballistic rockets, which can cross the Atlantic, which can attack any target in Europe ... jets and rockets imagine these combined as weapons, combining power, speed and manoeuvrability, a combination that could deliver *the* killer blow to every enemy of the Third Reich. The Germans are developing such an engine. If they get them in the air in numbers then we, America, Russia, and all our allies, will have no option, but to seek terms for a cease-fire with Germany. Surrender, gentlemen, surrender! Germany and its friends will rule the world. A frightening and terrifying image, I am sure you will agree. Regrettably, we are not quite ready to launch our own version yet, so we need to delay their progress a little longer. Group Captain Woodfield, would you like to carry on?"

"Thank you, Professor," he said, looking somewhat relieved. Woodfield was a big man, hard-featured and well made. He gave off an air of great strength and spoke with the carefully modulated tones of the British upper class.

"Everything you have heard so far frightens not only me, but also the privileged select number of people who recognise the facts. We have known the Germans have been working on something dramatic since before the first raid on Peenemünde, and it has taken a great deal of hard work and sacrifice to get the information we now have. We must destroy, at any cost, their chances of overwhelming the allies with these weapons."

He looked at the three young officers as if he were assessing their abilities.

"Nine months ago, guarded by units of the SS and the Wehrmacht, eight hundred slave workers arrived at an isolated valley in the Harz Mountains in central Germany. Their first task was to build hundreds of accommodation huts. This allowed the Germans to move in even more slave workers, thousands of them, to build the complex itself. In a very short time, they have built a massive industrial complex, including research facilities and an enormous production and test plant. How do we know all of this? Not all Germans have the same fanatical Nazi attitude to world domination as the moustached little house painter. We have received a supply of information from the area for a while. Combine luck, tragedy, unbelievable bravery and a hatred of evil and you come up with the answer to how we obtained our information. We got our breakthrough four months ago. A Dutch-Jewish engineer, a forced-worker, recognised certain aspects of their programme. He had already made contact with a small local group of German Jews and he communicated his suspicions on to them. They had the freedom to start their own secret underground line of communication, and so when that information could be passed on to the allies, it was."

Again, he paused to consider his audience.

"Now comes the lucky bit. The Germans have played their trump card. Since we have targeted their rocket launch and production sites, they have created a deterrent to bombing this factory complex. They extended the camp again and thousands of allied Prisoners of War moved in. They transferred, from many Luftwaffe guarded camps, four thousand-five hundred US airmen and over three thousand RAF POW. However, as we know, RAF chaps are an industrious and ingenious set of people. So, it wasn't long before London was receiving messages."

He looked at the three flight commanders in turn.

"The Germans are developing and producing test vehicles of terrifying power at this site. They are weapons that *will* win the war for them. We do not know exactly how far they have developed them, but we really cannot wait to find out. We have to stop them *now*! Moreover, you, gentlemen, are the men to do it! This entire situation is taking place in a gorge-like valley, high in the mountains in the heart of Germany. Regiments of SS, regiments of anti-aircraft batteries and Mother Nature herself protect it. The geography of the site makes certain that a successful high-level bombing raid is almost impossible. The mountains, a narrow gorge with a massive overhanging wall, and the presence of a very large number of susceptible people, make it necessary to find an alternative way to destroy – *completely* – this facility."

Here he removed his glasses, pulled a brilliant white handkerchief from his tunic sleeve and proceeded to polish with vigour his clouded lenses.

"The alternative, we believe, is a precision, low-level attack; this is where you come in. You have carried out, very successfully, several low-level precision operations and my Boss, ACM Harris, believes Five-Nine-Nine is the ideal squadron for this op."

He turned to AVM Nelson and slowly smiled. Turning back, he said,

"We have code-named it 'Operation Parliament', and the attacking aircraft will be known as 'G Force'. However, somebody high up has suggested that as the operation will take place in November, the destroyers of parliament will have the operational name 'Guy Fawkes'!" He smiled at the seated officers. "Air Vice Marshal Nelson, the floor is yours."

Air Vice Marshal Horace Nelson was of the old RAF. In fact, he was of the old Royal Flying Corps, having served for the last two years of the Great War as a pilot of distinction in the RFC before the forming of the RAF in 1918. He had then served with 'Butch' Harris in the early 1920s whist in Mesopotamia, helping him to develop the first ever heavy bomber, a converted cargo aircraft, the Vickers Vernon biplane. Nelson had saved the lives of many British troops by turning a blind eye to a Harris's order and carrying out a single-handed bombing raid on an attacking Arab force, driving them back from the susceptible troops. Unfortunately, small arms fire ruptured his fuel tanks and he crash-landed in the desert, badly injuring his right eye, leaving him blind in that eye and scarred across and above his eyebrow. It then took him four days to lead his remaining crewmembers out of the desert and walk to civilization. The medal ribbons, led by a plain, purple ribbon carrying a small metal cross on his left breast, indicated that experience and his bravery.

"Thank you, Group Captain," he paused. "Yes, gentlemen, you are going to blow up the Houses of Parliament!"

Now everybody smiled.

He carried on, "But you're not going to blow up the whole of Parliament."

"Shame," was the stage whisper from Johnnie Sanderson, bringing smiles to his colleagues' faces.

"There are two main areas of this facility and we have named them the 'House of Commons' and the 'House of Lords'. No doubt to your delight, you will be attacking the House of Lords. These are, for security reasons, the only details you will be given for now. I promise you a full and comprehensive briefing nearer the time. Your CO, Group Captain Thompkins and Wing Commander Picton, will give you the tactical information you will require and your training schedule. You are but small in number, but you will take on a very big responsibility and I know, as does Air Chief Marshall Harris, you have the talents, the ability and the courage to succeed. Thank you for your time, gentlemen."

The group of dignitaries rose, collected their papers and pulled on their hats. Picton called the men to attention and saluted the two Air Vice Marshals. AVM Nelson touched the peak of his cap and moved down the room. As they passed through the carved double doors, AVM Rice turned to Nelson and uttered,

"I just hope to God, Horace, that they succeed, and they have better luck than Guido Fawkes and his cronies."

"If they don't, the future will be very grim for all of us."

Two RAF police corporals, who had been guarding the doors against eavesdroppers, silently, closed the impressive portals.

What had just taken place had stunned the three junior officers; their brains were struggling to take in the magnitude of the information given to them. How could the three of them, three lowly squadron leaders, save the world? It was complete madness!

"All right, chaps, please be seated." Picton indicated their chairs to one side of the table while Group Captain Thompkins and he sat on the other side. He removed his cap and placed it with care and precision on the table in front of him.

"I can imagine what is going through your minds at this time," he smiled. "No, neither we, nor the Air Ministry have gone totally doolally." His smile faded to a grey-faced reality as he looked over to his senior companion. "Group Captain?"

"It is a great honour we have been given, gentlemen, and I will make sure that every opportunity is given to you and your crews to carry out this prestigious mission. You will start vigorous training Monday next. I must emphasise observance of the strictest discipline. We cannot have anybody slacking or making stupid, repetitive mistakes. Crack down hard on any infringements of the rules. Also, remember, this mission depends on every member of the squadron being part of the team. ... Tomorrow, you and your other flight leaders will report to the briefing room at Elkington at zero-eight-thirty hours for the first training brief. I know that you *are* the men for the job and *our* squadron will not let the Air Ministry, the Prime Minister or the country down in its hour of need. Good morning, gentlemen."

He stood up, replaced his cap and touched its peak with his leather-bound swagger cane in salute as the four officers stood to attention. "Wing Commander."

"Thank you, sir," replied Picton, as the Groupie ambled out of the room.

When he had left, Picton told them to relax and smoke if they wanted to. All three of them guiltily lit up a cigarette, even Johnnie Sanderson, and he usually smoked a pipe! Picton cadged a cigarette from Bill Askin and a light from Joe Kendrick.

"Well, gents, that was enlightening if nothing else."

"Did you know about this, Harry?" asked Johnnie.

"Yes, I knew our selection was for a special op, but I didn't realise just how important it was. Some of the tactical details I am aware of and it entails us flying in close formation, at low height and at high-speed through a very narrow gorge."

"The op involves the whole of the squadron, divided into five flights of six aircraft in two vic formations, leaving two aircraft as spares. These will be the crews with the least experience or those who do not come through the training well. The code name for the raiding party is 'Guy Fawkes', but we will use the initials, GF, George-Freddie, except me. I will lead the first six aircraft of 'A' flight, my recognition sign will be 'Guy Fawkes One'. Johnnie you will lead the next six, GF Two. Bill, the next six from 'B' flight, GF Three, and your second-in-command, Bill, 'Gunner Hargreaves will lead the next six, GF Four. Joe will lead the back-up flight of six from 'C' flight, GF Five, leaving two spare aircraft and crews. Everyone okay with that?"

They nodded their approval.

"You know as much as I do now. Our meeting tomorrow, with the CO and Ray Britton, will fill in the schedule for the next few weeks. ... Okay, chaps, I think you have had enough thrown at you for now. I want you to go back to Elkington, talk to your ground crew flight chiefs, and make sure that every kite is available for Monday morning. Go and brief your 2 i/cs, have a good night's rest and I shall see you all tomorrow morning. Remember, 'Loose tongues cost lives'! Thank you, gents."

He collected his papers together and left the room.

"Well, as my rear gunner would say, 'Bugger me!'" said Johnnie, mocking Yorky's accent.

\*\*\*

Johnnie and Ginny dined together in the mess that night and he nonchalantly, but tentatively asked her if she was on duty over the next couple of weekends.

"And why would you be asking me that, I wonder?" she smiled at him.

"Well ... er ... you did mention ... um ... er ... that we could possibly spend some leave time together ... somewhere."

"Oh yes, I did, didn't I? Yes, that would be lovely," she said with a mischievous smile.

"Great, wizard, I'll try ..."

She interrupted him. "But it won't be this weekend or next weekend, darling. I have duty for four days starting tomorrow and then I am on nights. I'm sorry, sweetheart, but maybe we can snatch a couple of hours together, if you want to, that is?"

"Yes, of course I do. It was just that I thought we could spend a weekend ..."

She put her fingers to his mouth to stop him talking.

"I know, darling, don't worry, we will find the right time soon, I promise."

The next morning, the five flight leaders met with Thompkins and his second-in-command, Wing Commander Ray Britton. It surprised Johnnie to find Ginny sitting next to the WingCo. She greeted him with a smile. It turned out that Britton would be in charge of the training, with Thompkins having a watching brief.

"Before I lay out the timetable for the training," Britton said, "I would like to tell you we are aiming for the full moon on the 12$^{th}$ of November, and not the 5$^{th}$, unfortunately," he smiled. "That means you and your crews have five weeks to get ready."

"Ray, as you know, I have some knowledge of the op and what the requirements will be, but five weeks, that seems a very short time scale," said Harry Picton.

"My thoughts exactly when the Groupie told me, Harry. Then he explained the bigger picture to me, and that is even more hush-hush than this is. All I can tell you is that we are just part of a larger exercise. This, gentlemen, is the type of sortie you only get once in a blue moon. I believe that the time allowed is realistic for the skills and levels of experience we have in the squadron. It will not be easy; in fact, it will be bloody hard work."

He smiled, and went on, "Talking about moons, the moon will be right from the 5$^{th}$ November until the 19$^{th}$, with the full moon on the 12$^{th}$, and these dates are, of course, strictly confidential. I might add there will be no involvement in any further bombing sorties not connected to this mission, for the next few weeks. But don't make any plans for the weekends."

Johnnie looked at Ginny and grimaced.

"You will be busy. All thirty-two squadron aircraft will take part in training up to the last week, when we shall select the final thirty that will go on the sortie. Those who do not go will most probably be the least skilled and the sick and lame. But I want every crew capable of doing the job, I want every man totally committed to his job and I want every aircraft fit to do its job."

The Group Captain interjected.

"Right, Wing Commander, I will leave you to cover the minutiae of the training schedule. By the way, gentlemen, Miss Murphy here will be our liaison with Air Vice Marshal Nelson and Group Captain Woodfield of Intelligence. You don't need me, do you?" he asked Ray Britton.

"Er ... no sir, not at the moment."

"Right then, I will tend to other duties. Good morning, gentlemen and lady."

They all stood as he exited the room.

Wing Commander Britton then went on to spend the next three hours breaking down each week's training aims and achievement targets in precision bombing, formation flying, navigation and ground gunnery, finishing with:

"There will be a full crew briefing at 0800 hours, here tomorrow, Monday morning, where we will tell them the very bare bones of the sortie, the need for specialist training, the training schedule, the fact it will be a low-level job and the vital importance of their efforts. We will also remind them of the Official Secrets Act and its consequences."

He looked towards Harry, who said, "As I said earlier, we shall be flying in five flights, but what you didn't know is that each flight will be flying eight seconds behind each other at two hundred and fifty miles an hour. Three abreast at fifty feet apart. Oh, and by the way, our height will be two hundred and twenty feet."

"Formation flying in a Lanc! I know some squadrons that can't fly in the same county without banging into each other, never mind fifty feet apart," laughed Joe.

"Your immediate task is to teach your flights to fly in tight formation at two hundred and fifty miles per hour at two hundred feet. They did well for the Château-Thierry op so I have every confidence in them."

He leaned back and lit a cigarette, drawing the smoke in deeply.

WingCo Britton took over.

"We should all be ready to start at 0800 hours tomorrow morning. Each Friday, we will go through a post-mortem of the week's efforts and each Monday morning there will be a squadron brief to emphasise the major points of the week ahead. The weekends will be used to bring up to scratch any problems, and problem crews, identified during the week. God knows when we will get a weekend off, never mind some leave!"

He finished with a smile.

Ginny smiled sadly at Johnnie.

Johnnie and Ginny spent time together, if you can call being in a pub full of riotous aircrew spending 'time together', but they enjoyed their snatched hours in each other's company.

Both knew that the next few weeks would be busy and the opportunities of spending time together could be rare.

# 21 ... Training

The large briefing room was full to overflowing with aircrews, some even standing down the sides leaning against the wooden walls. The two hundred and twenty young men were keen to know what the point of this briefing was. The unusual sight of a flight of 'Snowdrop' policemen both outside, checking everyone's ID, and inside, acting as guards on the doors, sent the buzz of conversation round the room. Absence of the normal maps and diagrams on the small raised daïs made them wonder if they were not going to hear the now infamous words, 'The target for tonight is ...' Each crew had tended to gather round its Skipper, cigarette and pipe smoke drifting up to wreath the rafters.

To the normal accompaniment of scraping chairs, the crews got to their feet and came to attention as a 'flight' of senior officers entered and made their way to the front. The fact that two of the senior officers were Air Vice Marshals surprised the crews. Squadron OC, Harry Picton, came to the centre of the podium and waved the crews down saying,

"Be seated." After a pause, "The target for tonight is ..." he paused again and smiled as a low groan swept across the room. "There will be no bombing targets or ops for you over the next few weeks."

After a moment's stunned silence, the room exploded to the sound of cheering, shouting and whistling. Smiling he waved them to silence. "That doesn't mean we will let you loaf around doing nothing. (Groans) The squadron is to carry out a special op, something very different from your normal day-to-day bombing run. Air Officer Commanding One Group, Air Vice-Marshal Rice, will explain ... Air Vice Marshal?"

"Thank you, Squadron Leader Picton."

He moved towards the front of the daïs, an imposing figure with a long face, a clipped, blunt moustache and narrow hooded eyes.

"Yes, gentlemen. Bomber Command has nominated Five-Nine-Nine for a special operation. One of the most important our group has ever undertaken. Air Chief Marshal Harris and the War Committee have selected the target. They know it will be very difficult to attack and very difficult to destroy. But they are confident that Five-Nine-Nine Squadron are the men for the job."

Some ironic cheering greeted his words.

"Over the next few weeks you will be working hard. You will be flying in difficult circumstances, you will be facing great danger, but I am sure you will face those dangers as you have already done so many times in the past, with tenacity, temerity and unbelievable personal courage. Good luck, gentlemen."

The Station Commander, Thompkins, now addressed the gathered aircrews, his cut glass syllables gracing his audience.

"The next few weeks *will* be hard, but I know that the men of this squadron are well and truly capable of absolute success on this crucial and decisive mission. What is your mission? Air Vice Marshal Nelson from Air Chief Marshal Harris's tactical staff will explain it in more detail."

He moved to the side leaving centre stage for the ACM's advisor.

"Thank you, Charles. I can only give you a certain amount of information now, because most of it still top-secret. However, I cannot emphasise to you how important this raid is. The success of this mission, against a very challenging and dangerous target, will greatly harm the enemy's ability to win this war. You will learn later exactly, what the target is. In the meantime, I ask that you commit yourselves totally to your comprehensive training schedule over the next few weeks. I shall be seeing you on a regular basis, checking that they ..." he indicated the other officers on the daïs and smiled, "... are treating you well and that you are doing what you're told." Again, an ironic cheer brought smiles from the 'Big Wigs'.

"ACM Harris is taking a personal interest in this mission and will be monitoring your progress closely; he also said something about seven days' leave after the op."

Even louder cheers and whistles greeted this news. A smiling AVM Nelson sat down.

Harry Picton now took the stand.

"Your target for this week ..." he waited for the expected groan of derision, but it did not occur, the aircrews had realised that whatever was in the pipeline for them was very serious. There were times and places for levity, this was not one of them. "... is to learn to fly very close to each other, very low and very fast. That is all I want you to concentrate on this week. Over the next few weeks, your training will get harder. Your levels of concentration will be stretched to the limit, as will be your abilities. Nevertheless, believe me, gents, by the end of the next few weeks of training, you will be able to put a Lanc through the eye of a needle. Flight commanders will take you back to your flight huts for further briefing. Thank you, gents.... Flight Commanders please stay behind.... Attention!"

The senior officers left the room accompanied by the usual scrape and squeal of chairs. When the aircrews had departed, Harry Picton addressed the three Flight Commanders.

"Get them in the air as soon as you can. Let's capture their enthusiasm and eagerness and put them to good work. Remember that losses are inevitable; the next few weeks will expose the weaker links; so be ready, gents."

By early afternoon, the squadron was airborne, including Harry Picton leading the first six of 'A' Flight's machines. Johnnie had briefed the whole of 'A' flight and was now leading off the second six aircraft in two straight flights of three abreast. He had explained to his pilots that instead of flying in the normal vic three aircraft formation, of one leading and two wingmen to the side and just behind, they would be flying in a straight line three abreast formation, this would offer a smaller target to the enemy gunners as they swept over them at two hundred feet.

That first week they had to learn how to keep station when flying straight and level, and how to turn as if they were one aircraft. They had to keep the same height and the same constant speed with fifty feet between them, half the wingspan of a Lancaster bomber. By the Friday morning, they were all reasonably efficient at flying in formations of three, although the week was not without a few scary near misses.

The Group Captain and WingCo Britton watched the squadron as they did their last passes over the aerodrome on Friday afternoon.

"Well, sir, we've got through the first week without mishap and they're shaping up very well."

"Yes, but we've still a long way to go yet, Ray. We'll see how they get on with their formation flying in the dark."

It started very well. The moon was in its first quarter and the skies were clear and would be for the next few days, so the Met men said! Johnnie led his flight of six Lancs on a cross-country exercise the next night, flying the contours of the Pennine Hills, and was very pleased at the way his pilots and their crews performed, especially the two new replacements that had joined only ten days ago. There were some 'hairy moments', as one of the new pilots, twenty year old Flying Officer Tarquin Scott-Baker, had described his very narrow escape from collision with Johnnie's roommate, 'Ginger' Bere, as they turned sharply up a narrow valley. The Sunday night exercise was not so successful. Two aircraft from Bill Askin's flight did collide as they turned over the airfield on their first take-off. Both were able to land safely, thankfully, not badly damaged, however, the crew of the newly replaced H-How of 'C' flight, flown by Flying Officer Dennis Shepherd, was not so lucky. They all bought it when their aircraft pancaked and exploded after having part of its starboard wing sliced off by Pilot Officer Jimmy Anderson's E-Edward when they went through unexpected low cloud on top of the Cleveland Hills on the Yorkshire Moors. Jimmy Anderson managed to get his kite down at nearby RAF Wombleton near Helmsley, with everyone on board unharmed.

The report at the post flight debriefing was that besides the fatal crash, several 'near misses' had occurred, so Harry Picton suspended night flying, but insisted they carry on with practising their formation flying in daylight. He called for a Flight Commanders' meeting the next morning.

"What the hell went wrong last night? Saturday night everything's fine, they were doing well. So what was the difference last night? We have lost a good crew and an aircraft, and damaged three more. If we carry on like this, by this time next week, there will be no bloody squadron left!"

"The only difference I noticed last night was the moon, there were times when cloud shrouded it and it was not as bright, but we fly like that all the time," said Bill Askin.

"We are fine in daylight, flying in close formation; I just think it will take us a long time to get used to flying that close at night. If we can open up the distances between aircraft then gradually close up the gaps over the next few weeks, that might help," said Jo Kendrick.

"The trouble with that," said Harry. "is we haven't got the time. The schedule is full as it is."

After batting ideas round the table for half an hour, 'Gunner' Hargreaves came up with a suggestion.

"Skipper, I don't know if this is for general knowledge or not, but my bomb aimer, 'Bunny' Warren, reckons that Six-One-Seven trained during the day for their night op by covering the windows of the aircraft with blue cellophane film, and the crews wearing yellow tinted goggles. When combined, apparently, it turns day into night, but in an emergency, you simply remove the goggles. Would it be worth having a word with them about it? It might help us initially. We are flying bloody close to each other in the dark and we're not used to that."

"Bloody good idea, Gunner, I'll get on to it immediately," enthused Harry.

The next afternoon, twelve Lancaster bombers, led by WingCo Harry Picton, took off with the cockpit windows covered in blue film and the pilots, flight engineers and bomb aimers adorned with yellow tinted flying goggles.

"By God, it works, Skipper," said Chalkie. "It really does. You would think it's a moonlit night. Amazing!"

"Jock, how do you find it?"

"It's quite strange, Skipper. You know it's daylight out there, but we're in the dark, strange. It's like having very black sunglasses on, but it's not, if you know what I mean. I suppose it's like flying in soft moonlight; rather unreal because you know you're flying in daylight."

"Yes, I see what you mean, but it does work."

They flew round for an hour to get used to the effect of the film and goggles, and then formed their vics and carried out various turns and manoeuvres, all without incident.

"This really works," said Harry over the RT. "Let's get the rest of the squadron up here."

For the rest of the week, the whole squadron practised night flying by day, without further mishaps. The squadron was going up together and flying in perfect formation. However, could they do it at night, for real?

They answered the question that weekend when they removed the blue film, ditched the yellow goggles, and yes, they could keep their stations on each other safely at speed, at a low height and move in formation. Over Saturday and Sunday, they flew for nearly eight hours in formation, flying from Scotland to Cornwall, Ireland to Norfolk at night, at low-level and at the correct speed.

Harry decided that all the crews had done extremely well and had earned a rest, so declared Monday as a day off for everyone except his three flight commanders.

"Right, gents, they have all done extremely well. The next stage is to get them flying a similar course to the one they will be flying for real on the day. The Directorate of Bombing Operations and the boys from the photoreconnaissance have found us a likely valley in which we can practise. In fact, they have found two for us. One, with a target, similar to our factory, and one that will get them to fly in a tight situation."

He took out a map and spread it on his desk.

"Here's the first valley, in Bilsdale, the Rye Valley," he said indicating with a pencil to the North Yorkshire Moors. "As you can see, it goes from Stokesley down to Helmsley. There's RAF Wombleton," he indicated the nearby airfield where Jimmy Anderson had recently put his damaged aircraft down.

"What about the weather up there, Harry? It cost us dear the last time," said Johnnie, referring to the accident.

"That's why we've got the other one to go at. That's here, look." He pointed to the valley that cut across Saddleworth Moor, near Huddersfield. "There's a giant wool mill up this side valley, ideal for our purpose. I want to get the chaps used to flying in a restricted situation in formation. Let's do it in daylight first so they know what to expect. Then tomorrow night, after they have experienced a few trial runs, we'll do it in the dark. Actually, as you know, we still have a big moon tomorrow so that will help. We then keep doing it, repeatedly, for the rest of the week until they can do it blindfold if necessary. Any questions so far ...? No? Then sort out the best approach courses and the timings. I suggest we divide the two valleys between us, but I'll leave that to you gents to sort out."

Johnnie led the first flight through the Rye Valley in North Yorkshire and it was tight. Although the valley did not deviate violently, its twists and turns demanded 100% concentration from the pilots and navigators, who provided a running commentary on the topographical features for the pilots. The sides of the valley rose up to nearly 1,250 feet and it was less than 2,000 feet wide. Johnnie's wingmen were obviously nervous as they flew down the narrow valley fifty feet apart and at two-hundred miles an hour, as per Johnnie's orders. Nevertheless, as long as they remained level with his height, he was not overly worried about keeping the height of two hundred and twenty feet or two hundred and fifty miles an hour, as would be required on the day. There was time to tighten up those aspects of the operation later. Three times, he led them through before he was happy to pass on to the next exercise.

The approach to the Saddleworth Moor valley was very different. Whereas the approach to the Rye Valley had been across the flat lands of the York Plain, this approach was over the high hills of the Peak District. They picked up the main road that ran from Manchester to Penistone and swung towards Holmfirth. The turn into the little valley was the first time the flight had to turn in tight formation in anger, so to speak. Their training had paid off and they came round beautifully all in the correct attitude to each other. The giant wool mill presented itself within two minutes directly in front of them. Its two towering smoke stacks rose majestically above the red brick multi-storied Victorian edifice. The multitude of windows threw back the light of the setting sun as they thundered over the grey-slated roof.

"Why the hell would they want to build a bloody factory here, in the middle of nowhere?" asked Jock from his forward station.

"It's not in the middle of nowhere y' bloody Sassenach, it's in God's county. It's where the workers live," defended Yorky, proudly.

"Aye, and that's why so many bairns round here have a naturally woolly skin and cloven feet," cackled Jock.

"All right, chaps concentrate on the job," said a pacifying Johnnie, opening his R/T. "GF two to flight. The next time round will be a mock bombing run. Take station and timing from me."

He kept his six aircraft attacking the mill for the next hour, to the obvious concern of the workers below. A couple of times their turns were not perfect and one in particular caused Yorky to comment, "I'll be buggered, that was a bit close, Skipper. I could have exchanged cartridge belts with the mid-upper on H-Harry as we turned!" he exclaimed.

They came back over the Pennines to Elkington without further incident.

After refuelling, of both the aircraft and the crews, the Squadron took to the night skies. By the time Johnnie's flight had reached the Rye Valley, the moon was like a giant silver disc in the sky, turning the October night into a shining, magical, metallic mirage-like world. Their flight through the valley was as if in daylight. The first and second passes were perfect with the giant bombers weaving and turning like performing air display bi-planes entertaining the crowds as they thundered up the valley at two hundred and fifty miles per hour. Johnnie purposely kept them at what he hoped was two hundred and twenty feet, and the way the crews performed pleased him.

A great start to the week. He hoped they would keep up the standard as the week wore on.

"I tell you what, Skipper, those last couple of turns were perfect; it was like watching Tiger Moth trainers displaying at a Cranwell passing out parade," commented Yorky.

Johnnie's NFT the next morning brought up some minor electrical faults with Gloria and she was laid up for the night while the Chiefy and his team sorted out her problems. Not that he minded a night off, or his crew. It would do them good to relax and, inevitably, enjoy themselves.

When Johnnie and Ginny met up that night in the snug at the Royal Oak, Johnnie could not help but notice she appeared to have a glow about her. Her hair shone, her cheeks flushed pink and there was a sparkle in her emerald eyes. She clutched his hand as they sat on the old pine settle beside the roaring fire. The buzz of laughter and singing drifted to them from the bar through the warm fug of pipe and cigarette smoke, which temporarily cleared as the church-like front door opened and let in a blast of cold winter air.

"When is your next leave?" she asked him quietly.

"Oh, not for a few weeks yet, end of November, after this next sortie I should think, at the earliest. Why?"

"Well ... I've been thinking," she said softly. "If you had some leave coming up we could ... spend it together."

"Yes, I would love to do that, but as I said, nothing until November."

"So you can't arrange anything before then?"

"I shouldn't think so, not with this Guy Fawkes thing. I suppose I shouldn't mention that really, should I?"

"As I'm the intelligence officer involved I think I can forgive you. Or I could have you Court Martialed and shot, I suppose, if you don't want to spend time with me, that is?"

"Of course I do," he laughed, kissing her fingers. "Let's do something this weekend, shall we?"

"What have you in mind?" she asked coquettishly.

"Oh ... oh, nothing like that, er ... nothing like ... erm ..." he stumbled.

She laughed, deliciously enjoying his flustered embarrassment.

"No ... No ... I thought we might spend the day in Ludworth, you know ... have a look round. There's an Autumn Market or something on over the weekend in the town centre. We could grab some lunch somewhere if you like?" he proposed, his high colour fading.

She grasped both his hands realising he had totally misunderstood her intention, and said, "Yes, that would be lovely." She laughed again.

The next day he was back in the air in Gloria, her electrics sorted and the crew refreshed from their night off, although most of them had spent it with Ginny and Johnnie down at the 'Oak' until well beyond 'kick out' time. That night they resumed their night flying exercises.

At the Friday morning de-briefing, it pleased Harry to report to both Thompkins and Britton that things were going well. The night flying, after their use of cellophane and goggles, had been very successful. AVM Nelson, who also attended, was particularly interested in the levels of morale and motivation of the crews. Harry reassured him that the squadron was keen and eager to get on with the job.

"I'm delighted at the progress you have made over the last couple of weeks and so is the Air Chief Marshal. He asks is there anything you need to help you."

"No, sir, not at the moment, although I would be interested to see the weapon we're going to use though."

"What's your training plan for next week, Harry?" asked Nelson.

"We start to practise formation bombing at night on the ranges, sir."

"I would like you and your flight commanders to come and watch the trials of the penetration bombs you'll be using. Is that possible, can you spare them and the time?"

"Er ...yes, sir, it's possible. Where are they being carried out?"

"Down at Dungeness Point."

"When would you want us down there, sir?"

"First thing Tuesday morning. Would that be okay?"

Harry was not used to Air Vice Marshals asking his opinion.

"Yes, certainly, sir, no problem."

# 22 ... Bombs and Bullets

"Is he in, Jimmy?"

"Yes, he's in," shouted Harry Picton through his open office door. "Come in, Johnnie. What can I do for you?"

"Hello, Harry. I would like to beg a favour, if I can?"

"Fire away, my old son, fire away."

"As you know, I'm walking out with Ginny Murphy, you know the dark-haired Waaf from Intelligence."

"Oh, I know! Believe me I know! As does most of the squadron. You jumped a queue of about two hundred gents who have drooled over her for months, you lucky beggar. What's the favour?"

Johnnie's face flushed crimson.

"I was hoping you wouldn't need me at all tomorrow. I kind of promised to take her into Ludworth for the day."

"Yes, that'll be fine; we've got nothing on till Monday. Oh, by the way, we will be going down to Dungeness on Monday, because first thing Tuesday, on the orders of AVM Nelson, we are witnessing the trials of our new bomb. Let the other two know will you? In the meantime, yes, enjoy yourselves. Where are you staying? The Mason's Arms?"

"No ... no ... nothing like that. We're only going for the day, that's all!" He flushed even more, his face and neck now bright red. Harry laughed at his discomfort and slapped him on the back.

"More bloody fool you then! Yeah, go on, have a nice day and night." He laughed.

They spent the morning strolling through the narrow streets of the little market town and wandering between the gaily-canopied stalls of the bustling outdoor market. After a late morning drink in 'Ye Olde Whyte Swanne', they picked up the wonderful aroma of fried fish 'n chips which led them to a side street shop displaying a chalkboard by its door proudly declaring, 'Freshly Caught Grimsby Fish Frying Now!'. Walking through the town, back towards the market, eating fish and chips from newspaper was something neither of them had done for years. They were enjoying the almost childlike pleasure of eating in the street.

"If my mother could see me now she would disown me," giggled Ginny. "'Eating in the street is for common people, Virginia, not for us'," she mocked.

After they had finished their risqué street meal, Johnnie suggested they go to a local beauty spot Algy had told him about it. As they made their way back to Ruby, Johnnie asked a passer-by where Hubbards Hills was.

The young man smirked at him. "Yes, mate, just follow the road round the church and pass the 'ospital and the old mill on yer right, an' you'll come to it. Enjoy yer self." he sniggered.

"What was that all about?" asked Johnnie as they got back in the car.

"Oh, at times you are wonderfully innocent, Johnnie." she said with an adoring look.

He drove as instructed and soon came to a stone track with a hand-written sign, 'Hubbards Hills'. They left the car on the rough ground above the track, crunched down the pathway skirting the wide, shallow, frozen pond, and soon came upon a little stream that was obviously feeding the pond. It tumbled along the flat grassy bottom of a narrow V-shaped wooded valley. Tall, winter-grey beech trees covered the slopes, and the little stream added its musical tinkling to the peaceful still air of this hidden gem. They walked in comfortable silence with Ginny holding on to his arm with both hands. A sudden 'plop' came from the little stream and they watched, delighted, as a plump, round water vole paddled furiously towards the other bank and disappeared into a hole.

"I wonder if that was 'Ratty' from Wind in the Willows?" she asked.

"If we keep quiet," whispered Johnnie, "we may see Mole and Toad. Poop! Poop!"

"Oh, you!" she laughed, slapping his arm gently. "Look at that sweet little chalet over there. Do let's have a look at it."

Beneath the giant beech trees, away from the meandering stream, sat an open fronted chalet made from logs, like a Canadian chalet house. It was a shelter from bad weather, but when they walked through the long grass and sat on the wooden bench that ran around the three walls inside, they realised that young men had brought their sweethearts here for years. Carved initials, some paired with others or surrounded by hearts, covered the wooden walls.

"Now you see why that young man smirked at us when you asked the way."

She ran her fingers over a large carved heart that held the message, 'GHH-L-EG'. "I wonder who they were?" she asked. "And where they are now?"

"Who knows? He could be a heroic soldier, serving overseas, fighting the wicked foe and she could be sitting at home weeping over her knitting."

"Oh, you have no romance in you," she laughed, hitting his arm, in fun, then pulling it around her shoulders.

After a while she said,

"Johnnie, you know when I said it would be nice if we spent some time together if you had some leave. Well ... if we can't go away together for a few days, I don't mind if it is only a weekend."

"Harry said I was not needed until Monday, so we can have another day together tomorrow, if you would like to."

"Johnnie, I'm not talking about going out for the day. I'm talking about the night."

"Well, we could go to a different pub tonight, if you don't want to go to the Royal Oak?"

"I am going to hit you in a minute, you buffoon."

"What?" he laughed, "What are you on about?"

"I'm talking about the time being right. You know what I mean!" She looked down, shyly.

"The time being right, oh ... oh! Oh my God! Yes ... well ... yes."

"The penny's dropped, at last."

"Where would you ... er ... how do you ... I don't know what to say," he laughed. "I'm normally good at responding to surprises, when I'm in the air, but I can't think what to say, except are you sure, are you really sure? I mean I don't want you to think that we have to ... you know."

"Just shut up, and the next time we both have a weekend when we're not on duty, you can try to organise something. There is no hurry; I am not going to stop loving you if we don't ... 'do it' now, you lovely man."

She kissed him, softly at first, and then in a way he knew that the time was right.

\*\*\*

Monday lunchtime saw the three flight commanders and Harry Picton emerging from the cross-track tunnel to climb the stairs to the southbound platform of Ludworth railway station. The late afternoon train to Kings Cross was already an hour late, and it had only to come from Grimsby, sixteen miles up the track. They squeezed into a freezing compartment and settled down for a long, cold journey. Their conversation was severely restricted by a garrulous oracle of knowledge, a bespectacled, rotund man of florid features smelling strongly of whisky, sitting opposite them. He spent the next few hours 'entertaining' them, as he explained how he would conduct the war if he were in charge. They were mightily relieved when the tunnelled approaches of King's Cross station darkened their world.

The next morning, after spending a night in the United Servicemen's Club, they found themselves shivering on the pebbles of Dungeness Point. A tall grey haired 'boffin' with thick glasses was explaining to AVM Nelson, and several other senior RAF and Naval officers, what was about to happen. Along the shoreline, at right angles to the sea, were two sets of tall, three feet thick, concrete walls, looking like abandoned sea defences. After a few minutes, the 'boffin' announced:

"Here they come."

Two Lancaster bombers appeared out of the morning's gloom flying side-by-side, parallel with the shore.

"They're going like dingbats out of hell," said Bill Askin.

"What do you reckon their height is? Two hundred?" asked Harry.

"Not far from it," answered Johnnie.

"Two hundred and twenty." called out the tall grey haired 'boffin'. "And their ground speed is two-fifty."

Three large, plump bombs, with surprisingly sharp nose cones, suddenly appeared from the bomb bays of the racing aircraft.

"My God, look at that!" exclaimed Johnnie.

The bombs had larger than normal fins at the back, curved like the blades of a ship's propeller enclosed in a broad metal ring. This caused them to spin immediately they left the aircraft, but what amazed the watching airmen was the speed of the bombs. They appeared to hang underneath the aircraft for ages before slowly falling away in a long, slow parabolic trajectory before smashing their way through the three concrete walls like knives through butter and burying themselves in the shingle beyond.

The 'boffin' leapt in the air with a 'Yahoo' of success to the mild embarrassment of the senior officers present.

"Yes, thank you, Mr Wallis, please congratulate your staff on a job well done," said an elderly Air Marshal.

AVM Nelson walked across the pebbles to the four bomber pilots.

"Impressive, what?"

"Very much so, sir, I presume that's our weapon?" said Harry.

"Yes it is. We will be getting some dummy ones to you hopefully next week so you can start your own trials at Donna Nook. As you can see, they are very effective. Clever fellow that Wallis, clever chap."

"Will we be able to drop live versions, sir?" asked Ben.

"Yes, hopefully, Squadron Leader, but not many, I am afraid, too expensive, believe it or not."

"Well, I suppose there is a war on, sir," said Johnnie, whose comment raised a scarred eyebrow from the AVM.

"One of the bomb development team will be coming to Elkington next week with the dummy bombs to explain the way they work. I shall be coming down on Friday for an update, Wing Commander."

"Yes, sir."

"How are things going?"

"The squadron is progressing well at the moment. Hopefully it will keep that way without any major problems ahead, sir."

"Good. I was very sorry to hear about Flying Officer Shepherd and his crew, I have seen your report. Bad show, what?"

"Yes, sir, a bad show, as you say, they were a top crew. Their replacements are arriving today though; another good experienced crew, sir."

The rest of the week saw the crews pounding up and down the Lincolnshire coast in the dark, carrying out formation bombing exercises over the range at Donna Nook, just up the beach from Saltfleet's windmill. Wireless operators refreshed their knowledge of aerial gunnery as well; Algy enjoyed clambering up into the front turret to blast away at the orange-painted targets. On the real operational bombing run that is where he and the rest of the wireless operators would be, giving the maximum firepower to every aircraft as they approached their target.

On one of the practice runs, Johnnie was not really concentrating; he was thinking of Ginny. Flying at fifty feet above the sea, in the dark, demanded total concentration from any pilot, even one with Johnnie's skills. She had said the time was right and about spending some leave together. His mind was not on his flying. He had to think of somewhere he could take her, somewhere special. The Mason's Arms in Ludworth was out; he dreaded the thought of taking on the battle-axe of a receptionist; no, somewhere romantic, London, Yorkshire Dales? He decided he would talk to the flight's 'Romeo', Algy, to see if he could come up with some suitable suggestion.

"Skipper, if we get any lower, this kite is going to turn into a submarine!" said a slightly alarmed flight engineer sitting next to him.

Johnnie pulled Gloria back from the foam. "Sorry, Chalkie, I was miles away."

"I much prefer you to stay at my side, Skipper, if you don't mind, especially when we are skimming over the North Sea at two hundred and fifty miles an hour."

They both laughed, although Johnnie was a little embarrassed at his momentary distraction.

Later, as they were having breakfast, he made his plea to Algy.

"No problem, old boy. I can put the old thinking cap on and come up with some little love nest for you two star struck lovers. Leave it with me, Johnnie."

The squadron continued their runs up to the North Yorkshire Moors and over to Saddleworth Moor, but now each run would end with an actual practice bomb drop at Donna Nook with twenty-five pound smoke bombs, focussing on getting the height and speed right.

Johnnie and Paddy were walking back to the flight hut after lunch on the Thursday. G-George had returned early to Elkington with an engine suffering from fuel starvation. The rest of the squadron was still buzzing the targets at the bombing range. Ginny and another WAAF officer came out of the doorway at the rear of the control tower where they had been working. Ginny waved, and the two young women began to walk towards them.

The harsh, angry snarl of foreign engines, the clamour of machine gun and cannon fire stopped Johnnie and Paddy in their tracks. It could only mean attacking aircraft, and two twin-engine Dornier fighter-bombers ripped through the air towards them. The black-crossed planes roared across the airfield at zero feet, side by side, their machine guns and 20mm cannons spitting fire and death. The first casualty was the Group Captain's Spitfire, it exploded in smoke and flames, as did the bowser that had refuelled it as its load of high-octane aviation fuel ignited and tossed it in the air like a child's toy.

Johnnie froze, his arm raised, pointing towards the girls as he realised they were directly in front of the fighter-bombers flight line and the trails of bullets and shells were quickly tracking towards them across the airfield. Paddy grabbed him, threw him to the ground, and screamed at the two WAAFs.

"Get down! Get down!"

The girls turned towards the attacking aircraft, shocked at the sudden violence hammering towards them. In panic, they turned and ran back towards the shelter of the control tower, but they were too late. The airmen watched in horror as a trail of shells, ripping up soil and concrete, sprinted towards the two running WAAFs. In an overwhelming assault of violence, the bullets and shells smashed into the control tower and tore through the ground around the two girls, hurling them to the concrete in a fan of crimson gore and death.

The noise of the two fighters drowned Johnnie's anguished scream of "No!" as they roared above his head, their guns yammering in demonic anger, ripping up the perimeter track and spraying the nearby hangar and buildings. The blue-bellied marauders tore across the airfield strafing the storage areas and the main operations block before banking away and turning for the coast, leaving death and damage across the camp. Belated ack-ack fire from the camp's air defenders stuttered in frustrated, impotent revenge. Johnnie and Paddy scrambled to their feet and raced towards the girls' blood-splattered bodies. Paddy got there ahead of Johnnie, knelt between the girls, and looked up at his Skipper and friend, as he skidded to a halt.

At least three bullets had hit Ginny's friend, ripping open her chest and smashing through her head. Ginny lay beside her, face down, one leg twisted underneath her blood soaked body.

"They're dead."

"No! She can't be," cried Johnnie.

He collapsed on to his knees beside Ginny, picked her up and crushed her to his chest; her body limp in his arms, her face and upper torso covered in blood. Tears of agony ran down his cheek as he rocked her backwards and forwards in his crushing grief.

"No, no, no!"

He did not hear the strident clanging bell of the green ambulance, or the squeal of its brakes as it stopped alongside them. He continued his rocking, grieving embrace of his beloved Ginny. Her friend was lying on a stretcher, her body hidden, covered by a blanket. He looked up as he felt a hand on his shoulder.

"I'm afraid she's dead, sir." A medical orderly knelt beside him. "I'm sorry, sir. Let's put her in the ambulance."

"No ... No ..."

Suddenly, Ginny's arms locked round his body and her hands grasped the material of his battledress tunic as if she would never let go.

The medical orderly rocked back and looked up at his colleague.

"Christ! She's alive!"

Desperate sobs, which seemed to come from the very depths of her soul, wracked her body. Johnnie's tears of grief turned to tears of relief. She was still alive. They clung to each other desperately, tears and blood staining their faces.

He went back to the sick quarters the next morning to see her. The attack had dazed and shocked her, but he thanked God she was not hurt. By some miracle, the fighters' missiles had completely missed her. As the two of them had turned and started to run, Ginny's colleague had been slightly behind her and had taken the brunt of the attack, the blood and gore that had covered Ginny was that of her unfortunate friend, Cathy.

The nursing sister told him off for sitting on the side of her bed. So, as there was no chair, he knelt beside her, clutching her hand between both of his. Ginny smiled at him.

"It looks like you're going to propose to me."

They both laughed and she squeezed his hand tightly and began to cry, softly. Johnnie tried to comfort her.

"You're all right, darling, you're all right."

She sobbed quietly. "I know, but Cathy isn't, is she? I had her blood all over me. She's dead."

"She didn't know anything about it, she died instantly. She would not have felt a thing. It is a miracle you are okay, my darling. Let's just think about getting you up and about."

"Yes, I suppose so."

"Mind you, you might get a medal for your war wounds. You did bang your head and graze your knee, and you laddered your stockings when you fell down."

She laughed through her tears at his black humour.

"Fool."

As he left the sick quarters, it dawned on him how much he truly cared for her; he had felt desperate when he thought she was dead; the pain had been almost unbearable. Her remark about him proposing to her had made him think about their future.

The next day they discharged her from the sick quarters and put her on 'light duties'. Johnnie was now determined to take her away as soon as possible, away from the airfield for at least a couple of days; a change of scenery would help her recover from the shock of the attack. He chased up Algy for an answer to his plea of last week.

"Yes, old man. All sorted," was his answer, "Nice little thatched cottage in the country, not more than twenty miles away. She will love it, my popsies do. Roaring fire, candlelight, big feather bed, can't go wrong, old man."

"No ... I don't mean for ... you know ... that. I mean it will be a nice change for her after the raider business."

"Yes, I believe you, old man, I believe you. Thousands wouldn't, but I believe you," he laughed and clapped Johnnie on the back. "When do you want it?"

"Next weekend, if possible, I shall have to ask Harry though."

"I don't think that will be a problem. When you arrive there, the key is on the ledge above the door. Piles of firewood in the woodshed round the back; the bathroom is a bit rustic, but at least it has one. Fresh linen in the cupboard, pots in the kitchen. Hope you can cook on a wood-burning stove? Mind you, I don't think you will be doing a lot of cooking, will you? Enjoy, old man, enjoy." He said, with a broad grin on his face.

On Sunday, Johnnie took Ginny into Ludworth again. It was the first time she had been out since the attack and she seemed to have recovered well. The sound of a slamming door or a sudden loud noise would make her flinch, but she looked and sounded as if she were well on the way to a speedy recovery.

He suggested to her that they could go and have a look at the church he flew over most days. It had always struck him as a beautiful building, rising majestically from the centre of town with its golden cockerel proudly surveying the landscape from the top of the magnificent spire. He parked Ruby in the little cobbled street next to the arched doorway, pushed open the heavy studded door and entered the cool tranquillity that is an English church. The cherubic sound of choirboys singing greeted them, the music soaring up to the church's vaulted ceiling as they sat in one of the old pews at the back of the nave.

They knelt in prayer for a few moments, giving thanks that they were both still together.

"I used to love to sing in the choir when I was a boy."

"Of course, your father is a vicar; this must almost seem like home."

"Yes, it's something that's been with me all my life, the sounds, the smells, the tranquillity, the grandeur of the columns and pillars, the majesty of the stained glass windows; it has a magic all of its own. Let's just sit and enjoy the choir practise."

The majestic chords of the organ filled the cathedral-like aisles of the ancient parish church.

After a while, Ginny asked in a whisper, "What's that they're singing now? It's beautiful."

"It's called Brother James' Air. It is an alternative tune to the Crimond for the twenty-third psalm. Listen."

'The Lord's my shepherd, I'll not want ...' The sweet, clear sound of the choir swept over them as they sat hand in hand at the back of the magnificent temple. They both said silent prayers again for Ginny's survival.

As they came out of the church, Ginny asked. "Can we go to Hubbards Hills again? It's a lovely day,"

"Yes, why not, in you jump." They bounced down the lane that brought them to the small parking area above the still frozen pond.

They wandered through the steep-sided valley; the little stream tinkled over its stony bed, and trapped between the leafless, giant beech trees, the remains of small drifts of snow glinted in the sunlight. Johnnie finally plucked up the courage to broach the subject of time, hesitantly.

"After what happened last week I wondered if ... well ... maybe you would like a change of scenery ... you know somewhere different for a couple of ... urm ... days."

"Well a change of scenery normally does mean somewhere else, darling. What are you suggesting?"

"Well ... urm ... Algy has a friend who has a ... cottage in the country and wondered if we would like to ... urm ... borrow it for the weekend."

She hesitated, shyly. "Oh ... I see ... you mean?"

"Well ... urm ... only if you think the time is right ... I mean, if you feel well enough to go away for a .... It's entirely up to you, of course," he flustered. "Not to do ... urm ... you know, just to spend the weekend together. I thought it might do you good ... urm ... to get away for a while," he added hurriedly.

She stopped walking and turned towards him, took hold of both his hands and looked up into his flushed face.

"I believe the time is perfect, you wonderful man, absolutely perfect." She reached up on tiptoes and kissed him tenderly.

## 23 ... Bombs

On the following Monday morning, Harry Picton summoned the three flight commanders and Gunner Hargreaves to the squadron office.

"How is your little waaf, Johnnie?"

"She is OK now, Harry, thank you, but she was badly shaken by it all."

"Weren't we all? We were bloody lucky the squadron was on exercise and not parked around the airfield. A lot of aircraft could have been lost."

"You don't think Jerries got a whiff of 'Parliament', do you?" asked Bill Askin. "That's why Elkington was hit."

"No, I don't think so; we would have had a few more visitors by now, if they had."

He scraped a match to flame and lit a cigarette.

"The Royal Aircraft Research Establishment and RAF Intelligence have worked hard on our behalf, apparently."

"I thought that was an oxymoron, Skipper?" said Gunner.

"What was?" asked Harry.

"RAF Intelligence," he said with a cheeky grin.

Harry grinned. "Very funny, smart arse, as the Yanks would say? Right then, there will be a squadron of Pathfinder Mossies coming with us, but it has not yet been decided exactly what they will do. If we send them all in first to light up our way, they could wake up every flak and heavy machine gun in Germany. If we send in one Pathfinder, on his own, there is a chance he will not make it and we will be literally left in the dark. What do you gents think? In fact, don't answer that yet; let's have the full story first. Just lift that box on to the side table, will you?" He indicated a large, square wooden box on the floor.

Johnnie and Gunner picked up the cloth-draped box and deposited it on the table. Harry carefully removed the cloth to reveal a perfectly formed model of the proposed target. They all crowded round to inspect it. He took out a sheaf of papers from his leather briefcase and spread them on the table. Addressing his notes, and using a pencil as a pointer, he described the target and the area around it.

"This is what they have produced for us, they say it is an exact model. 'Parliament' is a factory and research complex in a gorge, or a 'Schucht', in the Ilse Valley on the outskirts of the small town of Ilsenburg, in the Hartz Mountains, some fifty miles southeast of Magdeburg," he read. "The town is at nine hundred feet and the mountains either side of the gorge reach over fifteen hundred feet higher. The valley itself runs northeast to southwest. At the crest of the valley is the three thousand seven hundred and fifty feet of Brocken Mountain,'" he carried on reading.

"The factory, and its accompanying research facilities, is on the northeast side of the gorge, southeast of the town." He used the pencil to point. "'The House of Commons ... the POW camps and workers' accommodation, are to the southeast, south and southwest. In front of the factory is the scientists, scientific workers and guards accommodation, a series of some fifty wooden huts. These, and the factory complex, make up The House of Lords.'"

He referred to his papers again.

"'Surrounding the House of Lords are at least two regiments of Flieger Abwehr Kanonen.' Flak guns to you and me. 'Some twenty forty-four millimetre and ten eighty-eight millimetre guns are in place. Down in the valley beneath the town, protecting the road and an engineering factory, are more gun emplacements. We're not sure how many yet,' it says here! 'It is also believed that three light ack-ack gun emplacements are on top of the factory itself. It seems they are 20 millimetre quadruple barrelled units. The nearest fighter station is fifty miles away at Attersee, near Salzburg.' As you can see, the protection is heavy. But that is just the start of our problems, gents."

"Just a piece of cake so far, Skip!" exclaimed Bill.

They all laughed and the tension seemed to ebb away leaving a residue of relaxed confidence.

"I presume we are using the bombs we saw at Dungeness?" asked Johnnie.

"Yes, but I will come on to that. Let me describe the design of the factory. It is about eight hundred feet wide by three hundred feet deep and just less than one hundred feet high. The four boiler house chimneys are about one hundred feet in from the sides, and, as near as damn-it, two hundred feet apart. They and their boiler houses are fifty feet behind the factory and stand at nearly one hundred and ninety feet high, because of the gorge."

"The factory is in three sections. In fact, it is three factories in one, because each section is a complete individual unit. If one or two sections stop working, then the other can continue developing and producing their prototype jet/rocket. That is why we are attacking in threes, line abreast; it means we cover the whole of the factory. Dividing each section is an arched blast wall, constructed of three feet of reinforced concrete. This is to protect the production and development teams from internal explosions and to offer further protection if bombed from above, but, and it is a big but, we believe these walls are not protection from a lateral attack. We saw the mock-up of these down at Dungeness."

He looked round the gathered airmen.

"So, instead of trying to flatten it from above, as we usually do, we're going to try to flatten it from the side, well, from the front, to be pedantic. With what? To answer your question, Johnnie, yes, we shall be using the bombs we saw, a new type of four thousand pound high explosive penetrator bomb, developed in the same stable as the 'Upkeep' bouncing bomb of Dam Buster fame. More of that at a later date when you start to practise dropping it."

"Will we practise dropping the real thing, Skipper?" asked Joe Kendrick.

"Yep, after using dummies first though."

Gunner laughed. "We've got a few of them in the squadron as it is,"

Harry continued. "This is a true team effort, gents. We are going to practise the actual method of attack and the crews will work even closer together than they normally do. The pilot will point the aircraft in the right direction of course. The navigator will be responsible for getting us to the right spot at the proper time, the air bomber for fixing the height and range and deliverance of ordnance, the flight engineer for speed, and the wireless operator will operate the nose turret so that all guns are useable for attacking the ground defences. As you see, a total team effort. So, get your people trained up in their individual roles and then make them interchangeable in case of injury."

He now turned back to the model.

"Now we come to the attack itself. We shall come up this valley here, and turn beside this mountain with the giant cross on the top. You cannot miss it, it is three and a half miles from the target and the Mossies will mark it for us. The approach to the target is simple. As you can see, there is a bloody great waterfall directly in front of it. That is nine-hundred feet above sea level and one mile from the factory. It also represents the centre line of our approach and allows the middle aircraft of the formation to line up exactly with the target. This is where the gorge walls start to close in and this overhang increases as you go further into the gorge until it almost covers the factory. The most experienced Skippers will fly that inside line, actually flying underneath the overhang to deliver their bombs."

All four flight leaders looked at each other, knowing it would be them.

"The boffins have decided our height and speed and will confirm the drop point distance at the end of their trials this week. Going in before us will be the two flights of three Mosquitos; the first flight will attack the ack-ack posts on top of the factory with their machine guns and cannon, we hope taking them all out. The second flight will, if needed, drop flares and markers to illuminate the target, but will also attack the gun positions on the roof. We will then follow them in. Now the two starboard aircraft must turn and climb immediately after passing over the factory to allow the inner one room to get out from under the overhang and climb away before decorating the mountain in front with bits of bomber and aircrew. Get your pilots used to this scene, gents, come and inspect this model as often as you like, I know I will be, get the situation into their brain, so they can see it in their sleep. Now what do we think about the Mossies putting TIs down?"

"I suppose it depends on whether you're talking about Parramatta flares or Wanganui?" asked Bill.

"I think the question is, never mind whether its ground markers or sky markers, do we want markers at all?" asked Joe. "We're going in on a full moon, and at this time of the year the moon is very bright if it's a cloudless sky."

"And we're going in very low, Skipper," added Gunner.

"What about deciding when we actually do the mock runs with the mock-up bombs later this week? The moon is quite good from Thursday, Friday," suggested Johnnie.

"Okay, let's do that," said Harry, in his normal positive way. "Practise this safe exit from the target after dropping your load, getting the two outer aircraft up and away, allowing the inner one to turn and climb from under this overhang." He pointed at the daunting cliff that towered ominously above the factory.

Back in the flight hut, Johnnie explained that point to his pilots and their crews, pointing out how important the move was.

"When we get out on the range this afternoon that is exactly what we will practise. We will be dropping three twenty-five pound practice bombs each run, which will not fly like our nominated weapon, but it gives us the opportunity to rehearse the scenario before we load up with the big boys. We will repeat this afternoon's performance tonight in the moonlight."

"What size are the 'big boys', Skipper?" asked New Zealander, Sergeant Pete Tyndale, one of the newer replacement pilots.

"It looks like we will be using four 4000 lb penetration bombs, especially designed for this op."

"Will we need any modification of the bomb bay?"

"No, Pete, they will fit our normal 4000 lb cradles."

For the next couple of days, Johnnie and the other flight leaders worked their crews hard, making sure that the outer aircraft moved quickly out of the way as soon as they had dropped their bombs. However, they were all having difficulty in flying at two hundred and twenty-feet exactly. The altimeters fitted were not accurate at very low heights. Pilots normally flew by sight if they wanted to maintain low levels, and judging the correct height by eye was not easy.

On the Thursday morning of that week, a convoy of RAF lorries pulled up outside the bomb dump and unloaded some thirty practise mock-up bombs. Then one of the two civilian technicians from the Royal Aircraft Research Establishment, who accompanied them, explained to the pilots and air bombers, who had gathered in the briefing hut, the physical features of their prodigies.

"These are code-named 'Figgy Puddings'," proudly declared the senior technician.

"Figgy Puddings?" asked Harry, in surprise.

"Yes, 'Figgy Puddings'," declared the rather petulant technician. "The High Capacity Penetration Aerial Flight Weapon, a derivative of the 'Plumduff'," he sniffed. "They contain a four thousand pound mixture of RDX and Amatol high explosive, but these practice weapons have a concrete filling to represent the true weight," he added quickly. "As you can see, the nose of the weapon is very different from any other weapon. Besides having a pointed and elongated front, they have external rifling grooves that act as a virtual concrete penetrating screw. The offset curved tail fins are aerodynamically shaped to spin the weapon at their maximum revolutions as soon as they leave the plane."

"Planes are used for smoothing wood, we fly *aircraft*." said Harry, sniffing and grinning at the airmen.

"Urm ... yes, this high-speed rotating action helps to maintain their airspeed as they leave the bomb bay; this, combined with the concrete screw effect, allows the weapon to penetrate up to four feet of reinforced material. To achieve that effect and to guarantee accuracy of flight and contact with the desired target, the plan is to drop them from a height of two hundred and twenty feet precisely, at a speed of two hundred and fifty miles per hour and exactly six hundred and sixty yards from the target. The Operational Research Section of Bomber Command has worked out the weight, height and number of weapons required for breaking through the concrete of the target and creating the greatest damage."

He grasped the lapels of his jacket and beamed at his audience.

"So it doesn't blow your *'aircraft'* sky-high as you fly over it. There is a timing fuse fitted." He emphasised the word *'aircraft'*. "This consists of a fuse-pistol, a vial of acid, a strip of celluloid and a detonator. As the weapon leaves the *'aircraft'*, a linen cord, attached to the bomb bay, drags the safety device from the pistol; this activates the fuse by rotating a pulley that screws down a bolt on to a small glass vial of acid. The acid eats through a thin strip of celluloid. When the celluloid ruptures it releases the firing pin, which then strikes the detonator and ..." he waved his hands upwards to replicate an explosion. "All this happens at a previously determined time set by the armourer. Any questions?"

"How many 'live' bombs did you bring with you for us to practise with?"

"We make aerial *'weapons'*; soldiers throw bombs, and the answer to your question, Wing Commander, is none. Too expensive; there is a war on, you know," he sniffed.

"Snotty bastard," said Harry to Johnnie as they made their way back to the squadron office. "That's the trouble with civil servants; they think they're the only buggers fighting this war."

When he and the flight commanders got back to the hut, they agreed they would carry out the first trials with the 'Figgy Puddings'. If they got it right or wrong, they could then advise their crews.

Later that day, the five Lancs loaded two each of the bombs in the bomb bay. A line of flags on the range, to represent the release point and another set six hundred and sixty yards further along the beach at Donna Nook, represented the target. Harry had reiterated to them how important it was to maintain the correct height and speed. The first few runs were pretty close to disastrous. Not one bomb out of the five dropped was within a hundred yards of the target. Even the berating issued by Harry before the second run did not improve the results very much. They all returned to Elkington in a disappointed and confused state.

Back in the squadron hut, they sought to fix the problems.

"The speed part of the equation is fine," said Harry. "It's the height that's the problem; I think we're all guessing. Our altimeters are just not accurate enough at that height."

"I don't know, Harry; I think the main problem is the release point. I bet if we put someone on the line of that release point, they would see that every one of us would be releasing our bombs at a different time," argued Joe.

"I believe you're both right," said Johnnie. "But I think it's more than that. Not just the height or the drop point, what we have not considered is a sight line. As we attack in threes, each aircraft will have a different sight line; we're all aiming for a different part of the target." He stood up and went to the model. "Look, do we use a sight line *on* the chimneys, or to the left of them, to the right of them? Do we line up on the roof of the factory, the front, or what? You're right, Joe, how do we mark six hundred and sixty yards exactly in front of the target for our release point? How do we make sure our height is two-hundred and twenty feet, exactly? The bombsight we have is no good at that height and distance, and our altimeters are unreliable at that height."

"It's all right for these boffins to come up with a grand plan and fancy 'weapons', but has anybody thought about how we deliver the fucking bombs on target?" said a frustrated Gunner.

"Look, AVM Nelson will be here tomorrow. Let's have another run early tomorrow morning, see what happens and then have a chat with him. OK?" asked Harry.

\*\*\*

"The trouble is, sir, we need something to help us get our height spot on, and … an accurate way to estimate our distance from the target to the release point, our bombsight is totally inadequate at the height and distance involved. It's all guesswork," stated Harry to AVM Nelson the next morning. "Everything else is OK. The gents are brilliant now at formation flying, turning and climbing. The turns at two hundred and fifty miles an hour, and fifty feet apart, have provided a few hairy moments, I might add. We can control the speed easily, it's just these other vital elements we can't get right, height, sighting and distance."

"Yes, we realised that you would have problems there and wondered how you would get along without any special aids. You have performed extremely well up to now, and help is on the way. The boffins have been working on a new bombsight especially for this operation. It will give you your height and drop point. It is undergoing trials at this very moment down at Dungeness. You saw it being used when you came down for the bomb trial."

"With all due respect, sir, we are one week away from the op, shouldn't the trials be complete by now?"

"I have been informed that today's trials are 'fine tuning' and you should have the new sight by Monday morning without fail. Put it this way, if they are not here by then, a few people will be singing falsetto by Monday lunchtime, what!" he said smiling.

After AVM Nelson and the senior officers had left: "It looks like we may have underestimated our boffin friends, Skipper, but if we haven't we could always resort to spot lights, forked sticks with nails in them, or bits of string and chinagraph pencils." said Gunner, alluding to the sights used on the Dam Busters raid.

"Believe me, Gunner, I'd already thought about that."

# 24 ... Pond Cottage

With a conspiratorial wink from Harry and his blessing, Johnnie picked up Ginny from her quarters and set off in Ruby for the cottage early on Friday afternoon. Algy's directions were spot on and he soon found the turn off from the main road about twenty miles from Elkington.

"Algy said down this old coach road, through the ford, past the pub, round the pond and 'Pond Cottage' is up on the right overlooking the stream and pond. Well, here's the ford and there's the pub."

They splashed through a small shallow stream and passed 'The Angel Hotel', a large, old, black and white coaching inn. Pretty cottages lined the narrow lane and half a mile into the village, they came across a large, almost circular pond.

"Oh, stop, Johnnie; it's beautiful, please stop."

He pulled up alongside the single low wooden rail that surrounded the crystal-clear water.

"Algy said it's called 'Seven Spring Pond'. I suppose there are seven springs rising in it. Yes, look."

He pointed to where the surface of the water gently bubbled as a spring gurgled up through the gravelled bottom of the shallow pond. Dark green waterweed waved sinuously in the flow of other springs scattered across the bed of the pond. They bubbled to the surface, glistening in the late afternoon sun. On the far side, a small wooden sluice gate held back the waters like a little dam; the water fell over it streaming away through grass and reed-lined banks behind the old cottages and houses.

"Oh look, some ducks. What wonderful green heads they have. What are they?"

"Mallards, I think. I'm surprised they haven't graced someone's cooking pot by now," he said with a smile.

"Oh, don't be horrid. Hello, duckies," she called, as the little flotilla paddled towards them.

"They're looking for something to eat; we'll bring some bread down to feed them tomorrow, shall we?"

"Yes, that will be lovely. Is that the cottage, do you think?" she asked, pointing to a small thatched one, standing back from the pond overlooking the little dam and stream. It had been lime-washed a pale rose-pink, and a neatly trimmed lawn ran down to the water's edge, where a large weeping willow tree's branches gently swept the surface.

"Yes, I think it is. Come on, let's find out."

They jumped back in Ruby and drove round the pond and into the gravelled area in front of the cottage.

"Pond Cottage, that's what the sign says, we're here."

They approached the little porched doorway and Johnnie found the key where Algy had said it would be. He realised that both of them now felt slightly apprehensive. He smiled encouragingly at Ginny and unlocked the door. It opened directly into a wonderfully timbered room; a large inglenook fireplace was the first thing that caught the eye. A couple of armchairs and a large cushion-filled sofa were cosied up to the fireplace. In front of the window that overlooked the pond was a small dining table, surrounded by four ancient-looking wooden, high-backed chairs. Brass and copper bric-à-brac of another age, long gone, cluttered the uneven black timbered walls.

"It's beautiful, darling; oh, it's beautiful."

She skipped across the flag-stoned floor towards a half-open door while Johnnie brought in their luggage.

"Oh, do come and look at the kitchen, it's positively ancient," she giggled.

"I'll just pop these bags upstairs," he called to her in the kitchen.

A hesitant, and slightly nervous, "Yes, darling," came back to him.

When he came back downstairs, he lit the wood-burning stove and the fire; soon embryonic flickers of a flame were illuminating the gloom of the enormous fireplace.

"There are enough logs out the back to keep us going till Christmas. And, by the way, I've found an old water pump just outside the back door, but I hope we've got taps for our water."

She laughed. "Yes we have, and I hope there is a bath upstairs. Is there?" she asked, slightly concerned.

He walked over to her, put his arms around her, and kissed her on the nose. "Yes there is, you can have a nice long soak when the water gets hot."

She nestled into his chest making little mewing sounds of pleasure.

"Are you sure about this, sweetheart?" he asked gently, stroking her hair, "I can always sleep down here, you know. I wouldn't mind."

"Oh yes you would," she laughed. "Yes, darling, I am sure. This is a perfect place for us, just the two of us, alone. No crews for you to worry about, no noisy aeroplanes to disturb our peace and quiet, just the two of us together."

She kissed him with love and a tingle of suppressed excitement.

They scraped together a meal of bread and cheese, opened a tin of Spam, courtesy of the officers' mess stewards, and found a stash of wine and some homemade pickles in the walk-in pantry in the kitchen. Both the wood stove and the fire were now burning merrily as they settled on the sofa in front of the crackling fire.

Warmed by logs, wine, and the love they both felt for each other, they held each other tightly as the kisses they exchanged gradually grew into a smouldering passion.

She whispered softly. "Let's go upstairs,"

He awoke to find her delicious naked body wrapped around him, her leg thrown over his, her arm over his chest, her dark-tipped breasts crushed luxuriously against his ribs and her raven-haired head snuggled into his neck. He lay perfectly still, not wanting to break the magic of the moment, her warm perfume washing over him. The night had been perfect; their lovemaking had been tender and caring after their first shy awkwardness, and her first brief cry of pain. It had grown into a glorious, passionate joining of bodies and hearts, which climaxed in shuddering cries of mutual ecstasy. The thoughts of their erotic union were having an effect on his body and the warmth and pressure of her silken inner thigh was not helping the situation. As if by telepathy, she stirred and stretched, forcing her soft body against him. Her hand slid across his stomach, found his manhood, and moaned in pleasure at its readiness. She raised herself over him guiding his firmness into her willing body, her newly awakened passion eager to consume him.

The morning was cold and crisp. A frost had whitened the lawn and the willow tree's branches, whilst the winter sun seemed to make the air itself glisten and shimmer. Ginny was feeding and chatting to the ducks as Johnnie stood at the kitchen door with a hot mug of tea in his hands watching her.

'I love that woman, my God I do,' he thought, 'God knows what I would have done if that bastard Jerry fighter had killed her.' He shuddered in horror at the remembered scene of her sprawled on the ground covered in blood and his sense of hopelessness and loss. 'I just hope I am around her for a very long time.'

He called to her, "Darling, I'm starving. Shall we walk down to the village shop and see if we can get something for breakfast?"

"Well, you did expend a lot of energy last night, and this morning, didn't you?" she said, with a cheeky smile.

They walked round the pond hand in hand and stopped at a little thatched cottage that was the local post office and shop. A small bell tinkled as they pushed through the door and a wonderful smell of freshly baked bread assaulted their noses and Johnnie's stomach rumbled in protest.

"My word, you sound 'ungry, duck," laughed a round, apron-adorned woman behind the counter.

Johnnie and Ginny looked at each other and smiled.

"We've not had breakfast yet and the smell of that fresh bread is causing havoc down there," he said, pointing to his stomach.

"You'll be stayin' at Pond Cottage then, I suppose?" she asked in a friendly way.

"Yes, a friend of ours arranged it for us, for the weekend."

"Would that be that wonderful Spitfire pilot with the white silk scarf and wonderful 'andlebar 'tache?"

"Spitfire pilot?" said Johnnie, in surprise.

"Yeah, quite a hero, isn't he, but very modest. He says yar have to be when yar... now what did he say it was, summat to do with cards.... An ace, that's it, yes, an ace, and he's so 'ansome."

"Yar talkin' about Squadron Leader Algernon, duck?" said an equally round man, who appeared from the back room of the shop, dressed in a bloodied blue and white striped butcher's apron, sharpening a wicked-looking knife with a steel.

"Yes, these people are friends of 'is."

"Ay, he's a grand lad, that one. One o' the lads that beat off Jerry and won us the Battle 'o Britain, y'know, a real 'ero."

"Yes he is," said a struggling Johnnie.

Ginny had turned her back to him and was intently studying items on the shelf by the door, her shoulders shaking with suppressed laughter.

"Are yar in the raff wi' 'im, then?" the butcher asked.

"Yes, I'm in the raff, but I'm on bombers, I'm not a hero like the Squadron Leader."

"Aye, but yar lads do a grand job as well of course, but yar've got to depend on them fighter lads to keep yar safe, 'aven't yer?"

"Yes, we certainly have, we certainly have."

"'Ee comes here quite often, brings his cousins with him. Gets them out of the city, he says, gets them away from the bombin'. He has quite a few cousins y'know. Must come from a big family. He's related to the King, y'know, got a double-barrelled name, like all of them toffs, 'is dad's a Lord and ee's a 'onourable something, Yeah, a grand lad is the Squadron Leader."

"He's certainly something like that," smiled Johnnie.

"Anyway, duck, what can I get yar?" asked the woman.

"Well, we're looking for something for breakfast. I don't suppose you've got any eggs, have you?"

"Ay, duck. How many do yar want?"

"Two would be very nice, if you can spare them," said the recovered Ginny.

"Yar can 'ave 'alf a dozen, if yar want. We keep our own 'ens round the back; we've allus got lots," she smiled.

"Half a dozen would be fantastic," said Johnnie.

"Would yar like some bacon wi' them eggs?" asked the butcher, with a conspiratorial smile.

"Bacon and eggs, oh, yes please, and some of that wonderful bread I can smell. I don't suppose you have any spare butter, do you?" asked Ginny.

"Well, seein' as your friends with the Squadron Leader, I'm sure we can find yar some, duck. Can't we 'Erbert?"

"Ay, 'course we can. I'll slice that bacon fer 'ee. Thick?"

"Oh, yes please."

"Is there 'owt else, duck?"

"No thanks ... oh, yes, a pint of milk, please. We've been using 'Klim' and I hate dried milk."

"I'll need yar coupons for that, duck."

Ginny handed over her ration book and the woman took out just a coupon for the milk and handed it back, winking and saying, "Ta, duck,"

The butcher came back through the curtains with the bacon wrapped in greaseproof paper.

"There y'are, duck, I put a couple of sausages in there for yar as well," he winked at Ginny as well. "Just charge 'em for a couple of rashers, Ada."

Johnnie paid up and they both thanked 'Erbert and Ada profusely, and walked back towards the cottage with their ill-gotten gains.

"Squadron Leader! I'll bloody squadron leader Algy when I get back. Brings his cousins here to get away from the bombing!" He was laughing so much he had to wipe away the tears. "Related to the King, oh dear, that is the best one."

The pair of them rocked with laughter.

When they got back to the cottage, Ginny insisted on cooking breakfast for him on the wood burning stove.

"Oh, my God!" she cried. "Johnnie, come here, look at this!"

Johnnie rushed through to the kitchen thinking something was wrong.

"What? What is it? Are you okay?"

She showed him the contents of the greaseproof paper parcel.

"My goodness me, how many rashers are there?"

"Four and four sausages but, look at these!"

She held up two enormous, thick pork chops, both with half a kidney attached.

"Algy can be a bloody Air Vice Marshal if he wants to be, he's certainly got the influence."

They both giggled and said 'Thank you, Algy'.

After an enormous breakfast of bacon, two eggs, sausage, fried kidney, fried bread, baked beans, bread and butter and several mugs of hot tea, Johnnie suggested they walk it off by exploring the village.

Ginny's new bread-eating friends followed them round the edge of the pond, quacking noisily for attention. They left them to wander past the dozen or so cottages and houses that led down to the ford. As they passed the Angel Hotel, Johnnie pointed out the sign that said 'open to non-residents for dinner'.

"Shall we try that tonight?"

"Johnnie, darling, I couldn't eat another thing all day after that wonderful breakfast."

"You might have expended some more energy by then, sweetheart." He grinned and she cuddled up to him.

By the time they returned to the cottage, around lunchtime, it had turned bitterly cold and there was greyness about the sky that threatened snow. Johnnie stoked up the fire and the stove with more logs from the woodshed and piled more of them in the inglenook for later use. They did not need lunch, but they certainly expended some energy and dozed luxuriously until very late afternoon.

When they came downstairs, it was dark outside and Ginny went to close the curtains in the lounge while Johnnie stirred the fire back to robust health.

"It's snowing!" she cried in delight. "Oh, look, it's snowing."

She ran to the front door and threw it wide. Standing underneath the thatched porch, she held her hands out to catch the enormous snowflakes that fell silently from the dark sky. There were already a couple of inches of soft white blanket covering the ground. Johnnie came and stood behind her.

"This just makes it perfect. I love the snow and I love you," she pulled his arms around her and leaned back against his chest, watching the gentle giant snowflakes falling, drifting and dancing in the night.

"I love you," he said softly in her ear.

A few moments later, he asked her gently, "Why are you crying?"

"Because this is perfect and I know it can't last. I don't want it to end, but I know it will," she sobbed.

"We can make it last at least until tomorrow night though."

"I don't just mean this weekend, you chump, I mean us, I mean us being together. I would die if anything happened to you, if you didn't come back from an op, if you are posted missing. I know it will end."

She turned and buried her face in his chest and sobbed. He led her back into the cottage, sat her down on the sofa and just held her tight until the tears washed dry.

Half an hour later, she said.

"I'm sorry, darling, everything seemed so perfect and I am so happy. It was just the thought of losing you that overwhelmed me, I'm sorry." She reached up and kissed him gently.

"You're not going to lose me. Gloria will look after me and bring me back to the airfield every time we go out. I'll always come back for you, just you wait and see."

She laughed. "You and that ruddy plane! Sometimes I'm sure you think more of her than you do of me."

"Well ... she has a great undercarriage and she does exactly want I want her to do."

"Oh does she now! I bet she can't do this though."

She ran her fingers slowly up the inside of his thigh.

Later, they dressed and ventured out into the snow-filled night. Flurries of snow followed them into the Angel Hotel's bar, but soon melted to droplets of sparkling water as they shed their coats and settled at the bar with a giant roaring fire at their back.

With the calories of the breakfast burnt off, they were both starving and enjoyed their supper. By the time they walked back to Pond Cottage, it had stopped snowing, and the moon, although not full, was shining brightly and lit their way back through the thick, white, virgin blanket.

That night saw them make love tenderly, gently, taking time to pleasure each other, to enjoy each other's bodies, finally falling into the satiated sleep of lovers, under the thick, warm Eider-down quilt.

Sunday breakfast, a walk through the snowy village, a late lunch of pork chops came and went much too quickly for them, but they knew they had to start back to Elkington before dark, before more snow fell.

Johnnie locked the door and returned the key to its rather obvious hiding place, whilst Ginny stood looking back at Pond Cottage. She knew that for the rest of her life, no matter what happened, she would always remember the happiness she had found here. With a quiet tear, she slid into Ruby's passenger seat, alongside the man she loved.

## 25 ... Fine Tuning

Air Vice Marshall Nelson was true to his word, and several people at The Royal Aircraft Research Establishment did not need to worry about their manhood, with the new bombsight fitted to all aircraft by Monday lunchtime.

That morning, the same 'snotty' civil servant, who had explained the 'Figgy Puddings', now began his explanation of the bombsight to the gathered pilots, air bombers and wireless operators in the briefing hut.

"Let me introduce you to the 'PABB Mark Three'. 'Periscope Aligning Box Bombsight Mark Three'," he explained.

"Periscope, does the wee bugger think we fly submarines?" asked a whispering Jock.

"It's all done by mirrors, gentlemen." The civil servant sniggered at his own joke. Nobody else did. "It's very simple, you look down the eyepiece, and with the aid of the mirrors you see the target in front of you. You pre-set the calibration for height and width of the target, and the sight calculates the release distance you need from your target, and when the target fills the frame, you release your weapons. As simple as that. Here are some blown-up drawings, if you will excuse the pun." Again, he sniggered.

A photo projector at the back of the room threw its beam on to the white screen rigged up on the front of the stage. A square image appeared with suspended lines on all four sides inside a graduated frame. Two chimneys rose from the bottom of the square to the top and touched the vertical lines at the sides.

"As you can see, your aiming mark is the midpoint between two chimneys. If you're too high, there is a gap at the bottom of the sight." The projector flicked through more images. "If you are too low, there is a gap at the top, if too far left, a gap on the right, too far right, a gap on the left. It is as simple as that, gentlemen."

There was an instant response from his audience as they too realised the sight was so simple to use.

"For use in practise, you can adjust the vertical lines in and out depending on the distance between the chimneys and the horizontal lines up and down depending on the height of the chimneys. There are calibrations on both the vertical and horizontal planes."

He looked directly at Harry Picton, with a smug smile playing around his lips.

"To obtain the correct distance from the target to release your weapons, you set the vertical lines at the width of your aiming point, say two hundred feet, and when those lines correspond to the chimneys, you are exactly at the correct distance from them. When the horizontal lines match the roofline and the top of the chimneys, say one hundred feet, you are exactly at the right height. When both come together, that is your release point and you press the tit."

The level of noise rose dramatically as people, intelligent people, grasped the simple, yet brilliant concept that solved their major problems.

"Any questions, gentlemen?"

"How is it fixed in the aircraft?"

"You will find that it has replaced your normal mark fourteen sight, and it uses the same fixing, so there is no undue vibration."

"How do you adjust the horizontal and vertical lines within the sight?"

"Very simply by two adjusting knobs either side of the sight. These change the angle of the mirrors inside. We have one here, set up on a model of your target. You can come to the front and try it out dry."

He indicated to his colleague to uncover the bombsight on its stand in front of the model. There was a sudden rush of enthusiastic airmen, but he held them back.

"Not so fast, gentlemen, not so fast, it is vital that you check, for yourself, that you have calibrated the sight for your target correctly, both on the ground and, even more importantly, before your final bombing approach. If the circumstances of your target change, then you can quickly reset the system. Right, I suggest each crew comes out together to familiarise yourselves. Wing Commander, any comments?" he smiled graciously.

"No sir, as you say, a brilliant, simple answer to our problems."

He stood up to address the room.

"Right, gents, after you've played with this one, we will be carrying out practice runs in the daylight this afternoon on the mill on Saddleworth Moor. We picked that as a practice target because the building is of a similar height to the real target, and although it has only two chimneys, they are, as near as damn-it, the same size as well. Tonight we will again test the sight in the moonlight, but on the range at Donna Nook. Balloon Command is setting up four small static barrage balloons to represent the chimneys of the target, at one hundred and fifty feet apart and two hundred feet high, with smaller balloons attached at one hundred feet to represent the roofline of the factory. One of our friendly Mosquitos will keep illuminating the target with white flares. Do not prang the balloons, gents. One point, if the bomb aimer gets put out of action in any way, the wireless operators will take over their duties, so Skippers, make sure they also use the sight tonight."

Jock and Algy soon got the hang of using the new sight in daylight, finding it easy to use and very accurate when they were guiding Johnnie on to the target. However, the night exercise was much different. The moon was bright and the balloons easily picked out in the light of the flares the Mosquito was dropping. They quickly realised though that the flares were destroying their night vision and flying that low and fast was already very hairy. Back on the ground, Harry called in his flight leaders.

"Well? What do you think about the sight?"

They all agreed it was successful, but the flares were a problem.

"Looking at that model," said Joe, "to get out of that gorge we've got to turn and climb with aircraft very close to us. If we've just flown through flares, we will be as blind as bats. I would suggest we forget the flares, Skipper, and hope for a good moon."

"I agree with Joe, Harry, if we are going in on a full moon, why do we need flares?"

"Rest of you feel that way too?"

They all answered, yes.

"Okay, no flares. Tomorrow night we will try it on the mill. Stand by for a long night, gents."

Ginny and Johnnie sat in the bar of the officers' mess later that night. A group of officers was noisily enjoying themselves round the bar, but they were sitting next to the fire in armchairs. They wanted to sit together so they could touch each other, even just hold hands, but the rules of the mess were plain.

"The weekend was wonderful, darling," she spoke softly. "It really was. I feel like a different person, for some reason," she giggled deliciously.

"I wonder why," he laughed. "Yes, it was wonderful. You wore me out, you insatiable hussy."

"Oh, look who's talking. I couldn't even get a decent night's sleep without being bothered."

"We didn't go there to sleep, did we?"

Before she could answer, Harry interrupted them.

"Hello, you two love birds. How did the weekend go?" he asked as he sat down.

"It was lovely. Thank you very much for letting him go."

"My pleasure," he smiled at Ginny then turned to Johnnie. "We put in some good work today. I must admit I was very impressed with that snotty little ba ... that boffin and his sight. So simple, I wonder why it hasn't been tried before."

"Yes, I thought ..."

Ginny interrupted them and said with a smile.

"If you two are going to talk shop, I'm going to my bed. I need to catch up on my sleep."

As the words came out of her mouth, she realised what she had said and blushed deeply. Johnnie choked on his drink and Harry slapped his thigh, roaring with laughter. She grabbed her bag and fled.

"Oh, that was classic, that was," said Harry, wiping away a tear. "The weekend was *that* good then?"

The next night, Johnnie led his flight of six over the Pennines to Saddleworth Moor to have dry runs using the bombsight in darkness against the mock target. As they approached the mill, he ordered them to change from their vic formation to line astern, as there were only two chimneys, as opposed to four on the real target. This allowed them to practise sighting up on real chimneys in the moonlight. Gloria swept towards the target with Jock calling directions from his nose position. The moon was ideal and the mill, with its towering stacks, showed up clearly.

"Up ... up ... steady ... steady ... left left ... steady ... down ... steady ... steady ... Bombs gone!"

When the two wingmen in their Lancasters carried out their run, they pulled up and turned away immediately as if to allow Johnnie to follow safely underneath them. The second wing of Johnnie's flight followed seconds later, copying the actions of the first wing.

"Well done, B-Wing," called Johnnie on the R/T. "Round again, but try to keep it a bit tighter A-Wing. B-Wing keep up, remember, eight seconds behind each aircraft, no more."

For two hours, the squadron filled the valley with the roaring magic of Merlin engines, as they also did for the next two nights. They would fly to the moor and carry out two or three attacks on the mill in single file, then cross back to the Lincolnshire coast and drop the dummy 'Figgy Puddings' for real in their three abreast formation at the balloon-marked target on the wide sand flats. Each time they got more and more adept at using the new sight and getting very close to the target itself.

At the last practise briefing, on the Thursday afternoon, Harry Picton congratulated the crews on their bombing results. The squadron, as a whole, had achieved an 85% success rate for hitting within twenty yards of the target. The most successful crews were the B-Wing of Harry's Guy Fawkes-1 flight, pilots Ginger Bere, Taffy Morgan and Bob Hirst, with an incredible 92% success.

"Well done, you three. I knew that GF One would be the best, of course, look who's leading them," bragged Harry. "Well done again, gents. That's a free night at the Oak for your crews when we get back from the op."

Johnnie wondered how many would be there to collect Harry's prize; the risks on this op were very high, not just the close formation flying with the danger of collision. Bombers flying so low over Germany in bright moonlight were an ack-ack gunner's perfect target, especially with the deadly heavy machine guns of the light ack-ack.

"It's your last chance tonight to iron out any last-minute snags," continued Harry. "When you take up your kites for the NFT today, make sure everything is one hundred percent, so that the ground crews have time to put any problems right. Talking about NFTs; to confuse the German listening stations that monitor our ground radio test transmissions, tomorrow we will carry out wireless testing in the morning and afternoon, if we only do it the morning, they will know there is a big raid planned for tomorrow night. That is it for now. Remember, one hundred percent concentration tonight. We do not want any casualties at the last minute. The op briefing will be at 1900 hours tomorrow. All right, off you go."

The final trial runs went well, no incidents and no casualties. Wing Commander Harry Picton decided that an early finish would benefit everybody, so by eight o'clock the officers' mess was starting to fill up.

Johnnie and Ginny found a table away from the crowd and chatted quietly.

"Will you be waving us off tomorrow?"

"Yes, I don't suppose you know what time you will be taking off?"

"No, not yet, we will find out at the briefing. You'll be at that, won't you?" he asked, almost as a plea.

"Yes, I'm helping the SIO with the latest flak reports. I will see you before you go, darling. I am on duty all night in the control tower; I will be there to see you come home as well."

He smiled at her and longed to hold her, but the mess rules were strict.

To get away from prying eyes Johnnie walked her back to the WAAFs' quarters through the snow-covered camp. They found a quiet sheltered corner of a building and briefly held each other, kissing longingly.

"I wish we were back at Pond Cottage."

There was sadness in her voice, a wishful longing.

They said their goodnight and parted, each to their own bed and warm thoughts of Pond Cottage.

# 26 ... Final Briefing

Posted on the squadron notice board the next morning were the battle orders. Thirty aircraft would be going on ops that night. Two aircraft kept back as spares were F-Fox and I-India from 'C' flight. Flight Sergeant Bill Simpson and Pilot Officer George Geddes and their crews had the night off. Their Lancs would be bombed and fuelled ready to go should any of the other aircraft fail to take off.

The captains' brief was at 1815 hours, as was the wireless operators', half an hour after the navigators and bomb aimers had their separate briefs and the main briefing for all would be at 1900 hours. The crew of G-George took her up for the standard Night Flying Test at 1100 hours and reported in the Flight Snag Book 'No problems'. Johnnie checked with the Chiefy that he had issued an order for ground crews to carry out further radio transmission tests that afternoon to help disguise the op that night.

At 1845 hours, the crews made their way to the briefing hut. It was a part of a complex of wooden and brick-built huts all connected by footpaths just to the north of the flight huts. The aircrews dining room, which issued the ration-packs for the op and served their pre and post flight meals, the parachute store and map store were directly off the briefing room, while the store that issued the survival kits and Mae Wests was alongside. The main hut was the crew hut. Around two sides of it were their personal lockers, and these contained their flying suits, boots, helmets and equipment. They also left their personal possessions here when they were flying and any item that could identify their squadron or airfield. The testing rigs for intercom and oxygen masks were in a small room to one side. In the body of the room, scattered around, were armchairs and settees, begged, borrowed and stolen from various sources and a few small tables. On ops nights there were always a couple of WAAF stewards issuing gallons of strong tea in tin mugs from the steaming, shiny urns. These mugs of tea always contained a large shot of rum when the crews returned in the early, grey mornings for their post-op de-briefing. A mug of rummed tea in one hand and a cigarette in the other, while they calmly told of their terrifying exploits over enemy territory.

The intimidating 'Snowdrop', Flight Sergeant Pidkin and two of his staff, were present at the entrance door to the briefing hut, along with several others surrounding it. All public phone boxes in the immediate area of the camp were strangely 'out of order', and no phone calls allowed from the camp itself. The main gates were secure and no one, but no one, permitted to leave the camp. The need for tight security reflected how important this operation was.

The RAF police checked all ID cards and carried out a roll call when all the crews were in the briefing hut. The briefing for 'Operation Parliament' was about to begin.

"Stand to Attention!"

The scrape and squeal of chairs was the entrance fanfare for the flight of senior officers as they made their way down the polished, tan-coloured corticene floor covering of the central aisle.

Air Vice Marshal Rice, Air Officer Commanding 1 Group: Air Vice Marshal Nelson, Tactical Staff Officer Bomber Command: Group Captain Woodfield, Air Intelligence: Group Captain Thompkins, Camp Commandant: Wing Commander Britton, Camp 2i/c and Wing Commander Picton, Officer Commanding 599 Squadron, mounted the raised daïs. Accompanying them were the two 'boffins', Professors Richard Kemble and Charles Ankers and the tall grey haired man called Wallis the flight commanders had seen at Dungeness. All, but Picton, sat in the row of chairs arranged to one side of the platform. Down on the floor, sitting in the first row of chairs, were the various briefing officers and their assistants. Johnnie had already seen and exchanged shy smiles with Ginny who had briefly turned to search the hall for him.

Picton approached the back of the platform and pulled the cords that removed the black curtain masking the large map of Europe. Red and white tapes described the outward and homeward routes to and from the target.

"The target for tonight is ... Ilse Schucht. A river gorge in the Hartz Mountains of central Germany."

A buzz of conversation greeted his words.

"In that gorge," he carried on, "is a very important factory ... to the Germans that is, and it is vital we destroy it. That is why, for the last five weeks you have trained, you have rehearsed and you have practised how to destroy that factory. I would like to introduce Group Captain Woodfield from Air Intelligence at the Air Ministry, who will explain the background to our operation, Group Captain?"

"Thank you, Harry. Wing Commander Picton and I go back a long way. We were Pilot Officers together at Cranwell, many moons ago, or so it seems now, eh, Harry?"

"It does indeed, sir," said a smiling Harry.

Woodfield carried on in his refined accent.

"As Wing Commander Picton stated, the location of the factory is a gorge in the Ilse River valley above the small town of Ilsenburg. Slave and forced labour have been constructing the factory over the past ten to twelve months. Its test and research facilities have helped the Germans to develop futuristic and terrifying weapons. ... Some of you witnessed the launch of a ballistic rocket over Peenemünde back in October. Well, gentlemen, we are talking about similar weapons to those, and some of an even greater devastating power that could substantially affect the outcome of the current unpleasantness we are experiencing."

"He calls it an 'unpleasant experience', I call it fucking war," whispered Chalkie to Jock.

Woodfield looked directly at Chalkie, as if he had heard his comment. Chalkie defiantly held his eye contact.

"If we can destroy this facility we could radically change the course of this war. ... How many times have you heard that hackneyed phrase before departing on death or glory sorties? This time we are deadly serious. They are developing and producing weapons of immense power and range. They will be able to attack targets across Europe and Britain and even the east coast of America directly from Germany and the occupied countries. We have to stop them *now*. And you, gentlemen, are the ones to carry out this 'gunpowder plot' and destroy their ability to develop these weapons."

He paused as the murmur of conversation rippled round the room.

"The factory was purposely constructed in this gorge. They think it is bomb proof, especially now, as they have brought in seven thousand five hundred US Army Air Force and British RAF prisoners of war and billeted them next to the factory, alongside thousands of foreign workers. The mountains themselves partially protect the factory; a massive overhang on the west side shields it from a direct overhead assault. The POW and workers' camps protect it from the north and northeast, Brocken Mountain and the twisting gorge protect the northwestern approach. The only way to hit it is from the front, the southeast, in the way you have practised. It is not bomb-proof, gentlemen." He looked round the room. "And you will prove that."

"The code name for this target is 'Parliament'... Yes, gentlemen, you are going to blow up Parliament!"

A roar of approval greeted this announcement making all the 'big-wigs' smile openly. Woodfield raised his hands and waved the crews to silence.

"We have code-named the POW and worker camps as the 'House of Commons' and the factory, research section and the barracks area, specifically the scientists, skilled labour, SS and Wehrmacht accommodation in front of the complex, as the 'House of Lords'. Your target will *be* the 'House of Lords'."

Another roar of approval echoed round the hut.

"Yes, yes, I thought you might like that," he was still smiling. "Your squadron, for this operation, has been given the code name 'Guy Fawkes'."

Again another roar of approval startled the 'Snowdrops' standing guard on the outside of the building.

"They'll be saying we're gonna bomb that old bugger, Winnie, next," said Yorky to Dusty.

"Operation Parliament is vital to the allies' success in this war, and I, for one, have every confidence in Wing Commander Picton and yourselves in carrying out a successful mission. Thank you, gentlemen."

He sat down to the sound of excited chatter.

The Senior Intelligence Officer climbed up on the platform accompanied by Ginny. Her reception was predictable; the place immediately erupted with whistles, cheers and ribald comments, which she studiously ignored and concentrated on the papers in her hands.

"All right, all right, calm down you animals, calm down."

When he had gained their attention, he carried on. "You now know why we are bombing this target and how important it is. To state the obvious, it is vital that you get your aircraft and your bombs to that target. There are but thirty of you, so every aircraft needs to deliver every bomb to the target. Therefore, you will be flying at low-level all the way to your rendezvous point at two hundred miles an hour, hopefully under the Jerry radar. The Nav leader will take you through the details of the course and headings and Section Officer Murphy will show you the hot spots ..."

Before he could say another word, the aircrews exploded in cheers and whistles. Even Ginny could not resist laughing and blushing.

"She will show you the hot spots for flak, night fighters and searchlights, you bloody animals," he laughed.

Ginny went towards the back of the platform, took up the wooden pointer, and used it whilst saying:

"We are sending you through the Egmond gap. Those experienced crews will know that this is the gap in the enemy's Kammhuber defence line and is relatively clear of guns and lights. When you reach the Dutch coast, just north of Egmond, there are twin radio masts two hundred and fifty feet high at your point of crossing. Pass to the north of them within five hundred yards. However, be very careful not to hit the guide wires to the northern mast, the anchors are two hundred and fifty feet out on all sides. As you can see by the red and green overlays the hot spots..." She waited until the whistling and cheering had died down. Using the pointer, she carried on "... are either side of your planned track except for here at Lingen and Minden and again south of Hanover. Scattered all along your route are several fighter airfields, but at your height, you will be under their radar and hopefully they will not pick you up. Another hot ... another area for your attention is Hamlin and Osnabrück, after you have turned for home. Guns and lights."

She used the pointer.

"Just before Ilsenburg, to the northeast, there is a factory that manufactures ..."

She turned to her notes to find the information she required. As she did so, she glanced up and caught the eye of Johnnie who blew her a silent kiss. Her face flushed and she suddenly had a hand full of thumbs as she shuffled her papers, but she eventually found the correct piece.

"... Yes ... it manufactures piston rings for Heinkel engines and is quite heavily defended with light and heavy ack-ack, but because of your speed and height, we think you will be over and gone by the time the gunners are aware of your presence. We cannot say that for the target itself. As you approach the target, you will pass over the small town of Ilsenburg; the reconnaissance photos show some heavy 128-millimetre guns as well as 88s and 44s, all down the gorge, on both sides. On top of the factory itself, are three Flakvierling quadruple barrelled 20mil cannon, which, although hand fed, are still capable of putting up a high rate of devastating fire, especially effective at short-range. These will be the primary target of the Mosquitos and front and mid-upper gunners of the first flight of bombers. There are also four batteries of searchlight, four lights in each battery, just to the southwest of the town."

She hesitated and looked around the room, wondering how many of these brave young men would make it back for breakfast tomorrow. Her eyes stopped at Johnnie.

"A well-defended target, gentlemen ... good luck."

She again glanced at Johnnie, but this time with sad eyes. There were no whistles and cheers as she finished, just a murmur of conversation as they absorbed the information she had imparted.

Flight Lieutenant Johnson, the Bombing Leader took the stand.

"Right, chaps, the geography of the place. Thank you, Section Officer Murphy."

He took the pointer from her and she removed the cloth covering a large detailed map of the target area standing on an enormous wooden easel. She climbed down from the platform and took her seat in the front row.

"The mountains that protect the target are three thousand seven hundred and fifty feet high and overhang the valley floor, which is less than one thousand yards wide at that point," he said using the pointer to indicate. "A small town is to the northeast and the protective cliffs are to the south. The POW and workers' camps are to the north and northwest side of the complex. So high-level bombing is out of the question. Particularly after the criticism we came under from our allies, especially the Poles, when over five hundred civilian Polish forced labour workers were accidentally killed in the bombing of Peenemünde."

"One mile directly in front of the factory is a waterfall. Before the war, it was a tourist attraction. Its double fall creates a foaming white ribbon, perfect to see in the dark and it marks exactly the centre of the factory. There will be no use of flares or TIs over the target. It is vital you keep your night vision, so the PFF will drop red ground markers over the last turning point, here, and one and a half miles from the target, here, before the waterfall."

"Sorry to interrupt you, Flight Lieutenant," said Harry Picton, standing. "But we have had a change of heart on marking the last turn and the last mile. We now feel the mountain with the cross and the whiteness of the waterfall will be enough of a marker, no need to risk our night vision."

"Okay, sir, but can I suggest we keep them in reserve just in case?"

"Yes, Okay."

"Our friendly Mossie bus drivers, there at the back, will drop them, if we need them," he indicated towards the back of the hut.

Eighteen aircrew of the Mosquito Path Finder Squadron stood up and took a bow to the whistles and friendly jeers of the crowd.

"Their code name for this op will be 'Beefeater' and their leader will be 'Beefeater One'. They will also mark the rendezvous point over Oschersleben and attack in front of the squadron taking on the machine guns on the factory roof, details of both those later. The ordnances you will be dropping are four thousand pound high explosive penetration bombs."

"Weapons, dear boy, weapons!" was the sarcastic cry from his audience, who burst out laughing

He smiled and carried on, "You will each carry four of the *'weapons'*," he emphasised, "so beware at take-off, you are carrying sixteen thousand pounds of ... I'm bloody frightened of calling them bombs now!" he laughed. "You are carrying sixteen thousand pounds of *bombs*, instead of your normal ten to twelve thousand pounds. As they leave the bomb bay, a cord, secured to the bomb cradle, rips away the safety pin and starts the delay fuse countdown. The air bombers have already received the delay times on each of their individual loads; the armourers will set this. All the bombs will detonate at the same time two minutes after the last aircraft drops its load. The idea is to achieve maximum effect and damage. So, for God's sake, do not be late! As you know, approach speed is exactly two hundred and twenty knots, for those of you still flying wooden bi-planes that equates to two hundred and fifty-three miles an hour."

A few cries of 'Thank you' wafted up from the floor.

"And, as you know, your bomb release height is exactly two hundred and twenty feet. You will be flying below radar level all the way there. The only time you will come above two hundred feet will be when you make your final rendezvous and turn over Oschersleben at three hundred feet. This will be marked with 'Christmas Trees' at five thousand feet. It is forty miles from there to the start of the gorge, which is the final turning point, and the Initial Point of the bombing run. Two mountains mark this. One of them, as you know, has an unmistakable massive iron cross on the top. This you leave on your port side and turn forty degrees to starboard down into the gorge at a height of two hundred and twenty feet, and your speed should now be the optimum. The Turn Indicator will be a red ground marker, if we need to use them. Here, you will turn on, again, your formation and navigation lights to help you get your spacing correct. You will have already checked your bombsight, as you are now only three and a half miles from the target. You will be able to line up on the waterfall and the factory chimneys as soon as you complete your turn, as rehearsed. Using the bombsight, you can start getting your height exact and the release point distance of six hundred and sixty yards will be the easy calculation. At one mile, exactly in line with the centre of the factory, is the double drop of the Ilse Falls."

He moved closer to the enlarged map on its easel and used the pointer.

"Leading you into the gorge will be six of the 'wooden wonders', who are ferociously armed with four, point three-o-three machine guns *and* four twenty mil Cannon. They will strafe the gun positions in the gorge and the Jerry machine-gunners stationed on top of the factory roof, God help them. We believe there are three quadruple-barrelled twenty mil guns up there. Front and mid-upper gunners, these are your targets as well. Remember, to your right, as you go in and as you pass over the factory, are the huts of the POWs and forced workers. Avoid these at all costs. Gunners be careful; do not get carried away and spray their positions. The huts in front of the factory are fair game. Rear gunners; give these a good going over.

"Getting out of the gorge is dodgy. As you know, the port aircraft of your flight will be flying under the overhang and has to come to starboard as soon as he has dropped his load, then climb and turn to port to come up and over the end of the gorge and over Brocken Mountain. This, I remind you, is three thousand seven hundred and fifty feet above your head. The centre and starboard aircraft make sure you get out of his way very quickly. Remember the starboard wall of the gorge is still eighteen hundred feet above you. The gorge is one thousand yards wide, but narrowing and climbing very quickly and turning to port all the time.

"The three remaining Mossies will bring up the rear, dropping two, two hundred and fifty pound explosive incendiaries apiece and will strafe the gun positions and the accommodation huts.

"'Z' hour is exactly 0305 hours. Just remember, that in Nineteen-forty we were lucky if we put our bombs within five miles of the target from fifteen thousand feet! You will be *placing* them exactly on the target from two hundred and twenty feet. Who says we have not progressed? Any questions? ... No. If you have, see me later. Good luck chaps."

It was now the turn of the Navigation Leader to take control of the pointer.

"Gentleman, navigators, air bombers and captains have gone through their bits and pieces already, of course, so this is to pull all that info' together. Your heading from here will be one-one-five degrees at a height of one hundred feet until you cross the Dutch coast, here." He used the pointer and indicated the spit of land north of Amsterdam that protected the Zuiderzee.

"As you have already been warned, watch for the radio masts and their guide ropes. To help you, white Wanganui flares will illuminate the masts, briefly. From there you will turn on to one-zero-eight degrees and cross the Zuiderzee, or the Ijsselmeer, to give it its correct name, at a height of two hundred feet taking a straight course to Oschersleben, looking as if your target is Lübeck, Hanover or Magdeburg. In fact, another Mosquito squadron flying a few minutes behind you will peel off and carry out a diversionary attack on Magdeburg. There will also be a spoof attack on Hanover by Lancasters from just down the road. They will, also, I believe, carry out nuisance attacks on Essen and Dusseldorf. The main distraction for the night fighters will be a large raid on the 'Big City', Berlin, by just over five hundred aircraft.

"At Oschersleben, you will rendezvous with the escorting Mossies and form up into your final bombing formations; your TI here is red over green Wanganui 'Christmas Tree' flares. Between 0252 to 0254 hours, you will turn on to two-four-zero. The first flight will make its final turn into the gorge no sooner than 0304 hours. The TI here will be a red ground marker, that is if we need to use one, that's IF! Oh, and by the way, the bloody great iron cross on the top of the mountain on your left, the 'Ilsestein'… leave it there. The locals like it. The starboard mountain is the 'Wertenberg'.

You know the dangers of flying through the gorge; there is no point me going over them. After you have dropped your bombs, you will climb up and over Brocken Mountain and turn over the town of Herzberg. You should recognise it; there is a large Schloss there. From here, your heading, directly back to the Egmond Gap, is two-eight-eight degrees. You may want to put some height on as you come over Hamlin and the southern outskirts of Osnabrück to avoid the flak and lights there. We shall look forward to seeing your cheerful faces sometime after 0500 hours tomorrow morning. Safe journey chaps."

The Flying Control Officer informed the crews that they would be using the main southwest-northeast runway, runway one-nine. The first flight of three would take-off at 0030 hours, followed by the rest at fifteen-second intervals. They would circle the airfield until all thirty aircraft were in the air and then form into their vic formations before setting off for the coast on their designated heading. Until they were one hundred miles from the Dutch coast, they were to use formation lights as well as navigation lights to keep them together, and, of course, strict radio silence until the final turn.

He wished them luck and handed over to the Meteorological Officer, whose forecasts normally generated, inevitably, some doubt and cynicism. Although this time, he had some incontrovertible information to impart. Beside that there would be light cloud over the sea, clearing as they went further into enemy territory, the sky would be perfectly clear with bright moonlight all the way from then on. There would be light winds from the northeast and snow would cap the Hartz Mountains, especially Brocken Mountain, down to around two thousand five hundred feet.

"Gentlemen, you have been given a 'Z' hour of 0305 hours. Tonight's full moon will occur at precisely 0303 hours. The reason this is relevant is that when the full moon is at its zenith it will illuminate the gorge you are flying down for ten and a half minutes only. Either side of that window, the gorge will be in the shadow of the moon and in total darkness. If you miss that window, you might as well come home, because you will be flying blind in a dangerous narrow gorge in total darkness and you will probably not come out alive, never mind having no chance of hitting your target."

Harry Picton now stood up and emphasised this point.

"That is why, chaps, your timing is absolutely vital. You have rehearsed flying in formation at eight second intervals over a given point. We have a very short window of time to hit after flying nearly five hundred miles. After we make our final turn into the gorge, we must hit that target every eight seconds. It will take over two minutes for us all to pass over the target and for the Mosquitos to follow us through. If we make this, it will get us all over the target and away from all the flak guns protecting that factory, before they have realised we are there, hopefully, and before the gorge plunges into darkness.

Because the fuses of our bombs have been pre-set, we must go through the gorge as fast as we can, exactly on time. This will guarantee maximum damage to the target when our bombs explode together. Do not forget, only eight seconds separate each flight's bombs from the flight behind. They will explode two minutes after the last Mosquitos pass over. The reason we have gone for 0305 hours is that it gives us a very small leeway on the timing.

"Whatever you do, if you miss your drop, do not go round again thinking you have time to drop your load, because you will not have the time! You will miss the moon or be caught in the blast and anybody that happens to will get a royal bollocking from me."

Everyone laughed as he broke the pent-up tension.

"Okay, gents, I'm sure you all remember Air Vice Marshal Horace Nelson. Air Vice Marshal?" he said, inviting him forward to address the aircrews.

"Thank you, Wing Commander. As you know, I head up one of the tactical advice teams of the Target Selection Committee at the Air Ministry, and report directly to Air Chief Marshal Harris. He has asked me to relate to you his thoughts on this operation and is sorry he cannot be here with you today."

He pulled a sheet of paper from his tunic pocket, unfolded it and read:

"*'In August 1940, Sir Winston Churchill said of Fighter Command, during the height of the Battle of Britain, 'never was so much owed by so many to so few'. But when you succeed in 'Operation Parliament' you will give encouragement, hope and the opportunity for a total victory against the tyranny of Nazi Germany, and for that you will have the gratitude of right-thinking people all over the world. God bless and good luck.'* Signed; Air Chief Marshal, Sir A.T. Harris KCB OBE AFC, Air Officer Commanding-in-Chief, Bomber Command."

He folded the paper and replaced it in his tunic.

"The Prime Minister, Air Chief Marshal Harris and I, expect that every man will endeavour to do his duty to make sure that the delivery of this strategic and vital blow against Hitler's 'Wunderwaffen' succeeds. I will not dwell on the consequences of the 'if nots', gentlemen, they are too dreadful for rational thought. I know you will do your utmost to make sure your mission is successful. Need I say more, gentlemen? All that remains for me to do is echo the Air Chief Marshal's blessings. Good luck and God bless."

The Station Commander, Group Captain Thompkins now stood and addressed the aircrews. His cut-glass accent caressed his gathered comrades.

"Gentlemen, you are about to embark on the most important operation that this illustrious squadron of ours has ever undertaken. You have trained long and hard over the last few weeks. We have lost some of our old comrades, but we have embraced *new* comrades into our family brotherhood. I know, that you will carry out your duties, this bright moonlit night, in the way you have always performed them, with courage, tenacity and professionalism. We do not forget – those of us who sit in authority – that you are all volunteers to a man, and you face the dangers of your missions with unflinching bravery. I salute you."

He came to attention and snapped up a salute that would have made the terrifying 'Snowdrop' Flight Sergeant quiver with excitement. To the surprise of every aircrew member present, Group Captain Woodfield, AVM Nelson, AVM Rice and Wing Commander Britton joined him in the salute, and the civilians with them stood up. Harry Picton called the gathered assembly to attention and returned the salute on their behalf.

## 27... Operation Parliament

As they filed into the aircrew dining room for their traditional egg and bacon supper, Yorky said, "Well, I'll be buggered," without attracting the crew's normal response. "I've never been saluted by so many AVMs before."

"How many AVMs have saluted you in your career then, Yorky?" asked Chalkie, with a grin.

"No, y' know what I mean. 'Ave you ever known that to 'appen before, Skipper?"

"No, Yorky, I haven't. But I thought it was a nice touch from the old boy."

"Ay up! 'Ee's just walked in. Bugger me; he's sitting down to 'ave a meal with us. Would you credit it? Did you know that every time there's an op he stands by the caravan and salutes every aircraft as it takes off?"

"I don't know if you've noticed, Yorky, but he is always waiting for us at the debriefing when we come back as well, no matter what time of day it is," said Dusty.

"I think all this just goes to show how important this little jolly is," said Algy. "It certainly sounds like they expect some of us to get the chop, if all that talk from your little Popsie about guns and lights is not duff gen, Skipper."

"I think you're right, Algy; they do see this as a big sortie, but I think it's just another op for us."

He deliberately ignored Algy's reference to the 'well-defended target' that Ginny had emphasised.

After their meal, they crossed over to the crew room and joined all the other crews dragging on their flying suits, parachute harnesses and Mae Wests, with the gunners struggling to don their electrically heated Irwin suits that stopped them from freezing to death. Most of the aircrews were using the flying boots issued to them that featured a lace-up black leather walking-shoe with detachable zip-up suede and sheepskin lined upper section. This contained a hidden knife so the upper could be cut away leaving a normal shoe, much less obvious than a pair of flying boots if you were trying to avoid capture. They all made sure their flying suit pockets contained their personal escape packs. Johnnie knew of some aircrew that carried revolvers or small automatic pistols stuck down the side of their flying boots. He had a thin rubber map of northern Europe tucked down his right boot. In his left boot, he carried a small curved container with his emergency rations in. Those that felt inclined handed over to Jimmy Green, the Adjutant, a letter or will form to pass on to their next of kin if it was their turn not to take part in the debriefing session in the early hours of tomorrow.

As they dressed in their flying gear, they went through the emotions that every warrior since time immemorial has gone through in that hour before battle. That fear of the unknown, the fear of the known, that gut-wrenching feeling, which has a dramatic effect on the bowels of even the bravest of men, that sudden surge of nervous excitement, of uncertainty, that feeling of inadequacy, that stab of fear. The hour before battle.

The WAAFs staffing the parachute store had noticed how muted the friendly banter they normally exchanged with the aircrews was this time, but there was always the exception, the one airman who could not resist the hoary old joke.

"What shall I do if it doesn't work, sweetheart?"

"Bring it back and we'll change it, darlin'."

They all filed outside to wait for the transport that would take them to their aircraft waiting on their dispersal pads. Snow was blowing fitfully across the airfield. It was cold. They stood around sharing out the sweets from their ration packs or chain-smoking. Some people were laughing at unfunny jokes, some just quietly stood there, deep in their own thoughts, some stamping their feet and swinging their arms in the cold winter air trying to keep warm. Johnnie and his crew scrambled up on a crew bus with 'Ginger' Bere and his crew. There was very little conversation as the bus bounced round the perimeter track until the WAAF driver stopped the bus calling out, 'G-George'. The two crews wished each other 'all the best' as Gloria's seven charges jumped down and walked towards her, a dark menacing shape in the gloom of a November night. The moon was yet to rise and the only light came from the open door of the small dispersal hut fifty yards away. A torch flashed, a voice called out.

"Are you ready to do the pre-flight, sir?"

"Yes, Chiefy, everything Okay, I presume?"

"Yes, Mr Sanderson, no problems, bloody cold wind though."

They walked round the bomber together as Johnnie carried out his pre-flight ground checks. He signed the Chiefy's Form 700, noting that the fuel load was the maximum of 2,154 gallons. In the meantime, Jock had inspected his charges suspended from the open bomb bay, ensuring that they were firmly secure and the fuse lanyard to each 'weapon' was attached. The armourers had spent the afternoon going from aircraft to aircraft loading and setting the fuses of the bombs, making sure that the timings for each one had matched the proposed flight order. The air bombers would use the switches on their release board to arm the bombs as they crossed the North Sea.

As the crew of Gloria waited for the first green flare from the tower to tell them to climb aboard, they gathered in the thin snow around the sheltering tail, lighting up cigarettes and pipes.

Johnnie stood beside the sleeping giant on its concrete dispersal pan, the chilly November evening air misting his breath. Reaching inside his flying suit, he pulled Ginny's lock of hair from the breast pocket of his tunic and gently rubbed it between his fingers, feeling the soft silkiness. Before he returned it to the pocket next to his heart, he kissed it and under his breath whispered, "Until later, my darling."

He was not to know how long that later, would be.

He pulled out his 'flying pipe' from the same pocket and his tobacco pouch from the side pocket of his tunic, slowly filled and tamped the pipe. The striking match flared in the darkness causing the attending ground crew some momentary concern. He enjoyed the organic taste of the fresh tobacco. The aromatic hint of vanilla calmed the ground crew, who smiled and muttered something about the Skipper enjoying a last gasp before his flight. No one noticed the red-ribboned lock of black hair fluttering to the cold, snow-covered ground, before blowing away in the wind to disappear into the black night.

Algy placed one of his favourite Turkish cigarettes in his ivory holder and flicked his American Zippo lighter, whose flaring flame highlighted the pale faces of his apprehensive comrades. The distinctive foreign scent of roasted tobacco drew derogatory comments from his colleagues comparing it to what camels leave in the desert besides footprints! He went to tuck the white silk scarf closer around his neck to keep out the winter chill, but as he touched his bare neck, he remembered he had used it the night before to tie a kinky young lady to her brass bed head. She was the wife of an artillery Captain serving in North Africa, while Algy was serving her! He smiled at the memory and looked forward to reclaiming his scarf tomorrow night.

"Do you realise, lads, this is the fifteenth sortie towards our tour? I'm surprised we've lasted this bloody long. I didn't think we'd even make thirteen," said a morose Dusty.

"Oh, you're such a cheerful bastard, Dusty, you really are," was Chalkie's comment. Still, he wondered why he had said 'touch wood' and patted the wooden doorway of his billet hut when he left earlier this evening; he had never been superstitious; why now?

"I thought this was our sixteenth, Dusty?" said Yorky.

"Yeah, but remember the RAF only counts the Friëdrichshafen and La Spezia sortie as one," said Dusty

"Oh yeah, tight buggers, good old RAF. Well, remember wot they say, lads, 'Join the navy and see t' world, join the air force and see t' next!"

His hand slipped inside his Irwin flying suit and checked that the chicken wishbone was still in his pocket.

A flare suddenly bathed the night with its eerie wavering green light.

"Git on board liddle doggies, git on board," chanted Yorky. It had become part of his boarding routine now.

Johnnie tapped his lucky 'flying pipe' against the leading edge of the starboard tail fin to empty the still-glowing tobacco from it, but swore as the stem of the pipe snapped off in his hand. He picked up the empty bowl as the embers hissed in the snow, and cursing again put it back in his tunic pocket.

Jock went to relieve himself, as he normally did, on Gloria's tail wheel, but a sudden flurry of snow convinced him he was not that desperate to go.

They went to scramble up into Gloria in their normal order, Jock, Johnnie, Chalkie, Paddy, Algy, Dusty and finally Yorky, but Dusty said, "Hang on, Yorky, I'd better 'water the wheel' before we go."

He turned and started to relieve himself over the tail wheel, despite the weather.

"I'm not standin' 'ere in the bloody cold waitin' for you," laughed Yorky, and climbed up the ladder into the fuselage and made his way aft. It was the first time they had broken their normal boarding routine. He scrambled over the tail spar and after closing the bulkhead doors behind him, clipped his parachute to the starboard side of the fuselage, just before his turret. As he did so, something fell from his flying suit, unnoticed. He struggled into his turret, reached behind him and slid the doors shut, ensuring he had locked them, isolating him in his little Plexiglas world. After clipping on his safety harness and plugging in his heated suit, he started the pre-flight checks on his guns, ammunition and turret.

Dusty had followed Yorky up the short boarding ladder, and pulled down the metal frame holding his mounting step and heaved himself up into his lofty outpost that is the mid-upper turret. His feet resting in the stirrups, he fastened his safety harness on and carried out what is always his first action. He took out the photo of girlfriend, Mavis, kissed it and went to jam it into the fixings of his starboard gun. However, for some reason the photo slipped and disappeared out of sight behind the gun. He tried to pull it out, but his hands were too big, it would have to stay there until he stripped out the guns tomorrow. Anyway, he thought, she is still with me.

Paddy had settled in behind his anti-dazzle curtain and was preparing his pencils, maps and charts. He pulled, from his trouser pocket, the monkey fist that had kept him company and given him comfort both at sea and in the air for many years. It was a silly old seaman's custom, he knew, but ... for the first time he noticed, the tightly woven strands of cord were starting to fray, unravel and part, the result of his regular caressing. He smiled to himself, muttered something about 'the luck of the Irish', and put it back in his pocket.

Johnnie started the pre-flight checks, as did the other members of his crew, and twenty minutes later they had all reported to him that everything was 'A-OK The starboard inner engine was normally the first to fire up and would burst into life immediately; however, tonight it struggled to catch. After being primed for the third time, it finally roared into life. As it did so, Chalkie commented, with a smile:

"For a moment there, I thought the old girl didn't want to do this trip, Skipper."

The other engines appeared reluctant to start as well, but after a few minutes, they were all throbbing healthily. Chalkie had a reason why he was keen to do this trip. He hoped they would kill as many Krauts as possible, because in two day's time it would be the third anniversary of losing his family to German bombers.

Thirty minutes after the first flare, the second lit up the dark Lincolnshire sky, and the giant black birds of war started to lumber round the peri track towards the runway threshold. In front of Gloria, two flights of three Lancs thundered away down the runway. Fifteen seconds later, the Aldis lamp from the flight caravan flashed green. Johnnie checked the navigation and formation lights were on, set the directional compass to zero, double-checked the QFE was correctly set, ran up the engines against the brakes and called 'ready for take-off'. On Chalkie's answer of 'Ready for take-off', he released the brakes and opened the throttles slowly until they were against the gate, asking Chalkie for 'full power'.

"Full power," he repeated and slid his hands under Johnnie's on the throttles to make sure they did not slip back when Johnnie took his hands off to pull thirty-two tons of bomber into the cold night air.

They passed the red and white chequered control caravan beside the runway and its normal farewell committee of onlookers and the Group Captain frozen into a rigid salute. A flash of white and a pale face caught Johnnie's eye and he realised it was Ginny waving her handkerchief in farewell. They had not spoken at all today; just exchanged glances and smiles at the briefing. He wished he had had the opportunity to say goodbye.

His feet were dancing on the rudder pedals as Gloria 'wagged her tail', he eased the yoke forward and the tail wheel left the ground. Paddy started to call the airspeed when it reached 70 mph and every three seconds after that, until Gloria heaved her substantial frame into the winter sky at 110 mph. She climbed laboriously into the night, her bomb load of 16,000 pounds holding her low over the falling hills of the Wolds. He recorded in his log, 'Airborne at 0031 hours 13.9.1943 Elkington.'

They climbed to a thousand feet and circled the airfield until white over green flares climbed into the sky from Wing Commander Harry Picton's bomber, the signal to head for the English coast and take up their flying formation. They slid down the Wolds to the flat plain of Lindsey to level off at two hundred feet. As soon as they crossed the coast, just north of Mablethorpe, Johnnie ordered his gunners to check their weapons and test fire them.

"Algy, take station in the front turret and test those guns as well."

"Okay, Skipper."

He scrambled underneath Chalkie's control panel, carefully avoided standing on the prone Jock and heaved himself up into the turret, his feet held above Jock in makeshift stirrups.

He cocked the two .303s and after notifying Johnnie of his intentions, squeezed the triggers, and the hammering chatter of the two Browning machine guns and the brassy clatter of the empty cartridge shells falling through the chutes into the collection bags, rewarded him. After a few minutes, he made the guns safe, locked the turret facing forward and crawled back to his radio station to monitor the airways and the Fishpond radar.

When he had left the nose cone, Jock reported to Johnnie.

"Bombs selected and fused."

Silence returned as those that could, searched the bright sky for other aircraft, friend or foe.

They dropped to a hundred feet and charged across the North Sea at two hundred miles an hour. The Path Finder Mosquitos of their escort squadron were just starting to line up on the peri track back at Elkington, their twin Merlin '25' 1,635 horsepower engines roaring defiance as they raced down the runway and gracefully swooped into the winter night. They would overtake the Lancs well before the first turn, and their comrades, who were to lead the attack, would follow them later. Their cruising speed was nearly three hundred miles an hour.

All of Gloria's crew were busy with their duties, checking equipment and systems, radios and radar, guns and gauges, maps and charts. They were too busy to think of the dangers ahead; too busy to think about the batteries of guns waiting for them in the 'Ilse Schucht'; too busy to think about coming home; too busy to think about dying; they just got on with their jobs, even though the fear was there, always … just controlled.

When the navigator, Paddy, told him they were one hundred miles from the Dutch coast, Johnnie turned off the navigation and formation lights after flashing them once to remind the rest of his flight, flying close behind him.

"Thank you, Michael, how long to the masts?"

"Twenty-six minutes, Skipper," Michael, answered him instantly, anticipating the question.

The Pathfinders had dropped white sky flares to mark the turn and to illuminate the masts and the first fifteen aircraft of the squadron turned on to their new heading. Ginny had warned them to keep well clear of the guide wires of the northern mast, but Pilot Officer Fred Mercury, in Q-Queenie of GF4 from 'B' Flight, somehow managed to touch one with his starboard wing. At two hundred miles an hour, and just one hundred feet high, the thirty-two tons of men and metal did not stand a chance and ploughed straight into the earth, exploding on impact with a secondary explosion almost instantaneously as the bombs they were carrying detonated. Flame, smoke and debris filled the air, causing chaos to the fourteen following Lancs flying just seconds behind. They tried desperately to avoid the explosion and each other as they took violent evasive action. Although they were all very skilful pilots, the chaos of the situation inevitably took its toll.

As the ripple of panic spread backwards, the last trio of GF5 had very little airspace to flirt with. Flying Officer 'Froggie' French slammed the control column into his stomach and called for his engineer to power 'through the gate' as he heaved D-Dog up and to port. He narrowly missed his two wingmen, Jimmy Anderson in E-Edward and Isaac Cohen in G-George 2, who were not so lucky. They turned into each other and filled the night air with fire and death as they slammed into the ground with an enormous explosion that lit up the Dutch countryside for miles. In the time it takes to check the airspeed indicator, twenty-one young men were dead and their bodies burnt beyond recognition.

The moon had risen and the brightness of the silver orb and the glow of the funeral pyres lit up the night sky as the glaring white flares dimmed and died. The rest of the squadron had no option, but to reform as fast as they could and close up together back at one hundred feet and thunder their way over the Zuiderzee.

"What the hell happened back there, Yorky?" asked a shocked Johnnie.

"Bugger knows, Skip. It looked like someone hit the radio mast, but I don't know what happened after that. There were two more explosions, but I didn't see any flak going up."

"Okay. That should have told Jerry something is happening, if he didn't know before now. Keep rubber-necking everyone, if there are any night fighters around, that will bring 'em running."

The twenty-seven remaining aircraft of 599 closed up into formation and flew over the Zuiderzee, through Holland and into Germany.

As they passed just north of the small riverside town of Lingen, searchlights flicked on and swung across the sky and a few desultory ack-ack guns banged away in hope, but the squadron was miles past by the time the gunners had realised they had been flown over. Twenty minutes later the guns and searchlight batteries defending the approaches to Hanover and Braunschweig came to life. The earlier passage of bombers heading for Berlin had alerted them, but the squadron passed safely to the south of these oft-bombed cities. The turning and rendezvous point of Oschersleben was minutes away.

"Twenty minutes to RP and turn, Skipper," reported Paddy.

"Red over green sky markers directly ahead, Skipper, five miles," informed Jock from the nose fifteen minutes later.

"I see them, Finlay."

"Two minutes to turn, heading will be two-four-eight, Skip."

"Thank you, Michael. Stand by everyone, fifteen minutes to target. Algy, take station in the front turret," ordered Johnnie.

They arrived at the turning point a few seconds after 0252 hours.

"They do look like Christmas trees, don't they, Skipper?" remarked Chalkie, as the gently falling red over green flares high above them slowly drifted down.

The six Mosquitos that would lead them into the gorge swept up to take their station at the head of the attacking formation.

"Guy Fawkes leader to all GF aircraft, Guy Fawkes leader to all GF aircraft, escort in place, escort in place, tally ho, tally ho!"

Harry's RT call readied 599 Squadron for their turn in formation.

"Turn ... now, Skipper," said Paddy.

In the clear, bright moonlight, Johnnie could clearly see the other aircraft making their high-speed turn in perfect formation, sliding from their staggered vic formation to line abreast. For the next twelve minutes, they would keep on this course until the final swing on to the target. They increased their speed to two hundred and fifty miles an hour and closed in to fifty feet apart.

All three gunners on board Gloria, and the other twenty-six Lancasters, double-checked their guns, cocked them and made sure ammunition chutes were clear of obstacles and checked their illuminated sights. Bomb Aimers were double-checking calibrations of their SABB bombsights and checking their release boards were okay. Navigators had their eyes glued to stopwatches, counting down the minutes and seconds to the next turn, notifying their pilots as they neared the end of their last timed run from the turn over Oschersleben.

"Two minutes to final turn, Skipper." Repeated every eight seconds.

As the squadron, led by its 'Wooden Wonders', thundered over the Heinkel piston ring factory, a few miles before the town of Ilsenburg, alarm bells, Klaxons and sirens erupted into the night, bringing running troops to their 'Flieger Abwehr Kanonen' and searchlights. By the time they had manned their guns and lights the squadron had flashed past and were beyond the town. The alarms from the factory though, had alerted the anti-aircraft stations and searchlight batteries all through the valley. Hundreds of soldiers were pouring from their billets, sleepy-eyed and dishevelled, pulling on their uniforms and helmets galloping to their defence positions.

The R/T crackled into life as the Squadron Leader, Wing Commander Harry Picton called.

"Guy Fawkes, Guy Fawkes. This is Guy Fawkes Leader, on lights, repeat, on lights. Take note, Beefeater One has confirmed there will be *no*, repeat, *no* TIs dropped for final turn."

The two flights of three sleek, powerful, heavily armed, twin-engine De Havilland FB Mk VI Mosquitos swung in perfect harmony into the Ilse Gorge at precisely 0304 hours on the morning of November 13, 1943, in bright moonlight. So bright, it was almost like daylight, allowing the pilots to see every detail of the giant iron cross on top of the Ilsestein Mountain.

"GF One A, GF One A, turn ... NOW!"

Immediately obeying Harry's order, Frank Hubbard and Tony Rance, the first three giant bombers turned together into the gorge, like a trio of display aircraft a quarter of their size. Following, eight seconds behind, 'Ginger' Bere in F-Freddie and his two wingmen, Bob Hirst and Taffy Morgan turned on his order.

"GF One B, GF One B, turn ... NOW!"

Three and a half miles to the most important target 599 Squadron would ever attack.

Johnnie turned on his navigation and formation lights, as did every other war bird. He saw the bulk of Ilsestein with its huge iron cross coming up clearly in front of his flight of three. Eight seconds after his roommate, Ginger, Johnnie issued his order to his wingmen, Mike Hunt and Peter Montgomery.

"GF Two A, GF Two A, turn ... NOW!"

Every eight seconds, the flight leaders gave the same order and within one minute and twelve seconds, twenty-six Lancasters, six leading Mosquitos and three trailing Mosquitos were in the gorge filling it with the terrifying roar of one hundred and twenty-two Rolls Royce Merlin engines at full power.

The twenty-seventh Lancaster, Squadron Leader Bill Askin, leading the first vic of 'B' Flights GF3, had problems before the last turn into the gorge; he suddenly started to lose power to both of his port engines, he pulled out of the turn at the last minute and flew straight on after giving the order to turn to his flight. His two wingmen made the turn, as did the rest of the squadron.

Ahead, the factory complex and POW camp suddenly plunged into darkness, sirens wailed, orders screamed out and men ran. The POW camp inmates had no doubts that the raid was finally happening.

Jock was already sighting up on the distant factory and would soon start to instruct Johnnie for the final run in. He double-checked his stopwatch and called,

"One minute to bomb release."

Johnnie did not need to respond; he was too busy concentrating flying through the ever-growing walls of the narrowing gorge. Standing out in the moonlight, a perfect guide to the factory, were the stark, white waters of Ilse Falls, its double tumbling cascades as good as any ground marker flare.

The first storms of flak came without warning. Red, white and orange balls of fire were streaming from the top of the factory. The foremost three Mosquitos had opened up with their fearsome armoury of weapons in return, punching lead and fire at the guns and their gunners on the roof. The second trio of Mossies' cannon and machine guns hammered yet more lead at the doomed German artillerymen, blowing their sandbagged positions apart.

The first giant Lancasters, flying through what to them, seemed a very narrow and confined space, joined in the battle. Harry Picton and his wingmen's gunners were spraying the anti-aircraft gun positions along the bottom of the gorge.

The flak gunners in front of the factory now opened up with a vengeance, but their shell fuses had been set too high and they were exploding hundreds of feet above the gorge. A few of the lighter flak guns were putting up a tremendous rate of fire, starting to throw up a curtain of hot steel and lead across the approach of the bombers, but most of the gunners were still leaping on to their guns and loading them as fast as they could.

The Mosquitos had done an excellent job on the multi-barrelled guns on the roof of the factory. Ten dead men surrounded the two starboard guns, which lay broken and twisted while two more Jerry gunners lay dead beside the port side gun, the one under the overhang, but it was still pumping lethal 20mm shells at the fast-approaching aircraft.

"BOMBS GONE!" screamed Harry Picton's bomb aimer, his voice almost lost in the cacophony of machine gun chatter.

Newly promoted, Corporal Heinrich Schlep of the XVth Flieger Abwehr Kanonen Regiment, scrambled from his barrack hut just in front of the factory and, alongside his colleagues, was desperately trying to bring his 44mm anti-aircraft gun into action. Around him, the other guns were already firing as fast as they could. The crash of the guns, the flash of fire from the pumping barrels and the flying empty brass shell cases all added to the confused storm of battle around him. His eyes, drawn upwards by the shouting stutter of the enemy machine guns and the defiant roar of the attacking aircraft, were wide with terror.

The bright moonlight allowed him to witness every terrifying detail of the three giant bombers thundering towards him. Four enormous, green painted bombs seemed to slide from the belly of each aircraft. They started to spin quickly, appearing to hover beneath the aircraft, before, as if in slow motion, they fell away and glided downwards heading directly for him, or so it appeared. He screamed and fell to the ground curling into a ball behind the sandbags that surrounded the gun as the twelve, one and three-quarter ton bombs passed a few feet above his head. They smashed through the front and the roof of the factory and drilled their way through the reinforced concrete blast walls, burying their dormant, but deadly, destructive force, deep inside the factory to await their awakening calls.

Corporal Heinrich Schlep did not have time to realise he had fouled his field-grey trousers, before the stream of bullets from the next flight of 'Terrorfliegers' killed him and his colleagues. They were not long out of training and had never fired their gun in anger.

Harry Picton died swiftly and violently. A quadruple stream of bullets ripped through the front of A-Apple destroying the cockpit, the nose cone and the turret and the four men sitting in them. His bomb aimer was the first to die followed by his wireless operator manning the front turret, the burst of 20mm bullets ripped Harry's body apart alongside that of his flight engineer. A-Apple slewed across to starboard and skimmed over the top of the factory, narrowly missing one of the chimneys and his wingman, Frank Hubbard. The mid-upper and tail gunner of Harry's stricken bomber were still pouring fire from their guns as A-Apple careered into the ground in a sliding, slithering charge. It hit the perimeter fence of the POW camp, ripping up nearly one hundred yards of barbed wire, taking with it two of the machine-gun watchtowers and destroying some of the huts, before exploding in a ball of fuel-fed fire. Frank Hubbard and Harry's other wingman, Tony Rance, pulled up and away from the factory, then turned hard to port to escape the grip of the gorge. Flight Sergeant Frank Hubbard clicked over to R/T.

"Guy Fawkes one leader has pancaked, repeat, Guy Fawkes one leader has pancaked!"

The mid-upper and nose gunner of 'Ginger' Bere's F-Freddie, flying eight seconds behind Harry, hammered away at the last remaining Jerry gun on the roof and it quickly fell silent. His flight had delivered their weapons on target and screamed away up the gorge, the two wingmen quickly getting out of his way allowing him to pull out from beneath the overhang.

Searchlights had now joined the party and their beams were sweeping up and down the gorge, adding to the terror and confusion, frantically trying to lock on to a target, but the aircraft were flashing by at two hundred and fifty miles an hour a few feet above their heads. The swinging lights, the streams of tracer, the exploding flak, the roar of aero engines, the stuttering shouts of machine guns, the cacophony of war was terrifying. For a moment, Johnnie had a flash of insane clarity in this bedlam of violence, and found himself paraphrasing Tennyson's epic, 'Cannon to right of them, Cannon to left of them, Cannon in front of them, Volley'd and Thunder'd' … Flew the six hundred!'

It was now Gloria's turn to deliver, at high-speed, over seven tons of high explosives, along with her wingmen. Algy and Dusty were concentrating their fire on the accommodation huts and ack-ack guns in front of the factory, while in the rear turret Yorky's hands tightly gripped the triggers of his blazing guns, pouring thousands of rounds down at the anti-aircraft batteries that lined the gorge, as were his colleagues in the bombers alongside him.

German flak guns were now fully manned and putting up heavy fire towards the streaking bombers. Nevertheless, the squadron was returning an effective and terrifying barrage of lead and fire. All eight Browning machine guns on each aircraft were spewing forth their vengeful bullets at the stationary targets below them. Their height and speed were saving them from the hail of lead and fire. By the time the German gunners had picked a target, it had flashed by, and they had to re-align their sights for the next one.

Jock had the two left hand chimneys closing in perfectly in his bombsight; they were sitting next to the graduated lines at the top and bottom of his viewer. The chimneys touched the vertical lines of the sight, 660 yards. He pressed the tit!

"BOMBS GONE!" He yelled.

Johnnie started to turn to starboard to get out from the overhang, but Flying Officer Pete Montgomery in I-India next to him and H-Harry next to him, had not started to move.

"Jesus, move you bastards!" screamed Chalkie, waving frantically at them from less than fifty feet away.

The Australian, Mike Hunt in H-Harry pulled up and to starboard as Johnnie almost pushed I-India physically after him. The overhang was coming at them very quickly; Johnnie kicked the rudder over and sideslipped from under the mountain.

Jock, lying prone in the Plexiglas cone, had scrabbled backwards in a futile effort to escape hitting the rocks that were looming directly in front of him. As Gloria slid away and up, he made the rest of the crew aware of his feelings.

"Fuck me, Skipper that was fucking close!"

"You think you were close, Jock, you should have sat up here," called Dusty. "I think I've shit myself!"

"Yes, sorry about that chaps, that did get a bit hairy, didn't it."

The rest of GF2 of 'A' Flight dropped their bombs and got out of the gorge without further damage.

The German gunners were starting to find their range now and the light flak guns were hitting more aircraft, but again the bombers' speed and height were to their advantage, as one gun could not stay on them for more than a couple of seconds.

Bill Askin's remaining wingmen went through okay, as did two of GF3B, but the flak guns at the falls badly damaged the third aircraft, R-Roger piloted by John Titchmarsh, who was struggling to keep the bomber in the air. Though bleeding badly from a wound, his bomb aimer managed to release his weapons, but John could not get R-Roger out from under the overhang. The bomber exploded on impact with the mountain leaving a burning stain of fuel and debris.

'Gunner' Hargreaves and his flight dropped their load eight seconds behind them, but the second flight of GF4 lost Flight Sergeant Jimmy Campbell in V-Victor, a friend of Jock McGuffin, and Pilot Officer David (Jones the pilot) Jones in W-Willie. The first batteries of medium flak guns, which were now on the ball, had hit them both hard. V-Victor had slammed into the ground after passing over the waterfall and W-Willie had smacked into the waterfall itself. Neither crew survived.

'C' Flight had started badly. They had lost two aircraft at the radio masts at Egmond and although Squadron Leader Joe Kendrick, leading GF5 had led the first flight through the turn, the flak guns two miles from the target took out his two starboard engines. He tried to claw up and out of the gorge, but his port engines were slewing him to starboard, pushing him into his two wingmen. His choice was simple although dramatic, his colleagues or he and his crew. He rammed his foot hard down on the port rudder pedal, turned the wheel hard to port, pulled back violently on the control column, desperately trying to bring A-Able out of the gorge and away from the other two aircraft. He almost succeeded, but realised he could not escape the grip of the gorge and cried out, 'Sorry, lads!' as he touched the wall with his port wing. A-Able exploded in a massive ball of fire that cascaded into the bottom of the gorge, the crews of the two ack-ack guns directly underneath, screamed in terror as the burning wreckage and fuel engulfed them. His two wingmen went on to drop their bombs and escape the gorge; they survived because of his sacrifice.

Twenty seconds after the last remaining pilots of GF5, Flight Lieutenant Jock Giblin, Pilot Officer 'Bluey' Coogan and Flying Officer 'Froggie' French had negotiated the corridor of fire and lead, and dropped their bombs squarely on the target, the last piece of the jigsaw that was 'Operation Parliament' dropped into place. The last three Mosquito light bombers thundered through the gorge at over three hundred miles an hour, firing four Browning machine guns and four Hispano cannons each, filling the gorge with yet more deadly firepower, revenging the loss of so many RAF aircraft. As they rocketed over the target, they released their six 250 pound incendiary bombs on to the accommodation barracks and factory with devastating effect. They should have drawn the curtain on this attack, but one Lancaster bomber wanted the last say.

Squadron Leader Bill Askin's flight engineer had diagnosed their loss of power two minutes earlier as a fuel problem and rectified it by swapping fuel tanks. The engines regained their thunderous power and Bill turned again for the gorge. He followed the Mosquitos by just over a minute. A new curtain of steel and lead greeted M-Mother, 44mm, 88mm and 20mm guns threw up everything they could muster, hammering the last bomber. Bill's flight engineer and front gunner never heard his bomb aimer shout 'Bombs Gone' for they were dead. As were the rest of the crew two seconds later when the 'Figgy Duffs' already dropped on the factory received their awakening call, as the last drop of acid broached the cellophane strip and released the spring-loaded firing pin. It hit the copper-firing cap, which ignited the detonator that set off the first bomb of the one hundred and eighty-six tons of high explosive that had buried itself deep in the bowels of the factory. It erupted in the blink of an eye, directly under Bill Askin in M-Mother, blowing her and her crew to smithereens. The explosion was enormous; every bomb erupted simultaneously.

Doctor Irwin Schwatzwald, head of fuel technology at the factory, sat at his desk and looked up to stare through the high window of his office when he heard the unusual sound of approaching aircraft. He then became concerned at the sound of gunfire coming from directly overhead. A one and three-quarter ton bomb appeared through the three-foot thick anti-blast wall of his office in an avalanche of concrete, brick, wood, plaster and dust, burying itself in the floor in front of him. Strangely, he wondered why there were two red and one light green band painted around the casing towards the front of the bomb as he calmly picked pieces of plaster and concrete from his desk. He was still sitting there, in a state of complete shock, two minutes later when the world erupted around him. The bombs ignited hundreds of tons of his rocket propellant, carefully stored in fire and bomb-proof bunkers, or so he and the German authorities believed.

The overhang of the mountain deflected some of the force of the explosion, but the giant mushroom-shaped column of flames, smoke and debris punched high into the night sky. The narrowness of the gorge amplified the unbelievable sound of the explosion; it roared and echoed over Brocken Mountain, and forty miles away in Magdeburg and Hanover people looked up in alarm. The blast wave that swept up the gorge and the mountain pushed Gloria violently upwards. Johnnie fought hard to keep her in a steady climbing turn. Yorky and Dusty, who had spun his turret to face aft, both yelled out in excitement and surprise.

"It's gone up, it's gone up. Jesus, look at that!"

"Bloody hell!" exclaimed Dusty. "What a bang! Christ, there are bits and pieces everywhere. Look at the smoke. It must be going up thousands of feet!"

Individual bombs hitting the building had caused damage without even exploding; they had drilled through the three feet of the concrete blast walls as if they were butter. Every individual chamber had received at least one bomb, and when the 'Figgy Duffs' had erupted, the offices, production lines, experimental sections, fuel dumps and test facilities blasted apart. The exploding rocket propellant had increased the power of the blast tremendously. Even the giant chimneys had helped the destruction by toppling on the test sheds behind the factory. The blast devastated the factory, obliterating the barrack accommodation huts and eliminating hundreds of soldiers, scientists and staff. There was not one wall of the complex left standing, and the German's had thought the factory was bomb-proof.

Although he would never know, Harry Picton had enabled hundreds of POWs to escape from their prison camp. As she crashed, A-Apple had ripped a huge hole in the barbed wire fences, allowing the RAF and USAAF prisoners to swarm through and disappear into the woods and hills of the Hartz Mountains. Blast damage and falling debris did cause casualties unfortunately in the POW and worker camps, but thousands of civilian forced workers were able to scatter and escape their slave labour.

The site would never recover. Operation Parliament was a total success, but the cost had been high. Of the thirty Lancasters that left Elkington, only twenty-one came out of 'Ilse Schucht'. Twenty-one aircrew members had perished at Egmond, and forty-two in the gorge. One hundred and forty-three POWs and slave workers had died in the camps. A high price to pay for one operation, but many thousands of lives saved worldwide.

Johnnie knew Harry had bought it, but did not know who else had gone. He circled above Brocken Mountain.

"This is GF Two leader come in GF Three leader" he called over the R/T.

"GF Two leader, this is O-Orange. GF Three Leader didn't make the turn, over."

"Okay, O-Orange. Come in GF Four leader come in GF Four leader. This is GF Two leader."

"GF Two leader this is GF Four leader, I am OK, but GF Five leader has bought it. You're O/C now, Johnnie, out," replied Gunner Hargreaves.

Johnnie was now the Senior Officer and the Officer Commanding the Squadron. He turned Gloria up and over the snow-covered Brocken mountain climbing fast. He flew back over the gorge and saw the flames and a column of smoke pouring thousands of feet skywards. No guns or searchlights responded to his flight, the site was completely devastated. His impression was a gorge filled with fire, smoke and men running for the hills.

The moon slid from its zenith and the shadow of Broken Mountain slowly pulled the blanket of darkness over Ilse Schucht, the torch of destruction illuminating the wreckage of the 'bomb-proof' factory. Algy climbed down from the turret, patted Jock on the back and returned to his radio shack, while Jock climbed into the turret for the journey back home.

"Algy, send the signal to group."

"Ok, Skipper."

He tapped out the Morse code signal indicating the success of the mission.

'Guy Fawkes Leader to Woldimp, Guy Fawkes Leader to Woldimp, Bonfire, bonfire, bonfire.'

Back in Elkington, the duty radio operator, surrounded by senior officers and VIPs, called out excitedly:

"It's bonfire! It's Bonfire!"

Johnnie clicked the intercom microphone to R/T broadcast. "Guy Fawkes leader to all aircraft, this is Guy Fawkes leader to all aircraft. Good show, chaps, you got the bugger! Now you can all piss off home! Good luck, Guy Fawkes leader, out."

How many aircrews would get back safely to Elkington he wondered, there was still a long and dangerous journey in front of them, and half of Germany was now wide awake.

# 28 ... Home at Last

Johnnie turned Gloria and rolled down the snow-covered slope of Brocken Mountain, the glare of the burning factory sliding out of sight as the mountain shielded them from the scene of their success.

"Turn on to two-eight-eight, Skipper. That takes us back to the Egmond Gap," informed Paddy.

"Two-eight-eight, thanks Michael, report everybody."

The crew of Gloria reported calmly back to their Skipper that they were all okay. Although full of adrenaline from the attack, they were surprisingly restrained. Johnnie knew it was the after effect of unrelenting fear. They had all carried out their duties brilliantly, bravely and boldly, they were grateful that they had not let their comrades down. Although fear had sat there, right on their shoulders, their training, experience and faith in each other had not allowed *that* gremlin to grab hold. They were now satisfied, relieved that they had done their duty, and that they had done their job; the target destroyed; they were alive. All they had to do now was to get home. A large number of their colleagues would not be joining them.

The dash for the coast was now on. The heavy raid on Berlin should have kept the bulk of night fighters away from their proposed flight path home, but there was always the danger of searchlight-aided flak and the sound of the explosion would have alerted every gun, searchlight and fighter station for miles around.

Their track would take them just south of the ancient city of Hamlin, and Johnnie hoped that Gloria was not the new Pied Piper for night fighters. Apart from some desultory flak, they passed Hamlin without incident. The quiet before the storm, thought Johnnie. A few minutes later, as they passed Herford and approached Osnabruck at 12,000 feet, without warning flak burst and cracked uncomfortably close to them. "I spoke to bloody soon," he said to himself.

The flak was thick. 88mm and 110mm anti-aircraft shells exploded in fury-filled smoke balls, spitting fire and deadly shrapnel in an unending barrage of noise and death. Obscene black smoke balls of expended flak stained the sky. Johnnie fought the shock waves that tossed the Lancaster in every direction as flying metal raled against the skin of the aircraft with a wicked intention.

A blast of heavy flak slammed the tail of Gloria suddenly and violently upwards, pushing her in to an unnatural vertical position. Acrid smoke and the rotten-egg stench of cordite filled the fuselage. Paddy's unlocked swinging chair crashed him painfully into his table, as charts, pencils and other navigation equipment scattered on the floor. The violent movement threw Algy forward on to his radio table, banging his head painfully on the radio receiver unit. Johnnie was struggling with the controls as Gloria tried to dive to earth, his feet fighting the rudder pedals to try to keep her straight as she attempted to go into a spin, his hands pulling back the yoke to combat the unasked-for dramatic dive.

"Chalkie, for Christ sake, give me a hand with the yoke."

Chalkie grabbed the control column with both hands and together they hauled on the yoke. The altimeter was unwinding furiously, the engines screaming in protest. It took them many long seconds to pull her back to straight and level. Chalkie checked the engine gauges and dials and reported that the engines were okay. When Johnnie had returned some form of normality to the situation, he shouted,

"Yorky, what the hell has happened?"

"Yorky, talk to me. What has happened? Rear-gunner, come in! Talk to me! Yorky!"

The intercom only hissed and crackled.

"Algy, go and check on Yorky, find out what the damage is back there."

Paddy picked up his scattered equipment and rearranged his table, rubbing his bruised ribs.

"Dusty, can you see what happened back there?"

"There's something not right, Skipper, but I can't see what it is. There's a bit of damage to the starboard tail-plane and fin, but it doesn't look too bad, but something is not right."

Algy made his way over the main spar, ducked under Dusty's turret and struggled through the smoke-filled, claustrophobic fuselage towards the rear-gunner's turret. He bounced from side to side as the exploding, stinking flak, jerked the aircraft around the sky. His head throbbed and he wiped away the blood running down his face from his cut forehead.

Johnnie continued his fight with the yoke. He could feel the stiffness and reluctance in the controls; one of the rudders was obviously damaged; Gloria wanted to hang to starboard, he altered the rudder-trimming tab to compensate, but with only little effect.

Algy reached the bulkhead doors that separated the tail section of the aircraft from the main body. He tried to open them, but they refused to move. He struggled with the jammed doors, heaving with all his might and yelled for Yorky to help him. He peered through the small window in the starboard door but could not see Yorky and carried on trying to force them open. They suddenly smashed backwards, throwing him to the floor, he was immediately aware of a freezing, cold blast of night air. He struggled to his feet and stared into a black abyss. He staggered back and gasped in shock, his throbbing head forgotten.

"Oh, my good God!"

He scrambled back over the tail spar and plugged his intercom jack into the system and shouted,

"He's not there, Skipper. The whole bloody turret has gone! He's not there, Johnnie!"

"Can you see any damage to the tail-plane?"

"The tail-plane, did you hear what I said? Yorky and the turret have gone! There's a bloody great hole!"

"I hear you Algy, but I need you to assess the damage, okay? We have an aircraft to fly. Go back aft again and give me a damage report on the remains of York … of the rear turret."

"Will do, Skipper."

Another percussive explosion juddered Gloria and shrapnel sliced through the side of the fuselage by the aft door hatch, narrowly missing Algy as he tried to make his way back aft.

He could see clearly the damage to the rear of Gloria, Yorky's turret had just disappeared, leaving the stern ravaged and empty.

Suddenly, a brilliant blue light blasted the inside of the aircraft, stunning the crew into frozen, shocked statues, totally blinded by the sudden invasion of their dark world. The stark violent light held the Lancaster vulnerable and helpless in its ensnaring grasp. Everything caught in a blinding glare. Every rivet, every raw piece of paint-scuffed aluminium, every hidden corner and crevice highlighted. Intense rays of white light, like miniature spotlights, crashed through the shrapnel and bullet holes in Gloria's flanks, criss-crossing all the way down the fuselage.

The white-blue lead searchlight attracted other yellow lights like a magnet as they locked on to the floodlit bomber, enclosing it in a deadly cone. The crew was quick to recover from their rabbit-like entrapment in the light, but it had been a shock. The brightness still bathed the fuselage as Algy carried out Johnnie's order.

"I can't see any major damage, Skipper," he reported. "Besides the turret being blasted away completely, that is. There's nothing more I can do here."

The Plexiglas and armoured steel turret, the four machine guns and their fittings, Yorky's seat, the sliding turret doors, and Yorky, they had all disappeared, leaving a trail of wires and hydraulic pipes flapping and whipping in the slipstream. As he turned to struggle back up the fuselage, he fell against Yorky's parachute, hanging from the fuselage flank just behind the bulkhead doors; he patted it reflectively and noticed it had gone undamaged in the violent severing of the turret. Something pale caught his eye and he looked down. There on the floor underneath the 'chute was Yorky's chicken wishbone, broken, one of the wings snapped. He rested his head against the fuselage and closed his eyes. He thought of the good, honest

Yorky blasted into the cold night air, falling thousands of feet, and smashing into the ground below.

Was their luck starting to run out – his scarf, Yorky's wishbone, what next?

He managed to force the bulkhead doors almost to their closed position, but there was no way of securing them. He struggled up the body of the aircraft, pushed past Paddy and stood alongside Chalkie and to the side of the Skipper to give him his report in person.

"I think the ack-ack shell must have exploded right underneath the turret, Johnnie. There is nothing left of it at all. I don't think there is any damage this side of the bulkhead doors, but I can't secure them. I couldn't see the tail-planes or ailerons."

"Thanks, Algy."

The loss of Yorky hit Johnnie and Algy hard. They had both admired his courage and skill as a rear gunner, the most vulnerable place in the aircraft. Not once had he flinched from his duty even though he knew the odds of survival were stacked against him. Johnnie's first thoughts had been about the safety of the aircraft, but now the shock of Yorky's fate had hit him. He hated to think they were going home without him; they were a crew of seven, not six. It was no way for any man to die, on his own, falling through the black night sky, to be left behind broken in some foreign field. He swore foully, bitterly, and went back to flying his aeroplane, with a heavy heart.

"Is it true, Skipper, Yorky's gone?" asked a desperate Dusty.

"Yes, I'm afraid it's true."

"I knew something wasn't right, but I didn't think that he'd been lost. Fucking Krauts!"

Algy went back to his station and slumped into his seat, talking to no one in particular, 'as Yorky would have said, what a bugger'.

The searchlights had caught Gloria like a moth in a spider's web of light. Exploding flak, balls of smoke with angry orange-red centres spitting fire and slashing slivers of steel, were clawing closer and closer to the stricken bomber. One smashed into the port side just behind Johnnie and he felt the shrapnel striking the armour-plate of his seat back. Without that protection, the shrapnel would have riddled him. Michael 'Paddy' Doolan survived as his navigation equipment exploded around him in a shower of fizzing sparks and choking smoke. Another casualty was the parachutes of them both, pockmarked and burnt by red-hot steel. Paddy grabbed the fire extinguisher to the left of Johnnie's seat and subdued the hissing redness of the electrical fire in his nav. aids.

"You okay, Michael?" asked Johnnie.

"Of course I am, my son. You wouldn't be expecting anything else now, would you?" he laughed. "Not a single scratch ... yet."

"Cork screwing left!" shouted Johnnie.

Johnnie turned the control yoke hard to port and as far forward as it would go, pushing Gloria into a violent steep left hand dive, desperately trying to escape the clinging grip of the lights.

He pulled hard backwards to put the aircraft in a corkscrew-shaped climb, desperate to free the bomber of the ensnaring light. The cone of light still gripped them firmly. Johnnie threw her into another spinning dive to starboard before corkscrewing into a starboard climb. The damage to the rudder was making any violent movement difficult. By a miracle, the master light lost them as another Lanc crossed into its deathly beam. One yellow light kept with them for a few brief seconds before swinging away after the master light, in search of further prey. Gloria and her crew were left in the sudden comfort of darkness, the flashes of exploding flak seeming excessively bright in their temporary night blindness. However, they had not escaped the attentions of the enraged hornets' nest that was the flak defences of the German cities. It still crumped and banged round them; the flying steel from the exploding balls of anger was claiming many victims that night.

A Lancaster three hundred yards in front and just below them exploded as flak ignited the fuel tanks of the starboard wing. It fell through the black night air, highlighting, in its fiery glow, many scattered aircraft desperately running for home many dangerous hours away.

"Where the bloody hell did this lot come from? Where are we, Navigator?" asked Johnnie tersely.

"We're just south of Osnabrück," reported Michael.

"But where are all these Lancs coming from? They're not ours! I thought the diversion raid was Berlin, Skipper?" asked Chalkie.

"It was!"

Searchlights were striding across the sky, trapping Lancaster and slower Sterling bombers in their pointing fingers of light. Flak was bursting all around, explosions of smoke and shrapnel erupting in their obscene black bursts that littered the moonlit night. The German defences were throwing up a curtain of deadly steel.

Up above them, another Lanc had part of its tail-plane and port wing shot away. It lurched and staggered to port, spinning in a slow, deathly arc, slicing through the starboard wing of another bomber to its left. The burning Lancasters locked together like embracing lovers as they twirled and spun in a blazing waltz of death. No white canopies of life appeared. Fourteen young men either burned or fell to their deaths, trapped inside their aircraft by the unrelenting force of gravity.

"Oh, my God, did you see that, Skipper?" gasped Dusty in shock, from his grandstand seat above them all. "Poor bastards."

"Skipper!" shouted Jock, "Look up to the port quarter. About ten o'clock!"

Johnnie looked up to the left and realised he was witnessing a dual to the death. A twin-engine JU-88 night fighter had attacked a Lanc from behind and the bomber's port wing was blazing fiercely. The Lanc gunners had not given up and the mid-upper and rear gunner were firing round for round. The fighter was now in flames; he also, would not give in, and fired his guns to the end. His aircraft exploded seconds after the Lanc had gone into its death spin. Again, no parachutes appeared in the night sky. Sadly, none of the participants, German or

English, of that gladiatorial conflict, would be relating their story over a few pints in the mess later that night.

The bright moon shone on this scene of deadly aerial combat. The scythes of war were reaping a terrible black harvest from Bomber Command this night.

"We must have stumbled on to the bomber stream of another raid," said Johnnie.

"Skipper, they did mention a spoof raid on Hanover and Minden, but I wonder if this is the return stream from Berlin? It looks like they have been given the same track home as us, for Christ sake," said Algy. "Another cock up by 'the powers that be'."

"I think you're right, Algy," said Paddy. "'Never have so many been buggered around so much by so few,' to mis-quote our illustrious leader."

"Pilot to navigator, time to go home I think. What should my heading be?"

Before he could answer, more flak slammed into the sky surrounding them, rocking the aircraft viciously again. The outer-port engine spewed sparks and flame back along the wing's leading edge and thick smoke poured away from it. The propeller tried to free itself from the remains of the Merlin engine sending shuddering vibrations through Johnnie's hands.

"Chalkie, feather number one, quickly. Put that fire out!"

"OK, Skipper."

The flight engineer closed the fuel cock and pushed the feathering button in until it held. The Skipper closed the throttle. The propeller slowly windmilled to a stop and he switched off the engine ignition. The blades had turned edgewise into the wind to stop the circular motion that could destroy, by vibration, the engine and possibly the wing itself, but the fire raged on.

Chalkie calmly announced. "Master fuel cock off, prop feathered, fire extinguisher on."

"OK, Chalkie."

They both knew they only had seconds to stop the fire from spreading to the fuel tanks in the wing. Chalkie watched in horror as the fire engulfed the engine. Johnnie was ready to put the aircraft into a dive, if needed, to try to douse the fire. Chalkie hoped fervently that Johnnie would *not* put the aircraft into a dive, as he knew that the extra draught of oxygen would increase the temperature of the fire greatly and if the alloy skin of the wing started to burn, the wing would definitely explode. Many crews had come home telling the story of the dramatic dive that had extinguished a fire and saved them, but many more did not come home to argue the opposite.

The extinguisher kicked in and at last, the flames reduced and finally expired as they ran out of fuel.

"Fire's out, Skip. It will be OK now."

"Course for home, Michael, my heading is two-nine-five, come back to me soonest," instructed Johnnie. "Skipper to crew, Skipper to crew, I am going down to seven thousand feet to try to get out of this flak. We have lost number one engine, but the others are okay. Damage report from everyone."

Algy reported that his radios were still functioning after he had given them some emergency love and care. However, there was a 'bloody big hole' behind and above the electronic navigation aids, which had helped to protect both him and the Irish navigator from the scything blast of flak.

"There's also a big hole forward of the starboard door and some new ventilation ducts opposite on the port side."

Dusty Miller, from his lofty perch, reported slight damage to the tail-plane ailerons and starboard rudder, but nothing too drastic. Johnnie was already aware of the damage to the flight surfaces because Gloria was handling very differently. Jock, in his nose turret, assured Johnnie everything was okay from where he was.

"Keep on your toes for night fighters, gunners. Let's get our revenge, eh!"

"Seven thousand feet, Johnnie, course is two-eight-eight for the Dutch coast. By the way, we're on dead reckoning now, GEE and H2S are u/s."

"OK, Michael. Skipper to crew, gunners and Chalkie keep on oxygen to keep you sharp; we're at seven thousand."

Johnnie knew that one of the first senses affected by a shortage of oxygen was night vision, and he needed his two remaining gunners and engineer bright and 100% alert.

"She seems to …"

As he started to speak, all hell broke loose.

\*\*\*

Oberleutnant Carl-Wolfgang Schaefer, his navigator and defensive gunner, Stabsfeldwebel Hans Wiese and their wireless operator, Feldwebel Otto Schmidt had been in the air, as part of the Osnabrück Defence Squadron Nachtjagdgeschwader V, since their ground radar had picked up the first British bombers, some hundred miles out from the city.

They had already pounced on four Lancasters that night, attacking them from underneath, ripping apart the soft, vulnerable belly and fuel tanks with the high explosive and incendiary shells from the devastating twin 20mm cannon that rose at an angle of 65°, proud and erect from just behind the cockpit of his twin-engine Junkers 88 night-fighter. The pilot, looking through a periscope sight above his head, fired these angle-up guns, nicknamed 'Schräge Musik' or 'Jazz Music' by the crews, to devastating effect on the unsuspecting aircraft. This system allowed the night-fighters to creep up on the aircraft unseen, unchallenged from behind and below, and deliver their inevitable fatal attack.

20mm shells ripped through the soft alloy bodies and wings of the giant bombers, exploding fuel tanks and blowing apart the powerful Rolls Royce engines, sending flaming enemies to the hell they deserved. He was careful not to hit the bomb bay, as the exploding bombs could easily cause the bomber to fall on top of him. However, these bombers were heading home after dropping their women – and child-killing loads; the bomb bays were empty.

Searchlights had illuminated their last and fourth victim, permitting them to attack the blinded aircraft head on with the machine guns and cannons mounted in the nose. His first pass damaged a port engine and the tail-plane, but his second saw his last cannon shells destroy the two engines on the other wing. The Lancaster exploded into flaming scrap metal decorating the sky with its pyre.

He dived away in victory and immediately found himself below and behind another bomber. This one had an engine feathered; it had also lost its rear turret. His approach, he knew, would go unchallenged. He smiled in anticipated victory as he placed the fighter directly below the bomber, throttling back so as not to undertake it too quickly.

The shells left the twin upright cannons at a rate of 600 a minute. Oberleutnant Carl-Wolfgang Schaefer grinned as he fired his deadly, erect guns, but after less than one second, he exhausted his ammunition.

"Verdammt Hölle!" he swore savagely.

He had intended to turn his aim on to the wing tanks and blow another bomber from the skies. He dived quickly away to re-arm and re-fuel at his airfield, some fifteen miles away. He would then rejoin the attack on the hated 'Terrorflieger' of the RAF.

\*\*\*

The crew of Gloria had no idea the Junkers was below them until all hell broke loose. In less than half a second, it had fired eleven shells; nine of those had hit Gloria. The floor of the aircraft erupted in a storm of smoke, fire and shrapnel. The destruction travelled from the stern to the nose in a heartbeat. Small fires burned throughout the fuselage, which filled with swirling, stinking smoke and fumes, whipped into vortices by the onrush of the night air. The fact that the fighter had hit the fuselage and not the petrol tanks in the wings had saved their lives and Gloria, or so thought Johnnie.

The first of Oberleutnant Carl-Wolfgang Schnaufer's shells had ripped up through the root of the port tail-plane, but had not damaged the elevators. The next two armoured shells and had gone straight through Gloria, just behind the mid-upper turret without striking anything vital, except the Elsan chemical toilet.

Another one of the JU-88s shells had come up through the rear of the bottom of the bomb bay and passed straight through the roof above, leaving a jagged hole in the floor and a round, punched hole in the roof. One more had ripped apart the flare chute. The next one had hit something vital, Dusty. Algy had a very lucky escape; a shell had ripped through the front floor of the bomb bay and out through the roof of the fuselage, luckily missing him by inches. The next armour-piercing bullet came up between his legs, through his table, then through the main radio transmitter and exited through the astrodome. The last one ricocheted off the back of Johnnie's armour plated chair, punching him hard in the back and exiting the aircraft through the canopy.

When the noise had finished and the first shock had subsided, "Where the hell did that come from?" asked a shocked Chalkie.

"Health check, anyone hurt? Everyone report! " ordered Johnnie.

They all came back to him quickly.

"Michael, there's no reply from mid-upper; go and check Dusty's alright."

"OK, Skipper."

Jock spoke over the intercom.

"It must have been a night fighter that got below us, Skipper, probably a JU eighty-eight. I hear they have these machine guns sticking out of the top like a fixed turret. Now that's what I would call bloody unfair."

"I would agree with you, Jock."

Michael Doolan felt lucky as he had survived yet another Luftwaffe attack, but he knew in his heart of hearts his time would come soon. If not tonight, then tomorrow or the next time he was airborne. Funnily enough, he had never even considered death happening on the ground, or even on the sea, where he had spent most of his time before the war. His evasion of Nazi bullets and shells surprised even him, but he knew his time would come, and it would be in the air.

Algy was already back in the fuselage with a fire extinguisher in his hands fighting the small fires that were filling the body of Gloria with thick white, stinking smoke. He managed to subdue the flames and pointed towards Dusty's turret where blood could be seen dripping from the bottom.

As Paddy passed behind him, Algy said, "I think he's bought it, Paddy. There's an awful lot of blood beneath there."

The blast of icy air, rushing through the punctured sides and the gaping stern of Gloria, cleared away the choking smoke.

Paddy made his way to the turret. The shell had smashed through the floor of the fuselage and entered the bottom of the turret, bouncing off the inside of the armour plating skirt that protected the lower part of the gunner's body, but only from the outside. It had sliced through the canvas seat that Dusty sat on and entered his body from underneath, travelled through his torso to exit from his back and smash its way out of the turret through the Plexiglas cupola above his head.

Young Dusty Miller's body was a bloody broken heap, slumped, lifeless in his shattered turret, his dead fingers still on the triggers of his unfired guns.

"Holy Mary, Mother of God!" exclaimed Michael.

As he gently eased the body out of the turret, the photograph of Dusty's girlfriend, Mavis, fell from its hiding place, fluttering briefly around the shattered canopy of the turret, as if a butterfly trapped in a greenhouse, before the slipstream whipped it away into the darkness. Lowering him carefully to the floor of the aircraft, avoiding the dark pool of glistening blood, Paddy propped Dusty between two of the side former-struts, hoping he would not be lost through the hole in the starboard fuselage, and then made his way back to report to the Skipper.

"I'm afraid you're right, Algy, he's dead," shouted Paddy to the wireless operator as he passed him.

As he sat at his station and started to plug-in his intercom, he realised the flash and thump of flak had died away, replaced by the roar of the night air rushing through the many holes in Gloria's skeleton. Remarkably, the rest of the crew had escaped unscathed and the aircraft's damage was slight.

Paddy plugged in his intercom jack. "I'm afraid he's dead, Johnnie. He would not have known a thing about it. The turret is u/s."

"OK. Thanks, Michael. Skipper to crew, I'm afraid Dusty has bought it and his turret is u/s, so we are down to just one gunner now."

They flew for a while in silence, all lost deep in their own thoughts.

Jock, sitting in his exposed forward turret, was swinging it from side to side, quietly throwing out threats and curses in his heathen-sounding Gaelic tongue, as he searched the darkness for Nazi night fighters. He wanted to blast them from the sky. He wanted his revenge. He was now the only defender left; his fellow air gunners were gone. He had not known them for long, but they had, very quickly, made him feel very welcome, a part of the crew. Strange, he thought, how quickly these days that new colleagues become friends. Suddenly remembering he hadn't checked for his 'lucky heather', he patted and searched his pockets for the sprig of white heather his mother had sent to him after the last time he was on leave. He actually hated that he had kept it, such an obvious Scottish lucky emblem. He finally found it and pulled it from his breast pocket, but it was nothing more than connected twigs. The delicate white flowers and tiny green leaves were gone and the little branches were bare.

Chalkie was checking his oil pressure and temperature gauges, rpm indicators, fuel levels, coolant temperatures, listening to the very heartbeats of the three remaining engines. He was also trying to work out the repair schedule for the damaged Merlin, would it be possible to put in a new engine. That port inner was running a bit warm. 'Just hope it hangs on till we get home', he thought. He wondered how long it would take to get Gloria back in the air.... He was trying to block out the thoughts of his two crewmembers, they would not be making it back to base. It was hard to come to terms with; they had been friends and colleagues for nearly eight months. Now their luck had run out. That was three of the original crew gone now, how many more? He wondered why he had deliberately 'touched wood' before they left last night, he did not really believe in luck ... did he?

Michael was lost somewhere out in the Atlantic, with a fair wind and a lively deck beneath his feet. He hoped his luck would allow him at least one more trip to sea. Why he had never joined the navy now amazed him. Instead, he was freezing to death high above a foreign land surrounded by nasty people who wanted to shoot him, shell him and blast him out of the sky. 'And I'm just a peaceful, easygoing lad from the Mountains of Mourne'. He picked at the unravelling 'monkey fist'.

Algernon Rupert Willoughby-D'Arcy's thoughts were where they normally were, somewhere below his waistband. In particular, he was still thinking of the army captain's wife back in Ludworth and the fact she still had his scarf. He cheered up at the thought of retrieving it from her boudoir and maybe repeating their last performance. He fingered his neck, missing the comforting luxurious feeling of the expensive silk. He also deliberately tried not to think of the fate of yet another of his colleagues.

Johnnie Sanderson could not stop thinking about the two air gunners. What would he say in his letter to their families? What could he say to comfort yet another grieving wife, and a grieving mother? Dusty and Yorky were both so very young, younger than he was, mere boys really, just like his first air-bomber, Jan. Just crewmembers, no, they were his friends. They were all stuck in this dreadful man's war. He just hoped Gloria would make it home without losing any more of his lads.

He touched the pocket of his tunic underneath his flying suit, not realising the lock of black hair tied up with a small scarlet ribbon, was blowing aimlessly over the snow-covered airfield three hundred miles away. He swore when he remembered his 'flying' pipe had snapped in two.

The sudden cough and splutter from the inner-port engine brought everyone's senses to a heightened state of alarm! For the last hour, they had woven a cautious course across northern Europe from one safe corridor to the next, albeit at a much-reduced air speed, and they were still nearly two hours away from home.

The flight engineer checked the throttle setting and the petrol level in the fuel tanks, but the engine was starting to struggle badly and soon flames were licking round the cowling, hot oil was spewing back over the engine and wing.

"Kill it, Skipper or it'll take the wing with it!" shouted Chalkie.

"Is there anything you can do to save it, Chalkie?"

"No Skip. If it doesn't shake itself off the wing, it could set off the tanks."

"OK, shut down the fuel."

"Already done so."

Johnnie throttled back the engine while Chalkie feathered the propeller and when it stuttered to a halt Johnnie turned off the ignition switch as Chalkie pushed the fire extinguisher button to smother the engine before the wing suffered grave damage. Now they only had the two starboard engines left.

"It must have taken some damage from the same flak burst that took out the outer engine; the other two are running okay. Temperatures fine, revs are fine and fuel's okay. Let's hope they stay hale and hearty or else we're in for a long swim home," commented Chalkie. He stood up to peer across at the port engine. "Fire's out, Skipper."

"Flak to starboard quarter, Skipper!" shouted Jock from his nose turret, "Looks like someone's getting a taste of Jerry ack-ack."

"That will be Nordhorn, Skipper, some big factories there. We should miss them on this track; two-eight-eight should take us across the coast at Egmond."

"OK, Michael. ETA Egmond?"

"Thirty seven minutes, Skipper."

"Skipper to crew, we have lost number two engine, but the other two are running fine. We are going to avoid as much flak as we can as we head for the coast; our ETA is about thirty minutes or so."

Johnnie took Gloria to the south of Nordhorn to avoid the defences around the industrial town, swinging back on to his course towards the Egmond Gap, but it meant they still had yet to run the gauntlet of the corridor to the coast, and this area was notorious as the haunt of bomber-hungry night fighters. For thirty tense minutes, the crew held their breath; no night fighters found them, no staccato of machine guns, and no roar of cannon shells tearing apart the very fabric of their world. They just ran for home.

"Dutch Zuiderzee in sight, Skipper, dead ahead. Ten miles"

"OK, Finlay. Keep a sharp look out. You are our only defence now. Algy, is 'Fishpond' still operating?"

"Afraid not, Skipper. I've got my head stuck up the astrodome, or what's left of it, to try to spot any signs of night fighters in the area."

"Stand to everyone, if they are going to hit us, this is where it will happen, especially at this speed and height," warned Johnnie.

As they swept over the Zuiderzee and approached the coast, searchlights pierced the darkness, swaying across the night sky. The air blossomed with flak bursts, red and yellow tracer stitched the skies with its waving deadly fire. Most of it passed harmlessly above them or wide of them as Johnnie put the nose down to gain as much speed as possible. Soon they were away across the sea, away from the coastal defences. They could relax a little now, the North Sea below them and the welcoming coast of England less than an hour and half away. Their broken, blood stained aircraft was taking them home.

The twin-engine Messerschmitt bf 110 had followed a group of bombers back to their bases, near Lincoln, and the pilot had shot a Lancaster out of the air as it was landing at RAF Winthorpe, near Newark, on the Fosseway. He had then followed the old Roman road towards Lincoln and strafed two more airfields, exhausting his deadly 20mm cannon ammunition, before turning for the coast at high-speed, keeping very low over the flat countryside.

He roared over Gibraltar Point, just south of Skegness, and headed for home across the North Sea. After five minutes, he picked up the image of a lone bomber above and in front of him, silhouetted against the clear night sky, on its way home. He smiled as he climbed to attack. He was thinking that the RAF was making his job very easy tonight, but defensive radar had picked him up earlier and another type of twin-engine night fighter, a few miles behind, was streaking towards him.

"Bandit, bandit!" screamed Jock. "Coming in on port quarter, corkscrew right, now!" Jock's guns were his avenging angels as he pumped two streams of fiery tracer towards the attacking fighter.

Johnnie threw the yoke forward and turned hard to the right, stamping on the right rudder pedal, trying to make the aircraft dive violently to starboard. Before he could complete the manoeuvre, the Messerschmitt night fighter pumped a trail of machine gun bullets into them from stem to stern. If he had not exhausted his cannon ammunition earlier, he would have blown Gloria out of the sky. As it was, the stream of bullets shattered the bomb aimer's nose cupola into a thousand pieces, and blasted the escape hatch away leaving a gaping hole in the floor of the nose. The gun turret above, exploded into pieces as the bullets ripped into it and Jock McGuffin. He was barely breathing and the lifeblood was pumping quickly from his ravaged body as he fell from the smashed remains of his turret. At least he had fired off his machine guns in anger and revenge, but had paid the ultimate price.

A bullet ripped through the shoulder of Chalkie's flying-jacket, punching him sideways, leaving a bloody furrow in his upper arm. Bullets smashed through the canopy above him and the Skipper, holing and cracking it further.

Michael Doolan's charmed life carried on; his only wound being where a piece of shrapnel had sliced into the back of his hand. However, Algy and his radio equipment were not so lucky. Two bullets passed through the roof of the aircraft and destroyed the communication systems in front of him. Unfortunately, another two passed through his elegant, scarfless body, which now lay bloody and twisted among the debris and litter on the floor of G for George. The stream of bullets ripped through Gloria's starboard flank, tearing even more of her aluminium skin away. Several punched Dusty's body through the gaping hole in her side and he fell like a rag doll through the friendless dark to the cold sea.

The acrid smell of burning cables and scorched aluminium, accompanied by the strange metallic odour of fresh blood, hung in the smoke-filled air for a moment. The onrush of cold air from yet more ruptures to the aircraft's credibility, quickly cleansed it.

When Paddy had gathered his thoughts together, he turned forward to talk to the Skipper. He was shocked at the sight of both the other occupants of the cockpit covered in blood.

"Mary, Mother of God! Will you look at the pair of you?"

Chalkie was still in shock. His right shoulder and arm were soaked in blood, but he was complaining bitterly that the 'Bloody Krauts' had ruined his much-treasured American Irwin sheep-skin flying jacket. The Skipper was white-faced with blood oozing from a wound high up on his chest and a slashed open right thigh.

"Johnnie, are you with us? Can you hear me?"

Johnnie nodded, saying, "Don't worry about me. Is Chalkie all right?"

"He'll be okay in a minute, let's get you sorted first."

Paddy found the first aid kit and tried to dress his wounds. A sliver of metal, several inches long, was sticking from the wound in Johnnie's chest; he pulled it out and put a field dressing on the deep wound. He used his knife to cut open Johnnie's trousers and bound the leg tightly with a bandage. All the time Johnnie flew the bucking, twisting bomber.

"I'm fine, Michael, see to the others. Chalkie, are you okay?" shouted Johnnie, coughing.

"Yes, Skipper I'm okay, but the intercom's u/s. I'll check with Algy."

"Not till I've had a look at that shoulder, Percival. The Skipper needs your help up here. I'll check with Algy after I've sorted you out."

When he had attended to Chalkie, he returned to his navigation table to find it twisted and bent, as was most of the equipment on the port side of the aircraft. Algy's bloodied body lay crumpled on the floor alongside the remains of his radios.

Paddy swore foully. Although they were very different characters, he had liked Algy's carefree and irresponsible attitude in these times of short friendships and sudden death. He admired his knowledge as a radio and radar operator. He was his friend. He shone his torch down the fuselage to check Dusty's body, but his beam only found the gaping wound in Gloria's side.

He went to report to Johnnie, but dropped down below the flight engineer's blood splattered legs to check Jock. He stared in shock at the sight before him, a blood stained, smashed nose cone and turret. An aluminium spar was jutting out the side of the jagged hole that was the remains of the escape hatch; it had trapped Jock's body by his flying suit after he had slid from the shattered turret. His legs and lower body were hanging through the hole, but bizarrely the slipstream was causing his right arm to rise slowly up and down. For a fleeting moment, Paddy actually thought that Jock was waving to him. It was as if he was waving goodbye. With horror, he watched Jock's broken, bloodied body slip through the hole in the floor, to whip away in the rushing night air. By this time, Jock's heart had pumped his body dry of blood. He had no knowledge of his tumbling, lonely fall to the cold, cheerless North Sea below.

Paddy moaned angrily.

"Christ, will the dying never end?"

He straightened up and turned to face Johnnie.

"Johnnie, Algy and Jock are dead. Jock went through the floor of the nose."

"With his parachute?"

"No, I think he was dead when he fell through the floor."

"Through the floor!" he exclaimed.

"The attack blew off the escape hatch and there's a lot of damage to the floor."

"What about Algy?"

"He has taken at least two bullets to his chest; I don't think he would have known anything about it, thank God. We have also lost Dusty's body; he went out through the hole in the side."

"No ... No ... No! What a bloody mess," cried Johnnie, slamming his hands on the control yoke. He coughed painfully and blood stained his chin.

"Can you still navigate us, Michael?"

"I'll go and stick me head up what's left of the astrodome and have a look at the stars, Skipper."

"Thank you, Michael, thank you, we're not far from the coast."

He coughed again, this time screwing up his eyes in pain and wiping blood from his mouth.

"By the way, my friends, is this a good time to tell you that we haven't got a useable 'chute between us. So I hope you paid attention to the instructions about bringing home and landing a sick kite in your flying lessons, young Johnnie."

"Thank you, Michael for that little gem of knowledge," said Chalkie. "I wasn't thinking of leaving just yet, anyway."

Johnnie was becoming numb with shock, four of his comrades, four of his friends killed, another wounded. Three of them lost forever out in this black night, never to come home. The aircraft badly damaged and still a long way from Elkington. He prayed he could get the rest of them back safe. His chest was starting to burn and breathing was painful.

Fifty miles behind them in the middle of the North Sea, the twin-engine Mosquito night fighter was closing rapidly on the Messerschmitt, whose pilot and radar operator were complimenting themselves on a fine night's work. Cannon shells ripped through the two German crewmembers before they even knew the Mosquito was behind them. The Squadron Leader and his navigator watched as the Nazi night fighter exploded in smoke and flame, dived and knifed into the black North Sea.

They turned for home.

The Lincolnshire coastline appeared in the early morning light. Dawn was breaking behind them, somewhere over Europe.

"What time is it, Chalkie?

"0655, Skipper."

"Home in time for breakfast then, lads." He tried to make light of the situation, but broke into a fit of painful coughing, blood splattering the control yoke in front of him.

"Are you alright Skipper," said a concerned Chalkie, noticing the blood on Johnnie's face.

Johnnie nodded and mouthed 'Yeah, OK', and wiped his chin.

He turned Gloria north to run parallel with the long sandy beaches, passed over Skegness and turned northwest to head inland towards Ludworth.

Smoke erupted from the inner starboard engine and the revs dropped dramatically. Gloria immediately lost height. Chalkie grabbed the throttles and slammed them as far forward as he could through the gate to emergency power. To everyone's relief, the engine picked up again. Johnnie and Chalkie looked at each other sheepishly for they had doubted, just for a second, Gloria's ability to get them home on the two remaining engines, and now they had a twinge of guilt for mistrusting the old girl. Chalkie checked the fuel gauges, but they showed plenty of fuel. The engine coughed again, this time it left a trail of greasy smoke in the sky, but Gloria flew on. The snow-covered flatlands of Lincolnshire contrasted starkly with the darkness of the sea, the land's brightness giving hope, reassurance and confidence to them now they were nearly home.

"It must have been hit by that fighter," said Chalkie.

"Twenty miles to go, Johnnie. It would be a long walk, but as it's flying we are, we will be home safe and sound in less than ten minutes," chirped Michael.

Gloria flew on, slowly losing height and speed, but she was taking them nearer to home all the time.

Greasy smoke was now billowing from number three engine. Chalkie did everything he knew to keep that engine alive. He coaxed a few desperate revs from the dying motor, but the oil pressure was down and temperature in the engine was critical, as it struggled gallantly to continue pushing them onwards.

"What height have we?" asked Johnnie.

"Five hundred."

"Five miles to go ... there's Ludworth church ... turn for final approach, Johnnie."

The three hundred feet tall, graceful spire of the church was just five miles from the end of the runway. In the summer, the golden light of the early morning sun as it burst over the uninterrupted eastern horizon, gilded the giant cockerel weather vane as it sat on the very point of the spire, acting as a shining finger, pointing the way home. However, on this grey morning, the spire stood like a sentinel rising from the mist-shrouded valley of the town's setting. Dawn was leaching into the day as they turned for their final approach.

The engine appeared to pick up power a little after the shallow turn, as if Gloria knew that the end of her traumatic journey would soon be over, all three of the survivors looked at each other and smiled. They were going to make it. Gloria was taking them home.

"We're going home, Johnnie," said Paddy, putting his hand on Johnnie's shoulder.

"Not all of us, Michael."

Paddy was staring somewhere far away.

"But we all will, one day, Johnnie, one day."

"I hope so, Michael."

"We will, even if it takes forever."

Chalkie looked at him with a quizzical frown.

Johnnie was coughing again; the front of his flying suit now stained even darker with his blood.

The old windmill appeared out of the low-lying, early morning mist at the beginning of the wooded valley. They passed over it at two hundred feet, three miles to go. The airfield's welcoming flare path was lit up in front of them.

"Look at that, Skipper," said Chalkie, pointing forward. "Looks like Blackpool, doesn't it?"

The twin rows of flickering lights, two miles away, stood out dramatically against the whiteness of the snow and the two dark wheel tracks between the lamps indicated where other bombers had made it back home

"Wheels down."

"Wheels down, Skip," said Chalkie and, after a few second, "We've got two red lights on the undercarriage, Skip."

"Try bringing them up and down again."

"No joy, they won't come back up, still two red."

"Okay, try flaps twenty."

"Flaps twenty ... nothing, Skipper, absolutely nothing. No flaps. We've lost the hydraulics and the spare compressed air. No flaps and unlocked landing gear."

"This landing could be a bit hairy, chaps," said Johnnie, coughing.

The dark-grey, winter-dressed trees of the misty, wooded valley that led up to the runway, flashed beneath the wounded black bird of war, its ravaged body struggling to hold together for the last few miles of its final journey.

"One hundred and fifty feet, two miles to go," announced Paddy.

"Michael, send up a Verey flare just to let the tower know we've got problems," he said, coughing up more blood, struggling now to breathe.

"Okay, Johnnie."

He went back to the Verey pistol, in its holster on the port side of the main spar, found the cartridge he wanted from the remaining flares and loaded the pistol, fitted it in its firing position in the roof and pulled the trigger.

Ginny was in the control tower when the radio observer called "G-George on final approach."

The double red flare climbed high above the approaching bomber, indicating to the ground staff that it had damage and wounded were onboard. Ginny rushed out on to the veranda of the tower and clung tightly to the metal railing, straining to see Gloria as she struggled towards the airfield. The Duty Flying Officer came and stood next to her.

"My God, his engines sound rough; he really has got troubles," he said, not seeing the fear in Ginny's eyes.

She could clearly hear the coughing and banging of the struggling engines herself now.

"Come home, please darling, come home," she pleaded softly.

Johnnie had thought for a while he had said his last goodbye to his beloved Ginny, but he was nearly home now. He would get the chance to see her, hold her, and kiss her. He had promised her that Gloria would always bring him back to the airfield, and that was exactly what she was doing. He had been thinking over the last few days he should ask her to marry him, and he could not think of any reason why he should not ask her. He decided he would ask her as soon as he could. He smiled at that wonderful, warm thought.

Paddy had come back from the astrodome and was watching Johnnie smile. He smiled and said, "'The grey-eyed morn smiles on the frowning night, chequering the eastern clouds with streaks of light.' Shakespeare's 'Romeo and Juliet'. Johnnie, look to your right, dramatic isn't it?"

Johnnie snatched a glance at the eastern sky, streaked with the growing light over a distant horizon and thought, another dawn, another day.

The cold November mist, lying like a grey blanket, filled the valley that was their approach line to the runway.

Gloria suddenly plunged into this greyness, sucked down by the sinkhole effect of the cold air. Johnnie should have remembered the danger of this valley. The Duty Flying Officer at the briefings had reminded them on countless occasions. 'Beware of the sinkhole if your approach takes you low over the valley and its beech trees. Remember the country name for beech trees ... Widow Makers!'

He heaved back on the control yoke and Chalkie tried to coax just a few more revs from the struggling engines.

"Come on, my darlin's, come on, nearly home, sweethearts, nearly home, just a bit more my darlin's," he pleaded.

"Come up, come up!" cried Johnnie trying to peer through the thick greyness enveloping them.

Gloria did her best. First, the yellow-tipped, spinning discs that were her propellers appeared above the mist followed closely by the cockpit, and Johnnie, Chalkie and Paddy found themselves, sitting, isolated on top of the grey swirling world. Then the wingtips emerged as she fought her way out of the cloying grey shroud.

One and a half miles to go.

Bit by bit, inch by inch she crept upwards. The wings were now clear. Foot by painfully slow foot she clambered clear of the mist, but she was still below the valley sides.

"One mile to go," said Paddy.

Johnnie kept the backpressure on the yoke while Chalkie tried to increase the boost power and the bite of the propellers. She gradually clawed her way back into the sky.

"Oh thank you, babe, thank you, Gloria," said Chalkie; he grinned at a relieved Johnnie.

They were going home.

The inner engine disintegrated in a storm of flames and spinning metal. Gloria dramatically lurched and dropped down into the valley again. Pieces of the shattered engine smashed into the starboard outer engine, their last means of support. Johnnie heaved back on the yoke, crushing it to his belly, to try to gain some height.

"There she is!" shouted the DFO, pointing. "Christ! She lost another engine!"

They all saw Gloria's engine burst into flames, highlighting her passage over the misty wooded valley. They did not realise she now was left with only one engine, and that was badly damaged.

The strident clamour of alarm bells shattered the early morning as the fire engines and ambulance charged across the airfield towards the start of the runway.

"Please, Gloria, please," prayed Ginny, desperately. She held out her hand instinctively, as if helping to hold Gloria up in the sky.

"Not now, Sweetheart, not now!" Johnnie pleaded. "Come on, come on! Up! Up!"

He fought to wrench the yoke back even further, coughing violently. Chalkie heaved against the throttles, almost bending them in his effort to coax just one surge of life-saving power from the last remaining struggling engine. Paddy stood holding on to the back of Johnnie's seat and resigned himself to his fate, calmly thinking, 'Lancasters can fly on three engines, even two engines have brought us a long way, but a shattered aircraft cannot fly well on one damaged engine, even a Merlin engine, even one named after the greatest wizard of all time. That's for sure.'

Gloria tried to respond to their desperate efforts, her tortured engine screeching its protest, but the tall beech trees on the runway side of the valley appeared to reach up and grab the undercarriage. The starboard wing dropped suddenly, the heavy branches dragged Gloria down, the last spinning prop tried, desperately, to carve its way through the leafless branches. She managed to smash through the trees, but the tip of her starboard wing made contact with earth, cutting its own furrow in the chalky, Lincolnshire soil, leaving an obscene black scar across the pristine, snow-covered field. The wing crumpled and the fuselage broke in two as the port wing ripped from its roots. The fuel tanks ruptured, bathing the wreckage in high-octane petrol as she cartwheeled into the ground. The fuel erupted in a thunderous fireball, sending pieces of burning wreckage spinning high into the air. For several long moments, it came clattering down on the concrete runway, the perimeter track and the snow of the airfield. The wreckage of Gloria, the giant black bird of war, burned furiously, angrily, as if she was punishing herself for the failure to bring her crew home safely. Other smaller explosions wracked her as flares and machine gun ammunition added yet more punishment to her tortured frame.

Searchlights, flak and murderous night fighters had joined the attempt to end the crew's sorties on many occasions. Now they had succeeded, but with the added curse of an English beech wood.

"Good God!" exclaimed the DFO.

Ginny watched in horror as G-George smashed into the ground and exploded into a pall of smoke and flame. She heard him call her name as the percussive blast of hot air swept over the tower.

"No ... No ... No!" she wailed and slid down to the floor. "He promised he would come home, he promised!" She collapsed and cried out in heartbroken anguish, sobbing in desperation.

"Johnnie!"

The flickering shadows, cast by the ferocious flames, were performing the devil's dance on the wall and the windows of the control tower behind her.

The crew and Gloria had finally run out of luck, less than one hundred yards from the safety of the runway.

She had brought Johnnie back to the airfield as he had promised Ginny she would. She had brought Paddy, Chalkie and the elegant Algy home. But, what of the three of her crew she had not brought home?

# EPILOGUE

The rolling chalk hills of Elkington returned to their pre-war tranquillity at the end of 1945, when the RAF flew off for the last time. Lincolnshire and the Wolds were left scarred by the concrete, steel and brick of the many abandoned airfields scattered across the county, along with the many graves and souls of the young aircrew who had made the supreme sacrifice. The chalky soil of the Wolds felt the cut of the plough once again as Jack Richards and his father, and many other farmers, started the long, hard graft of returning the airfields to farmland. Peace returned to the rolling green hills around Elkington. The melodious sound of skylark, peewit and yellowhammer filled the skies once again. The thunderous roars and growls of the giant, black birds of war ... the Lancaster Bombers ... were gone forever, or were they?

\*\*\*

At the end of the old runway, its concrete surface now cracked, broken and etched with weeds, Jack turned off the powerful engine of the enormous modern tractor, climbed down stiffly from the cab and started to re-connect the giant six-furrow plough his son had left there the night before after he had finished his day of ploughing.

"Ah shouldn't be out bloody ploughin' at my time o' life, especially on a bloody cold and miserable mornin' like this. I'm bloody seventy-seven for Chris' sake," he grumbled. "Mind you, when I was a lad my old man would kick me out at five-a-bloody-clock in the mornin' with no brekfas'. Then I 'ad t' get the 'osses ready fo' a full day's ploughin'."

He carried on mumbling to himself as he connected the plough, but in truth, he wanted to work, particularly this morning. His irritable mood was, in fact, a way of hiding his sadness and grief, his way of coping with the impending death of the woman he had cared about for many years, even though he had known for weeks this day would come.

The noise startled him; he stood up quickly, turned and searched the sky over the beech wood that sat at the top of the valley below the end of the old runway. Then he recognised it, an unmistakable sound engraved on his memory, that of a Lancaster Bomber.

"Hello, it's back again then," he said to himself, as the sound reached him through the mist.

Every November for the last sixty years, always first thing in the morning, the ghostly sound of a struggling Lancaster bomber, its engines banging and coughing, desperately trying to bring its crew safely to earth, would crescendo to a desperate thundering roar. Then, as suddenly as it arrived, it ceased. Abruptly. Leaving Jack mystified and somewhat disturbed. He had heard it for the first time when he was a young man just after the war. However, this time it was different. The engines were not running rough, they did not sound as if they were struggling, they were not banging and coughing, there was no sense of impending disaster.

It was very different from all those other times ...

\*\*\*

'The Widow Sanderson', as the locals called her, and her young son, had moved into the village a handful of years after the war. She had lived with her parents near Lincoln, but they had perished in the flu epidemic of '46, and towards the end of the war, her sister had died whilst serving in the Wrens. It was just her and her son now. The small cottage in the wooded valley below the old RAF airfield at Elkington suited her well. It was a pleasant enough place to live. It had once been a gamekeeper's cottage and situated, as it was, at the bottom of the valley, down the lane from the village, alongside the little meandering stream, it allowed her to live her life quietly with her son and her memories. The tall beech trees of the wooded slopes ensured the valley was cool in summer and protected from the bitter northeast winds in winter. She had earned a small living acting as a bookkeeper for several farmers in the area, including Jack Richards, and they had become close friends after his young wife had died, leaving him, like her, with a young son to raise. The two boys had grown up, attended school together, and become good friends. Jack had tried to persuade her to marry him for years, but she had remained steadfastly single, be it that she used the name Mrs Sanderson; it was more for her son's sake and convention than any vanity.

She had lived there for over fifty years when the illness finally overtook her. When she first fell ill, earlier that year, Jack had helped the district nurse to look after her until her son had returned from his work in the Middle East to nurse her in her last months.

Not everyone has the belief or sensitivity to witness spiritual occurrences, but she, like Jack, was one of only a few select people locally that had, and they could hear the ghostly return of the struggling bomber. Since her first year in the valley, she was aware of the occurrence and knew exactly which bomber it was. It always appeared on the anniversary of the time and the day of Johnnie's crash. She thought nobody else knew, just her, she had never told Jack or her son. It was painful at first when she realised it was Johnnie's bomber, but after that first time she looked forward to hearing it. It brought him back to her, although the pain of his loss was, once again, raw, but she felt his love and her love blossomed again every year she heard it. That was why she could never accept Jack's proposals, although she was very fond of him; it would not be fair to him, her still loving another man. However, Jack had found out years before her true story, and her relationship to the ghost bomber. Nevertheless, he still kept on repeating his marital offer.

On that last night, he and his son went to see her.

"Thank you for coming, Uncle Jack," said her son, Jonathan. "I'm afraid she is fading fast, I'll be very surprised if she sees another day. She has fought so hard these last few weeks; it's as if ... as if she is waiting for something, as if she is hanging on ... she has been incredibly brave."

"I think she just doesn't want to go, Jonathan; she's been a stubborn woman for as many a year as I can remember," he said with a sad smile.

He sat with her for a long time, but she was barely conscious and he doubted if she knew he was there. Saying what he believed would be his last sad goodbyes; he kissed her just one more time and left.

She had been desperately ill for months, and he agreed with Jonathan, that for some reason she had struggled bravely to last until now and he wondered why. Jack's son kept his friend company through the late hours of the night until Jonathan had insisted he would be all right on his own with his mother. He then sat with her all through the rest of the night.

As the grey dawn started to lighten the eastern sky, a gentle smile came to Ginny's face and she painfully raised her hand and touched her son's cheek as he sat on the side of her bed. He was a tall man, his fair hair now streaked with grey, his soft hazel eyes smiled down with love on the once beautiful countenance of his mother, now yellowed and ravaged by disease, her emerald-green eyes misted with time and her raven-hair now thin and grey.

"You're so much like your father," she whispered. "I love you, Johnnie."

She had not called him that since he was a little boy, he thought, she had always called him Jonathan.

"I love you, mum," he replied, holding her small, thin, fragile hand in his.

She heard the thrumming of the Lancaster's engines approaching.

"I knew she would finally bring you home, Johnnie. I'm ready now," she whispered weakly.

As the sound of the bomber passed directly overhead, a flicker of a smile passed across her now peaceful face, her eyes closed, her hand went limp and her soul departed.

Four majestic Merlin engines were throbbing in perfect harmony, a symphony of mechanical magic, bringing the giant bomber back home. She slid out of the air, her natural habitat, and returned, for the very last time, to that world of earth-bound mortals. A double squeal of protest came from the mighty tyres as they made contact with their home runway. The aircraft bounced back in the air and the tyres squealed again as they made their final contact. The engine's notes dropped as the enormous aeroplane taxied towards the hard standing in front of the long-gone hangar. As the brakes came on, it rocked briefly and came to a standstill. One by one, the engines hoarsely coughed the spirit of life from the cylinders for the last time and rattled to a stop. Then there was silence ... except for a tick ... tick ... ticking, as the engines cooled in the crisp, November morning air. The faded and weathered painted image of a scantily clad young woman, smiled down from the nose of the bomber.

In the grey early light, seven, smiling ethereal figures, wearing flying suits, yellow Mae Wests, leather helmets and parachute harnesses, appeared to flow from the doorway of the Lancaster and hesitate briefly. One of them peeled away to join a young WAAF standing nearby, her arms outstretched and her face wreathed in smiles. He embraced and kissed her, they turned and walked hand in hand to join the others and then they, and Gloria, all seemed to meld into the early morning mist.

Jack Richards looked around the old airfield.

There was no sign of an aircraft anywhere ... no noise ... nothing ... just a swirling, curling, disturbance in the mist.

He suddenly recalled his father's prediction all those years ago, and realised he would never hear the Lancaster again. Ginny had fought so hard to last until this day, and now he understood. He knew she had gone, and why she had waited and the reason she had never accepted his proposals.

"You brought them home then, old lady? I knew that you would. You are all together now. Rest in peace, Ginny. Rest in peace, boys, and thank you."

He looked round the airfield, his cap in his hands, remembering the distant days of war.

It was the morning of November 13, 2003. It had taken Gloria sixty years to find, collect and bring home together the lost souls of her crew.

Like a faded echo, a sound whispered across the airfield, "Home at last, chaps, home at last".

## **THE END**

> "Went the day well?
> We died and never knew,
> But well or ill, Freedom,
> We died for you."

John Maxwell Edmonds
(1875-1958)

Inscription from a plaque in Tuddenham Church, commemorating a bomber crew.

# AUTHOR'S NOTES

This is a fictional story, but the basis of the story is true. The first raid on Peenemunde and the raids on Hamburg and Berlin happened in the way described in the story.

There was no RAF Elkington, there was no Johnny Sanderson, there was no 'Gloria' and there was no 599 Squadron.

However, there were forty-five bomber airfields in Lincolnshire alone, and thousands of allied aircrew flew, fought, loved and died like the crew of 'Gloria', MH393 G-George of 599.

In the period 16th July to 12/13th November 1943, covered by the story, Bomber Command flew 23,086 sorties and 789 aircraft failed to return. 5,128 (approx.) aircrew went missing, killed or taken prisoner.

Between 3rd September 1939 and 7/8th May 1945, [the War in Europe] Bomber Command flew 387,416 sorties, dropping over 955,000 tons of bombs, and 8,953 aircraft failed to return. Of the 125,000 aircrew that served in the squadrons, 55,573 lost their lives and 18,241 were taken prisoner or wounded.

# APPENDIX

## Serving members of the RAF mentioned in the story

Air Chief Marshal, Sir A.T. Harris K.C.B., O.B.E., A.F.C., Air Officer Commanding-in-Chief, Bomber Command. Royal Air Force 1942-1945.

Air Vice Marshal Sir Edward Rice KBE, CB. CBE. MC.
Air Officer Commanding 1 Group Bomber Command 1942-1945.

Air Vice Marshal the Hon. Sir Ralf A. Cochrane GBE. KCB. AFC. FRAES.
Air Officer Commanding 5 Group Bomber Command 1942-1945.

## Commanding Officers of 617 Squadron [The Dam Busters]

Wing Commander Guy Penrose Gibson VC. DSO and Bar, DFC and Bar.

Wing Commander George W Holden DSO. DFC.

Group Captain Leonard Cheshire VC. OM. DSO. DFC.

# Crew of 'Gloria' MH393 CD – G-George.

'**Gloria**'. Aircraft ID No. 393MH. Squadron ID letters, CD-G-George 'A' Flight 599 Squadron RAF. Built May/June, 1943 at the factory of Mr Alliott Verdon Roe (Avro) at Chadderton near Oldham in Lancashire. First test flight 30 June, 1943. Delivered to 599 Squadron, RAF Elkington, on Friday 16 July, 1943 by Air Transport Auxiliary pilot, Miss Serena Barrymore. Completed fifteen operational sorties, plus one Gardening sortie under training. Crashed due to enemy flak and fighter damage 13 November, 1943 at RAF Elkington, after 'Operation Parliament'. [Pieces of her wreckage still turn up whenever the field is ploughed.]

**Pilot.** Squadron Leader Jonathan James Sanderson, DSO and Bar (P) DFC 'A' Flight Commander August-November, 1943. Killed in crash after 'Operation Parliament' 12/13 November, 1943. Was awarded a bar to his DSO posthumously. Aged 24.
**Bomb Aimer**. Sergeant Frank 'Jan' Greasely. Killed on aborted raid to Hamburg 2/3 August, 1943. Aged 21.
**Bomb Aimer**. Flight Sergeant Finlay 'Jock' Lachlan James McGuffin DFM. Killed on 'Operation Parliament' 12/13 November, 1943. Aged 24.
**Flight Engineer**. Flight Sergeant Percival 'Chalkie' White. AFM. Killed in crash after 'Operation Parliament' 12/13 November, 1943. Aged 24.
**Navigator**. Flying Officer Michael 'Paddy' Doolan, DSO. Killed in crash after 'Operation Parliament' 12/13[t] November, 1943. Aged 26.
**Wireless Operator**. Pilot Officer Algernon 'Algy' Rupert Willoughby-D'Arcy. Killed on 'Operation Parliament' 12/13November, 1943. Aged 25.
**Mid-Upper Gunner**. Sergeant James 'Dusty' Miller, MiD. Killed on 'Operation Parliament' 12/13 November, 1943. Aged 22.

**Rear Gunner.** Flight Sergeant Gordon 'Yorky' Ward, DFM and Bar. Killed on 'Operation Parliament' 12/13 November, 1943. Aged 23.

## MEMBERS OF 599 SQUADRON.

July – November 1943. RAF Elkington, Lincolnshire.

Group Captain (later Air Commodore) Sir Charles Peregrine Thompkins KOB MM DSO DFC and Bar. Retired from the RAF in 1947. Knighted in 1966 for his work with the Royal Air Force Association. Died on his 79th Birthday 1 April, 1975.

Wing Commander Harry Picton, DSO and Bar (P) DFC and Bar, Squadron Commander.
Killed On 'Operation Parliament' 12/13 November, 1943. Aged 26. Was awarded a bar to his DSO posthumously.

Flight Lieutenant Jimmy Cook, DFC. Squadron Adjutant. Medically discharged from the RAF in 1945, took his own life in 1946, aged 27.

Flight Sergeant [later Warrant Officer I] Percival Horatio Pidkin, AFM BEM, RAF Police. Honourably discharged from the RAF 1953. Joined the Metropolitan Police Force, retired in 1968 and became a publican.

Section Officer Virginia 'Ginny' Murphy, WAAF. Discharged in March 1944 after discovering she was four months pregnant. She moved to the hamlet of Elkington in 1951 and lived there until her death from cancer on 13 November, 2003, leaving behind a son, Jonathan Algernon Sanderson.

# PILOTS OF 599 SQUADRON

**'A' Flight.**
**A-Apple.** Wing Commander Harry Picton. See above.
**B-Baker.** Squadron Leader Christopher Cooper, DFC AFM. 'A' Flight Commander July-August, 1943. Killed on Peenemünde operation 17/18 August 1943. Aged 23.
Replaced by Flight Sergeant Frank Hubbard AFM. Left RAF in 1964 as Squadron Leader.
**C-Charlie.** Pilot Officer Tony Rance DFC. Killed on raid to Nuremburg March, 1944. Aged 23.
**D-Dog.** Flight Sergeant Olaf 'Chin' Petersen (Canada) Killed on 'Operation Decapitation' 30/31 August, 1943. Aged 25.
Replaced by Flight Lieutenant Robert Hirst DFC. Aged 26. Left RAF in 1945 and joined a pharmaceutical company as a salesman.
**E-Easy.** Pilot Officer Dylan 'Taffy' Morgan. Killed over France on 6 June, 'D' Day 1944. Aged 23.
**F-Freddie.** Pilot Officer Anthony 'Ginger' Bere, DFC DSO. Retired from the RAF as an Air Commodore in 1963 aged 54.
**G-George.** Squadron Leader Jonathan James Sanderson. See above.
**H-Harry.** Flight Lieutenant Michael Hunt, DFC. (Australia) Went back to Northcote, Melbourne, Australia in 1945 as a 'Bush Pilot'.
**I-India.** Flight Sergeant James Baker. Killed on 'Operation Decapitation' 30/31 August, 1943. Aged 22.
Replaced by Flying Officer Peter Montgomery (Canada). Aged 24. Returned to Canada in 1945 to become a farmer. Killed in a car crash in 1965.
**J-Johnnie.** Sergeant Peter Tyndale, DFM. Aged 25. (New Zealand) Shot down on the way home from 'Operation Parliament' 12/13 November, 1943 by flak near Osnabruck and taken prisoner with his crew. All survived the war.

**K-King.** Pilot Officer Peter 'Pity' Mee. Killed in crash-landing at Elkington after raid on Watten 2/3 September, 1943. Aged 22.

Replaced by Flight Sergeant Ernest (Ernie) Ward AFM. Aged 23. Transferred to RAF Musical Services in 1945 and left the RAF in 1964 as a Bandmaster.

**L-Leather.** Flying Officer Tarquin Scott-Baker, DSO DFC and Bar. Aged 23. Left the RAF in 1945 and became a well-known actor of stage and screen under the stage name 'Scott Baker'. Starred in the 1950's film about Bomber Command, 'Operation Parliament'!

## **'B' Flight.**

**M-Mother.** Squadron Leader William Askin. DFC. Killed on 'Operation Parliament 12/13 November, 1943. Aged 23.

**N-Nan.** Flight Lieutenant Kenneth 'Gunner' Hargreaves DFC. Left the RAF in 1945 and joined the 'Ted Heath Big Band' as a professional trumpet player.

**O-Orange.** Flight Lieutenant John Welcome. Killed over Berlin 30/31 August, 1943. Aged 23.

Replaced by Flight Lieutenant Herb Stiefel (Canada). Aged 25. Returned to Canada in 1945 to form, with his brother, his own pharmaceutical company.

**P-Popsie.** Flight Sergeant George Stirling (New Zealand). Aged 22. Shot down on 30/31 August, 1943 on 'Operation Decapitation'. Three of his crew were killed, he and three others of his crew taken prisoner. He escaped and made his way back to England and re-joined the squadron in March, 1944.

Replaced by Flight Sergeant Robert (Bob) Goodwin AFM. Aged 32. Killed, coming home from 'Operation Parliament' 12/13 November, 1943. Crash-landed in the North Sea after being attacked by nightfighter. No survivors.

**Q-Queen.** Pilot Officer Fredrick Mercury. Killed on 'Operation Parliament' 12/13 November, 1943. Aged 22.

**R-Roger.** Flight Sergeant John Titchmarsh DFM. Killed on 'Operation Parliament' 12/13 November, 1943.

**S-Sugar.** Flying Officer Anthony 'Tich' Thomas DFC. Aged 23. Left the RAF in 1945, carried on his interrupted medical studies, and became a cardiovascular surgeon.

**T-Tommy.** Flying Officer Simon Goldblume DSO and Bar DFC. Aged 22. Left the RAF in 1953 to become a Colonel in the Israeli Air force.

**U-Uncle.** Flight Lieutenant Pierre Letrecque DFC. (Canada) Aged 25. Left the RAF in 1945, returned to Canada, and became a commercial airline pilot. Was killed piloting a de-Havilland DH 106 Comet in 1954.

**V-Victor.** Flight Sergeant Jimmy Campbell. Killed on 'Operation Parliament' 12/13 November, 1943. Aged 21.

**W-Willie.** Pilot Officer David 'Jones the Pilot' Jones DFC. Killed on 'Operation Parliament' 12/13 November, 1043. Aged 23.

**X-Xray.** Pilot Officer Michael 'Doc' Whaites DSO DFC. Age 22. Left the RAF in 1945 and qualified as a Doctor of Medicine in 1950. Became Consultant Dermatologist at Leeds General Infirmary.

### 'C' Flight.

**A-Able.** Squadron Leader Anthony Ian 'Joe' Kendrick DSO and Bar (P) DFC and Bar. Killed on 'Operation Parliament' 12/13 November, 1943. Aged 24. Awarded a bar to his DSO posthumously for his sacrifice.

**B-Beer.** Flight Lieutenant Angus 'Jock' Giblin DFC. (New Zealand) Killed over Berlin 2/3 December, 1943. Aged 23.

**C-Charlie.** Flight Sergeant Peter Pavle (Canada) Killed over Hamburg 27/28 July, 1943. Aged 26.

Replaced by Pilot Officer James 'Bluey' Coogan (Australia). Killed over Berlin 2/3 December, 1943. Aged 24.

**D-Dog.** Flight Sergeant Charles 'Chuck' Bowden (Canada). Aged 25. Killed over Hamburg 27/28 July, 1943. Aged 25.

Replaced by Flying Officer Peregrine 'Froggy' French. Aged 24. Killed, coming home from 'Operation Parliament' 12/13 November, 1943. Shot down by nightfighter over Germany, no survivors.

**E-Edward.** Pilot Officer James 'Jimmy' Anderson. Killed on 'Operation Parliament' 12/13 November, 1943. Aged 24.

**F-Fox.** Pilot Officer George Geddes, DFC. Aged 23. Left the RAF in 1954 and became a music publisher and agent.

**G-George 2.** Flying Officer Isaac Cohen. Killed on 'Operation Parliament' 12/13 November, 1943. Aged 29.

**H-How.** Flying Officer Dennis Shepherd. Killed in collision over North Yorkshire Moors on 10 October, 1943 while training for 'Operation Parliament'. Aged 22.

**I-Item.** Sergeant George Palmer. Shot down coming back from the raid on Peenemunde 17/18 August, 1943. Died of his injuries 3 September, 1943 as a POW. Aged 23.

Replaced by Flight Sergeant William (Bill) Simpson AFM. Aged 20. Left RAF in 1945 and became a professional footballer with Carlisle United.

**Plot the routes of 'Gloria' and her crew on their sorties.**

I suggest that you plot your courses on the 'Captains of Aircraft Map' in pencil to allow for corrections, if required. When confident it is right, then use a different coloured pen to indicate each sortie's route. Remember that pilots never flew 'straight and level'; they would vary their height and fly a weaving course as a protection from flak and fighter attack and to confuse the enemy radar, but for this exercise the direct courses are indicated.

You can also measure the distance of miles flown of each sortie.
Equipment required:
Map of Northern Europe [Captains of Aircraft Map ideally]
Compass
Protractor
Pair of Dividers
Ruler
Pencil
Eraser
Coloured pens

Explanation of details given;
Place of departure and its co-ordinates of Latitude (N) and Longitude (E) then the heading to steer to the next turning point. See the example below:

**Gardening.** 13/14 July, 43.
Elkington, position 53° 17'N 00° 02W---then heading 087°→ to 53° 27'N 5° 0'E[turning point]---then heading 75°→to 54° 04'N8°40'E[turning point]---then heading 262°→to Elkington, 53° 17'N 00° 02'W

**Hamburg.** 24/25 July 43.
Elkington 53° 17'N 00° 02'W--072° → 54° 40'N 7° 00'E---117°→53° 51'N 9° 45'E---153° →Hamburg 53° 32'N 10° 00'E--180° → 53° 15'N 10° 0'E-- 300° →53° 55'N 8° 00'E --262° → Elkington.

**Hamburg.** 27/28th July '43.
Elkington 53° 17'N 00° 02'W--80° →Heide 54°11N 9° 5'E--80° →Sth Kiel 54° 15'N 10° 10'E--147° →Lübeck 53° 52'N 10° 41'E--230° →Hamburg 53° 32'N 10° 00'E—288° →53° 55'N 8° 00'E--262° →Elkington.

**Milan.** 12/13th August '43.
Elkington 53° 17'N 00° 02'W--197° →Reading 51° 27'N 0°57'E----161° →Le Havre 49° 30'N 00° 5'E--135° →Bourg-en-Bresse 46° 12'N 5° 13'E--114° →Gran Paradiso Mountain 45°32'N 7° 16'E--90° →Milan 45° 28'N 9° 10'E--035° →Wildspitze Mountains 47° 9'N 11° 5'E--300° →Beachy Head 50° 44'N 0° 16'E---315° →Reading 51° 27'N 0° 57'E--17° →Elkington.

**Peenemünde.** 17/18th August '43.
Elkington, 53° 17'N 00° 02'W--136° →62° 00'N 00°30'E --119°→Rugen Island 54° 20'N 13° 45'E--160° → Peenemünde 54° 14'N 13°79'E--295° →55° 15'N 09° 30'E--250° → Elkington.

**Berlin.** 23/24 August.
Elkington 53° 17'N 00° 02'W --083° →53° 44'N 5°50'E--135° →52° 22'N 08° 5'E--095° →52° 00'N 13° 40'E--343° →Berlin53° 32'N 13° 24'E ---278° →53° 12'N 4° 50'E--274° →Elkington.

**Chateau Thierry 'Operation Decapitation'.** 30/31 August '43.
Elkington 53° 17'N 00° 02'W--197° →Reading 51° 27'N 0° 57'E---127° → Abbeville 50° 06'N 01° 49'E--135°→Chateau Thierry 49° 03'N 03° 20'E--315° →Abbeville 50° 06'N 01° 49'E--315° →Reading 51°27'N 0° 27'E---017° → Elkington.

**Watten Bunker.** 1/2September '43.
Elkington 53° 17'N 00° 02'W---103° →53° 00N 2° 30E---178° →De Panne 51° 06'N 2° 35'E---230° →Watten Bunker

50° 48'N 2° 12'E---268° →Beachy Head 50° 44'N 0° 16'E---315°→Reading 51° 27'N 0° 57'E---017° →Elkington.

**Peenemünde.** 18/19th September '43.
Elkington, 53° 17'N 00° 02'W---70° →Ribe 55°10'N 8° 44'E---93° →Bornholm Island 55° 00'N 15° 08'E---180° →53° 30'N 15° 05E---311° → Peenemünde 54° 14'N 13°46'E---340° →54° 53'N 13° 25'E---275° →55° 10'N 08° 5'E---250° →Elkington.

**Friëdrichshafen, Blida and La Spezia.** 24/25th September '43.
Elkington 53° 23'N 00° 00'E---197° → Reading51° 27'N 0° 57'E---133° →Beachy Head 50° 44'N 0° 16'E --- 115° →49° 00'N 6° 00'E---120°→ Friëdrichshafen 47° 39'N 9° 28'E---130° →Merano 46° 40'N 11° 10'E---180°→Trento 46° 04'N 11° 07'E---215° →Blida 36° 30'N 2° 49'E---35° →Viarèggio 43° 04'N 11° 07'E---310° →La Spezia 44° 06'N 9° 28'E---304° → Bourg-en-Bresse 46° 12'N 5°13'E---315° → Le Havre 49° 30'N 00° 5'E--- 340° →Reading51° 27'N 0° 57'E ---17° →Elkington.

**Mimoyecques Bunker**, France. 7/8th September '43.
Elkington 53° 17'N 00° 02'W---100° → 53° 00'N 2° 30'E---192° →Mimoyecques 50° 51'N 1° 45'E---265°→Beachy Head 50° 44'N 0° 16'E---315°→Reading 51° 27'N 0° 57'E---017° →Elkington.

**'Operation Parliament'**, Ilse Gorge.12/13th November '43.
Elkington, 53° 17'N 00° 02'W --=100°→Egmond, 52° 50'N 4° 39'E ---102°→Oschersleben,
52° 2'N 11° 15'E---248°→Ilsenstien, 51°52'N 10°41'E---248°→Turning Point, Herzberg 51° 42'N 10° 20'E---288°→Egmond, 52° 37'N 4°39'E---284°→Elkington

# NIGHT FLIGHT TEST [NFT]

## SCHEDULE

Current aircraft limitations and restrictions are not to be exceeded.

## GENERAL DATA

Pilot..............................................................
Engineer........................................................
Navigator......................................................
Basic Weight..................................................
Fuel Weight...................................................
Aircrew Weight..............................................
Other Load....................................................
Take-off AUW...............................................

## CIRTIFICATE OF AIRWORTHINESS

Certified that this aircraft has been flight tested in accordance with the appropriate Flight Test Schedule and that it is:
*a. Airworthy and functionally serviceable to the required standard.
*b. Airworthy and functionally serviceable subject to minor rectification and entered in F700 and does not require further tests.
*c. To be retested after rectification as entered in the F700.

*delete as applicable

Signed..........................................................
Name............................................................
Rank.............................................................
Date..............................................................

Ambient Air Temperature..........................................
QFE...............................................................
Pneumatic Pressure..................................................
Brake PressurePort............................................
Brake Pressure Stb..................................................

Emergency Air Pressure [1,000 to 1,200 lb/in]..................................................
Hydraulic Accumulator Pressure [220 lb/in]..........................................................
Voltage.........................................................

Fuel Contents No. 1 Port.........................................
No, 2 Port.....................................................
No. 3 Port.....................................................
No. 1 Stb.......................................................
No. 2 Stb.......................................................
No. 3 Stb.......................................................

Controls and Trim -
Check full, free & correct sense.
Satis/unsatis

## AFTER START

After starting No. 3 -
Close Bomb Doors satis/unsatis

At 1,200 RPM No.1 No.2 No.3 No.4
Oil Pressure [min 30psi] ...... ...... ...... ......
Oil Temperature [Min 15°c] ...... ...... ...... ......
Rad Temperature [Min 40°] ...... ...... ...... .....

Fuel Pressure Warning light on/out on/out on/out on/out
Magneto Dead Cut yes/no yes/no yes/no yes/no
Generator Charge ....... .......
Vacuum ....... .......
Voltage .......volts

## TAXIING

Check operation of:
Compass, Remote satis/unsatis
Magnetic satis/unsatis
DI satis/unsatis
Turn & Slip satis/unsatis

Maximum brake at each wheel port
...........psi
stb ...........psi

Function of brakes, judder and fade.
Captain's Port satis/unsatis
Remarks..................................
Stb satis/unsatis
Remarks..................................
Engineer's Port satis/unsatis
Remarks..................................
Stb satis/unsatis
Remarks..................................

PRE TAKE-OFF

At zero boost No.1 No.2 No.3 No.4
RPM ......... ......... ......... .........
Oil pressure[min 30psi] ......... ......... .........
Oil Temp [min 15°] ......... ......... ......... .....
Rad Temp[min 60°] ......... ......... ......... .....
Mag Drop Port [max 150] ......... .........
Mag Drop Stbd [max 150] ......... .........
Supercharger operation y/n y/n y/n y/n
Generator charge ...........amps

TAKE-OFF

Start timing at zero boost and brakes off
Open throttles to +7 boost.
Unstick at..........Knots IAS
Climb at 140 knots. With +4 boost and
2,400 rpm to 7,000ft
if possible
Time to 3,000ft ........min ......sec
Time to 5,000ft ........min ......sec
Time to 7,000ft ........min ......sec

CRUISING

At 3,000ft, fly at 150 kts and 2,000rpm

In steady conditions No.1 No.2 No.3 No.4
Boost ......... ......... ......... .........
Oil Pressure ......... ......... ......... .........
Oil Temp [max 90°] ......... ......... .........
Rad Temp [max 150°] ......... ......... .........

Supercharger Operation y/n y/n y/n y/n
Generator Charge ......... .........
Voltage ......... volts
Hydraulic Accumulator Pressure [600-1,000psi] ......... psi
Trim: Elevator Trim .........Div Nose up/down/neutral
Rudder Trim .........Div Port/Stbd/Neutral
Aileron Trim .........Div Port/Stbd/Neutral

STALLING

Aircraft clean. Pitch fully fine, throttles closed
Stalling Speed [onset of buffet] .........kts
Stalling Speed [full stall] .........kts
Wing Drop Port/Stbd/Neutral
Undercarriage and flaps lowered .........kts
Wing Drop Port/Stbd/Neutral

OPERATION OF UNDERCARRIAGE AND FLAPS.

At 150 kts straight and level time the following:

Undercarriage Down .........secs
Flaps Down .........secs
Flaps Up .........secs
Undercarriage Up .........secs
Bomb doors open .........secs
Bomb doors shut .........secs

ENGINES

At 2,000ft, 150kts and 2,000rpm

No.1 No.2 No.3 No.4
Boost ......... ......... ......... .........
Oil Pressure ......... ......... ......... .........
Rad Temp ......... ......... ......... .........
Feathering y/n y/n y/n y/n
Unfeathering y/n y/n y/n y/n
Generators ......... amps ......... amps
Remarks....................................................
..............................................................
..............................................................
..............................................................
..............................................................

..............................................
..............................................
..............................................
..............................................

## LANDING/SHUT DOWN

After Landing at 1,200rpm:

No.1 No.2 No.3 No.4
Oil Pressure ........ ........ ........ ........
Oil Temp ........ ........ ........ ........
Rad Temp [max 100°] ........ ........ ........

After shutting down engines 1,3 and 4.
Operate flaps fully down then fully up
Satis/unsatis

Fuel Contents No.1 Port........ Gals Used........
No.2 Port........ Gals Used........
No.3 Port........ Gals Used........
No.1 Stbd....... Gals Used........
No.2 Stbd........ Gals Used........
No.3 Stbd........ Gals Used........

Total flight time......................

Total fuel used......................

## INSTRUMENTS

Check each instrument for function:

| | |
|---|---|
| Compass | satis/unsatis |
| DI | satis/unsatis |
| A H | satis/unsatis |
| T & S | satis/unsatis |
| Altimeter | satis/unsatis |
| RCDI | satis/unsatis |
| ASI | satis/unsatis |

## RADIO

| | |
|---|---|
| UHF | satis/unsatis |
| VHF | satis/unsatis |

## GENERAL REMARKS:

................................................
................................................
................................................
................................................
................................................
................................................
................................................
................................................
................................................
................................................

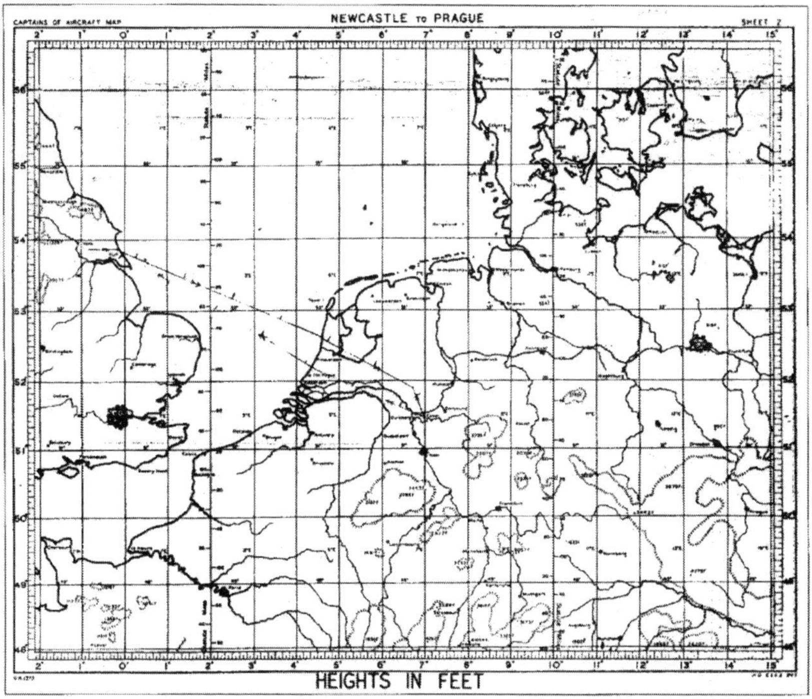

CAPTAINS OF AIRCRAFT MAP
NEWCASTLE TO PRAGUE
SHEET 2
HEIGHTS IN FEET